Boxed Secrets

Mary Jo Stanley

authorHOUSE®

AuthorHouse™
1663 Liberty Drive
Bloomington, IN 47403
www.authorhouse.com
Phone: 1-800-839-8640

First published by AuthorHouse   4/25/2011

ISBN: 978-1-4567-6290-2 (sc)
ISBN: 978-1-4567-6289-6 (hc)
ISBN: 978-1-4567-6581-1 (e)

Library of Congress Control Number: 2011906303

Printed in the United States of America

Acknowledgements

I would like to thank all of my readers of *Paper Secrets* for your loyalty and support. I could not have continued the story of Vivian and Louise without you and your faith in me. I hope you enjoy this sequel as much as I have enjoyed writing it and are pleased with the results.

I would like to express my appreciation to all the members of the Author House publishing family for assisting me with the various issues that arose trying to get this second book in the series completed in a timely manner.

Of course, I couldn't have done this without my husband, Ray, and my family. They have all been so patient and supportive during the whole process in getting this book written. Ray, you always told me that if people would just read the first one, they would want to read the others. Thank you for believing in me and my story. I would like to dedicate this book to the surviving WWII veterans, widows, or orphans. I want to thank each of you for all of your personal sacrifices.

Prologue

Vivian Black and Louise Pierce were childhood friends in the 1930 are when they were separated at a young age. Louise's father had died and her mother moved her family in with a widowed maternal aunt, by marriage. A short time later Belle Coleman became extremely wealthy when a major coal seam was discovered on her land grant. The two girls meet at college ten years later at which time Louise had become infatuated with the man Vivian loves. Conflict after conflict has erupted between the two by Louise's instigation but came to a full blown eruption when Vivian was given a sizable endowment by Louise's aunt as opposed to Louise, who thought she was more deserving. Louise will do whatever it takes to get even with Vivian, her perceived enemy and root of all her troubles. It appears that it had finally subsided with the marriage of each of the young women- Vivian to the man she loves, John, and Louise to the son of a judge, Alfred, an attorney.

With the death of Louise's mother, who had tried to be her conscience, few people are left that can stand in Louise's way of destroying Vivian who has become, in her mind, her nemesis. In November, 1944, Louise's mother, Bertie Pierce, died of cancer the day after Thanksgiving, naming her aunt, Belle Coleman, as the guardian of Louise's only brother, William. Vivian Black's parents were named as the ones to take her aunt's place if she should die before William reached adulthood. It was a natural choice for Bertie to make since Vivian and Louise had been best friends in their early years while their mothers had also been the closest of friends. Bertie bequeathed everything she had owned in her will as she had deemed proper.

She had been advised by Mr. Blakeman as to the legalities of her bequests and although her estate was relatively small, the custody of William, Belle's apparent choice of heirs, had brought controversy to the family. Louise had been left all of her mother's jewelry save one emerald ring that Bertie had specifically left to her best friend, Emily Black. Louise had coveted the ring and was furious when Belle had bought it for Bertie instead of her. She had been confident that her mother would bequeath it to her.

Vivian was left all of Bertie's shares in Marshall Steel while her only son, William, was left the remainder of the estate except for a single chest. It along with all of its contents bequeathed to Emily. Louise sued Belle for custody of William on behalf of her grandmother. She wanted Bertie's mother to raise William and wanted Belle declared insane for giving her money to Vivian. Alfred, Louise's husband went to a meeting and received some shocking news about both Louise and Belle. After hearing about Louise's escapades in college and the truth about Belle's relationship to Emily, he dropped both lawsuits immediately.

Emily, too pained from the loss of her dear friend, had waited to open the chest. When it had been delivered to the farm after Bertie's funeral, it had sat silently, unopened for several weeks. When she finally did open it, Emily found a few clothes, a quilt that Emily had made especially for Louise and Alfred as a wedding present, and a box of papers. Many things weighed heavily on Emily's mind as she looked over the papers. She reflected on her friendship with Bertie and its renewal the last few months of Bertie's life. Bertie wasn't the only one who had been disappointed in Louise.

She recalled all the troubles from the past years getting the farm going and how attached she had once been to Louise in those early years. She had been taken care of by Emily and Paul Black when her family had lived near them in a southern WV hollow near Jackson. Louise's dad had been what folks called a "mean drunk" who beat Bertie severely. Louise would spend nights at Emily and Paul's house when her father had a particularly bad night. Louise and the other members of her immediate family left the hollow after the sudden death of her alcoholic father in a wagon driven by Emily's husband, Paul. He had straightened out Belle's barn and set out a garden for them using seedlings he had started before returning home.

Louise didn't see her friend, Vivian, until they met again in college. She was spoiled and spent thousands of dollars on clothes for college. Apparently

Louise had gone to Comfield College to find a husband and set her sights on the man that loved only Vivian. He was from a rich Richmond family and despite her efforts to destroy Vivian's reputation; it was Louise who returned home in shame. She had been quickly married off to the son of a judge and yet she still tried to manipulate anyone or anything without thought of consequences to them trying to get John. She just tried to get information so that she could somehow get closer to John Williams, now married to Vivian. Emily's heart was heavy with the loss of her friend, Vivian's miscarriage, and the recent threat of lawsuits.

This is where the story begins with a single piece of paper found in the box a few hours after packing up the Christmas decorations. Emily Black, Vivian's mother, made a discovery of a box filled with special papers in the bottom of the chest bequeathed to her by Bertie Coleman Pierce, Louise's deceased mother and Emily's best friend. Pieces of paper can make a big difference in a person's life and these can often lead family members to some of the best kept family secrets. Without realizing it, Emily has found papers that her friend had hidden from her own children and wasn't sure of what they meant.

Chapter 1

Emily had sat down in her rocking chair with the long box of papers she had found in the chest. She unfolded a piece of high –quality paper upon which was written the number and location of a safety deposit box and let out a gasp when she read what Bertie had written a small note on the paper, *"Emily everything in the box is yours. Use it wisely. Bertie"* Emily looked further down the paper and saw a typed list of instructions with Bertie's signature that were on the bottom along with another signature of one of an unfamiliar name on the witness line and Emily saw that it had been notarized out of state. Mr. Blakeman was the attorney of Bertie Pierce's aunt as well as Bertie's and apparently she didn't want him to know about the piece of paper in the box.

Emily reflected on several things as she waited to discuss her find with Paul, her husband. Her mind was occupied with not only the loss of her friend to a battle with breast cancer the day after Thanksgiving, but also the revelations Bertie's aunt, Belle Coleman, the richest woman on the east coast of the US. Belle had recently made these revelations to Emily and Paul only when Louise had threatened to sue for William's custody. It still pained Emily to think of all the tragedies that had befallen Bertie during her lifetime and when it finally had seemed like things were turning around for her, she had died. Bertie had found a man that loved and cared for her in a gentle way, Judge Andrew Marshall. She thought 'Oh Bertie, why did you have to have so much pain in your life yet I have been blessed with so much love in mine? I had parents who loved me, a husband that adores me, and a beautiful, intelligent daughter that has made us as proud as parents could possibly be. Why couldn't your parents have been more like mine? Why hadn't they protected and loved you like they should have done? Why did your husband beat you and despise you just for wanting children? How did your daughter, raised by a woman capable of so much love, get filled with so much hate?'

Her thoughts were somber as she wondered if Bertie had actually known the truth about Emily's relationship to Belle. Belle was Emily's natural mother as a result of being raped by Bertie's father. Belle had been the widow of his brother when he had severely beaten her and raped her. She had no choice but to put Emily up for adoption, given the fact that her husband had been dead for almost a year when Emily was born. 'Oh my gentle, loving Bertie I miss you so much. I wish that I could talk to you right now,' she thought. 'I would have loved to have claimed you as my half-sister. You know I would have helped you more in those early years dealing with Jack Pierce. You had so much pain and so little happiness,' Emily sighed to herself and returned to look at the papers.

Paul, Emily's husband, entered the back door from their barn and saw Emily sitting in her chair staring into space with the box on her lap. They lived on a self-sufficient farm near Jackson. "Hey, Emily, what's wrong?" he asked.

"I decided that it was the right time to look into Bertie's hope chest and as I was going through it, I saw this box of papers. Look at this one-it has instructions about a safety deposit box at the Chase Manhattan bank. Here, read it," she said as she held the paper.

Paul scanned it and said right after he let out a whistle, "Hmm, I wonder what's in it."

"It's a curious thing that Mr. Blakeman didn't mention anything about this box. Of course I do remember that when he read from Bertie's will that it said something or another about whatever was connected to the contents of the chest was ours. Maybe you ought to call Mr. Blakeman and Belle and ask them about this safety deposit box," Paul said.

"I think that's what I'm going to do. I'll call and see if she wants to meet us at her house or at Mr. Blakeman's office," Emily agreed.

Emily called Belle and asked if she could meet with her and her attorney and Belle suggested that they meet at her home. "I found some interesting pieces of paper in the bottom of Bertie's chest that I want to show to both of you. Can I come down there now?"

"Certainly dear," Belle answered.

Paul drove Emily to Belle's in their '39 Ford and they conjectured along the way about what was in the box all the way to Belle's. "She left her jewelry to Louise, so it can't be jewelry. Maybe Bertie wanted to try to mend fences between Louise and Vivian from the grave. It won't be any shares of stock because she left those to Vivian. I still don't know why she didn't leave them to Louise. I can't think of anything else she could possibly have owned, can you?" Emily asked.

Belle was just as confused as Emily and waited for their arrival in her large Welfield home. Knowing how quickly Louise went through money, Bertie had known that she would just sell off the shares of stock and had advised Bertie not to give them to Louise. Bertie's jewelry, purchased in the past ten years by Belle, was worth a lot more than the stock and Louise hadn't mentioned them in her lawsuit.

Emily and Paul arrived at Belle's, a twenty room brick home on Sumner Street in Welfield, WV, and recognized Mr. Blakeman's '41 Lincoln parked in the driveway. They knocked on the leaded glass doors and the maid welcomed them and led both of them to the office where Belle and Mr. Blakeman were seated. Emily and Paul greeted Mr. Blakeman and Emily kissed Belle on the forehead. Belle and Emily had gotten close while Emily had taken care of Bertie during the last months of her life. Emily had nursed her friend of more than twenty years as tenderly and as best as she could. Emily had received a shock the last time she had seen these two when they had been forced to reveal that Belle had been raped by her deceased husband's brother i.e. Bertie's father, and had given birth to Emily. Emily had been adopted and her adoptive parents died without ever telling her she had been adopted. Belle had revealed the truth unwillingly, only to stop both of Louise's lawsuits.

Emily hadn't quite come to terms with all of this information that she was actually Bertie's half sister and Louise's aunt, but the piece of paper she held in her hand had her curious about her old friend and what she had found necessary to secure in a bank vault. Was it something of value or was it just something she had to hide from her children?

"I opened a box that was in the bottom of found Bertie's hope chest and found this piece of paper," she said as she handed the paper to Belle. Mr. Blakeman glanced at it over Belle's shoulder and said, "This is an agreement for a safety deposit box at a bank. What does that say Belle?" as he pointed to Bertie's handwritten note.

"It says 'Emily, Everything in the box is yours and use it wisely.' Mr. Blakeman, Bertie trusted me to use whatever is in that box wisely. Am I entitled to whatever is in the box or should the contents in the cedar chest have been listed specifically named in the will?" she asked the attorney.

"As I recall her will stated that you were bequeathed anything connected to the contents of the chest so whatever is connected to the chest, whether it was physically in the box or not, in my opinion it is rightfully yours," he answered.

Belle straightened after reading the paper once more and said, "I don't know anything about this safety deposit box. She never mentioned it to me. She must have gotten it on one of her trips with Louise when they were shopping for Louise's wedding. By the address, this is a bank near the Waldorf Astoria in New York where I have stayed for business meetings these past six or seven years. I have no idea of what it could possibly be in there, but I would be willing to go with you to find out." She turned to Mr. Blakeman and asked, "Are you sure that Emily is legally entitled to what is in that box?"

"Yes," he answered. "You will need to take a copy of her death certificate and a copy of the probated will naming you as an heir. You will need to have some sort of identification with you or Bertie's attorney attesting to your identity. I will be happy to go along with you as well."

"Well, I guess we are all going to have to go to New York 'cause Em isn't going to find out without me. She doesn't need to find out about anymore surprises and be all by herself," Paul spoke up.

"When do you want to go?" Belle asked. "Oh wait, what do we do with William?"

"Well, school is out until after New Year's and we could take him with us, couldn't we if we left tomorrow, that's the 27th and returned by the third?" Paul suggested.

"We could be in New York for New Year's Day!" Emily laughed.

Belle smiled and said, "Let's do it! Mr. Blakeman, we can manage to ride up in a regular sleeper car if I can't get my private rail car here."

"Oh I can get your private rail car here or we can drive up to Bluestone, and pick up the train there. Remember, your private rail car is stored in the Bluestone train yard. Which do you prefer?" Mr. Blakeman answered.

"Well, if we drove up to Bluestone we wouldn't have to wait for the next train and then we could get to New York in time to go to the banks on the 28th. Say, why don't we call up Vivian and John and see if they want to go with us?" Belle asked with excitement. It would be the first trip she would make knowing Emily was her daughter and thought perhaps it would be a good time to let Vivian and her husband John know that Vivian was actually Belle's granddaughter.

"I don't know about that. They may want to spend their first New Year's as man and wife in their own home," Emily stammered slightly.

Paul spoke up, "Now Em we will be going right by Charlottesville on that train and I know you want to see her every chance you can. Besides how many times will she get a chance to be in New York for New Year's Eve?"

"I could call her from here if you don't mind, Belle, and find out" Emily replied.

"By all means, call her. Call her right now!" Belle said excitedly.

Emily dialed Vivian's number and told her about the piece of paper she had found and the trip they were taking to New York for New Year's 1945. "Would you and John like to join us? We would have to return on the 2nd because William has school on the 3rd. When do you two go back to classes at the University?" Emily asked.

"We don't start until the week after on the 11th. Let me ask John, he's in the study, hold on for just a minute," Vivian said and Emily whispered to Belle, "She's gone to ask John."

After a minute or so Vivian returned to the phone and said, "John is all for it! What time do you think you would be coming through here?"

"Well if we catch the 9am in Bluestone, we should be there around noon or so," Emily answered. "We could call you from the Bluestone station and give you the route number of the train. We will be in Belle's private rail car. I'll call you tomorrow. I love you sweetie," Emily said and heard Vivian say," I love you too. See you tomorrow!"

"Well I guess we better go home to pack," Paul said. "What time do we need to be here?"

"I suppose we need to be leaving around 7 or so! Mr. Blakeman will call and get our rail car hooked up on the 9am northbound train. See you tomorrow and get plenty of sleep!" Belle said.

The couple left to prepare for the trip and talked once more about the contents of the box. Paul was a little anxious for Emily since he didn't like her to be unpleasantly surprised. Emily needed time to get used to being accustomed to the revelation of her natural mother and perhaps this was the perfect opportunity for them to really get to know each other a little better. He didn't say anything aloud, but his love for Emily would strengthen her as she was exposed to whatever was in those boxes. He hoped that both Emily and Vivian got closer to Belle. Her strength would help them as they encountered problems. Paul had a feeling it wasn't going to be good news in the box but said nothing! He was often teased by Emily that he must have gypsy blood when he got those feelings of foreboding. His parents had emigrated from Hungary and he smiled to himself as he recalled Emily calling him "a hard-headed Hunk" when she got mad at him. Most of the time he was easy to get along with but if he had his mind made up he wouldn't change it.

Paul pulled out their new suitcases from the attic when they arrived at the farm house and Emily began packing for their trip. Emily packed her trunk with items she had recently purchased. She packed several evening gowns including her light blue gown, suits, and pajamas, under clothes, jewelry and toiletries in a travel bag and then started on Paul's bags. She made sure to pack his black wool tuxedo, black tuxedo shoes and several suits bought only in recent months. If she had forgotten anything, they could buy it once they had gotten to New York. She placed their new winter coats on the back of the sofa along with Paul's new hat. She got their leather gloves out of the dresser and thought of when Bertie had given them the gloves and Emily's locket the Christmas before her death.

Belle had given land on top of another mountain, on which a Sportsman's Club with cabins and a main lodge that were located, to Emily and Paul. She had also given Emily a large sum of money to improve the club property which provided them with income from rental fees. Emily received more than a year's wages every off-season month from the rental property and during each of the summer and fall months she received around $5000 in fees. People came to the mountains to forget the war and to enjoy the peacefulness and protection offered by the Appalachians.

Emily told Paul he would need to call Josef Novak, their hired hand, and tell him that he would need to come and stay until the second of January. He left to call Josef while Emily finished packing. Emily then straightened up the bedroom and set the suitcases in the living room. Paul and Josef would have to move the trunk onto the back of the truck the following morning.

As she set down the suitcase, Paul was hanging up the phone and turned to tell her that Josef would be at their house around 6 or so the next morning. Emily had gone over to her chair to get the box of papers and return them to Bertie's hope chest. She was about to return the box into the chest when she decided to look into the box once more to see if there were other papers that dealt with other banks in New York. If there were, she might as well make the trip count. Sure enough, she found several other safety deposit box agreements, in addition to the one at the Chase Manhattan bank. The other safety deposit agreements were for Pittsburgh banks and another bank in New York. Each of them had a note attached written to Emily similar to the one she had shown Belle. One safety deposit box would be considered necessary, but more than three boxes seemed to be perhaps pieces to a puzzle, one that only Bertie Pierce had known about. What had her friend entrusted to her in those boxes? Why hadn't she just given the items to Belle or Mr. Blakeman for safe-keeping and why did she feel that she had to go to different banks and cities? It made absolutely no sense to Emily. She looked at the dates and the ones in New York were on different dates from the ones in Pittsburgh. The ones in Pittsburgh had been rented several months later.

Emily and Paul turned in early that night and set the alarm for 5am. Emily dreamed of Bertie looking 20 years younger and awakened with a jolt, 30 minutes before the alarm sounded, when Bertie was pleading to her to protect her children in Emily's dream. She rose to get breakfast and after eating, got dressed for the trip. Josef showed up promptly at 6 and he promised to take good care of everything until they got back. Paul gave him the front door key after loading the luggage and trunk into the car and they left for Belle's a few minutes before 6:30. Belle and William were just finishing with their packing and William had his chess set under his arm ready for a rematch or two with Paul when the Blacks pulled into the driveway. The driver loaded everyone's bags into the limo and they left for Bluestone at 7:25 when Mr. Blakeman arrived. He had brought copies of Belle's death certificates and a copy of her will.

They arrived around 8:30 in Bluestone and the private rail car was ready to be hooked up. Mr. Blakeman had wired the necessary funds for the hookup to the 9am train and had a confirmation that everything was ready. Mr. Blakeman had asked that a copy of the notification be sent to the Bluestone station master and was pleased when he was told that it had been done. Emily and Belle chose to stay in the limo while the men went into the station until the rail car was ready. Paul had brought his pipe and had forgotten to bring tobacco. He went into the station to the little stand that sold magazines, cigarettes, and tobacco. He lit his pipe and walked out into the cold with William behind him as his shadow. Mr. Blakeman chuckled as he watched Paul deliberately take a long stride and William stretch his preteen legs to stay in stride. The train was running a little early and since it would take only a few minutes to hook up Belle's car, they would leave the station on schedule. There had been few passengers to get on or off and they actually left a few minutes early.

Emily called Vivian from a pay phone to tell her that they were slated to arrive in Charlottesville around 1pm according to the schedule at the Bluefield station just before the train pulled out. Belle's secretary had made hotel arrangements for the arrival of the group at the Waldorf. She had a suite that she rented by the year and so it was always ready for her. She had paid for ten year's rent ahead of time with the understanding that if the rates increased she would pay any additional increases. She also liked the fact that the suite was only used by her or her family. She never knew, with all of her business interests there, when she had to go to New York on the spur of the moment and not having to make hotel reservations was one less thing she had to worry about. She absolutely refused to fly and always traveled long distances by train. Her secretary had already notified the hotel so that a limo was waiting for her group at the station.

William had mixed emotions traveling in the private rail car since this would be his first trip without either his mother or Louise, but it was also the first one with Emily and Paul. Paul told him to set up the chess board and Mr. Blakeman called out that he wanted to play the winner. William and Paul looked at each other and at almost the same time said, "Could you teach me how to play?" Everyone laughed and Belle and Emily watched as Mr. Blakeman explained the different pieces and how they could move. He briefly explained "check" and "check mate". He coached both of them through a game and started rubbing his head after about a half an hour. William and Paul had quickly picked up the moves of the pieces and the match quickly became intense. William said, "This is like going to war, isn't it Paul?"

"Well it is as far as strategy, movement of pieces and capturing pieces but no bloodshed. In chess, there's no destruction of property or innocent people suffering, starving, or dying. War is an ugly monster, William. Never forget that people's lives are at stake in war. Generals draw up maps and make plans, but it's the soldiers, marines, and sailors that do the dying and yes, sometimes even civilians. Many times, when people are badly wounded, they're just never the same. My father's father was killed in World War I as he was pulling his cart near Budapest. I didn't mean to get so serious, but I do believe my friend, that is check mate," he said as he moved his rook.

"Paul, you tricked me," William said.

Paul chuckled and said, "All's fair in love and war. You want to play again?"

William had his hands on his hips and said, "You bet!"

Emily shook her head and whispered to Belle that she didn't know who was enjoying the game more. Mr. Blakeman sat back and watched the intensity build once more at the chess board and heard "check" several times by both of them and finally "check mate" with that match going once again to Paul. Not giving up, William set the board up once again and asked Mr. Blakeman if he wanted to play. William played two matches with Mr. Blakeman who coached him along the way pointing out mistakes he had made and William finally got to say "check" and got so excited. Mr. Blakeman coached him through a check mate and William literally jumped up and down. The second game lasted almost an hour and Mr. Blakeman once more coached him and they ended up getting boxed in and it was declared a draw. Mr. Blakeman explained to William that in chess tournaments if there had been a draw, then how much time each player took to move would be compared and they used special clocks that timed each player's moves.

William was beginning to get tired and just then Belle pulled out a 750 piece jigsaw puzzle in its box from a wide tapestry bag that everyone could work on together. They could all work on the puzzle after lunch. The porter announced the lunch would be served when they reached Charlottesville in about another half an hour. After he left, Emily mentioned finding the other five box agreements and Mr. Blakeman asked to see them. Emily took them out of her purse and he wrote down the names of the banks and dates. He was going to try to retrace Bertie's steps in the order that she had made when she had signed the agreements. As luck would have it, she had opened the ones in New York apparently within a few days of each other last year in 1943 and the last two, the ones in Pittsburgh were opened earlier this year on the same date just a few weeks after Louise's marriage to Alfred Perkins. Belle listened carefully to the dates and knew that the last date was when Bertie had bought Belle the gas lamps that were on her vanity as a surprise. Belle recalled that in '43 that Louise had gone to New York for her graduation but then remembered that Bertie had gone with herself on a trip to New York to shop for Louise a birthday and graduation present in the early spring of '43. That must have been when Bertie had gone to the banks.

The puzzle with the bank boxes was getting more complex as they found out more information about them. The biggest question seemed to be why? Why had she gotten so many boxes in two different cities? All of them would have to wait until they actually saw the contents of each of those boxes to get any answers. According to Belle, Bertie never carried a lot of cash with her except when Belle had forced her to take some with her when they went to New York for business so that she could shop while Belle was in meetings. Belle smiled to herself as her thoughts turned thinking about the gas lamps Bertie had bought for her on their last trip together before Louise's wedding plans had taken over their lives. In everything she did, Bertie always put the feelings and the welfare of others before her own. Belle thought that perhaps the renting of the boxes was a means of protecting others. Belle missed her favorite niece by marriage each day since Bertie's death, and was comforted by the mere presence of Bertie's son, William. He was a lot like Bertie in his manner and temperament and thankfully didn't resemble his sister who seemed drawn to everything bad from the Coleman side of the family.

They were almost to the Charlottesville station and decided to wait on starting the jigsaw puzzle until Vivian and John had gotten onboard. Belle had told the porter while they were in Bluestone that two more would be joining her car and additional lunches had been prepared. The train had barely been stopped a minute than Vivian and John were both escorted into the private car. Shouts were raised by all when they came through the door and hugs, kisses, and handshakes were shared as well as holiday greetings. John sat across from Paul as he ate his lunch at the table with William as well and told Paul,"I am so glad you guys called. Since we have been out of classes Vivian has had a lot of free time to think about the baby she miscarried in September. She needed to see you guys more than ever! I was worried that she would get into a deep depression right after she miscarried, but she threw herself into her studies. The distractions of the various projects, readings, papers, and regular assignments had helped her a lot. We needed to get away from the house for a while and I thank you. We had a nice first Christmas together, but she missed you two so much."

Paul patted his hand and said, "Emily always seems to know when and how to help our Vivian. I guess it's her maternal instinct or something. We were both worried about her son, and we're both so glad you joined us. So, you had a super Christmas? Did you like our gifts? We both loved ours! Say, have you met William? This is William Pierce, Belle's nephew. He lost his mother, a good friend of Emily's, back in November." John shook William's hand and each said how glad they were to make the other's acquaintance. John waited until William was gone to ask if he was related to Louise. Paul assured him that although William was Louise's brother, he was nothing like her. Meanwhile, across the car Vivian, Emily, and Belle enjoyed their lunch at another table and Vivian just kept hugging her mom as she enjoyed her lunch while Belle and Emily sipped on cups of coffee.

"So did Mr. Blakeman know anything about this box?" Vivian asked.

"Apparently he didn't, so he has laid out a timeline and we believe the first ones were set up while Bertie was shopping for a birthday and graduation gift for Louise. Oh I didn't tell you, there are actually five boxes! The last two were rented right after Louise's wedding this year in Pittsburgh. I have no idea what we are going to find in them," Emily said excitedly.

"You mean to tell me that there are five of them! What in the world could she have put into those boxes? Well, I suppose it will depend upon the size of the boxes, you know. I know one thing and that is I sure missed you two," Vivian said and hugged her mom again. Belle noticed the extra hugs Vivian had given her mother and knew that the two of them had always been close and intended not to push or nose around to find out what had happened to cause this extra show of affection. It didn't take long before she heard Emily ask, "How are you feeling now dear?"

"Oh I'm all right mom. It's been hard now without having class work to keep me busy and I've had a lot of free time to think about it. I mean I would have been close to the halfway point soon. Father Schmidt, the campus priest, told me that we could have other children, but I can't think about that right now. We will try again and if God wants us to have a child then we will have one."

Belle closed her eyes as she realized the full impact of what Vivian was saying. Apparently she had suffered a miscarriage in the fall and knew that must have been what had caused Bertie to cry about so hard back in September, but had said she couldn't talk about it then. All the pieces fell into place about that mystery and she now understood why Vivian wasn't her typical upbeat self but was being overly affectionate with her mother. They were definitely close and Belle envied that closeness. She hoped and prayed that perhaps she could have a fraction of that sort of rapport with both Emily and Vivian one day.

Belle asked her what classes she was taking and Vivian told her that she had the second part of a literature class, biology, accounting II, Introduction to business practices, and an economics class. She had made all A's in the fall semester as did John. He had discovered that due to lack of enrollment, the school of law was closing after this semester until the end of the war. If John could find a lawyer that would accept him as an apprenticeship, he could still get his state law license within two years, otherwise he would have to wait until after the end of the war to go to law school.

Belle listened intently to John's dilemma and excused herself to speak with Mr. Blakeman. She asked him if he knew any attorneys in the Charlottesville area that were accepting law clerks as apprentices. "No I don't, but I have a brother that has a law firm and he lives in Farmington that's located a little northwest of Charlottesville. It's a little drive of about twenty minutes one way each day, but I can check with him. He has lived there for about twenty years now and he may know of an attorney looking for an apprentice," he replied.

"I would appreciate it if you would. Tell him if he knows of someone that I would like to personally recommend John for an apprenticeship to practice law in VA. I would prefer that it be someone who currently has a successful practice in corporate law. John will have to have knowledge of contracts if he is going to help Vivian as much as he can. He already has a good solid background dealing with wealth since his mother's family was one of the original Virginia families. His parents had inherited a successful and very large shipyard in Newport News and now they were one of the richest families in Richmond. John will protect Vivian, we just have to give him the legal knowhow of how to do it," Belle patted his shoulder as she spoke and returned to the other side of the rail car.

Paul, John, and William worked diligently on the puzzle while Mr. Blakeman was trying to think of other options for John to get his license to practice law. Belle had a personal stake in seeing that Vivian was taken care of and he knew how much she admired the young couple. With just a little bit of time, patience, and experience he knew that John would make a fine lawyer. Vivian had a good head on her shoulders and would succeed in pursuits she chose with the more than $20 million endowment she had received from Belle. She would not squander it and that's for sure. She was generous, but not to a fault. Her intelligence, pleasant personality, and capacity to love endeared Vivian to everyone that met her. Mr. Blakeman naturally had a higher regard for Vivian than he had for Louise. She had proven herself over and over again to be responsible in her decisions. Louise had been a big disappointment to Belle but luckily Vivian, Belle's only grandchild, more than made up for the disappointment.

Mr. Blakeman knew that Louise would probably get into more mischief once Belle was dead and gone. She had made several attempts to cause problems for Vivian and would have succeeded if Belle had not swallowed her pride admitting to actually being Emily's mother. Louise wanted the position and wealth of John's family but he had chosen Vivian over her. She hadn't accepted his rejection due to her own character flaws but rather felt that Vivian had blocked his interest in her. One way or another, Louise would try to come between them or cause pain or suffering for Vivian. Louise didn't take defeat easily.

Belle had always insisted that any aspect of her business ventures be above board in the larger picture and was certain that Vivian would continue to do business in the same way. Belle had bought extra ration stamps from the poor, but she chose the families that she purchased from carefully and bartered with them using money that they needed for medicines, clothes, or food for the sugar and coffee rations that they could do without. They didn't need coffee, but needed flour, salt, vegetables, and fruits. Belle paid double the price for the ration stamps and then didn't use them except for a few special occasions. Boxes with groceries and an occasional tin of coffee magically appeared on those families' back porches.

Belle was a shrewd businesswoman with the keenest business sense he had ever encountered but she never forgot her roots. She had diversified her holdings without any guidance from her attorney and made shrewd business maneuvers after doing her own research. She called it "not putting all of her eggs in one basket" but he called it building a good solid foundation. Her portfolio of holdings included various companies, stores, businesses, and even television and radio stations. The individual contracts for her holdings filled a large filing cabinet. She always insisted on having copies stored in various safe places in case of a fire or break-in at his office. Only Robert and Belle knew about the copies and where they were stored. Belle was more like a second mother to him and he protected her in every business or personal matter. She had trusted him when he was first starting his career and had been extremely generous to him over the years. There was a mutual admiration on Belle's part as well. He was like a son to her and he had never failed her when she counted on him for his legal finesse. He knew everything about Belle's personal and business life.

On the way to New York, Emily, Vivian, and Belle talked about their memories of Bertie and shared some of them with each other while the others worked on the jigsaw puzzle. After Belle and Emily had shared several of their own memories, Vivian recalled how Bertie would push Louise and herself on the swings at the little school at the end of the hollow. "Mom, do you remember how much Bertie loved strawberries? If I found a patch of wild ones, I would always take some of them to her. She would sit down with us on the edge of the porch and Louise, Bertie, and I would eat those berries with some sugar and cream. Another thing I will never forget was how Bertie would always share anything she had and made everything so much fun for everyone."

Belle surprised both of them when she said, "When Bertie came to live with me, did either of you know that she couldn't read or write? She could only pick out a few words here and there from Louise's primary books, but as

Louise read to her, Bertie was learning more and more words. After Louise practiced her writing and spelling, Bertie did the same late at night after Louise went to sleep. She didn't want Louise to know about her mother's illiteracy and I was proud of Bertie for trying to learn."

"Here I tried to help her all those years ago and wrote down directions over and over again of how I made jams or canned vegetables and she couldn't even read them. She should have told me," Emily said.

"Bertie was a proud woman that had been neglected and abused all her life; first by her parents and then by her husband. She didn't want anyone to know that her mother had never even bothered to send her to school for even one day. Her mother used her like a slave. She frequently beat Bertie for not moving fast enough. I guess Bertie didn't want to admit it to herself just how badly she had been treated and was ashamed that she didn't know how to read or write," Belle affirmed.

Emily started to mention how Bertie had hidden her pregnancy with William from Jack but decided that might be too painful for Vivian to hear at this time and chose instead to tell the story about Bertie and a mouse. She asked Belle if Bertie had ever told her the story about a mouse and when Belle shook her head no, Emily began the story. "Well, make no mistake Bertie was a true mountain woman. She could shoot as well as a man and was very strong, but she hated snakes. The only thing she feared more than Jack during one of his rages was a snake. Well, one day Bertie was working on the edge of her vegetable garden clearing rocks and saw a coiled copperhead about three feet from her hand out of the corner of her eye. Her hand was under a loose stone and she knew not to make a sudden move. The snake was about to strike when a little mouse came out from under the rock and scampered over her hand just as the snake struck at her. The snake bit it and poor little mouse didn't live long but Bertie quickly smashed the snake with the rock. She looked around since Paul had once told her they traveled in pairs and saw a second one about another three feet away and killed it with her hoe. Bertie dug a grave for that little mouse and planted a few daffodils over it. I had taken a few bulbs for her to plant in the fall, but she had waited until the last frosts of winter to plant them. There is a whole bed of daffodils right now up by her old cabin that spread from those few bulbs planted over that little mouse."

Belle chuckled to herself as she imagined Bertie with the strawberries and planting the daffodils. Silent tears slid down her face as she remembered how cruel Louise had been to Bertie, the woman that Belle had come to think of as a surrogate daughter all those years. Bertie had been a wonderful and devoted mother to both of her children. William had loved her; but Louise, she only had two great loves in this world, material things and herself. She acted as though she was better than anyone and was embarrassed by Bertie's lack of sophistication. Belle reflected upon the events of '43 and '44. She and Bertie had both been so ashamed by Louise's antics designed to hurt Vivian. Belle and Bertie had spent many evenings discussing Louise's shenanigans.

Emily had only found out in the last couple of months that she was Belle's only natural-born daughter. Belle had allowed Emily to be adopted by the Schmidt's – Ann and Nathan Schmidt. Belle had discovered their real relationship for herself in the spring of '44. She was investigating one of Louise's many lies about Vivian and had chosen only to reveal their relationship to Emily due to threats of those lawsuits following Bertie's death. Belle didn't want to take a risk that their relationship would be exposed in an open court. Louise had also done what Belle considered unforgivable; she had dared to challenge Belle's sanity. After Alfred was shown several documents and photographs of his wife's various escapades, the lawsuits were immediately dropped to avoid public scandal. Alfred and Louise did not know of Belle's relationship to Emily and Belle wouldn't do that unless it was absolutely necessary. At his point in time, William didn't know the truth about their relationship either. Louise would try to humiliate and hurt Vivian any way she could. Louise's lies about Vivian had ultimately been the means to learning the truth of Emily's birth and had then led Belle to find her only child and grandchild.

Belle thought that the best time to tell Vivian and John about their real relationship was when William wasn't in the room and perhaps had gone to a museum or shopping with the men. An opportunity would surely occur during their time in New York. She could not take the slightest risk of Louise finding out and ruining Vivian's chances of a peaceful life. Newspapers would love to get a story about one of the richest women on the eastern coast. If William found out he wouldn't say anything intentional that would hurt either Emily or Vivian, but Louise could coax it out of him if she suspected he had any sort of a secret that would in any way be to her benefit. Louise, who had blamed Vivian for any trouble Louise herself had gotten into or caused. Louise would humiliate Vivian without blinking her eyes. She never accepted any responsibility for her actions that had gotten her removed from Comfield College and it had caused a lot shame for Bertie and Belle.

Vivian's family had helped the Pierce family as much as they could when she was in elementary school, but Louise, in wanting to forget her humble beginnings, forgot their many kindnesses and had replaced those memories with fantasy ones she created out of her hatred of her own past. She had set her cap for John as soon as she had found out about his family and obvious wealth. She wanted him since he had the wealth and connections she craved and claimed that she was denied him, supposedly by his Vivian's schemes. She imagined that Vivian had spitefully taken John from her when, in fact, he had never given Louise as much as a second thought. He had recognized Louise as a husband hunter and had encountered numerous other women with the same intent. Vivian hadn't treated John any differently and had to be pursued by John instead of the other way around. Vivian had made a positive change in both John's attitude and grades. His parents loved Vivian for her positive influence on John. If Louise could hurt Vivian she would, indeed, she would enjoy doing it at any cost.

Belle hoped that William hadn't heard anything they had said about Vivian's miscarriage. Only The Good Lord knew what Louise would make of that piece of information. Louise took after her father and was as mean and ornery as he had been, and perhaps could even be worse. Jack Pierce had been raised to hate immigrants and never wanted to learn anything that they did differently from him and treated them with disdain. He had been a decent carpenter when he had first married Bertie, but had, unfortunately, fallen under the influence of alcohol. In his last years of his life, he drank more and more, became more physically abusive of Bertie, and had died in his sleep after one of his binges. Bertie's mother had been a bad influence on Louise as well.

Paul had used the family wagon when he had taken Bertie and the two children to Belle's home all those years ago. They had moved onto Belle's old family land grant and she had hoped that the children would do well under her influence. They had been there only a short time when Marshall Steel had a signed contract with Belle to mine an extremely large coal deposit on her property. They had moved into the large 20-room home in Welfield where William had thrived, but as time went by, Louise's behavior became worse and so did her attitude towards Bertie. Eventually, after the Comfield College fiasco, Belle had made arrangements with Judge Perkins, Louise's father-in-law, to get Louise and his son married. Belle knew that Louise would eventually become a bad influence on William if she stayed around him and so she had to act swiftly to get Louise out of the house. She had paid for a huge wedding and construction of a large house in Charleston, WV, that was completely furnished with the best furnishings that money could buy and yet Belle knew that it wasn't going to be enough for Louise and her obsession with never seeming to have enough. Belle had furnished Alfred's office near the state capitol. In essence, it amounted to her paying Alfred to take Louise off her hands.

Belle fell asleep in the upholstered chair while her thoughts had drifted to those early days with Bertie and the children and she slept for about an hour after leaving Philadelphia. As the train headed for New York, Emily also took a nap. Vivian looked at the faces of the two most important women in her life as they slept. She loved her mother and had a great deal of gratitude and respect for Belle who had given her an endowment that now opened so many doors for her and John's future. 'It's a shame that Belle hadn't had any children. She would have been such a wonderful mother,' Vivian thought, 'any children of hers would have been so strong-willed and well-disciplined that's for sure. She has been such a good influence on William. He's unspoiled and has good morals like Bertie and Belle. It's a shame that Louise wasn't more like her younger brother.' Vivian had last seen William when he was barely a 1 year old baby more than a dozen years ago.

'Perhaps that is what God intended all along when Bertie had moved in with Belle about twelve years ago. Indeed, God does work in mysterious ways. Jack had died, and Belle became wealthy shortly after Bertie had moved in with her. Belle got an instant family to take care of and had dearly loved Bertie and the children. She didn't have to live out her days alone,' Vivian's thoughts echoed in her mind as they neared New York, 'I'm glad mom has a new friend in Belle Coleman. She still misses her mother after all these years and its good for her to have someone older to advise her.'

She turned to see what the men were up to and saw that they had just about finished the jigsaw puzzle when they arrived at Grand Central Station. William yelled with delight when they put the last few pieces in just as the train stopped. He was so excited about seeing New York with Paul and Emily. He had mentally decided where the "men" were going to go, namely

Paul, John, and himself. An extremely intelligent boy of almost thirteen, he knew that there were several museums he couldn't wait to visit as well as the huge library he had read so much about. Neither Bertie nor Louise had ever been interested to take him there and he was determined to go this time with Paul and of course, John. He also wanted to see Ellis Island. Paul had told him on one of his stays with them, while his mother was going to different doctors across the country when she first gotten sick, that he and his parents had come to America when he was only a baby. William wanted to see where Paul's parents had actually stood on Ellis Island. He hoped to get Paul's help in buying a new suit. It was time for him to wear a suit and tie to church now and he needed a man's help. He had a lot of plans for them over the next few days.

Two limos were waiting at the station for their party and they arrived at the Astoria within a half an hour of arriving at the station. They would be staying in the hotel's Queen Suite, which is Belle's suite, with five bedrooms. Belle had instructed Mr. Blakeman to stay in the suite with them and to be available in case he was needed. She also did not want to risk any possible eavesdropping of conversations by any of the maids or other hotel guests. He could make arrangements for total privacy from all staff of the Astoria. The concierge had welcomed Belle and her party with open arms and a huge basket of fruits, caviar, crackers, and chocolates were on the suite's main desk to welcome them when they had arrived.

They each went to their individual rooms and after taking long baths in their individual bathrooms slept soundly except for Emily. She too had thought of how she was going to tell Vivian the truth about their relationship to Belle and had trouble falling asleep. Emily wasn't sure of how Vivian was going to take the news of Belle being her grandmother. Emily hadn't slept well since finding out and knew that she had to tell Vivian as soon as possible to get much needed sleep. Perhaps Belle would be willing to be with her to tell Vivian when the time was right. Emily had always been completely honest with Vivian, but wanted to make sure that William was not around when it was discussed. It wasn't something to be discussed of the telephone either. Perhaps, she thought, Paul could take William for ice cream or shopping. Emily hoped that John could be there as well as Mr. Blakeman when Vivian was told the truth of their relationship. Emily's mind was busy with thoughts of Bertie and the boxes and it wasn't until well after midnight when she finally fell asleep.

William was the first to rise after Paul and Emily. Paul had ordered coffee and a full breakfast of eggs, bacon, toast, juice, and sweet rolls for everyone from the kitchen. William knocked loudly on Vivian and John's door and softly on Belle's and said, "You guys are going to sleep all day. We have things to do and people to see, don't you know!"

Belle, already awake, was dressing when William had knocked on the door as were Vivian and John. John came tearing out the door and chased William who fled behind Paul as if he was afraid of John's intent. Paul said, "You're on your own there buddy! I believe he intends to tickle you until you cry for beating on his door like that! I can't say that I blame him!"

"Paul!" Emily scolded. "John, both of you is acting like, like children! Now sit down William, before I get after you! What on earth will the maids think?"

"Yes ma'am," they all said in unison and went to sit on their chairs. John kissed his mother-in-law's forehead and helped Vivian get into her chair. Mr. Blakeman had just arrived into the dining area and the maid quickly poured him a cup of coffee. Belle had laughed at the scolding and shook her head. They had a big day ahead of them. Belle, Emily, and Mr. Blakeman would go to the first bank to get the contents of the box. They would be bringing it back to the suite as soon as they could if there was nothing in it that would possibly upset William. Paul had his own plan for the guys and Vivian that day. Vivian would go to the spa and the men would get haircuts while the others went to the bank. Paul said, "Looks to me like you need to get your ears lowered William. What do you say to us getting a haircut while Emily goes to the bank? We can get some skunk water put on when we're finished!"

"Skunk water, what's that?" William asked.

"You'll find out," Paul teased. "Vivian, I thought you could use a spa treatment while they're gone!"

"Oh that sounds so good. I'll call and see if they have an opening," she said.

"Don't bother. I called down and made you an appointment myself last night," he said proudly.

"You made her an appointment for the spa? I don't believe it!" Emily said with a look of shock on her face. "Why didn't you make us one?" she said gesturing to Belle and herself.

"I did. Your appointment is for this afternoon," he smiled as he saw genuine surprise on her face. "What are you looking at me like that for? I have my moments," he said with a tilt of his chin upward.

"You sure do dear, you sure do," Emily said as she kissed him.

They enjoyed their meal and retreated to their rooms to freshen up for the big day ahead of them. Mr. Blakeman had all of the papers and Emily had the receipts for all of the agreements. They left to go to the bank while the others went to their destinations. Kisses were exchanged between the couples and William announced, "I'm getting too old for kisses."

Paul elbowed him and said, "You're never too old to be kissed by a beautiful woman, William, never."

The party rode down the elevator together. Vivian got off the elevator on the floor to the spa. Paul, John, and William got off on the next floor for the hotel barbershop. The last three were ushered into a waiting limo to take them to the Chase Manhattan Bank.

The bank was very thorough in checking over the documents and finally after about an hour, papers were filled out and signed. Bertie had put Emily's name as co-owner of the box and that expedited things. Emily was led into a room where the box was brought to her and placed on a table. The bank's clerk closed the door behind him. Emily opened the box and saw a small box and a stack of papers. The small box contained a beautiful loose cut blue diamond. The papers were bearer bonds attached to the Chase Manhattan Bank worth $5000. Bertie must have saved the money up and purchased those bonds on her trip with Louise. It must have taken her years to collect it. Emily opened the door and motioned for Mr. Blakeman and Belle to join her.

Belle looked at the blue diamond and smiled. She had given the 3 carat blue diamond to Bertie on Bertie's first birthday celebrated after moving into the house on Sumner Street. She had forgotten about it over the years and wondered why Bertie had never had it set. "I gave her that stone when we first moved to Welfield. She was supposed to have it set but I guess she couldn't make up her mind whether to have it set as a pendant or as a ring. Poor Bertie all this time she's had it and didn't get to enjoy it," Belle said with sadness in her voice.

"Perhaps she just liked to look at it," Emily said. "Bertie enjoyed looking at pretty things and often told me that nature provided the world with so many beautiful things and how much pleasure she got just looking at them. She raised flowers and yet she would never pick them. She liked looking at them and smelling them. I believe that she probably did the same thing with this diamond."

"I agree with you, Emily. The clerk said that Bertie came here often to sign out the box. She must have come just to look at it from time to time," Mr. Blakeman assured her.

"Look at these though. These are bearer bonds issued from this bank," Emily showed them. "Where in the world could Bertie have gotten so much money?" she asked.

"From me," Belle offered. "I gave her $500 for each birthday and $500 each Christmas. She used some of it to buy gifts for her children and must have squirreled away the rest and brought it to New York. She probably kept it in her hope chest. Louise wouldn't have touched the chest since it was so old-fashioned and William wouldn't have gone into his mother's room without her permission. She must have sensed that something was wrong with her health and didn't want to keep so much cash in the house and wanted it to go to you, Emily. I intended for her to spend it on herself, but Bertie was always afraid something might happen and then we would need money. Knowing her, she wanted to keep it safe for all of us. Well they're yours now Emily. She wanted you to have it."

"Can't I just give them to William?" she asked.

"Sure you can," Mr. Blakeman said. "But as bearer bonds, right now anyone can cash them," he reminded her.

"Well in that case perhaps we need to leave them here and bring William to the bank later and have the bonds cashed and reissued with bonds having his name on them. What do you think?" Emily asked. "She got them for the protection of her family and William will appreciate them more than Louise. What about the diamond? What should I do about the diamond?"

"You should keep the diamond, have it set as a pendant, and wear it from time to time to remember Bertie when you wear it. Louise has more jewelry than she can ever possibly wear. You can always give someone the pendant later," Belle observed. "Emily, Bertie loved you as a sister and wanted you to have the contents of this box. She obviously didn't want Louise to get either the diamond or the bonds. Don't you see, Bertie must have thought of you when she put that diamond in here? Louise wasn't impressed when I gave it to Bertie because it wasn't set. She was very young then and probably doesn't even remember it. Keep the diamond, Emily, in honor of Bertie."

"I already have Bertie's emerald ring to remember her, but I will have the diamond set as a pendant and wear it only on special occasions. I will let Vivian decide what to do with it when I die," she said with determination.

"Well that clears up this mystery. Let's return the box and return to the hotel. You may want to put the diamond in the hotel safe before we go out for lunch," Belle suggested.

They returned the box to the bank clerk and had arrived back to the hotel shortly after the others. Vivian looked quite refreshed and the men were handsome. Paul had decided on a shave as well and the men had gotten their shoes buffed. The men all smelled alike and William said, "We smell good, don't we? That's skunk water you smell! They put it on your hair after a haircut." Everyone laughed and Emily directed them to have a seat in the living room area. She shook her finger at Paul and he merely shrugged and said, "What did I do?" She gripped her lips tightly together and said, "Never mind."

"There were some bearer bonds and this diamond in the box at the Chase Manhattan," she announced. "I am going to have the bonds transferred to William's name. Anyone can cash in the bonds right now and I want William to have them. When he gets older, he can decide what he wants to do with them. He can keep them in the safety deposit box until then. I will check to see whether or not I can change Bertie's rental agreement to have my name and William's name put on it instead." William was surprised and said, "Why don't you keep them Emily? Momma would have wanted you to keep them."

Emily said, "She told me to use it wisely and I can't think of a better way than to put them aside for your college education. Paul and I both have all we need and besides, it was your mother's money that bought the bonds.

She must not have known how to give you money without Louise knowing about it. Louise would have wanted the money even though all of it had been gifts through the years to your mother. William, I don't want to speak ill of Louise, but rather I'm merely stating my opinion. It seems like she never has enough and manages to waste money as quickly as possible on some odd pieces of jewelry or clothing. I believe that Bertie would like for the money to be used instead to help make a future for you. Do you understand?"

William nodded and told her, "Yes ma'am and thank you."

Emily took out the small box with the blue diamond and said, "I'm going to have this set as a pendant. Belle had given it to Bertie when you first moved to Sumner Street. You were just a toddler then William."

William peered at the diamond and said, "It's the same color as your eyes Emily!" and as the others looked at the diamond they had to admit he was right. Belle smiled as she said out loud, "That's why she left it to you. I told you it must have reminded her of you."

"Vivian, I trust that you will see that it is handled appropriately after my passing," Emily said solemnly.

The diamond was passed around and each added their own comment about it. John had called for reservations for lunch and as they were leaving, Emily left the diamond with the concierge to be placed in the safe. A strange man in the lobby overheard her request and went to the pay phones.

Chapter 2

Alfred had been furious when he had returned from the meeting in Mr. Blakeman's office in Welfield after seeing various documents and photographs taken of Louise with other men in some run down bars while others had been taken in California with some movie star. He called out for Louise, "Louise, I need to see you in the library, now if you please!"

Louise swayed into the library and smiled as she closed the door. She was expecting to hear good news but sensed from the sound of his voice that something must have gone wrong with his meeting about her lawsuits. She had asked for custody of William, her brother, who had been left the bulk of Bertie's estate and wanted all of the endowments made to Vivian and her parents nullified. Louise thought to herself, 'Finally I have gotten even with Vivian and when I'm finished with her, she will have to go back to being nothing but a little farm girl. John will leave her and then I can take my place beside him. Any court would decide in my favor to be William's guardian, after all I am his sister and Aunt Belle isn't even blood related.' She had used the time to think about the case while Alfred had been away. 'The endowments to total strangers speak volumes on Belle's sanity. Who in their right mind would give away more than $20 million and property to total strangers and not to her own family? What made it so bad was that she had given it to the very people responsible for all of my problems. Oh I can't wait to make sure that Belle is punished for how she had mistreated me and forced me to drop out of college' Louise had thought over and over again during Alfred's absence.

For Louise, everything would be tied up nicely and then things would be as she thought that they should have been. She would gain control over a lot of Belle's holdings and in a few years after she died, Louise figured she would have it all. Vivian would be returned to her penniless former self and was sure of that. Louise could hardly wait for John to drop her and Louise would be waiting. Over and over the same thoughts had run through her mind. Later, she thought, 'In time I will divorce Alfred, of course, and chance upon John and renew our relationship. I know the truth of how he feels about me. That last kiss I got to share with him before Aunt Belle forced me to come home from Comfield, he couldn't have forgotten it, nope, and he just couldn't. He would have had to have been made of stone not to have been moved by that kiss. My relationship with John was interfered with and ended by Vivian before it even had a chance to start. Yes sir, everything was going to be as it should and John would have a real woman by his side. John needed someone who knew and understood how to take one's place in society. I have everything he needs in a wife. It won't be long before he realizes how perfectly suited we are for each other. Money should marry money, everyone with money knew that.'

"Oh Alfred I am so glad you're home. Well, what did Mr. Blakeman want to talk to you about? Are they going to settle out of court?" Louise asked with one of her sweetest smiles.

"Oh he had plenty to say and a whole lot to show me! Why didn't you tell me that you had been forced to withdraw from Comfield for a scandal? And what about these?" he questioned her as he tossed the photographs showing Louise shoplifting. "Oh and there are others, lots of them! Pictures of you with men taken all over the country!" he shouted.

"Where did you get those? Who took these?" she attempted to refute what he was saying as she recognized different stores in different cities and herself putting different items into her purse.

"Your Aunt Belle hired a detective. It's obvious from that group of pictures that you were stealing. How am I supposed to explain that away in court? Oh and there's more," he said a lot louder as he showed documents and photographs of her spending, drinking, and cavorting with strange men. "And if that wasn't bad enough there's the scandal with affidavits of a Mrs. Byrd and a Miss Adams telling of a conspiracy and your propensity for lying to discredit Vivian Black Williams, the daughter of your mother's best friend! With all this evidence, I had no choice but to withdraw all of the lawsuits."

"You withdrew them?" she screamed louder. "You made the decision without asking me? I can't believe you did that! Why didn't you call me first before dropping them? I can explain everything! On top of everything else that's happened, you decide to drop the lawsuits!"

"Did you honestly expect me to have these shown in open court? How can I counter so much evidence against your character? You're lucky that Belle didn't throw you out of her house with nothing! It's over, Louise. Now answer me truthfully, did you marry me because you loved me or was I made a fool of and tricked into believing that you loved me?" he asked earnestly.

"Why I married you because I loved you, dearest," she lied.

"You have to call your grandmother to have her withdraw her suit. Don't look at me like that; you didn't see all the evidence they had against her. All of this could come out in her suit for William's custody as well," he informed her. "I know you want your grandmother to have William and the money that goes with him for her own. Look at these. Did you know these little secrets of hers?" he shoved copies of signed affidavits from her aunts.

"I can't call her Alfred. This is the first I've heard of any of this, really!" she tried to sound sincere.

"I can't believe you Louise! You two are a real peach of a pair!" he countered. "Why don't you ask her about all of this? Ask her how she raised her daughters?"

"I can't, she committed suicide last night. I got the call right after you left. I don't know what happened but I am sure that Aunt Belle had something to do with it. I am all alone now if you don't believe that I love you. I loved her and now she's gone. Oh Alfred, I knew that I couldn't take care of William by myself and now, now I don't have a choice," she cried. No one knew how much Louise had loved her Grandma Coleman and had relied upon her for guidance for tricking Alfred into marrying her. The tears she shed now were real tears of sorrow in the loss of her grandmother as well as tears of self-pity. Alfred was a sucker for tears.

"Oh dearest, I didn't know. I'm sorry," he said as he quickly rose and came to her side. He couldn't stay angry with her for long seeing her obviously in so much pain. All of those documents were from the past and he was sure of one thing and that was how much he loved Louise and how much she loved him. "What can I do?"

"Her funeral will be on Friday. I can't bear it. I really don't know how I'm going to get through this. First I've lost mother and now grandma," she cried.

"I'll go with you to take care of things, darling. Now, why don't you go and get some rest. I'll put these in our safe where no one can ever use them against you. We'll go and stay at your grandmother's house or would you rather go to my parent's house?" he suggested.

"I can't stay in her house where, where she…" her voice trailed off.

"Very well I'll call mother and tell her we'll be in for the weekend. I have to make a few cancellations of appointments I have meetings set up with clients on Thursday and Friday and can get them postponed. I don't have to be in court until next week. Now go on, get some rest," he kissed her tenderly.

Louise closed the door and then smiled slightly to herself about her narrow escape. Belle must have had her investigated after she had become engaged and had a detective take those pictures. Louise knew about the other investigations but she had been younger and not as wise. It was lucky for her that Alfred hadn't noticed the one showing her engagement ring on her left hand in some of the photographs and the one from California with the actor that showed her wedding band. She had managed to cover them with her own hand when he was showing the pictures to her and was pleased that he hadn't noticed them. Thank goodness he hadn't remembered the trip to California where she was supposed to be with some friends when Bertie had gotten so sick. He must have been too upset to look at them closely. Satisfied with the timing of her grandmother's death, Louise had managed to wiggle out of the situation with a few tears.

Louise thoughts turned to her grandmother and she began sobbing once she reached her large bed and she wondered why Grandma Coleman hadn't called her if she had become so desperate. She and Alfred used separate rooms during her monthly cycles and only rarely slept together now. She cried herself to sleep and awakened two hours later refreshed and immediately had an absolutely brilliant idea. She would hire her own private detective to follow Belle! She must surely have some secrets, some things that she was hiding. Perhaps there was something that she could even be blackmailed with to loosen her purse strings. Louise decided to take care of that when she returned from her grandmother's funeral and was pleased with herself for coming up with the idea.

Louise was quite a pitiful sight when she went to attend the wake held in her grandmother's house. She had no memory of ever being in the house before and was shocked by its sad state. Louise's aunts, Lois in particular, had tried to clean up the living room for the wake, but the rest of the house was a real mess. Louise had selected and purchased the coffin on Thursday as well as a large spray of flowers on the coffin. Her grandmother's body was shielded by a piece of netting to distort where the mortician had tried to repair the area where the bullet had entered beneath her chin. The high collar hid most of the fatal wound, but the mortician had been asked to make it less noticeable by Mrs. Perkins, granddaughter of the dearly departed and he did a reasonable job.

Louise had been relieved when her Aunt Lois told her that the incident had actually occurred on the back porch rather than inside and Louise refused to look out onto the site. She had asked Alfred to let her go alone to the house until it was time for the public to come for the viewing. He would join her about an hour later.

The mortuary had brought several folding chairs and set them around the living room. The dingy curtains and worn furniture were worse than Louise could have ever imagined, but she bravely entered her grandmother's bedroom and was shocked by what she found! It was overflowing with a variety of new clothes, shoes, and miscellaneous finery. The huge, obviously new bed had a lovely comforter and the bedroom set was obviously well-made furniture. Why was this room so elegant while the rest of the house looked like such a dump? Where had her grandmother gotten such beautiful furniture? One thing was for sure and that was her three surviving aunts would be fighting each other over this furniture and the new clothing items.

Louise took another look around the bedroom and returned to the living room. A condolence caller had come by early and one of her aunts called out that she was needed. Louise's aunts claimed that they couldn't bear to be in the room with their mother's remains because they were so distraught. If the truth was told, they were all anxious to try to sneak out some of their mother's belongings without the others seeing. A terrible argument broke out in the bedroom as two of them were pulling on a satin covered pillow. Louise had heard the screams and had gone to see what was going on. "Enough, both of you, you should be ashamed of yourself acting this way on the night of her wake! Now put that down until we hear what is in her will! Until then nothing leaves, do you hear me nothing leaves this house!" Louise said with sudden great authority. Her two aunts dropped the pillow and rushed by her. Louise closed the door behind them and tried to compose herself before returning to the living room. She was grateful that no one else was in the house to hear the argument over such nonsense.

Alfred arrived about fifteen minute before the public viewing and tried to console Louise who was now sitting in the living room alone beside her grandmother. Judge and Mrs. Perkins came by for a few minutes and they made note of the fact that Belle and William were noticeably absent. Very few visitors came to the wake and Louise's aunts had left very early in the evening. Louise couldn't bear for her grandmother to be alone and she and Alfred stayed up through the night sitting in two of the folding chairs.

The funeral held the next morning was short and only a few mourners came to it as well. The mortician paid six men to serve as pall bearers and the cost was added to the price of the arrangements. Alfred stood beside Louise at the gravesite since she was so overwhelmed with grief. Her three aunts could hardly wait for the funeral to be over when one of them, Lois Townsend, asked, "Do you know when they will be reading her will?" The other two echoed her feelings that they needed to return to their home and didn't want to have to come back for it. There was a strange man who had been at the funeral that came up to the burial site and introduced himself as the attorney of the late Martha Coleman. He told the women, "I have been asked by the late Martha Coleman to take care of her last will and testament and can read it at your convenience." All of the aunts spoke at once and it was decided to meet at two o'clock that very afternoon. His office was near the courthouse in Welfield and Alfred agreed to be there as well, on behalf of Louise.

Louise and Alfred returned to his parent's home for an early lunch. Louise rested a short while before it was time to go for the reading of the will. She had decided that she wouldn't call on Belle or William on this trip. She was too hurt by the loss of her grandmother to think of anyone else and couldn't believe that Belle had been so cruel as to not let William attend his own grandmother's funeral. They had deserted her when she could have used their support. Belle had to have been the one who caused her grandmother to commit suicide. Her grandmother was looking forward to having William with her and never would have thought of doing anything like that on her own. They left the honorable Judge Perkins and his wife to go for the reading of the will around one thirty in the afternoon.

The will was short and sweet. All of the earthly possessions of Martha Coleman's were left to Louise Pierce. The aunts turned on her screaming, "That's not fair! It's not fair, not after we went through because of her. It isn't fair."

Louise looked at them coldly and said, "What about what you did to her? I know all about your statements, your lies you supposedly swore to. I know you made up all of it about her. That's what caused her to commit suicide. Rest assured them that if I see fit, I might let you have a few of those possessions that I do not want among you. I will only be keeping a token or two to remember grandmother." What she hadn't said out loud but had thought was, 'The bedroom set would look nicely in one of my guest bedrooms and they have the rest,' she thought.

Louise left the lawyer's office and returned to her grandmother's house with the aunts and let them go room by room dividing up the spoils. What they didn't want would be left for the next owner that moved into the house. When they entered Martha's bedroom, they tried flattery of every sort to try to convince Louise to give the bedroom set to them, but Louise firmly stated, "I intend to take the bedroom set to my house. You may have the linens and whatever you want from the closet or the drawers." The three women just about knocked each other down as they tore open drawers and the sad little closet door. A beautiful dark blue gown hung in the closet, but was too large for any of them. Louise remembered buying the gown for her grandmother to wear to her engagement party. Grandma Martha had looked so beautiful in it and Louise saw the lovely gown that she had purchased for Martha to wear to her wedding and wept because it hadn't been worn. One of Martha's daughters claimed the sewing machine while another wanted the full length Cheval mirror. Louise didn't want either since they didn't match the bedroom set. The eldest of the three wanted her mother's jewelry box and Louise dumped out the jewelry and handed the box to her. There was only one nice piece of jewelry in the stack and that was the piece Louise had bought for her to wear with the blue gown. It took only three hours for the women to make their selections and Louise was glad to have that episode done and over with.

None of the women had chosen to go into any of the dresser drawers since their mother had been much larger than any of them. Louise wanted to check to make sure that the drawers were still intact and pulled each one out. One of the new drawers was stuck and Louise pulled hard and a piece of paper fell out. It was a bank draft that had been signed by Louise's mother, Bertie. Why in the world would her mother be sending money to her mother especially $500? That was a large sum for her grandmother who had only a small income from a small rental cottage back in the mountains. Louise's grandfather had died before she was born and Bertie had never visited her mother. Grandmother rarely visited Bertie while Louise's father, Jack Pierce, was alive. Once Louise's family moved in with Belle she wasn't invited to their new home. In fact, Louise recalled how her grandmother said that Belle told her she wasn't welcome in her home. Belle was unfair to have kept their grandmother away from her and William. There were some other papers stuck behind the drawers, but they appeared to be nothing except sales receipts.

Louise took one last look around the bedroom and closed and locked the front door. Alfred had offered to go with her, but Louise couldn't bear for him to see the condition of the remainder of the house. Louise had never returned to the cabin where her family had lived in that miserable little hollow and the sooner she could forget this vision of squalor, the better. As Louise rode back to Judge Perkins' house she thought more about hiring the detective to follow Belle and felt that perhaps she needed to see what he could dig up about her mother, Bertie, as well.

The morning after the funeral, Louise rose with a feeling of nausea. She had told Alfred that she was having her period when, in fact, her monthly cycle was late and Louise feared that she might be pregnant. She didn't say anything to anyone and decided to wait until they got back to Charleston from Welfield to see a doctor. Louise thought about calling on Belle, but changed her mind. Surely her aunt would forgive her for the unfortunate lapse in judgment. Louise had finally called Belle's and was told that her aunt could not speak with her at this time but wished to convey her condolences on the loss of her grandmother.

Louise was livid and set her mind to contacting a detective almost as soon as she got back to Charleston. She would first go to the doctor and then once she took care of that would have to check for a detective. She would have to be very careful to make sure that Alfred didn't find out about either visit until it was necessary.

Louise secured transportation for the bedroom set just before she and Alfred left the judge's house and returned to Charleston. The trip was only about three hours long and Alfred went to the office to prepare for an appearance in court. Louise checked with the operator and was given the number of several gynecologists. Louise called several before settling on Dr. Thomas Gray with whom she made an appointment. Louise had been nauseous every morning and was sure that she was pregnant. She would need to have it confirmed and then would do what she had to do to make sure that Alfred completely forgot about all of the earlier unpleasantness with Aunt Belle.

Louise kept her appointment and the doctor confirmed she was pregnant. "You are approximately six weeks along Mrs. Perkins. Here is a list of foods you will need to eat and vitamins you will need to take. I will need to see you every month until you deliver the baby. We will discuss things more as you get further along."

Louise thanked him and went directly to a pharmacy to purchase the vitamins. Alfred would be so excited when he heard the news. Although he would make a fantastic father, Louise had no intention of ruining her figure for anyone, especially a baby. She had no intention of carrying the baby to term, but would use an old trick she had learned back in high school. Nobody would mess up her current arrangement of being Charleston's most beautiful hostess and that included some screaming brat.

When Alfred came home that evening, Louise dressed particularly nice in a gown with jacket and set the dining room with lit candles. She had purchased a glass baby bottle at the drug store and had it gift wrapped. She had it sitting on the chair beside hers and couldn't wait to break the news to him. She had ordered cook to prepare steak, asparagus with Béarnaise sauce, and parsnips, Alfred's favorite vegetables. Warm apple dumplings, another of Alfred's favorites, would be served for dessert.

"Uh oh," he said when dinner was served. "What have you done now, Louise?" expecting to hear bad news.

"Why, I haven't done anything dear," she claimed. "I was thinking today about where to put the Christmas tree. This will be our first Christmas together and the first in our new home. I want it to be perfect for us and I want to include some of both of our traditions. What do you think? What did your family do for Christmas?"

"Well we always put the largest one in the living room and put several smaller ones in each of our bedrooms," he said. "What about you? Where did you have your tree?"

"Oh, well, we only had one tree and it was always in the living room and there was a large wreath on the door. I would like to get a wreath dear for our front door, but would like to have one on the upstairs landing as well," she said so sweetly.

"Well what if we put the wreath on the door and a tree in the ball room? That way if we decide to have a holiday dance or party it would look lovely for our guests," he compromised.

"That sounds wonderful! I would love to have a Christmas ball. We could invite all of the judges and all those attorneys who came to our wedding that live in Charleston or in Huntington. Oh darling that would be so wonderful. Should we have our presents under the tree before Christmas or wait until Christmas morning?" she hinted.

"We could wait until Christmas I suppose," he said. "We always opened our presents after Christmas dinner. It doesn't really matter to me though."

"Oh well, I already have you a gift. Well, you might as well open it. I couldn't possibly get it past you now to hide it until Christmas," she said as she handed him the gift.

"But dear, Christmas is a still a couple of weeks away," he countered.

"Well, I want you to open this one today," she urged.

Alfred opened the box and looked puzzled for a moment at the bottle. A gleam of sudden understanding hit him and he rushed to her saying, "Really? When?"

"I went to the doctor today and he said it should be born in late July, around our anniversary. Are you happy darling?" she asked.

"But of course," he answered. "Maybe you should take it easy and not think about hosting a dance. I mean you will need your rest, dearest."

"Nonsense, I'm perfectly healthy and I enjoy planning parties. Please Alfred, I promise that I won't overdo it. I wouldn't do anything to jeopardize our baby," she begged.

"Well, if you think you will be all right and promise not to overdo it. It should be fine but mind you if you start getting fatigued you will let me know as soon as possible, I don't see why we can't just have a small affair," he bargained.

"But darling, people will talk if it's too small of an affair. You know that. We have an image to project and I intend to keep it. I will make the most of our money and splurge it on some items and improvise the rest. We will invite 100 people and most of those will be flattered just to be asked. Some of them, you know will certainly have other plans by this time. It will be wonderful, you'll see. It will be the talk of the town, I promise."

Louise immediately immersed herself into the planning of the party. She set the menu and had to use a local printing shop for the invitations and she stayed up late to address the invitations. After all, only 100 people would be invited and all of them were members of the Kanawha Country Club. She was downtown searching for favors when she noticed a detective agency located beside the small gift shop. She entered the agency and asked to speak with someone about an investigation. Arrangements were made and she was assured that the investigation of Belle Coleman would start the day after Christmas. Payments would be in cash and passed through a third party.

Louise left the agency and entered the shop next door where she finally found the most beautiful porcelain angel ornaments with 24K gold embellishments that would be perfect for her guests. She estimated that 60 to 75 guests would be coming and at $6 each she felt that they were appropriate as favors. Louise had ordered the rental tables, chairs, linens, crystal, china, and flatware. For the first time she could remember, she would have to follow a strict budget. She decided to use boughs of holly and evergreen around the room and would set candles among sprays of evergreen and glittered pine cones as centerpieces. She would serve salad with duck breast, French onion soup, beef tips with mushrooms, creamed spinach, garlic mashed potatoes, rolls, and fresh apple cake for dessert. She spared no expense on the wine for the dinner or for the band hired for the dance.

Three days before the dance the RSVPs stood at 70 and she was pleased. Others were either going out of town or were already committed to other events on that evening. Alfred's parents had already arrived and his mother was assisting her with the last minute details. Judge Perkins insisted on paying for the wine and band to alleviate some of the expenses. He reasoned that the young couple would need extra money to plan for his grandchild. Louise had chosen a ten foot tree that was decorated with lovely lights, ornaments, and garlands. Icicles were hung on each tip by a hired crew and Louise made sure that they were directed strategically in place.

Judge Perkins and his wife were so pleased to hear the news about the baby. Mrs. Perkins had gone out immediately to buy a few baby things due to her excitement and had brought them with her to show Louise. The judge had bought some special cigars and would hold onto them to hand them out when the baby was born. All the women guests were excited as Louise told them about her pregnancy and each one offered her their own piece of advice. Alfred beamed as he told the men and they congratulated him with slaps on the back.

The dinner and dance was a tremendous success and Alfred got several new clients as a result. Everyone loved their angel ornament and praised her for the fine meal and great band. Louise rested for several days following the dance and before she knew it, Christmas was only a few days away. Aunt Belle had given her wrapped gifts when she had dropped by for an hour and Louise was surprised when Belle had sent a card with a bank draft for $1000. She immediately took it to the bank to cash. She figured that she would be able to pay the detective's fees and expenses for at least six months, the balance still owed to the caterers, and have money left to buy Alfred's Christmas present. She had seen a beautiful Parker pen set at a jewelry store and was sure he would love it.

Louise was surprised when Judge Perkins and his wife sent them a check for $500 for Christmas and she told Alfred how nice it was that some of their relatives still acknowledged them around the holidays. She deliberately omitted telling him about the $1000 since he would have wanted an accounting of how the money had been spent. She was getting ready for the next round with Belle, Emily, and Vivian and sympathy was going to be her biggest ally where Alfred was concerned. She didn't want him to know about the detective she hired under any circumstances because he was so self-righteous he would force her to withdraw from the contract. Alfred had told her earlier, "Belle may just need some time to forgive you for threatening to sue her. When she hears about the baby, all will be forgiven you'll see."

Alfred presented Louise with a beautiful diamond and emerald bracelet for Christmas. He knew that emeralds were her favorite and he had surprised her with the matching diamond cocktail ring as well. By the end of January she figured that she would have the matching earrings if everything worked out according to her plans.

Two days after Christmas, her detective called to tell her that he had just learned that Belle and William were going to New York. "Do you want me to follow them?" he asked.

"But of course I do, just make sure that you aren't seen," she said.

Around noon of the 28th he called her again to tell her that he had just overheard Belle suggesting to some woman that was with her, she should put some diamond into the hotel safe before they left for lunch. Louise asked him to describe the woman and when he did, she knew it had to be Emily Black. Now what would Emily be doing with a loose diamond and why did the thought of a loose diamond seem to remind her of something? He told her that the two women were going to lunch with a man, a boy, and a young couple. Louise told him to check with the concierge to find out where he could find Belle and pretend to have some business with her. The detective hung up and agreed to do just that.

"I'm sorry but you just missed her. She just returned from the Chase Manhattan Bank and is going to lunch at Theodore's on 56th Street. She will be returning here after dining. Would you care to leave your card or a message?" the clerk asked the stranger.

"No, I'll go to the Theodore's and speak with her there. Thank you for your assistance," the detective said.

The detective took a cab to 56th street and smoked a cigarette as he watched from across the street for Belle to leave the restaurant where he would approach her. The longer he waited the thought occurred to him that instead of waiting he should actually go into the restaurant and see if he could get more information for his client while the others were with her.

The detective asked the restaurant's maître´d to seat him at a particular table that just happened to be close enough to Belle's table to hear any discussions. He ordered a Caesar salad and a cup of coffee. The young girl was heard to say, "But what could possibly be in the other four safety deposit boxes? Bertie was one of the most honest women I have ever known. Why would she spread out stuff in those boxes and why would she have them in different cities? Did she have that much cash?"

"No, I don't think so, but apparently she didn't want Louise to know about the boxes, that's for sure. Well, do we go to the National City Bank or Bank of New York next? The Bank of New York has an address on Wall Street and the National City Bank is on East 42nd Street. Bertie rented both boxes on the same day." Emily offered.

"We will have to go to both of them tomorrow. The banks won't be opened on Saturday," Belle said emphasizing the last part.

The detective was enjoying his $6 salad as he listened to the names of the banks. He would have to ask his client why his subjects were going to banks and what safety deposit boxes they were talking about. "Well I suppose we will go the National City first and then go to Bank of New York after lunch. That leaves Saturday to shop and enjoy New York without any worries about banks or secrets in boxes," the oldest woman suggested. From the way she was dressed, the detective figured she had to be rich, very rich. He had heard her name before but didn't know of the relationship between her and his client since their last names were different. The others in the party weren't slackers either. The boy who was seated by a serious middle-aged man had listened intently to what the oldest woman had said. The man must be a lawyer because he sure sounded like one and besides, he had that lawyer look about him. He didn't recognize the young and older couples either.

Well since he now knew their agenda for the next few days, he would follow them to the National City and see what they were up to. The detective finished his salad and paid the $8 for a salad and a lousy cup of coffee. He thought it was outrageous, but his client was paying his expenses, after all, and wouldn't think that they were steep.

The detective called Louise and told her what he had learned about safety deposit boxes and about some secrets of some woman by the name of Bertie. "Are you sure they said Bertie?" she asked with the sound of panic in her voice.

"Yes ma'am, the youngest lady said she couldn't believe that Bertie could have had any dark secrets because she was quote, the most honest woman I have ever known, unquote. They mentioned that there were other boxes in another city. So what do you want me to do?" he asked.

"Follow them and try to find out what is in those boxes! Call me tomorrow at this time. If my husband answers ask him if her wants to invest in some land or something! Use your imagination but do not, under any circumstances, tell him about this investigation," she demanded.

'That is one smooth broad' the detective thought as he hung up the phone. He went back to a tiny hotel in the cheap side of town and slept peacefully thinking what a score he had made with this client. She would pay him for the room and his meals plus $10 a day. She had flown him up to New York with a round trip ticket. Yes sir, he was going to be in the money for sure after he was finished with this case.

Louise was definitely interested in what could be in the boxes and wondered what Bertie had squirreled away in them. The only other places they could have been in were Pittsburgh, Chicago, Raleigh, and Bluestone. She would have to wait until tomorrow to hear any more information. Meanwhile, she had to do something fast about her pregnancy. She was already beginning to show a little and it already messed up her dress line. Oh well, it was nothing that a penny pencil wouldn't take care of.

By the next morning, Louise was having severe cramps and called her doctor while Alfred was home, "Is it normal to be cramping so much this early in my pregnancy?" she asked. "Okay, I'll meet you there. Alfred, we have to go to the hospital! The doctor thinks I may be having a miscarriage!" Alfred ran to get the car and drove like a maniac to the Charleston Hospital. By the time the doctor got there, the spontaneous abortion, as he called it, had occurred. He admitted her for an overnight stay after doing a D &C and spoke with both of them at once, "Sometimes Mother Nature takes care of problems on her own. There must have been something wrong with the fetus. Don't worry dear, you're young and you're healthy, once you heal, you can try again. I would wait at least another six months though before trying again. You will bleed for another two weeks or so and shouldn't have sex until then. I'm sorry for your loss and just so you know, there was nothing I could have done to save the baby."

Louise cried when the doctor left and Alfred comforted her, "Darling we'll try again. I know. We can go on a holiday in the spring. Would you like that dearest?"

Louise stopped crying long enough to manage to say, "If you think its best. Oh darling, I'm so sorry that we lost our baby. I was planning on going shopping for nursery items later this week, but not now!" Louise poured on the tears but she could tell that Alfred was truly devastated. He wanted children badly and had felt that he would be a good father. He thought, 'We'll try again in another six months or so, that should give her plenty of time to heal.' but said softly, "Get some rest now. I'm going to call my parents to let them know. I'll see you tomorrow. I love you darling."

"I love you too," she said demurely waiting anxiously for him to leave. 'At last' she thought 'I can have a moment to myself. Thank goodness I lost the baby before the doctor actually got here. He would have known what I had done if I hadn't delivered it in the bedpan. I'll have to be more careful next time.' Louise stretched across the bed and dreamed of what gifts would be coming her way to make up for the loss of a child. She was quite pleased with her performance. She should easily get a necklace or bracelet out of this and fell asleep with visions of her emerald earrings to match Alfred's Christmas gift.

By the next morning, Judge Perkins and his wife had arrived in Charleston. Alfred was with them carrying flowers and a wrapped jewelry box tied with a dark green ribbon. She hid her excitement as she opened the box and found the matching emerald and diamond earrings. She was disappointed that there wasn't anything else in the box and frowned slightly. She had hoped he would have gotten her a pendant. Alfred's mother asked, "How are you darling? We were so worried about you. Thank God your life wasn't in danger. I don't know what Alfred would do if something happened to you."

"I'm all right now Mrs. Perkins. I pray that we will have another chance one day," Louise answered timidly. It was mid-morning when Louise was finally released and she was taken upstairs with Alfred helping on one side and the Judge on the other. She changed into her prettiest nightgown and quickly fell asleep. About an hour later her private line in her bedroom rang. The only one it could possibly be was the detective. He said, "Hey where were you? I called and no one answered."

"Never mind about me, tell me what you found out about the banks?" she whispered.

"Well, they returned to the Chase bank and then went on into the safety deposit sections of the other banks yesterday. I followed them into the first one and got change from a teller and then waited across the street. I heard the older woman tell the driver to return to the hotel at once. They weren't carrying any bags with them, but whatever they got out of those two, if they carried it out, well it had to be either really thin or really small. They went right up to their suite and didn't talk at all about what they had found. Today they went shopping and I wore a disguise so they wouldn't notice me. They didn't talk about the contents anywhere they went either. Ma'am do you want me to keep following them or come back to Charleston and see what I can find out about this Belle Coleman?" he asked.

"I want you to follow them, you idiot! I don't care what you have to do I have to find out what was in those boxes. It must be something they don't want me to know! If I know my aunt, she will want to go to a show and do some shopping. You said they only mentioned those two other banks. She must be planning on spending New Year's Eve in New York. Try to get into that suite and see what you can find! Call me tomorrow!" she said a little louder than she intended. When Alfred came into the room, she pretended that she had awakened from a nightmare and he held her close and rocked her gently until she could calm down. "You are so good to me," she purred.

The detective hung up the phone and tried to figure out how he was possibly going to be able to slip into the largest suite in the fanciest New York hotel. He would have to do a little check of the staff members to see where they kept their uniforms and their keys this afternoon and then watch to see if Belle Coleman was indeed a creature of habit as Louise had claimed.

The detective secured a waiter's uniform used to deliver room service and he got a master key from a very attractive maid who was quite easily coaxed with a few sweet words and a $50 bribe. He told her he only needed to use the key for about half an hour and would bring it back to her before she finished cleaning the adjoining suite. He searched the suite and didn't find any new purchases other than a couple of shirts and a kid's suit. He found bonds with the name William Pierce written on them worth about $5000 and a copy of a wedding certificate for a Bertha Coleman and Jack Pierce. Maybe that's what had been in there- cash that they had converted to bonds. If it wasn't cash, then they must have whatever it was with them or had left it in the bank in the box. It must not have been too valuable if they had left it in the bank's vault. Certainly they would have taken it out of the bank and brought it with them to take to Welfield if it had been valuable or useful against his client.

True to his word, he called Louise and reported about the bonds and not finding anything else in the suite. "What kind of bonds were they?" Louise asked.

"They were war bonds, you know, the regular defense savings bonds! They could have gotten them anywhere. They had to pay about $5000 for them because they'll be worth more than $7500 when they're cashed in and they can't do that for another ten years!" he told her.

"I have to know what else they found. Go back to the concierge desk and see if you can find out where they are going. Introduce yourself to Belle as an old friend of mine. Make sure you tell her that you were sorry to hear about my mother's death. Ask her if I'm with you, she will probably tell you where they are going after New Year's. Call me when you know more," Louise commanded and then hung up.

Everyone had a successful shopping experience. Paul had gotten some new boots, dress socks, and several new suits, a couple of sweaters as well as casual pants and shirts. Emily had purchased a few dresses and a coat with a mink collar. She had gotten the blue diamond set into a platinum pendant setting at Cartier's and had purchased a platinum chain to match. Vivian and John bought a few new knickknacks for a shelf in the office and some clothes for the upcoming spring semester. John needed a few suits for interviews for his possible legal apprenticeship. William had needed several pairs of pants for school since he was in another growth spurt and his other pants were getting embarrassingly short. It seemed like he had grown an inch every month since school had started. William had asked Belle if they could go see the Ice Follies show he saw in a poster. Belle had arranged for tickets to the show as well as made arrangements for them to go skating after the performance. Only John knew how to skate and the others went along to watch. It would be kind to say that William didn't fall too many times, but he still managed to have fun. It had indeed been an eventful day for all of them.

The Blacks and the Williams had planned on going to St. Patrick's Cathedral for the eleven o'clock high mass on Sunday which was also New Year's Eve. William and Belle asked if they could join them. William enjoyed listening to all of the beautiful songs sung by the choir and the pipe organ and followed along in Emily's missal. In a high mass all of the prayers are sung rather than recited including the Eucharistic Prayer. Incense was used and William whispered that he liked that heavy perfumed smell. When Vivian, Paul, and Emily rose to go to communion William wanted to go but Belle caught his arm time and told him he couldn't go because he wasn't Catholic. All had sought to have a good time in New York and it was almost spoiled when William asked about the contents of the two boxes at the end of mass. "You never said what was in the other two boxes. What was in them, Aunt Belle?" They had left for lunch after church and were then going to return to the suite.

Belle answered, "They had different papers including Bertie's marriage certificate to your father. We left them at the bank except the wedding certificate since we thought that you might want to see it. I'll show you when we get back to the hotel."

William smiled and said, "I wish I had gotten to know my dad. I bet he was great. Mom wouldn't have married someone that wasn't, would she Emily? You know, Louise never talks much about him, but since he was your neighbor, you must have been good friends with him too, right?"

Emily carefully answered, "Your dad was a good carpenter and hard worker." She had no intention of telling William that in fact his father had been an alcoholic in his last years. He had beaten Bertie regularly, sometimes so badly that the doctor had to set her arm or wrap her chest tightly from broken ribs. He had been good with his hands in carpentry or with machines, but once he began drinking, the alcohol ruined him and his disposition. Paul had often said that it had rotted his brain.

John and Vivian sat across from Paul and Emily at the table while Belle sat across from Mr. Blakeman and William sat beside Paul. Conversation drifted to the upcoming fireworks and dinner from New Year's Eve and the highlights of their trip to New York. It had been fun and everyone, except for Belle and Mr. Blakeman, was going to circle Ellis Island and the Statue of Liberty on a ferry that afternoon.

Since Vivian, Paul, and Emily had fasted since midnight they were quite hungry and looked forward to their lunch. They left immediately after mass to eat lunch at the Arabelle Restaurant at the Plaza Hotel where Mr. Blakeman had made reservations earlier in the week. Belle particularly liked their soothing décor with conservatory style windows. When they returned to the hotel, true to her word, Belle showed William his parents' wedding certificate dated July 5, 1921. William thanked her for showing him and went with Paul and the others for the tour. Belle was going to rest while they were gone on the ferry.

The afternoon was spent on a ferry that was going to circle Ellis Island and then Statue of Liberty. Since it was now being used for immigrant internments, they wouldn't be able to actually go onto Ellis Island. William had wanted to look the place over, but understood when the ferry captain told him about the internments. William grinned as he stood in the front of the ferry and felt the wind on his face while the others were inside of the ferry trying to keep warm. The group returned and took a short nap until 9 pm. They had plans for dining at the Rainbow Room on the 65th floor of the RCA building on New Year's Eve and would be watching the fireworks from there. Emily, Vivian, and Belle had bought new gowns and accessories and the men were in their tuxedoes. Emily wore a lovely deep burgundy sheath with garnet jewelry; Vivian chose a beautiful silver lame gown with a sequined cape; while Belle's gown was elegant black velvet accessorized with her signature strand of perfectly matched pearls.

William was proud of his new tuxedo and bent his arm and offered it to Belle. Mr. Blakeman was on her other side in his tuxedo. She smiled and walked with both of them to the elevator. Vivian looked beautiful with her arm linked through John's as did Emily with Paul. Paul wore the new cufflinks that Vivian had sent to him for Christmas and the diamond tie tack she had bought for him. All of the men wore carnation boutonnieres while the women wore orchid corsages. They were just entering the lobby when a strange man called out Belle's name. Belle turned and a strange man said, "Excuse Mrs. Coleman. I thought that was you. I'm Jake Turner; I went to school with Louise, Louise Pierce. Is she with you?" he calmly said. Belle simply replied, "No, she isn't"

"Oh I'm sorry I missed her. It's been years since I saw her. I was awfully sorry to hear about her mother dying. Please tell her that Jake Turner sends his condolences," he said and turned to leave.

"Wait! We will be returning home late tomorrow and won't be going home until the second. I will let her know that I met you when I see her. Have a nice evening," she said and continued across the lobby to the waiting limo.

He immediately called Louise and told her that Belle's group was returning to Welfield early on the second and gave her only a little more information about the people in the group. He had described John and Vivian and she had no doubt of their identity when he described Vivian's lovely diamond rings.

"William probably has to go back to school on Wednesday. I forgot about that little weasel. Come on back to Charleston and we'll see what I can find out on my own. Oh, by the way Happy New Year!" she said as she hung up the phone.

She would wait a few days and call Aunt Belle to wish her and William a Happy New Year and to also let them know about her miscarriage. Aunt Belle might give her a bauble or two for her distress or better yet, cash. Well she had to get herself ready for the New Year, 1945.

Chapter 3

M r. Blakeman took William back to the hotel around 12:30am on New Year's after watching the fireworks display. William had enjoyed the fireworks from the Rainbow Room after such a delicious meal with his new best friends in the world, Paul and Emily. Belle had asked Mr. Blakeman to escort William to the hotel since his head was drooping from being so sleepy and told him that they would follow in about an hour or so. Emily and Paul waltzed a few more times near John and Vivian. They switched partners for the next waltz and after about an hour it was time to return to the hotel. Belle asked the driver to close the window separating them so that they could have a private conversation. He turned on the radio and focused on traffic.

Emily looked at Belle and started with, "Viv, baby doll, we need to talk with you about something really important. Do you remember when I called you after the reading of Bertie's will about the time of Louise's threats of a lawsuit? Well Belle asked us to come to Mr. Blakeman's office because she had something to tell us that she didn't want us to find out in open court. Belle, do you want to tell her?"

"Vivian, my husband died when I was very young and I never had the urge to remarry. Several months after Carl died, his brother, Bertie's father, came over to mend a fence or so he claimed. He forced his way into my house, beat me, and raped me. I had a broken arm that I had to get set and it was only a few months later that I found out that I was pregnant. I hid in my cabin so people wouldn't find out I was pregnant and know there was no way it could possibly be Carl's. That devil came back to rape me again and

47

I shot at him. He never bothered me again. A doctor by the name of Dr. Sherman came to check on me and when I had my baby and he talked me into getting my infant daughter adopted. He still gave me a birth certificate for March 23, 1902 and told me that he knew a nice couple that couldn't have children and I agreed to let them adopt her. That couple was Ann and Nathan Schmidt, your grandparents. Vivian, Emily is my daughter and you are my granddaughter."

Vivian was silent at first and when everything fully registered she sounded obviously hurt when she asked, "Is this why you gave me the money? You knew all this time and said nothing to me! You let me grow up not knowing I had a grandmother, how could you do that to me and to mom?"

Emily spoke up and said, "When Louise pulled her stunt at Comfield College and tried to get you expelled, Belle had a detective check into your background and eventually mine as well. She had no idea of our relationship to her until her detective told her my parent's names and my birth date. She didn't know I was her daughter until after she had us investigated at Louise's urging. She didn't know until a few months ago herself. She didn't want to tell me until she absolutely had to and that was when Louise had threatened to sue. She knew I loved my mom and dad and didn't want to attempt to replace them. It has taken me a little while to even begin to accept it."

"But how are you so sure, Belle?" Vivian asked.

"I was sent a letter from Emily's mother thanking me for giving her husband and herself the greatest gift. I showed the letter to Emily who recognized her mother's handwriting immediately. I also have an affidavit from Dr. Sherman stating that Ann and Nathan Schmidt were the adoptive parents of my daughter. Vivian, there were no other Schmidt's of that name anywhere else in the county and they were the only ones that lived in the house that the doctor wrote down as the address for me. My investigator was very thorough, you are indeed my granddaughter," Belle said tearfully. "I wouldn't hurt either of you for the world. I hated that man, but loved his daughter who took such good care of me and my home. Bertie became my surrogate daughter all those years ago. Somehow by sheer instinct I suppose, she found her way to you, her half-sister all by herself but without knowing it. There's more, that I think you should know. Bertie was raped by her father before she was ten years old. Martha Coleman sent him to rape me and had forced all of her daughters to have sex with their own father," she said with her head held down low.

John said in almost a whisper, "So that's why she committed suicide. We couldn't figure out why she would do something like that with the lawsuit pending. Does Louise know any of this?"

Vivian spoke quietly, "Oh mom, tell me she doesn't know. You know she will make my life miserable for sure."

Belle told her that Louise didn't know about their kinship and that was why they were telling her now while they were away from William. "Louise doesn't know the truth about her grandmother either," Belle admitted, "And neither does William. I don't intend to ever tell him."

Vivian shook her head slightly and said, "Belle, I am so sorry that I reacted the way I just did. I know he hurt you but I want to thank you to for the gift of life, but this is just so much to digest all at once. Mom, what happens if the press gets hold of this? What happens if... Oh no, that means that Louise is my cousin! This just gets better and better! This could ruin all of us! I mean what will the people of Jackson think? Mom, I just couldn't bear it if you were hurt by any of their gossip. John's apprenticeship could be in jeopardy."

"That's why we are telling you now, dear. I'm grown and neither Louise nor gossip can hurt either of us. We are innocent in this whole affair and it was Louise's grandparents that were to blame and both of them are dead. Just because someone says something mean, doesn't mean that it is true. Our friends will remain our friends no matter what they hear and those who don't want to be friends, well, they never were our friends," her mom spoke calmly.

"Well thank goodness it wasn't sprung on me in a courtroom. I honestly don't know what to say right now, I just don't know," Vivian sighed.

Paul spoke quietly and calmly, "Well, Bertie's dad died several years ago and he can't be punished and it cannot be undone. Belle is innocent in all of this and so is Emily. Viv, think about it this way, you have a grandmother. My folks died before you were born and so did Emily's. You always said you wished you had a grandmother. It's not the way it usually happens, but here she is and she loves you. Now that the initial shock is over we must make sure that William doesn't find out until he gets a little older. Think of it this way, not only is Louise your cousin, but so is William. Girlie, you just picked up a whole bunch of relatives!"

John had been awfully quiet and finally said, "Vivian, your mother has the most to lose by this situation and she has had to accept a lot. She isn't happy with the news but is willing to accept Belle. I know you Viv; you are full of love and compassion. Rather than be embarrassed, we should celebrate. Our family grew today although not painlessly to any of us. Consider it as sort of a merger, if you will." She chuckled a little at his attempt to sound like an attorney and said, "Some merger… I guess it could have been worse; it could have been a hostile takeover!"

She hugged Belle and said, "I loved you before I knew that you were my grandmother. May I still call you Belle?"

"But of course, in fact I insist," Belle smiled.

"I have a grandmother," she said in a whisper. "I have an honest to goodness grandmother," as she hugged Belle once more.

The two couples and Belle left the limo in good spirits and went straight to bed. Vivian had a difficult time falling to sleep as she tried to figure out how anyone could be as mean and devious as Louise's grandparents and yet they had produced a daughter as loving and gentle as Bertie. It was no wonder that Louise had turned out the way she was if she took after her grandparents. With the way her father had been and now finding out about her grandparents, Louise must have gotten some doozey of some genes from all of them. It now made perfect sense for Belle to have given her the large endowment. With a land grant, Vivian now knew that it had to be passed to a blood relative. Belle's legacy would live through Vivian and any children she might have.

At ten on the morning of New Year's Day, the maids were busy packing the luggage and trunks while Belle and Mr. Blakeman tended to some business affairs for 1945 while the others had sat down for their breakfast. She had no intention of ever changing her will now, especially after she had read the papers that were in those safety deposit boxes. Emily had replaced the letter and bill that had been in separate boxes and would put them along with her marriage certificate, Louise's birth certificate, Jack's death certificate, and William's birth certificate. There had also been miscellaneous bills of sale, a bill from a detective agency in Bluestone, and a folder. Belle would have to think long and hard about what to do with this information. What would Alfred do if he found out what is in those boxes? One thing was sure; Belle had no intention of letting Louise move back to her home. Everything would be returned to the boxes except for the blue diamond. Alfred and William must never know what had been hidden in those boxes.

Belle recalled how hard Emily had shaken as she had wept reading Bertie's letter in one of the boxes. It had shaken Belle up as well. Emily had always wanted more children but, after having Vivian, she had hemorrhaged so badly that the doctor had to do a hysterectomy in his office only a few days after her birth. Emily couldn't understand how anyone could, without thought, deliberately end a pregnancy like she had read about in Bertie's letter. Bertie must have suffered so much when it had happened, but had kept it quiet, yes, kept it secret. What else had she kept secret? Could it possibly be something worse? Belle had wept in the Queen's Suite as she recalled her gentle niece, Bertie, who had protected everyone she loved. She washed her face before she joined Mr. Blakeman to go over some business proposals for the New Year.

He had one in particular that immediately caught her eye. She had once mentioned to him that when the war ended that new businesses would be needed for the families of returning vets. She had decided that she would invest in some companies specializing in infant care. She knew that the war wouldn't last much longer and figured that there would be a baby boom when the boys returned from war. Baby bottles, formula requirements of evaporated milk and Karo syrup, lotions, shampoos, strollers, baby food, diapers, etc. would be in high demand. Belle had investigated all of them and had finally decided on investing in a company that made cradles, cribs, high chairs, and strollers. She was also interested in making high-end to low-end accessories for cribs as well. She could have the items sold in her department store and pharmacy that she owned and would need someone to oversee the project, someone who had a good head on their shoulders. She had initially thought of some of her managers but then she thought about Emily. Emily had been an excellent mother and had a good sense of style. She would know quality when she saw it and would enjoy the challenge. Paul was busy with the farm and had hired extra help for Emily to take care of the house. Since Vivian had gotten married in the summer, Emily had made great improvements to the Sportsman's Club and Belle had been very impressed with all of her choices.

Emily would run out of options soon with improvements to the lodge and cabins and since she had shown that she had a knack for business, she would need a project to take over. Belle would talk to Paul and Emily on the way home about the proposal. If Emily did as well with the plan as she had with the Sportsman's Club, all of the new companies would provide significant income for Paul and Emily. The group returned from a trip to Central Park and Belle shook her head when she saw what William was carrying in his hands. Paul had treated William to some hot dogs, hard candy, and chips. He had bought him some candy apples and a couple of comic books as well. Belle shook her head thinking what a stomachache William was going to get. However the belly ache never occurred and they ate dinner at 7 pm in the suite and left at 8:30 pm for the train.

The party left the hotel and arrived to Grand Central Station with about fifteen minutes to spare. When their train arrived at 9:15pm they entered the private rail car and were ready to relax and possibly get some sleep before arriving in Charlottesville. William wanted to read one of his comic books but was sound asleep before 10:00pm in one of the upholstered chairs.

Mr. Blakeman had informed Belle earlier that his brother had told him that he knew several attorneys that needed an apprentice. She encouraged him to share the information with John before they got to Charlottesville. Emily, Vivian, and Paul talked about the upcoming spring semester and the farm.

Paul was enjoying the trips to New York, Richmond, and Charlottesville and told Emily, "I'm thinking of hiring two more men to do my chores or perhaps leave the farm entirely. I was thinking the other day, we have been away from the farm for almost a month since summer and maybe we ought to just pack it all up and leave the farm all together."

"Where would we go?" Emily asked. "During our whole marriage we have lived on that farm and have made it a success. Sure our house is a little old-fashioned, but it's our home. I can't imagine living anywhere else. Going to the city is nice, but only for visits. I love returning home after being away for a while. Let's give it a little more thought, all right? We have worked so hard to get the farm the way it is now. I can't see leaving it after all those years of work."

"But Emily, you work yourself so hard each and every day and for what? We have a little money now and we can afford a small house in Welfield. It would take some adjusting, for sure, but we could do it," Paul said.

Vivian said nothing when her father had first mentioned leaving the farm but her silent tears told Paul a lot. Vivian loved the farm almost as much as Emily. Paul finally said, "All right, we'll stay. It was only an idea anyway. Well, I guess we can stay there until we can't run it by ourselves. We'll know when the time comes."

"Well, we could still buy a little house in Welfield before the price goes up on real estate. When the war is over, there will be a big demand for houses and the prices will go up. We could buy a two bedroom house and could rent it on a yearly basis until we're ready to leave the farm," Emily admitted, "Or we could just live in one of the cabins on the mountain at the Sportsmen's Club. They are all modern and we would still be in our mountains."

"You know what, that's a good idea. We wouldn't need but a three bedroom to have room for Vivian and John. Who knows we might have grandchildren to take care of one day. I tell you what; we'll wait at least another year before we make a decision, agreed?" Paul said.

"Agreed," Emily affirmed.

Vivian couldn't hold it in any longer and blurted out, "I am so glad that you're keeping the farm or at least for another year. I love that little farm and all of the chores that go with keeping it. It keeps me grounded when I visit and doesn't let me get so uppity."

They were going to be arriving in Charlottesville around 5 am and they went to bed to get several hours of shut eye. The porter came about forty-five minutes outside of Charlottesville to give them time to get freshened up and dressed before they arrived. Paul and Emily had arisen with John and Vivian to say goodbye. Belle waved from a window as the young couple exited to the platform. William had tears in his eyes when they had left and sat down beside Paul.

"Well, young man, how about a game of chess?" Paul asked.

"You bet," William answered.

While the chess game was in full swing, Belle and Emily were having a serious conversation about Belle's idea of investing in infant care products. Belle asked if perhaps Emily would consider heading the project over a cup of coffee.

"I don't know anything about heading up a project," Emily protested.

"Since the project is just starting, you can learn from the beginning and besides, Mr. Blakeman will be with you throughout the process. Oh please say you'll do it. We can do the majority of the work in Welfield and any meetings in New York or Chicago, I can go with you. Emily, I want to involve you more in the running of my affairs. You will have controlling interest of 90% in them and the other 10% will be in William's name. I'm not getting any younger you know. At least talk it over with Paul for now. We have a few more months before we will be ready to begin, but I want to get started before Easter." Belle pleaded.

Emily and Belle ate a leisurely breakfast with the men before arriving at Welfield. Belle had decided to ride the train into Welfield and felt that it would be a lot easier on everyone to ride comfortably to Welfield and avoid the curves of the highway. Paul and William packed up the chess set and checked to make sure that there were no pieces left out. William got out another comic book and Paul asked him to share and he read the other one. In what seemed like a very little time they were at the Welfield station.

Belle hugged Paul and Emily before they entered a car being driven by Josef. The three chatted about their New Year's party and the farm. It felt so good to walk through the front door where Emily could be a farmer's wife again. Belle and William were happy to be home once again and the maid helped them unpack while Belle checked with her secretary for messages. She noticed one in particular from Louise but had no desire to speak to her now, especially after what she had found out in New York. There was no way to predict what Emily would find in the Pittsburgh banks, but they had planned to go later in the spring when Belle had to go for a quarterly meeting with Marshall Steel's Board.

Emily unpacked the bags and placed the blue diamond pendant that was in a padded snap case in the bottom of Bertie's hope chest. Emily decided to only wear it on special occasions and especially on Bertie's birthday, Sept. 5. Emily called to Paul and asked if they could go to the company store to pick up a few essentials. Paul had first checked on the animals in the barn and then they left for the store. Emily needed to get coffee, flour, yeast, baking powder, and a few other items. They spoke along the way about Belle's new project and Paul encouraged her to seriously think about it.

Over the next few months John was accepted as an apprentice law clerk with an established law firm in Charlottesville. He would be starting it in May after graduating from UVA. Vivian's classes were going well and she had decided to go to summer school terms to finish early. Paul had hired a local fellow to help full time with the farm. Josef Novak and his widowed mother had been friends of theirs for years. Josef needed a job and Mrs. Novak could use the extra money to keep up their home. Josef was a hard worker and did everything to Paul's standards. The two got along well and Mrs. Novak kept house like she had been taught by her mother in the old country.

No other major events occurred in any of the families until March 13, 1945 just before noon. Josef was resetting a loose fencepost while Paul was in the upper pasture plowing when Bucky, the old blind mule, slipped on the moist dirt and tumbled. In a freak accident, the plow slid down the mountainside behind Bucky and Paul lost his footing and fell as well. He had the straps around his shoulders and was pulled down the mountain along with the plow. As the plow flew through the air and the blade of the plow dug into the ground, Paul's body followed landing on the blade. Josef saw the accident and immediately went to help him. Paul whispered, "Get Emily."

Josef ran down to get Emily and then he called the Marshall Steel doctor who was only about three minutes away. Emily ran to the upper pasture and held Paul's head as he searched her eyes and managed a weak, "Love you Em," and died in her arms. Josef had never known that a human being could let out such a painful sound as Emily hugged her beloved Paul and wept without restraint rocking his body back and forth. The doctor had arrived just moments later and tried to remove Emily away from Paul's corpse. It took both Josef's and the doctor's strength to break her grip from around his neck. Josef ended up just carrying Emily into the house where the doctor sedated her with an injection. Josef called his mother who said she would be there shortly. The doctor called Belle and told her about the accident. He asked if she could come to be with Emily and she and Mr. Blakeman were both at Emily's in less than fifteen minutes.

Emily was sitting in her chair staring at Paul's chair and his pipe. Josef had gone up the mountain to cover Paul's body with a sheet. The doctor called the mortuary and made arrangements to have his body moved. Josef had to shoot Bucky who had a badly broken leg and hip and it took Josef over an hour just to bury him. Mrs. Novak was with Emily when Belle and Mr. Blakeman arrived. Emily's body shook violently from her sobs despite the fact that she had already been sedated. Belle hugged her tightly and Mr. Blakeman just shook his head not able to think of any words of consolation. He walked out with Mrs. Novak onto the front porch and asked her what had happened. Mrs. Novak told him what Josef had told her when he had called. Mr. Blakeman knew that the next few days were going to be extremely difficult for his clients and would do what he could to make it easier on all of them. They went back inside so that Mrs. Novak and Mr. Blakeman could talk with Emily as Belle took it upon herself to call Vivian and John. Luckily, it was John who answered the phone.

"John, this is Belle. I'm fine dear. John there's been a terrible accident and I'm afraid to tell you that our Paul is dead. He was plowing in the upper field and that old donkey slipped and pulled the plow and Paul down the hill. Paul was impaled by the plow and died almost instantly. I am here with Emily and she's in a bad way. Do you want to tell Vivian or shall I? Very well, may I speak with her please? Hello Vivian, this is Belle. I'm fine too dear. Vivian…"

When Belle told Vivian she heard the phone drop and heard John's voice yelling, "Vivian, Vivian darling." Apparently Vivian had fainted at the news and John picked up the phone and said, "I'll be right back Belle. Come on Vivian, wake up honey, wake up," and she heard him try to waken Vivian until he eventually hung up the phone.

Belle went to Emily whose eyes now seemed to have lost their very spark of life from the sedative taking effect. Belle told her that Vivian and John knew about Paul and would be calling shortly to speak with her. Belle asked Emily if she would like to speak with Father O'Brien and Emily managed only a nod. Belle asked the operator to call the rectory of Our Lady of the Rosary in Jackson. Belle repeated the horrible details to him and Father O'Brien assured her that he would be there in a few minutes. Belle asked Emily if she needed anything and she quietly said, "Paul" and broke down once more. Belle was holding her tightly when the priest arrived and he talked with her for over an hour.

Mr. Blakeman called the funeral home and made an appointment for the family to come to make arrangements. He called the local Marshall Steel office as well as their main headquarters in Pittsburgh asking for guards to be posted at the entrance of the farm. He called Belle's secretary and asked them to make arrangements for a family dinner after the service at the country club and to call the local newspaper offices and local radio station.

There were going to be too many visitors for the small parish social room in the basement of the church or to all come into Emily's home for the wake. He asked Belle's secretary to come to Jackson after making the other calls, and gave her directions on how to get to the house. He also told her to tell the guards at the foot of the hill that she worked for Belle Coleman. She would be taking care of all of the details for the family dinner.

Vivian called Emily while Fr. O'Brien was there and no one could console either of them separated by the hundreds of miles of phone wire. Vivian told Emily that she and John would be leaving in just a few minutes and should arrive by 4 that afternoon. Emily couldn't think from the medication and Belle took over the decision-making, asking for her input along the way. She decided to have the wake at the parish church since it would be so hard for visitors to get up the hollow where Emily's house was located. Emily made a list of some of Paul's friends to be pall bearers to include: Mr. Allen Jones from the company store, Josef Novak their handyman, Henry Jansen the caretaker at the Sportsman's Club, Alex Carter the butcher at the company store, Laurence Snyder an usher at Our Lady of the Rosary, and Sam Szajak another usher at Our Lady of the Rosary. All of them had known Paul for years and all were honored to be asked by Belle's secretary and accepted immediately. John and Mr. Blakeman would have their hands full with Emily and Vivian and weren't asked to be pall bearers. Marshall Steel posted company guards at the underpass to protect Emily and Belle in less than 30 minutes after Mr. Blakeman's call to Pittsburgh.

Mr. Blakeman had picked up William from school to bring him to Emily's shortly after Belle's secretary had arrived. The young man sobbed so hard in the limo and ran directly into Emily's house. He hugged her very tightly and wouldn't leave her side. Belle had made a pot of coffee and a guard knocked on the door with a box containing food and small cloth wrapped packages of coffee that was beginning to arrive from the neighbors during the first hour. It was decided that the food would be brought to the cabin by one of the guards who would escort no more than fifteen people at a time to the house. Absolutely no reporters or photographers were to be brought up to the house. If the company guards didn't recognize them, they were not to be allowed to the house. Additional guards were posted by the front and back doors in case a reporter tried to sneak down the rail tracks and climb to where the cabin was located.

The mortician arrived with two guest books around twelve thirty in the afternoon. One for those bringing food to be set up where the guards were posted and the other one was set up in the cabin. A huge spray of roses and carnations were hung on the Black's front door. Belle's secretary stayed to answer the phone and took pages of notes and messages. Allen and Maggie Jones arrived around one o'clock and Maggie tried to console Emily whom she had known for more than twenty years. Mr. and Mrs. Jones were asked to stay and were happy to oblige for one of their best friends. Maggie made coffee and some sandwiches, but neither Emily nor Belle could eat. Maggie and a neighbor from the ridge washed dishes as each group left and the next one came.

Vivian and John arrived around 4pm and Vivian and Emily sobbed for a long time wrapped in each other's arms until they were near exhaustion. The sedative had worn off and Emily began to get more lucid in her thoughts although she had difficulty focusing on discussions. John felt helpless in consoling the two women while Belle sat beside William on the couch. He would have to be strong for both of them even though he missed Paul so much. Paul had been more like an older friend to John than a father-in-law. It had been almost a year ago when John had been welcomed into the cabin for the first time when he had come with Vivian for spring break. He had felt so comfortable in that little cabin of a house and John recalled how Paul had taken him hunting. It was those thoughts and memories of happier times with Paul and Emily that gave him comfort as he tried to take care of the two most important women that had been in Paul's life. He tried to call his parents and the housekeeper told him that they were out of town in the western part of the state.

One of the local visitors went to sit in Paul's chair and William hollered out, "Don't sit there! That's Paul's chair!" and then he broke down once more. Every folding chair in the living room was quickly filled and it was decided that callers would have to be rotated every thirty minutes or there would be no room for the family. Mrs. Jones continued to make pots of coffee and some sandwiches, but neither Emily nor Vivian would eat anything fixed. She got help from a neighbor who lived on the ridge to wash dishes as each group left and dried them for the next group that arrived.

Belle tried to get Emily and Vivian to at least try to eat part of a sandwich between groups of callers, "You have to keep up your strength both of you. I'll eat something with you. Come on I'll fix something for you, myself."

It was eight o'clock in the evening, when the guards were changing shifts that they decided it was time to start turning people away that had come to call. The family needed to rest and had to be near exhaustion by now. The next day would be a difficult one for them and for all of the community, but they knew how hard it was going to be for Emily and Vivian Black that they all had known for many years. Word had spread swiftly and many of the guards had cried when they heard the news. All of them had respected Paul and many had been the recipients of the generosity of the Blacks years before they had been endowed with a small fortune and property. The next shift of guards would stay, but visitors would be asked to return in the morning after noon. They told the callers that the wake had been tentatively set for the evening of March 15th or 16th and would be at the Catholic Church in Jackson. The funeral would be on the day following the wake with burial in the Catholic section of the Jackson cemetery. That was all the information that they knew at that point in time. An update was to be given shortly before noon and would be announced on local radio stations.

Little rest was had by any staying in the Black's cabin. William had insisted on staying with Emily and Vivian. He was sleeping in the room that had once been prepared for John the year before. John and Vivian slept in her old bedroom and Emily tossed as she wept through the night for her beloved husband. Belle had returned to her home and promised to be at the mortuary the next morning to help Emily with the selection of the coffin and vault. The great expense and metal shortages would not stop Belle from getting the finest casket made and if necessary, she would have it rail expressed from Pittsburgh.

The next morning, Emily drank a cup of coffee and ate some of a single piece of toast as Vivian ate little more. Maggie Jones, Mrs. Novak, and Josef had arrived at eight in the morning to help out in any way that they could and were only slightly relieved when both of the women had eaten a few bites of toast and a poached egg.

The family had been told that they needed to be at the mortuary to select the casket, floral spray, and make arrangements at ten o'clock. They also had been asked to take something with them for Paul to be buried in. When Emily opened the closet door and saw Paul's suits her desire to do this one last act of love drove her to be strong in selecting one of his new beautifully tailored black suits, a white starched shirt she carefully pressed, and a red tie. It was the first tailored suit he had ever bought in New York and had been so proud of it. She also selected some of his new underclothes. She got his rosary of black beads and put it into her purse. Paul would be buried with his rosary that he had recited each night of their marriage without fail. She selected his black shiny shoes and black socks he had bought in New York in December just before New Year's Eve. Paul liked to wear the thinner dress socks but didn't like to wear garters to keep them up. Emily smiled to herself as she remembered when they had returned home after Vivian's wedding he told her that he had to get those things off first. He could always make her laugh with his quips and idiosyncrasies. He had referred to the black suit as his monkey suit.

Vivian stood beside her mother as she made the selections and agreed totally with her mother on every choice made for her father. She reached for one of Paul's shirts and could still smell the cologne from the suits or as he called it, "skunk water". "Mom, I can still smell dad. These clothes smell like dad! Oh mom, I miss him so much! I'm sorry mom. I was going to try to be strong for you today, but I can't help it! I just miss daddy so much."

She broke down hugging her father's shirt and Emily hugged her daughter saying, "It's okay darling, I miss him too and always will. God made only one Paul Black and sure did put a lot of goodness and kindness into that one man. God must have broken the mold when he made my Paul. He was such a good and decent man and I don't know how I'm going to live without him. Oh Vivian, if I had only agreed to move from this place when he wanted to when we were coming back from New York, this wouldn't have happened. He would be with us now if I had agreed with him."

"Oh mom, it was an accident. You aren't to blame, no one is. Come on mom, I need you to understand that it wasn't your fault. I love you, momma and we will get through this together," she kissed her mother's temple. The two finished gathering the items and the suit and shirt were carefully hung up to avoid wrinkles. The two went into the living room with their handkerchiefs in their hands to dab their swollen eyes.

William was sitting at a table with John and they were playing a game of chess. William suddenly looked much older that morning and took his duty of watching over Emily seriously. He had told Belle that he would take care of Emily in Paul's stead and he meant it. He had bathed and dressed early that morning in the clothes Belle's maid had packed and sent to him the evening before. Belle's driver had brought the clothes and the guards had gently knocked on the door to hand several suits and a travel bag to the young man.

The family was driven to the mortuary in Belle's Pierce Arrow limo. Mr. Blakeman had driven Belle to the mortuary and she was waiting there for them there. The director of the mortuary took them into his office and offered his condolences on behalf of the funeral home. Emily had handed a bag to one of the mortuary assistants that contained the under clothes and shoes. Another assistant had greeted them, and John handed him the wooden hangers with Paul's suit and shirt. Emily had Paul's watch and rosary in her purse and asked John as she handed them to him to tell them to make sure that the items were to be placed with Paul. She made John promise that he would tell them that Paul had worn his watch on his left wrist and the rosary should be wrapped around Paul's right hand as if he was reciting it. William sat next to Emily and she began to shake after handing the items over, he held onto her arm tightly. To William, she had emotionally become his second mother and Paul had been the only father figure he had ever known. He loved both of them for taking care of his mother during her illness. It was a shame, he thought, that they couldn't be related to him.

A book was brought out that contained pictures of the various caskets and cloth samples for the interior. A brass crucifix would be pinned on the inside cover when the coffin arrived if the family wished it. Vivian agreed with all of the choices Emily made and both women were told that it would take about three days for the special coffin to arrive. Belle asked to use the phone and a few minutes later the director received a call that the casket, with an attached crucifix, would arrive the following day. The wake was then set for the evening of the 15th at Our Lady of the Rosary to begin promptly at 6pm for the public and 5 pm for the family. The funeral mass would begin at 10am in the church on the 16th.

Holy cards were selected with Paul's name, birth date and date he died printed on the back and various pictures of the Blessed Mother or Sacred

Heart on the front. Emily estimated that they would need around 500 of the cards. The family spray would be solid red roses. Paul had loved roses of every color, but he had always preferred the wild ones to the ones from a florist. Emily remembered how he had planted several rose bushes around the cabin for Emily during their first years of marriage. The wild rose bush that climbed up and over the front porch and had just started budding was one of the first he had planted.

Emily recalled for the group how Paul had had the greenest thumb and had started many of the rose bushes with cuts from other bushes. He was amazing in getting things to grow and took such joy from watching them produce flowers, fruit, or vegetables. He would carefully dry seeds and start seedlings in a small greenhouse he had made out of some boards and an old window. Emily requested that one small sprig of that wild rose bush was to be included in the family spray.

As Emily made each selection for the funeral service, she would look to Belle and Vivian for their approval. "How will we get word of his death to his relatives in Europe?" she asked. With WWII active in Europe, it was going to be difficult to send word to several of his cousins that were still in Hungary. She would have to wire them but she would have to look through his letters to get their addresses.

When they finished making all of the arrangements at the mortuary, they had to go to the Country Club to select a menu for the dinner that would be following the burial. After eating half of a sandwich at the club, Emily asked the club manager for a buffet to be prepared with fried fish, salmon, macaroni and cheese, green beans, and rolls. The burial would be on Friday and she and her family abstained from meat on Fridays. No bacon or ham was to be added to any of the side dishes. She asked for coffee and iced tea to be served as the only beverages. Desserts would be Paul's favorites, pound cake and apple pie. It was Lent and Emily knew that the majority of the guests would be Catholic and many may have given up sweets for Lent. Belle estimated that about 300 would be arriving for the post-burial dinner but that it could be as high as 500. She decided to have the club plan for 500. It was always better to overestimate than under estimate and the extra food would be given to the poor in the area. Belle was paying for the cost of the dinner and had insisted upon paying for the casket and its transportation cost as well. She would tell the helpers to divide the food that was left at the end of the dinner into family-sized portions and take them to the company store for distribution. She wanted everyone to eat their fill and knew that those who had benefitted from Paul's gifts of produce, eggs, and meat might not be able to attend.

Their last stop was at the rectory. Father O'Brien had asked them to join him for a late lunch and his cook had prepared some fried chicken, potatoes, and creamed peas. He told her about the funeral rituals and the role the family would play. He would have to bless Paul's body before it was carried into the church for the wake. About an hour before the funeral, the coffin would be closed and sealed and taken to the rear of the church. The choir would be singing the Requiem mass and it would last about an hour and a half. Emily hadn't been to many Catholic funerals but knew there would also be a special service at the gravesite as well. Father O'Brien had made arrangements for interment in the Catholic portion of the local cemetery. Marshall Steel employees were used to open and close the grave site.

They ate lunch reminiscing about Paul and his many contributions to the church and the community. Emily asked him to keep any flowers that were in baskets to decorate the church. He reminded her that during Lent flowers weren't present and suggested that perhaps she could give them to other churches instead. Emily wrote a check for $150 to pay for Easter lilies and spring flowers to surround the altar for Easter in Paul's memory. The group left the rectory and returned home around 2 pm.

Vivian and John walked together up to the upper pasture where Paul had died while Emily tried to get some rest. Vivian wanted to see the location where her father had died and walked up the mountain with John and Josef. Josef had carried bucket after bucket of water up the hill the day of the accident trying to wash away the blood off of the plow blade because it was too heavy to move without a mule. It had stayed put where it had landed and the blade was still sticking up with the handles sunken into the muddy soil. Vivian stooped to pick some dandelions and made a ring by weaving the stems together and placed it upon the blade. She walked further up the hollow and showed John the Pierce's cabin where Bertie, Louise, and William had lived all those years ago. The roof had almost completely caved in on the front part and Vivian recalled the visits she and Emily had made each summer with the Pierces. John liked the quiet and solitude of the surroundings and while Vivian picked daffodils around the cabin he followed the path to a spot where there had been a garden. When Vivian was finished picking a bouquet, they walked further up the mountain along a path. Apparently someone had been coming to the old Pierce place regularly and Vivian figured it must have been her dad. They followed the path as it continued on up to the top of the mountain to where Jack Pierce was buried. Vivian was surprised to find his grave well tended and said, "Daddy must have done the upkeep as a special favor to Bertie."

She would have to ask her mom when she returned to the house why he had done it for so many years when they hadn't heard from the Pierces until only about a year ago. John had listened to Vivian's questions and understood more about the family he had married into. He was so proud to be part of this decent, loving family.

John and Vivian looked over into the next valley and could barely make out the roof of Emily's cabin. They walked slowly with their arms linked and Vivian lovingly placed the daffodil bouquet beside the plow blade. She spoke openly about Paul and how difficult life was going to be for her mother. When the couple returned home, Belle was making dinner while Emily had gone to try to rest. William was sitting on the couch listening to the radio.

It was around four o'clock when Louise called the Black's residence. She had called Belle's house and had been told by the housekeeper of the tragic death of Paul Black. She planned to offer her condolences and somehow mention her miscarriage in late December in her call. Belle was close to those Blacks for some strange reason but Louise couldn't understand why. She knew that Belle would be vulnerable at this time and was attempting to make a gesture, albeit an empty one, at being decent for a change. Louise spoke sweetly on the phone offering her condolences and asking if she could do anything to make the loss easier for those that loved such a dear man. Belle was polite yet curt with her responses. She declined any assistance and promised to relay the condolences. Belle told her she was sorry for the miscarriage and hoped that she would be successful in any future pregnancies.

Louise had no plans to return to Jackson, but if she went to Belle's while she was still vulnerable from her loss of that Paul Black she could possibly get a lot of information if not from Belle, then from William. The private detective hadn't found anything about Belle or Bertie but she was sure that there had to be secrets. Why else would her mother have had so many safety deposit boxes? She hoped that if there was any jewelry in any of them then, she was entitled to them and could sell them for much needed cash. She was hopeful for additional funds; after all, Bertie's will stated that she was to receive all jewelry. Louise wanted to know all about what was in those boxes but didn't want to risk a lawsuit to find out. She already knew about the diamond and since diamonds were sold in a jewelry store she reasoned that it should be hers. If only she could remember why the mention of the diamond seemed to stir a vague memory, then she could act. She searched her memory for something familiar and gave up when she got a headache instead. Louise knew gemstones and was aware that a blue diamond would be worth a lot of money and the amount would of course depend upon the clarity, cut, and carats. Perhaps Belle would just hand over any jewelry found in the box or be coaxed to do so with little trouble. She would have to play it smooth with that old bat.

Louise and Alfred were planning on spending Easter in Welfield, Easter fell on April 1 and she could just arrive a few days early to help her mother-in-law with the plans for the holiday. She was thinking 'What an April fool's Day it could turn out to be if I could fool Aunt Belle into revealing what had been in the boxes. Perhaps William knew, and of course, if William knew then he would be sure to spill everything. I could go a few days early and treat him to some ice cream, etc. and coax it out of him. That sounded even better than trying to get anything from Belle Coleman. He would be the easiest to pry something out of and definitely with the least amount of trouble.'

She smiled to herself and called Alfred's office to tell him about Paul Black's horrible accidental death and claimed that she wanted to visit with her brother. She hadn't seen him since their mother's funeral and felt he would be quite upset about this Paul Black dying. "He's the one that kept William when mom and Aunt Belle went searching for a cure for her cancer."

Alfred told her that they would talk about it when he got home. She smiled to herself as she thought of all of the possibilities she would have with getting William to talk. While she waited for Alfred to come home, she would have to do a little shopping, Louise style. She would buy William a few volumes of the latest novels and a few comic books. He loved the Ace comics the best, especially "Four Favorites". At least, she knew that much about her brother. She really had ignored him for most of his life, but had enjoyed reading his comic books. She would have to buy him several comic books, especially some of the new releases. He would be excited about getting them and wouldn't pay a lot of attention to her questions. Although he was a lot more intelligent than Louise, she was a lot sneakier. Getting information from William was easiest when it didn't seem as though she was trying.

Chapter 4

Emily and the family arrived promptly at 4:45pm to the church on the evening of the wake their limo following the hearse. Father O'Brien greeted them as the casket was carried from the hearse to the back of the church by the pall bearers and it entered into the church in front of them. He placed a white cloth over the casket and walked around it sprinkled it with holy water and said prayers. The altar boys assisted the priest with the ceremony and left to change from their black cassocks and white surplice to street clothes as the mortician and his assistant rolled the casket to the front of the church in between the communion rails. He folded the white cloth carefully over the bottom half of the casket and placed the family spray on a stand at the bottom of the coffin. He opened the lid and arranged items that had shifted from the trip from the Welfield mortuary. His assistant placed the kneeler in front of the casket and put touchier lamps on the two ends of the coffin. There were numerous floral arrangements around the back of the coffin in baskets as well as on stands. When all was ready, the director motioned to the family in the back of the church who came forward slowly. Emily and Vivian walked together with John holding onto Vivian and William next to Emily. Belle and Mr. Blakeman followed them only a few feet behind.

Emily leaned over the coffin and softly kissed Paul's lips as she whispered to him so that none of the others heard her words. Paul looked so natural and so handsome in his new suit. Emily made a few adjustments to a few strands of his hair as she spoke softly about how much she loved him and always would. She spoke to him as though he was still alive and mentioned that Vivian and John were there along with Belle, William, and Robert Blakeman. Emily cried onto Paul's vest and finally her whole body shook from her loud sobs as she tried to hug him when she told him that she couldn't go on without him. She could hardly believe that her Paul was in the casket looking so peaceful while her world had fallen apart.

Vivian couldn't believe how serene her father looked and whispered to John, "He looks like he's asleep." She wept as she listened to her mother's soft voice of endearments to her beloved and when Emily sobbed even harder Vivian turned and wept onto John's shoulder. "My wonderful, wonderful one," she had whispered to Paul. When Emily's sobs stopped, Vivian saw that she had knelt down to say prayers and kept her hand on Paul's. Vivian quietly knelt beside her as John and William stood silently behind them. Emily turned silently to Vivian and the two hugged as they looked down at Paul. John helped her return to a chair sitting in front of the front pews to receive visitors.

John returned to the coffin to be near Vivian and when she saw his peaceful face, her façade of calm faded and she was inconsolable as she cried out, "Daddy, oh daddy, please don't leave me daddy. What are we going to do without you? Oh God, why did you have to take my daddy? Why? Oh daddy, my sweet daddy. I miss you so much! Why did I make you stay? I'll never forgive myself for making you stay there, never." She tried to hug him and John watched his tiny wife cling to her daddy as her body shook from her sorrow. Her body finally relaxed and she turned as John held on to her as she asked repeatedly aloud, "Why? Why did he have to die now? He was so good and I need him so much. I don't know what I'll do without him. John, why did God have to take him from us?" She had spoken with anger towards God and then thought of her mother and Father O'Brien's words of consolation so she spoke softer, "Daddy, I loved you so much and I promise that I will always remember you and everything you taught me. I will do the best I can and might ask you to help me from time to time. God loaned us to you for only a little while but I know if anyone can find a way to help us when we need it the most, you will. Oh daddy, my daddy, I miss you so much. I'll take care of mom, I promise." She finally left the coffin and John helped ease her to her seat beside Emily.

William was heart-broken as he had watched Emily and Vivian's sorrow and wasn't afraid to show his own. He had wept silent tears at first and used his handkerchief to wipe them and then his small shoulders began to shake and he openly sobbed. Emily got up from her seat to comfort him and he sobbed so hard on her shoulders until she quieted him down. "It's all right, William. He's not in any pain. Look at him, he looks so peaceful now, doesn't he?" William nodded and blew his nose once more before he leaned down and buried his curly head into her shoulder.

"It was so nice having him around. We had so many plans, you know. He was going to take me hunting and fishing. He promised to teach me how to smoke meats. Now, I'll never get the chance to do any of those things," he said pitifully.

"We'll all miss him dear and you can come to the farm anytime you want. I'll need the company, you know, now that I'll be all alone. Let's go sit down now, Vivian needs us," she said and William returned her to her seat beside Vivian. Vivian had heard her mother's last words and was trying to hold herself together now for her mother. William slowly turned back to the coffin and placed his hand upon Paul's and vowed, "I'll take care of both of them. I promise I will. In fact, I give you my word and my word is my bond. You told me once that a man was only as good as his word and I intend to keep it. No one will hurt them, ever. I promise you this; if someone wants to hurt them then they will have to go through me." He turned to find Belle nearby and said that he wanted to pray but didn't know what he was supposed to say. She whispered that they would say the Our Father together to themselves and they did.

Belle cried silent tears as she looked upon the man that had become like a son to her for such a short amount of time. He was one of the nicest men she had ever met. She didn't know how, but she would have to help Emily get through this difficult time. She wept openly as she leaned her gray head onto William's shoulder. Mr. Blakeman had come in with his wife and helped Belle to a seat beside John who was sitting on the other side of Vivian. William had pulled a chair over to sit on the other side of Emily.

John had gotten up, silently looked down upon Paul and softly said, 'Thank you for welcoming to your family and for letting me marry Vivian. I will do my very best to take care of both of them, but buddy, you sure are a tough act to follow. I wish we had had more time together and I'll never forget you.' Aloud he said, "I loved you as much as my own father and will miss your wit and advice. I pray that one day I will become half the man that you were."

There was a crowd of almost a thousand that eventually walked through to pay their condolences. The rosary started promptly at 7:30 pm and there was standing room only as Father O'Brien led the rosary. At 8:00pm a steady stream of mourners came by with endless anecdotes of Paul's generosity and keen sense of humor. Over and over men, women, and even some children told Emily and Vivian how much they respected Paul and how much the community would miss him. Emily found out some things she hadn't known about Paul. He would always get an ice cream from the pharmacy when he went to the company store and he would also buy a cone for any child that happened to be in there. She finally knew the explanation for his lack of appetite when he had returned for lunch after going to the pharmacy. She also found out that he liked to go all the way to Welfield and visit veterans that were recuperating and take them candy bars and comic books. She was comforted by all of their stories and smiled at each one who shared them with her.

The family would be staying through the night at the church and Belle asked Mr. Blakeman to escort Emily to the basement to get a bite to eat just before midnight. Emily ate a small amount of tuna salad and drank a glass of milk. She would be fasting until she received communion at the funeral mass the next day. Vivian had come down with John and followed suit. William stayed with Belle and waited until they returned before he went with Belle to get something to eat. He didn't want to leave Paul alone for even a minute. There were few other mourners there throughout the night. Allen and Maggie Jones stayed at the church as well as Josef and his mother.

The Filbert Resort's caretaker and his wife sat in the back of the pews in the dark so as not to intrude on the family. He wanted to be there since he and Paul had become good friends while Paul helped with improvements to the grounds around the club himself. He hadn't acted like an employer to the caretaker, but had behaved more like a coworker. Paul had respected his ideas and toiled hard right by his side on many projects. The caretaker had lost a good friend and didn't want to leave him or his family just yet.

When dawn arrived, the sun's rays entered through the stained glass windows and rested upon the coffin. Emily and Vivian both noticed the bright colors and used that particular time to look at the floral arrangements and messages on the cards. The mortician mentioned that it was time to get ready for the funeral so Emily went up to say some final words. She let Vivian go first and she was finally face to face with her dead husband for the last time. Her last words of, "I'll always love you. Take care of him, God. Wait for me Paul. Pray for me that I make you proud. I love you." She leaned into the casket and kissed him one last time. The mortician had told them the previous day that the coffin would be closed around 9:00 and they may want to be out of the sanctuary when it occurred. She left to freshen up around 8:55 in the only bathroom that was in the church's basement and Vivian and Belle followed her lead. Vivian found that she had no more tears left and was physically exhausted from crying and had chosen to simply kiss her father's forehead and left. William and John chose to stay and watch as the kneeler and torchiers were removed and the coffin was closed and sealed. The coffin was moved to the back of the church and once again covered with the white cloth. All flowers were removed to another hearse except for the family spray that would cover the coffin on the way to the cemetery. It took almost fifteen minutes to remove all of the flowers, chairs, and stands and already mourners were being directed to their seats. It had taken four assistants and the owner with the help of the pall bearers to get it done so quickly.

The family would be seated in the front pew and a velvet red cloth with a large embroidered R was placed on the pew to the right and another on the front pew to the left for the pall bearers. They would follow the coffin in as it was rolled into place as the choir would sing the "Requiem" entrance hymn. Several songs were sung in Latin and in English. One of them had an English translation of "Day of wrath oh day of mourning, fulfilled is the Savior's warning..."

Promptly at 10am the bell was rung as the altar boys and Father O'Brien entered from the sacristy in his black vestments. Everyone in the crowded church rose and the funeral began. Emily would remember little from the funeral except the readings that Father O'Brien had chosen. He gave a beautiful homily. The service ended at 11:30am. The family processed out after the priest, altar boys, and pallbearers who followed the now uncovered coffin to the hearse. Emily and Vivian both seemed to be in some sort of trance until they reached the cemetery. The priest sprinkled holy water on the grave site and said some final prayers. At the end of the graveside service, Emily leaned over and removed a rose from the spray to be pressed and kept in her bible. Vivian got a rose and so did Belle and William. They walked down the hill to go to the cars and drove straight to the Jackson Country Club for lunch. There were almost 500 mourners that attended the lunch. There would have been more, but most of the men had to work and their wives, who didn't have driver's licenses didn't have rides. Many of the women of the parish had ridden together and assisted the club's staff with the serving of the food.

The family ate their dinner together and after each of the mourners paid their last respects to the family it was almost three o'clock in the afternoon before they could return home. So many people who hadn't been able to get to either the wake or the house had wanted to speak personally with Emily and Vivian. Neither of them turned away from speaking to any of the guests. Once more Emily heard stories about Paul that she hadn't known about. So many told about how he had helped them one way or the other. Some of the widows told how he had done physical labor to get their gardens in shape after their husbands had passed away. Numerous times Emily repeated phrases like, "That sounds so much like Paul. He loved helping others…Thank you for coming…I'll call you if I need anything…You are very kind for saying that."

Emily was exhausted when they finally returned home and fell asleep almost as soon as her head had hit the pillow. William went to the room he had slept in for the past two nights while John helped Vivian get to bed and suggested she sleep. Belle had returned to her home but promised to return later in the evening. She promised to come around 7 with a dinner her cook had prepared. Mr. Blakeman would return with her, to make arrangements for the reading of Paul's will. John stretched out on the couch ready to answer the phone while Josef's mother finished cleaning up the kitchen. John's parents, Henry and Catherine Williams, had called around three and told him how sorry they were that they hadn't been there for Emily and Vivian. They had gone to the mountains to check on their cabin that was being built in western VA and hadn't left a phone number to be reached. They had stayed at the Hotel Roanoke as part of a short holiday. When they had returned to Richmond, they had received his message about the accident and Paul's subsequent death.

They told John that they were leaving on the next train from Richmond and would be arriving in Welfield the following morning. They had made arrangements to stay on Filbert Mountain at one of the Sportsman Club's cabins for the next two weeks. There were several other calls mostly from his relatives and John wrote down messages from each of them.

It was around six when Belle and Mr. Blakeman returned with several boxes of casserole dishes filled with grilled salmon fillets, potatoes au gratin, peas, rolls and a tossed salad. There was a half gallon of strawberry ice cream for dessert. Belle arranged the casseroles on the table and called out, "Ya'll need to wash up for dinner."

Emily, although she had rested several hours after the burial, appeared worn and haggard. John went to get Vivian who had been resting from their room and helped her to the table. No one sat in Paul's seat and William pulled up a side chair to sit directly across from John. They began the meal in silence but as they began remembering some of the stories they had heard the previous night, the group became more animated. William recalled how Paul used to sneak him candy just before meals on his visits and Paul's first reaction to cotton candy, "He told me it looked like the inside of cat tails but tasted sweet." William laughed as he reminded them of his first chess game with Paul, "We had given up and decided to just play checkers with the pieces until Mr. Blakeman straightened us out."

John recalled for them his hunting expedition with Paul and how Paul didn't know how many times he had shot a rifle before and tried to give him instructions. "You should have seen his face when I tried to milk my first cow. Paul had laughed heartily at my first awkward attempt and eventually broke down showing me how to warm my hands first. He loved doing work on his farm and taught me a lot each and every time I came here. Emily, do you remember our first trip to New York together? He was like a fish out of water at first, but liked riding the subway almost as much as he liked the limo. He made friends so easily. Paul could fit in anywhere he went," John shared.

They ate dinner and then as Emily, Belle, and Vivian washed up the dishes, John and William sat in the living room and turned on the radio. A radio show was playing some old tunes and the song "My Wonderful One" began playing. Emily froze as she listened to the words and smiled as silent tears ran down her cheeks, she mouthed the words the best she could while wiping the dishes,

"My wonderful one that I love you so

Awake or sleeping

My heart's in your keeping

And calling to you soft and low

My wonderful one

Whenever I'm dreaming

Love's love light a-gleaming I see

My wonderful one

How my arms ache to hold, dear

To cuddle and fold you to me

Just you, only you

In the shadowy twilight

In silvery moonlight

There's none like you, I adore you

My life I'll live for you,

Oh, my wonderful, wonderful one"

She told the others how she and Paul had danced to that song while on their honeymoon and said, "He whispered to me during that dance that I was his wonderful one." It was one of those memories that she would cherish for as long as she lived and Vivian hugged her mother saying, "I have never heard that story before, mom." The family talked until well after midnight and Belle left with William who promised Emily that he would return to the farm the next morning and would stay for the weekend. He would help Josef with some of the chores and hugged Emily and Vivian tightly before he left.

Around eight the next morning, Josef quietly knocked on the front door to ask what Emily wanted him to do with the milk from yesterday. He had taken it home and had put in his refrigerator along with the eggs. He had already collected the eggs and milked the cows that morning and would do as he was told. Emily told him to keep them as well as the milk and eggs from today. She told him that she expected William to arrive any minute and advised him to take the milk and eggs to his mother's neighbors. She told him about her plans, "We have to go to the lawyer's office for the reading of Paul's will around ten this morning. If you could get William to help you pick out a new mule, I'd appreciate it."

William arrived with a suit for Sunday mass along with two sets of work clothes. As soon as he saw Josef he set out to lead the cows to the west pasture and then to clean out the stalls. The chickens needed to be fed and the pigs slopped. William was pleased to be doing work that Paul had shown him how to do. He and Josef left to get a new mule while Emily, Vivian, and John left in Belle's car to meet Belle, who had been picked up by Mr. Blakeman at 9:30. The will left the bulk of his estate to Emily to do with as she wished. To Vivian, he left his pocket watch and asked her to take care of Bucky.

Vivian cried as she heard Bucky's name. He had been an old blind mule from the mines that Paul had rescued. Bucky had always only responded to her or to Paul. Vivian had always snuck him a handful of oats when she visited. Paul used the mule as his own way to reduce usage of gasoline with the tractor. She had forgotten to ask about Bucky after the accident and Emily told her about having to be put down because of his injuries in the fall. John was surprised when he heard his name mentioned as the recipient of Paul's pipe and stand along with his tie tacks and cufflinks. John had admired the pipe once, and although he didn't smoke, Paul thought he would like it. To William, Paul left his collection of comic books and several pairs of gloves. To Belle he left several jars of honey that she had told him she loved to have with her waffles. Paul left $12,500 for Our Lady of the Rosary to build a decent parish hall. He had checked with Father O'Brien and that was the amount that could build a reasonably large parish hall. Paul left his Hungarian missal to his friend, George Groch and his pole diggers, tools, and wheel barrow to the caretaker of the Filbert Mountain resort. He made other small bequests to neighbors and asked that his friend, Allen Jones, was to be given $1500 to take Maggie on a special holiday.

Emily decided on the way home to donate Paul's clothing to war refugees and was pleased when she called Father O'Brien and he agreed to make the arrangements. She gave a few of Paul's handkerchiefs to Josef and found that Paul wore the same size shoes as Josef and gave him several pairs as well. Vivian began helping Emily box up the clothing but wanted to keep a plaid shirt that he had always worn when they picked blackberries. It was the only long sleeve shirt he wore in the summer and it protected his arms from the briers. She had so many happy memories of her dad, and wanted to hang on to him for just a little longer. She asked for one of her dad's bottles of cologne that she could open and smell from time to time. Emily had set several bottles aside for William and Paul's St. Christopher medal. Most of Paul's clothes were relatively new and little memories were attached to them, but Paul's old sweater Emily couldn't let go of just yet. Paul had worn it the morning he died after coming in from the barn to take the chill off and had hung it up before going to plow. His hat still hung beside the sweater and she couldn't bear to part with either of them and felt comfort seeing them on the hook. It was as if he would be returning any time soon.

Packing up the clothing was taking longer than she had expected, but little surprises were found inside Paul's suit pockets. That meant that pockets in each pair of pants had to be checked for sticks of gum or wrapped hard candy. Emily was so relieved when Catherine and Henry Williams, John's parents, finally arrived around 9:30 that morning. Henry joined in to assist with the chore of packing up Paul's clothing. Catherine held onto her tightly as Emily related the events of the past few days. Vivian was also comforted by both of her in-laws who were extremely fond of her. While Catherine helped Emily, Henry was introduced to William who had just come in to wash up and use the bathroom.

Emily presented Henry with Paul's new riding apparel to be kept at their Richmond home for his guests. She also gave him one of Paul's Harry James albums that Henry had admired just last summer. Catherine helped Emily sort out Paul's clothing as well as his socks, shoes, and toiletries. Emily decided to divide the various toiletries between Josef and the caretaker. She set several pairs of socks aside for Josef who had been so faithful a helper in the past year or so. Josef was a lot stockier than Paul and couldn't wear his clothes or jackets. When the task was finished, John and Henry carried the boxes out to Paul's old truck and drove the boxes to Father O'Brien who addressed the boxes. They took him in the truck with them to immediately mail the packages. Henry and John paid for the postage as Father O'Brien wrote Emily's return address on each of the boxes. They ended up with eight large boxes and two smaller ones. John then asked Father O'Brien to accompany them back to the cabin since Emily had asked to speak with him. On Saturday's the Jackson post office closed at noon or whenever the last mail truck arrived and they had gotten the packages on time to get on the truck. They assured him that Emily had said it would take only about an hour of his time.

Emily smiled slightly when she first caught a glimpse of Father O'Brien and invited him to join them for lunch. William joined them for lunch after washing up in the back like Paul had showed him the previous summer. They had a light lunch of sandwiches made with one of Paul's hams, potato soup and fried apples made with butter and cinnamon. They finished off the ice cream Belle had brought for them the night before. William and Emily were both concerned that Belle had not returned on Saturday while the elder Williams' couple was disappointed since they had been anxious to meet her.

Emily handed Father O'Brien the cashier's check made out to a local lumber yard that also sold brick and mortar for $12,500 and told the priest that it was Paul's wish that a parish hall be built. Emily had asked her banker about getting the check for the church and he informed her that if the check had been made out to the church, Father O'Brien would have been obligated to send a large portion to the diocese. "Paul wanted the money spent on the parish and this was the best way I could get it done," Emily told him. Father O'Brien could hardly speak from the shock of the large donation. He knew that they needed a hall for wedding receptions, church functions, and catechism classes for his growing membership and had begun plans for fund-raisers. Instead of waiting at least four or five years, they could begin immediately. He thanked her over and over for the generous gift and she said, "It is from Paul, too, Father."

Vivian promised to have windows and doors ordered to suit the needs of the parish as well as to fully equip the kitchen in order to serve large crowds. Emily would order nice tables and chairs that could be used for wedding receptions, dinners, etc. as well as extra linens for the tables. There would be separate rest rooms for the men and women fitted with toilets and sinks. Father O'Brien was speechless hearing those offers and accepted the generous gift on behalf of the small parish, "I thank you on their behalf and the future members who will benefit from the hall. God will bless you for your generosity, both of you."

Construction costs would be paid entirely by Emily and Vivian and therefore it could start shortly after Easter. Father hoped that it all could be completed by Christmas so that the parish could begin using it as quickly as possible. Marshall Steel had already surveyed the property site and had found the best location for the facility. They had promised that they would provide the plumbing and electricity for the building when it was constructed. Father

O'Brien was driven to the rectory and the family decided to return to the cemetery with John's parents to Paul's grave.

Emily walked with her arms linked through Vivian's as they walked towards the grave. Flowers were stacked up high on his grave and all of the women wept for some time over their loss. Vivian pointed out the small sprig from the wild rose bush and tears welled up in all of their eyes as Emily explained the story of the wild rose. Catherine wept along with them for she had greatly admired that pleasant farmer and his wife who had helped her to understand what was needed for her family to become closer and how to make a house, a home. She and Henry held onto Emily and John helped Vivian return to the '39 Ford. William stayed behind for a few minutes alone at the gravesite. John and Henry returned to walk with him and they had a few moments to share their mutual admiration of Paul. William left with his head held down trying to hide his tears and Emily hugged him as soon as he got into the car and he broke down once more into loud sobs.

John and Henry stood behind at the grave for a few extra minutes. Henry spoke to John as they turned to leave, "You have a great burden on your shoulders now son. He was a wonderful man, a good, decent human being. I am sorry I have not been more like him in the past but I promise you that I am going to try to be more like him in the future. Those women will really need you now that Paul is gone and I know you won't let them down."

They had a quiet afternoon as several businessmen from Welfield and Marshall Steel came by to meet privately with Vivian and Emily. When the guests had left, Mrs. Novak had prepared supper for the group. After dinner, Belle called and apologized for not joining them. She told Emily that Louise had called to say that she was coming for a visit to Welfield and wanted to visit William. Belle told Louise that William wasn't at home at the moment and would not be returning until late on Sunday. Belle didn't mention to Emily that Louise spoke to her as if nothing had happened and hadn't bothered to ask that her condolences be forwarded to Emily's family once more. Belle was not sure of Louise's sudden interest in William or herself but she was certain that it certainly wasn't due to any feelings of affection. Louise was up to something. Belle had spent the biggest part of Saturday on the phone with detectives and Mr. Blakeman. Whatever she was trying to start, Belle was intent on stopping. Neither Emily nor Vivian needed to deal with any further problems from Louise, especially now. Everyone was emotionally spent and went to bed early. Sunday would bring another onslaught of support and emotion from the parish members after mass the next day.

Louise had gotten the comic books for William and planned out how she would approach him about what had happened in New York. She awakened to go to church with Judge Perkins and his wife and was quite pious as the minister gave his sermon. She appeared moved by his words of strength in faith and love while, in fact, her mind wandered about various scenarios. Later, she made sure to be particularly attentive to the Judge and his wife's conversation at lunch. They spent the afternoon reading the paper and listening to the radio. Around four o'clock in the afternoon she asked if arrangements could be made for her to visit with her brother. She admitted to them that she had been guilty of neglecting him since the death of her dear mother and grandmother. "He is the only family that I have left other than a few aunts and cousins that I don't see very often. I miss him terribly," her pleas sounded so sincere.

At six o'clock she called Belle and was given permission to see William at seven o'clock, but was told he would have to go to bed by nine since he had school the next day. Louise didn't think it would take longer than an hour to talk to him and get the information she needed. She had the comic books wrapped in a bright paper and ribbon and handed them to her brother who was quite excited when he saw them. While he was talking about them she mentioned that she had wanted to bring them after Christmas, but he had unexpectedly gone to New York.

"I had a miscarriage while you were in New York, William. I couldn't come to visit sooner since I was having female troubles. Alfred and I are going to try again, you know," Louise claimed. She craftily steered the conversation so that he would relate to her what he had done while in New York asking questions about where he had gone and whether he had done any shopping. She seemed interested as he told her about New Year's Eve and her eyes lit up as he told her about the fireworks.

"It must have been exciting for you to be in New York for New Year's!" she hinted. "But why on earth did you go to New York? We never went to New York in all the years we lived with Aunt Belle on New Year's Eve, so why did you go this year?"

"Oh Emily found some papers in mom's hope chest about some safety deposit boxes and some of them were up there. Did you know that Paul

Black died? I really, really liked him. He enjoyed "the big town" as he called it. He loved it so much there. We had so much fun together in New York with John and Vivian. He taught me so much when I stayed on the farm last year. I'm really going to miss him. It's been so tough on all of them with him dying so suddenly," he told her.

"Oh, I'm so sorry to hear that. Did you say that John and Vivian were with you?" she tried not to sound too interested.

"Oh yeah they were there. They are both so nice. Did I tell you that Paul and I tried to play chess on the train and Mr. Blakeman taught both us how to play chess on the train? Paul beat me every time but taught me a lot about war and stuff. Louise, do you know how to play chess?" William asked innocently.

"Oh no, I'm not smart enough to learn. Did you do any shopping in New York?" she continued.

"Paul, John, and I shopped while Emily, Aunt Belle and Mr. Blakeman went to the bank the first day. I got a haircut too with them and Louise, I hate to admit it, but it was so nice to have someone treat me like they were my dad," he answered. "I'm really going to miss him, sis."

"Well of course you are. Well, why didn't you go with them to the bank?" she pushed thinking, 'I wish he would stop talking about that man.'

"Oh I went with them in the afternoon to sign some papers for some war bonds. Emily got me some war bonds from money they found in one of the boxes. When they went to the other banks there were just a bunch of papers. Aunt Belle showed me a copy of mom and dad's marriage certificate and our birth certificates that they found in some other boxes. We watched fireworks from a restaurant on New Year's Eve! It was really neat! Paul treated me like a grown up and John treated me like a brother. It was one of the nicest days of my life," he admitted.

"I'm sorry all this happened after you had such a good time. Maybe we need to spend more time together, huh?" Louise offered.

"Sure, do you want to do something together after school tomorrow Louise?" he asked.

"Why that sounds like fun! How about going for an ice cream soda after school? Maybe we can find some more comic books at Murphy's. Well, I come around 3, ok?" She kissed his cheek and called to Belle, "May I come back tomorrow to take William for an ice cream soda?"

Belle was working in the office looking rather tired and Louise asked, "Are you ok, Aunt Belle?"

"I'm just a little tired. It's been a very long and difficult week with Paul Black's death that's all. I really liked him a lot and it's been hard on William as well. Paul and Emily kept him on the weekends, while I was taking Bertie to the doctors in New York, Chicago, and Durham. He really became attached to Paul and Emily during that time almost as much as I have. Listen, I have had some rough days ahead and it will be fine to take William for ice cream sodas and now if you excuse me, I will bid you good night," Belle stated as a dismissal.

"Good night, Aunt Belle. Do try to get some sleep tonight. I'll be by around 3 and promise me, Aunt Belle, promise me that you will take care of yourself," Louise said with such sincerity that it almost sounded like the real thing.

Louise walked to her car thinking about what William had said about a wedding certificate and birth certificates being in the boxes. Strange that those would be the only things in the boxes; there must have been something else, there just had to be. William had mentioned a bunch of papers and found it peculiar that Aunt Belle didn't want William to know more about them. It was also odd that William hadn't mentioned anything about the diamond the detective had told her about. What was it about that diamond that seemed familiar? Perhaps if she could see it, then she might remember. If it was in a necklace, then it definitely should be hers. She would ask William about that tomorrow while they enjoyed their sodas. As she pulled into the Perkins' driveway, she thought of something else. Aunt Belle hadn't bothered to mention her miscarriage and that was odd, very odd. She would have thought that Aunt Belle would have offered something to cheer her up. She would somehow work it into her next conversation with Aunt Belle.

While Louise was entering the Judge's residence, Belle was thinking about her visit and spoke briefly with William. "It was nice of Louise to come by to visit. What did you two talk about?" she asked.

William continued, "Louise bought me some comic books and asked me to go get an ice cream soda tomorrow. She said she wanted to bring me these at Christmas but we were gone to New York. Anyway, I told her about learning how to play chess and asked her if she could play, but she said she wasn't smart enough to play. She asked me if I went shopping in New York and what I had bought. I told her what I bought and about going to the bank to get those bonds. I told her about the fireworks and stuff. Oh, she did ask something about what we found in those banks and I told her there were just certificates in those boxes. She told me she miscarried. I could have been an uncle."

'So she seems a little more than just curious. How on earth had she found out about those boxes?' Belle thought. She would have to ask Louise about that young man they had met in New York. 'What did he say his name was? Oh yes, it was Jake Turner. He never did say what he was doing in New York. Now what were the chances of meeting someone from Welfield in the lobby of the Waldorf Astoria? They were pretty slim at best. I bet he was hired as her detective. Louise was getting more devious in her methods. I will have to be very careful in the future.'

"I'm sorry to hear that but I'm glad that you had such a good time. Now it's time to go to bed. You have school tomorrow and you have had some rough days here lately young man," she said gently.

"Good night, Aunt Belle. I love you," he hugged and kissed her on the forehead.

"Good night, William. Sleep well, and William, I love you too," she admitted.

Belle slept quite well and the next morning watched William get onto the school bus. She had a second cup of coffee and called Emily. Vivian answered the phone and told her about their visit with Father O'Brien. Belle asked if it would be convenient for her to visit and when Vivian asked Emily, Belle had to smile as she heard an "Of course she can," in the background. Belle wanted to make use of the time and opportunity to spend with her daughter and granddaughter. "I'll be up there by ten. Do you need anything?" she asked.

"No, we're fine. We just want your company!" Vivian answered.

Belle would go to see Emily in the morning to talk with her about Louise's visit. Emil was sharp and could possibly figure out what mischief Louise was up to now. But first, Belle would ask a few of Louise's old high school friends about Jake Turner before Louise got a chance to get to them and ask them to lie. She immediately went to her office after breakfast and called two of them, and both said the name didn't mean anything to either of them. She called the Welfield High principal who told her that no student of that name was in any of their records. She thanked them for their time and was sure now that he had to have been a private detective hired by Louise. Belle couldn't help but think, 'Louise needed to be careful or she might just get what she is asking for and it wouldn't be what she was expecting, no ma'am, it wouldn't be that at all.'

Belle freshened up and put on her hat and gloves. She called her driver who came around to drive her to the cabin. When Belle arrived, she was pleasantly surprised to meet John's parents. They were very impressed when they saw her Pierce-Arrow limo and knew who she was before they had gotten out of John's Lincoln. Henry and Catherine Williams were both considered members of High Society and Belle recognized their name vaguely from articles in the New York Times Society pages. When Henry mentioned the shipbuilding in Newport News, she knew where she had heard their names. Their shipbuilding firm's name had been on some of the largest contracts for Marshall Steel. She made a mental note to check with Mr. Blakeman to make sure that there wasn't anything illegal about those contracts and didn't want to be accused of nepotism with any of their contracts.

Emily still looked pale, but at least appeared to be perhaps a little more rested. She hugged Belle tightly as soon as Belle got through the door. Vivian offered everyone a cup of coffee and a chorus of yeses was heard. John helped her pour the coffee while he and Vivian had hot tea. Belle listened to the conversation and found out that the Williams were staying in a Sportsman Club's cabin. Belle asked Catherine how the little canary was and after a slight smiling pause was told it was still singing its little heart out. Henry told her that he was having a cabin, similar to the one they were staying in, built in the Shenandoah Mountains near Roanoke. They were enjoying themselves in conversation when Catherine asked, "Why don't we go to the Jackson Country Club for lunch, our treat? You are too tired Emily and we need to get you away from your house for a few hours."

"You know, I haven't been to the club for lunch in a long time, "Belle said.

"Well, I say we go then. It would be good to get out of the house for a little while. We have a ton of leftovers for dinner to get rid of, though. Perhaps you can help us out with some of that Catherine," Emily offered.

"As long as it includes some of Paul's ham I won't mind at all taking some of them off your hands," Catherine agreed. "It's important for you to get some down time after this past week."

Everyone got ready and Vivian put on just a little perfume and makeup while Emily combed her hair and only put on a little lipstick. They rode in Belle's limo while Henry and Catherine followed in John's car.

The country club wasn't very crowded for lunch since it was still a little too chilly for most golfers, and the party had a delightful lunch together. As they were preparing to leave, who should enter the club but Louise Perkins with her mother-in-law, Mrs. Perkins. Louise waved and came over to say hello to her aunt and was dying to meet those well dressed people who were with her. She had recognized Emily and Vivian immediately and saw John Williams come out from the rest room just as she had crossed the floor. She assumed that the strangers must be John's parents and she excused herself from her in-laws at that precise moment to freshen up. She knew that she looked great in her carefully chosen ensemble and smiled to herself when she noticed just how dreary Vivian looked. Louise left the ladies' room and kissed Belle on the cheek and asked to be introduced to her companions.

"Catherine and Henry Williams I would like to introduce you to my grand niece, Louise Pierce Perkins. She is the daughter of my niece by marriage, the late Bertie Coleman Pierce. I was married to Louise's uncle," Belle explained the relationship.

"How do you do," Louise said in her sweetest tone. "I was so sorry to hear of Mr. Black's sudden death and was shocked, just shocked by the news. Emily, Vivian, if you need anything, anything at all, don't hesitate to call me. I'm staying at my in-laws, Judge and Mrs. Perkins."

"Certainly," Emily barely managed to say. Emily didn't know what to say to the girl who had tried to ruin her daughter in college by bribery, conspiracy, lying, and stealing. This sudden show of concern was puzzling to her to say the least. She looked over at Vivian who said, "Louise, if we need anything I assure you that we will add you to our list of all the people who have already offered to help us at this time."

As Louise turned and the others were out of earshot, Vivian leaned over and whispered to her, "You'll be on the bottom of the list, dearie," and walked out of the club behind the rest of her family.

Louise was a little shocked by the rebuke, but could not appear to be too disturbed by Vivian's remark when she waved to John and his parents. After all, she had just met John's parents and was sure that she had made a favorable impression. She was deep in thought when she returned to the table, 'I wonder where they are staying. There's definitely not enough room at the Black's house and there isn't a decent hotel in the area. They must be staying up at the Sportsman's Club. Perhaps I'll speak to the Judge and have them invited to their house for dinner.'

Louise sat down and said, "Well, wasn't that nice seeing Aunt Belle. Did you know that I went to school with Vivian Black? Aunt Belle just introduced me to Vivian's in-laws. They are the Richmond Williams, a prominent family in the shipbuilding business, I believe. Vivian and I were best friends when we were younger. It is so sad about her father dying in that horrible accident."

Judge Perkins said, "Well, perhaps we should invite all of them to dinner. What do you think dear?"

"I believe that Vivian Black Williams will want to stay with her mother at this time. It wouldn't hurt though to invite the Richmond Williams to dinner though. What did you say their names were?" Mrs. Perkins inquired.

"Catherine and Henry Williams are their names and I believe they are staying at the Sportsman's Club. I'm sure if you call, the caretaker could tell you if they are guests there," Louise said innocently.

"I'll call up there this afternoon. I'd like to know more about the shipbuilding business," Judge Perkins offered.

Emily had a large stack of sympathy cards from Pittsburgh, New York, and Richmond in the mail and she was faced with a mound of thank you notes to write. She and Vivian would have several days' worth of notes to finish over the next week or so. The guards had set the cards inside a basket beside the front door off of the front porch.

When Emily and the rest of the party came into the house, Emily rubbed her face with her own hands and Catherine noticed how pale she looked. "Are you all right, Emily?" Catherine asked.

"I'm all right. I just didn't expect to run into Louise Pierce today of all days," Emily said.

John explained, "Louise is the one that caused all of those problems for Vivian last year at Comfield. I can tell you this much, she isn't normally like she was today. She was trying to make a good impression, because I know that she is actually like a snake. When she is acting nice, she is up to something and is getting ready to strike, so look out. She's what dad calls a man-eater. She went to college looking for a husband and for some reason she set her eyes on me for a while. Thank goodness she's married now."

"Well I'm glad you told me. She certainly was dressed in a very expensive outfit and I have to admit that she seemed to be so nice. She had me fooled with her impeccable manners," Catherine noted.

"My niece does not lack in social graces but does lack immensely in the integrity department. I am sad to say she is not one to be trusted and could even be described as a wolf in sheep's clothing," Belle admitted. "John's right where Louise is concerned. The friendlier she is, or seems to be, the more dangerous she becomes."

Shocked by what they had just heard, Catherine and Henry both made mental notes at the same time not to be seen in public with this Louise Pierce Perkins girl. So she had been the one that had tried to get her hooks into their John. Thank goodness John had found Vivian who had been such a good influence on him before John got mixed up with Louise. Louise had to be pretty bad for her own aunt to apologize for her character. Belle left shortly after two in the afternoon in order to be home by the time William's bus arrived.

Louise showed up promptly at three to take him for the promised ice cream sodas. She appeared to be in a particularly good mood after meeting John's parents and had decided to get more information about them from William. But first, she had to raise the question about the diamond.

While at the soda fountain Louise mentioned, "You know I was thinking about mother and remembered a beautiful diamond she once had. Do you remember it? I believe it was a blue one."

"Sure I do, it's the one they found in one of those boxes in New York. It was a big blue one that Emily brought back home with her after she had it made into a pendant when we were in New York. Aunt Belle said it was one of the first gifts she had ever given to mom," William said without pause.

"Oh yes, I remember now. Mom didn't know whether to have a ring or pendant made with it. Do you want to go to Murphy's? They sell comic books you know," she said. 'So there was a blue diamond and she's trying to claim she had it made into a pendant. I knew it. So they think they can cheat me out of a pendant that's part of my inheritance. I'll just mention that I didn't see it among mom's jewelry and watch Aunt Belle's reaction. She may just bring it down to me at the Perkins' house. It must be worth a small fortune and I can certainly use the money right now. Alfred's practice isn't doing as well as it should be. We should be on easy street by now. After all, it's been almost a year since he opened his practice. Just how long does it take to make a successful law practice?' she thought to herself.

Louise bought several comic books and bags of candy for William in Murphy's. She brought up the subject of John's parents and William only said a few words about them since he was distracted now by the comic books and candy. They went into a jewelry store on Main Street and she asked to see some diamond jewelry and a money clip. She asked William to select a money clip while she looked at some diamonds. The jewelry store clerk she chose to speak with was the oldest one that worked there and brought out several nice pieces of diamond jewelry for her to look over. In the course of the conversation, she managed to ask about colored diamonds. The clerk had a few pink diamonds and a very small blue one and told Louise they didn't get larger colored diamonds because they were so expensive. Few people could afford larger blue diamonds. Louise smiled and thanked them and decided that she had changed her mind about the pendant but purchased a money clip for William and paid extra to have his initials WP put on it. The clip would be ready the following day and Louise assured the clerk she would be the one to come by to pick it up.

William was excited about the money clip and when he got home he had to tell Aunt Belle. "All the boys in the ninth grade only have wallets; I'll be the first to have a money clip instead of a wallet."

Belle thanked Louise for taking William out and asked her to sit down and visit for a while. Belle began the conversation with a simple, "I was so glad to see the Perkins again at lunch. They both look well. How have you been lately?"

"Oh I'm much stronger now, thank you. After losing the baby, it was quite a difficult experience for Alfred and me, but the doctor said that we could try again in another six months or so. You know, while I was recuperating, I was thinking about our early years with you and I just happened to remember that you gave mother a beautiful blue diamond. It wasn't among mother's jewelry and I am sure that she had it set in a pendant or ring. I mean, what woman would hold onto a diamond that hadn't been set?" she asked.

"Ah yes, the rather large one I gave when we first moved to Welfield. I don't recall her getting it set. If she had, I am sure she would have worn it at some event over time if she had it set. But knowing Bertie, she would have kept it unset simply because she didn't get around to it or couldn't make up her mind. By the way, I meant to tell you. I met a very nice young man while I was in New York, his name was Jake Turner. He asked about you and sent his condolences on the loss of your mother," Belle said watching Louise's face for any sign of misgiving, but saw none. Instead Louise said, "Why imagine that, good old Jake Turner and in New York! How was Jake? We had several classes together in high school. He used to help me with my math."

"He seemed like a nice fellow and I was wondering what he was doing in New York. He didn't tell me of course," Belle said.

"I believe he works there, but I'm not sure," Louise said.

Belle pried a little deeper, "I thought it was rather odd that he should just happen to be in the Waldorf Astoria lobby when we were there. Could he have been waiting on someone that was staying there perhaps?"

"Oh that must have been it. Imagine the odds," she said with a forced smile.

Louise changed the subject back to their lunch and mentioned how nice the Williams couple seemed to be. "I adored her dress and would love to know where she got her shoes and purse," Louise said. "Perhaps I could call her and ask her but I don't know where they are staying," she hinted.

"They are staying at the Sportsman's Club but will be spending the next few days with Emily and Vivian. Vivian will be returning to Charlottesville next weekend and they are staying an extra week so that Emily won't be alone. Vivian's spring break ends next weekend and she has to go back to classes. I'm sure that if you ask Vivian that she would more than happy to let you know where her mother-in-law shops, because they are very close you know," Belle hinted knowing darn good and well that Louise was trying to get to know the Williams a little better and trying to cause trouble for Vivian.

"Well the least I could do would be to take them to lunch at the club or dinner. They must feel a little out of place with Paul gone and be bored with Emily and Vivian writing thank you notes or taking care of the farm. Judge Perkins said he would love to meet them and wanted me to ask them dinner at their home," Louise admitted.

"Oh, I don't think that's a good idea right now. Perhaps next time would be more appropriate, after all they are here to comfort Emily and are not here merely to make a social call with their acquaintances," Belle advised. "It wouldn't be prudent to approach them at this time Louise."

"Well perhaps you are right, but I can't deny the judge from at least meeting them. When I told him that they were in shipbuilding, he practically insisted that he meet them. I'll call them and let them decide, and then I won't look bad in front of the Perkins. You could join us, if they accept," Louise cooed.

"My calendar is very full right now. I have to go to Pittsburgh later this month for a board meeting and have other projects I'm working on as well. Call them if you wish, but don't be disappointed if they turn you down," Belle said with a slight warning tone.

"Well I must be going. If you happen to run into Jake again, tell him I said hello and thank you for his kind words," Louise said as she kissed her aunt's cheek.

Belle could barely keep from laughing out loud at the audacity of Louise. There was no such person as Jake Turner who had ever been enrolled at Welfield and that, was lie number one. She probably had arranged for her "miscarriage" and that, was lie number two. Lie number three was she had no interest in Catherine Williams' shoes but wanted to try to learn more about them and therefore about John. Obviously, Louise was still bent on getting John. 'I thought when she married Alfred that she would forget John. She must be over-extended and needs money and that's why she has taken the sudden interest in William and mentioned her miscarriage to me twice. Yep, she needs money. Well, perhaps if I give her some money she will lay off any ideas about John for a while.' Belle thought. 'I can spare the money, and perhaps I can keep a closer eye on her if she comes to the house for a visit more frequently. When she's on her own she is a lot more dangerous, money will give her a false sense of security. I can definitely watch her while she is around William as well. Louise isn't the only one to get information on her visits,' she shook her head as she dived into the stack of legal papers needing her attention.

Chapter 5

Louise wasted no time calling the Williams at the Sportsman's Club who politely declined the invitation. She was disappointed but decided that she wouldn't give up so easily. She would merely see if she could manage another chance encounter with them. She would go to the country club each day and perhaps run into them there. She turned her thoughts to what Belle had said about the diamond and decided to approach that subject with more caution. Belle wasn't easily fooled and it would be hard to pry any more information from her. 'I'll just continue to pretend to be interested in William, after all, he will be inheriting part of her money as well and I want to have a few cherished memories together when she's gone.' She congratulated herself on the idea of the money clip and decided to have $50 in small bills put into the clip before it was wrapped. Indeed you could catch more flies with honey instead of vinegar.

William was delighted with the surprise of the money in the clip. Louise had put four tens and ten singles onto it to make it look like he had a lot more money. William had really enjoyed her visit and really needed affection at this time, but unfortunately it wasn't genuine, and he was too young to realize that. On her last visit to Belle's house, before returning to Charleston, Belle gave her a check for $25,000 to help her "deal with her miscarriage and the adjustment to married life" as Belle called it. Louise was pleasantly surprised since she had only expected a few thousand and made it a point to thank her several times. She owed the private detective $1000 for the next six months and she laughed to herself that Belle was actually paying for a detective to investigate herself.

Belle suspected that Louise would use the money for a detective and since it would have to be one in Charleston, Belle's own private detective found one that fit Belle's description beside a gift shop in Charleston. The name on the sign was Jake Turner. Belle was surprised that he had actually used his real name when introducing himself and thought that he had to be relatively new to the business. Belle's detective confirmed that Louise had been in the hospital overnight in late December and had been in a private room on the OB/GYN floor.

Belle called Emily and told her what she had found out about Louise. Emily was silent as Belle told her about the interview with William and then said, "It doesn't surprise me, how about you?" Emily was glad she had called and asked if she and William could come to visit for a little while. The Williams were coming down for dinner and Emily had come to a big decision and wanted to talk it over with Belle.

Belle got ready while William got into one of his new suits. He would be escorting Aunt Belle to dinner and was so excited to be going to Emily's. Emily had set the table with her crystal and china and silver. She had asked the chef at the country club to fix a dinner for nine. Vivian and John were leaving the next day and she wanted to have a special private dinner at home. Emily had called Mr. Blakeman and invited him and his wife as well. The Blakemans would have to get a sitter for their son, Robert Jr.

When she came out in her blue evening gown and Bertie's blue diamond as a pendant she was all aglow. She intended to make this dinner a celebration of Paul's life and had an announcement to make in his honor. When they were all assembled, that is Vivian and John, Belle and William, Henry and Catherine, and the Blakemans, Emily held a glass of wine from the bottle that Mr. and Mrs. Williams had brought last year. She asked them to raise their glass to "To Paul Black my beloved husband. May he rest in peace knowing how much he was loved and admired by so many. May he be pleased with the decisions I have made this day, to Paul!" A chorus of "To Paul" as the crystal glasses clinked one to the other. They sat down and Emily took out a letter with rather strange writing on it. It appeared to be in a foreign language. Emily opened the letter and read a translation she had gotten from Mrs. Novak. She had tried to notify Paul's relatives in Hungary about his death and had found a letter dated only a few days before Paul died from his parent's old village. It had arrived the day after his funeral.

Dear Paul Blecoe,

May God bless you and your family this day and every day. I am afraid to hope that you are indeed my late neighbor's cousin. I pray that if you are the son of Elizabeth and George Blecoe who left in 1902 from the port of Fiume having lived in the village of Baksa in the Kassa District with an infant named Paul, then God has indeed blessed my dearly departed neighbor.

If this is the correct Paul Blecoe, then I have the burden of telling you that your cousin Kristof Blecoe was arrested and sent to a prison camp in Auschwitz for inciting locals to rebel against the Nazi regime, and has died in the camp. His four year old grandson was hidden and is now left an orphan and needs a home. I am too old to raise the child and am hoping that you will send for him. I can get him safely a passage to the United States if war ends soon. I include his birth certificate for you. Please let me know, his name is Paul Miklos Blecoe. My address is:

> Tivadar Dudas
>
> 123 Magyar Street
>
> Baksa, Kassa

Soviet forces freed our village from a German unit. If you want him mail to me soon, I can send the boy.

God bless you and your family. Tivadar Dudas

Emily said, "I know it sounds a bit awkward, but it was the best Mrs. Novak could do. I have answered this with a telegram. When I looked through Paul's papers I found letters his father had received from this Kristof Blecoe in this village. I have wired $500 for the transportation of the boy to America. That was enough to bribe the local officials because I received an answer in a wire this morning that told me to expect the boy by Easter. He is arriving next week on Holy Thursday at Ellis Island. I am going to pick him up and wanted to know who would go with me to welcome my new son, Paul Miklos, to my house?"

Vivian was speechless at first and then looked from John to Belle and then said, "Mom, are you sure this isn't some sort of scam?"

Mr. Blakeman spoke up, "I have called and spoken through the American embassy to Mr. Dudas myself. He is an elderly man that hid the boy in his cellar when his grandfather, Paul's cousin, was arrested. The little boy's parents and a baby brother were killed during a bombardment of the city in the early part of the war and he has no other relatives. They are trying to get as many children with relatives placed so as not to be a burden on the Russian government that is in control there, now. He wired me the information I requested and the boy is legitimate. If Emily wants to adopt him she can do so and it will be final after only six months. With the number of refugees coming into this country, it will not be difficult at all."

Belle tried to smile and said, "Emily, darling are you sure about doing this so soon after Paul's passing?"

Emily said emphatically, "The letter came the day after Paul's funeral and I know that Paul would want me to do this and other things as well. We had talked about leaving this farm and I have decided it's time to leave. I cannot stay here where I lost him. I don't feel like it is my home but rather, in my heart, it feels like Paul's murderer. I am going to move into Welfield where I can still be close to him, but I cannot leave him or the area. I have nightmares and cannot continue running the farm by myself, even with Josef's help. If you can offer a solution I am open to any and all alternatives. I will return from time to time back here when the pain is not so sharp. I just can't bear to stay here any longer."

Vivian was more shocked by the possibility of losing the farm than the adoption. "Mom I understand that you can't take care of the farm by yourself, but can't you just hire extra people now? Why don't you come with me and John for a while or stay with Belle?"

Emily explained, "I can't be a burden on anyone. You and John are still newlyweds and I won't intrude. Belle will have Louise visiting from time to time and I just can't face her right now. I can and have hired some help that will live in the house. Mrs.Novak and Josef will live here from now on, free and clear. I will come up for visits during the summer months when the fruit is ripe and make preserves as I always have, but I just can't live here, my dear. She will set aside butter and honey from the farm for our use, but I can't stay in my bedroom many more nights. I have so many wonderful memories with your father here, but they cannot erase the last one I have of seeing him on that plow. I cannot get rid of that vision when I last saw him alive. Baby, I just can't stand another night here. It's over, my life and all of my dreams are buried with Paul. All of it ended when he was buried. Please try to understand how I feel." Emily was getting more and more distressed and Vivian quickly rose and hugged her tightly. "I know mom and I understand. This is just a house now and not your home. Without dad, it has become more like a tomb, hasn't it?"

Emily kissed her cheek as Catherine spoke up and said, "How can we help?"

"Well, I found a lovely six bedroom house on Virginia Street that is the last house on the street near the top of a hill. It has three stories to it and is located only a few houses up the mountain from Judge Perkins as a matter of fact. I have made an offer and it was accepted yesterday. I can move in anytime. I wanted to be settled into the new home before the little boy gets here. I know that I will also have to buy a bedroom set for him as well as clothes, etc. I don't know what he will need, but probably everything. If you can help me with all those things, then I would appreciate it," Emily searched their faces as she made the last statement.

William piped up, "Well, I can help you with his room. I know what boys like. Perhaps I can go with you to pick out some stuff for him. You might want to let him chose a lot of things when he actually gets here. I mean what if he hates green and you paint his walls green. You can be sure, he won't like pink!"

Everyone laughed at that last remark and Emily managed, "I kind of figured that one out myself dear!"

Catherine said, "Are you going to hire a staff at your new home?"

"Well I hadn't thought of that but I guess I'll need a maid for that large of a house and I suppose that I'll need a driver and cook as well. I don't know what to do with Paul's car and truck. I thought of just leaving the truck since the Novak's will need the truck. I could learn to drive, but who would teach me?" she asked.

Mr. Blakeman spoke up, "I can teach you how to drive and my wife will help too! You could hire a driver for long distances. But you may want to get a new car first. The newer models are a lot easier to drive than that '39 model." His wife nodded in agreement.

Belle spoke up,"Why don't we see if we can get a plan made of how to pack up while you work on your driver's license? I'll see if I can find a maid that comes with recommendations as well as a cook. You are a marvelous cook, but having a young child, a business, a farm, and other obligations you are going to need a lot of help. You may want to hire someone to do your yard work. I have a good worker that comes on Mondays, Wednesdays, and Fridays and is free on Tuesdays and Thursdays. If you have to go to New York dear, and it is not quite two weeks away, how are you going to get all of this done by yourself?"

Emily took a deep breath and said, "I have already asked a moving company to pack up most of my things I have from my bedroom and a few other things. Everything else will stay here. I will have to buy several bedroom sets, a dining room set, living room set and parlor set. Vivian, I wanted to offer you your father's chair. Do you want his chair?"

"Mom I have no room for the chair, but I think I know where there is a perfect spot. Why not put it in William's room?" Vivian quickly suggested. William had been slightly disappointed when Emily had asked Vivian and when he heard the offer he immediately said, "Oh yes, I have plenty of room at Aunt Belle's and I will take really good care of it!"

"Catherine, if you could help the movers pack here, I could unload the stuff from the kitchen that Josef can load up on the truck. I am going to have to buy new towels and linens but will need to be at the new house to place the new furniture," she hinted.

"But of course, this is an exciting and sad time for you dear. When I think of home, I will always remember this little cabin, but your love is what made it what it as happy as it was. If you surround that little boy with your love, you will make a new home quickly. Paul will live now through his little cousin. Now we have a lot of plans to make so we better get busy," Catherine said.

John finally spoke up and said, "Emily, you don't need to go to New York by yourself. I don't start my apprenticeship for a while and would be pleased if you would accept me as your escort. We can stop in Charlottesville on the way back on the train and Paul Miklos can meet his new sister."

Emily said, "I believe I'll just call him Paul Michael. He will have his given name on all papers, but I know how children can be cruel. If I adopt him with his given name they may make fun of him. What do you think?"

William spoke up quickly and said, "Most of the kids don't care what your name is but the older people are the ones that can be mean. You better ask him although I figure he will have a lot to handle and probably won't understand English. He's been through a lot and changing his name might be a little too much if you know what I mean."

Henry had been listening carefully and said, "You are wise beyond your years, young man, and I say let the youngster decide. Your right William, he probably can't speak English. You may want to have a translator with you when you pick him up."

"Oh I hadn't thought of that, but who could I take? If Paul was alive he would be able to talk with him. He still spoke Hungarian with his friends when he didn't want me to know what he was talking about! Perhaps I could ask Mrs. Novak to go with me! She speaks fluent English and Hungarian! I will call her in the morning!"

"So when do we start?" Catherine asked.

"Well, the house is empty and since I have paid cash for the house, I can move in as soon as I like. Would you go with me to look at it?" Emily asked. "The electricity and water will be turned on tomorrow along with the phone," she quickly added.

A chorus of "yes" was heard, and Emily said, very well, "We will meet here at nine in the morning. Belle, William, and Mr. Blakeman can meet us at the house. The address is 278 Virginia Street. Is that all right with everyone?" Everyone nodded and the dinner progressed with great excitement and the sharing of ideas about items to add to the list.

At nine the next morning, everyone was crowded into either the '39 Ford or John's Lincoln. They met Belle, William, and Mr. Blakeman at 9:30. Emily gave them the grand tour of the house. William immediately identified which room would be Emily's and which should be Paul Miklos' room. He suggested changing the wallpaper to a stripe or plaid and to definitely not to keep the pretty floral paper that was in there now. The four smallest bedrooms were each larger than Emily's current bedroom. The three bathrooms upstairs had recently been remodeled with new wallpaper and bead board and so nothing needed to be done to them. The third floor had three more rooms that could serve as servant's quarters or extra bedrooms if needed. Catherine suggested that she keep them as servant's quarters so that they would be available to her at all hours. If Emily hired a couple, a maid and a butler, it would be an ideal way to run the house. The downstairs floor had a large living room which had a wide doorway that led into the dining room which had another door that led into a hallway off which was another bathroom, office, den, and parlor.

The kitchen was separated by a swing door that had another door on the opposite end leading to a butler's pantry and small storage closet. The kitchen had a huge six burner stove and two ovens. The extra large refrigerator was separate from a large freezer and was included in the price of the house. The cabinets in the kitchen and baths were made of solid oak as were all the doors, frames, and windows in the house.

The extra wide front door had a wide half moon shaped stairway of five steps faced with brick leading to it. The steps ended at a brick walkway that curved towards the driveway. A brick edged driveway led to a two-car garage that had a small apartment over it. Henry told her that if she hired a full time driver then the driver would keep the car and garage clean and neat.

The full basement contained a huge coal furnace that heated pipes that led to radiators throughout the house. Each radiator had a metal grill inserted into the oak radiator covers. The finished basement's ceiling was covered with wall board and the wall was covered with drywall and had bead board on the bottom part and wallpaper on the top. The previous owners had used the basement in the summer as a playroom for their children as well as summer office. There were phone lines throughout the house and an extension was in the basement office section as well.

Vivian had to admit it was a nice house, but she still mourned the loss of her parent's home. What would Emily leave there and what would she take? She made suggestions to her mom about furniture placement in the large rooms. They could now go to the furniture store to select furniture since they had a feel for the house. The large living room would need large scale furniture. Since Emily had no formal dining room furniture that was something else to consider.

William was tremendously helpful in choosing furniture for the little boy's room. He suggested getting a twin bed, a chest of drawers, night stand, and dresser as well as a matching desk. "He's going to have homework and will need a place of his own place to do it," he spoke like an expert. He also volunteered to test all of the couches and chairs as well as mattresses. Emily selected a mahogany set with twelve chairs and matching sideboards and a tea cart for the dining room. She bought a large cherry round table for the foyer, a living room set of damask fabric of several sofas, wing back chairs and a love seat. She also bought a large desk and leather desk chair for the office and furniture for the servant's quarters. She purchased another corner cabinet to match the dining room set, sofa tables, lamps, and large area rugs. Everything was in stock and would be delivered to the house the next day. Assignments were made to assist in the placement, Henry and John upstairs, Catherine and Vivian on the second floor and Belle and Emily the bottom floor. The day was spent and they decided to go to the country club for dinner.

As luck would have it both of the Perkins' couples were also at the club as were the Williams of Richmond and Charlottesville, Belle, William, and Emily were greeted by Emily's new neighbors. Judge Perkins was pleased to have someone in the house that had set empty for the last six months. The owner had died and none of the children wanted to return to Welfield and had finally put it up for sale. They had tried to sell it at too high a price and as he heard, the estate sold it for only $60,000. Louise was not pleased that Emily would be so near, but then she thought, it would give her more opportunities to see John. She ignored the fact that he didn't do more than give her a curt nod in her direction, but she thought that he was merely doing that because Vivian was around. His parents didn't appear to be too friendly towards Louise and that didn't surprise Louise, but surprised her in-laws. Vivian and Emily must have used their time with the Williams couple to get sympathy so they could bad-mouth her. She would bide her time when she could make her own impression on them when neither Emily nor Vivian were around. Each group ate their meal without any further communication.

The movers showed up two days later on the Friday before Palm Sunday. The furniture was delivered on Saturday, in place, and all of the boxes were unpacked. Belle had found a maid and cook for Emily as well as a butler who was married to the cook. She had also found a driver for Emily. Emily had been too busy to learn to drive, but planned on learning after her trip to

New York the following week. The maid, Mrs. Carlson, made up all of the beds and hung the new draperies and curtains that Emily had purchased at the department stores in Bluestone. She bought neither outdoor patio furniture nor any furniture for the basement thinking she would wait until summer to do that. She wanted to make sure that during the April rains that the basement didn't leak.

Emily felt strange sleeping in the new house, but with Vivian and John nearby, it was a little easier. Breakfast cooked by someone else was a different experience for her as well. Oh she had experienced room service in New York, but having it done in your own home was certainly a lot different experience. She looked around the dining room and living room deciding to bring out the table scarves from her small chest and got her crochet basket out to crochet some others. Catherine suggested ordering damask tablecloths for the dining table and matching napkins from stores in New York or just going to New York a few days earlier and buying them herself. Some quality lamps, artwork, crystal candelabras, framed photographs, vases with fresh flowers would add a lot to the home. Emily missed her hand-loomed rag rugs and simple furniture, but knew that Mrs. Novak and Josef would take good care of them. Wall sconces and mirrors would add to the atmosphere as well to the home of a woman of means. She could select those now that she had the furniture set in place and had a vision of how to make her home elegant, yet inviting. She didn't want it to look too much like a museum. A home was a place to relax and enjoy daily living with one's family.

Emily had planned to fly to New York from Pittsburgh. She had agreed to go to Pittsburgh on Tuesday with Belle so that they could go to the other two banks by train to discuss the infant care project. Emily would need something to occupy her mind while Paul Miklos was in school. In just two months he would be free for the summer. She wanted to hire a tutor to help with his English, and reading of his ABC's. She knew he would be behind and had plans to have him repeat the first grade, but would need the two months to get used to the American school and possibly even make a few friends. She would wait for confirmation of the boy's arrival before leaving for New York by telegram.

On Monday, a telegram arrived that it would be an additional month before the boy arrived, since there supposedly were problems with German mines in the port that had to be cleared. He would be arriving in early May instead of April. That gave Emily more than enough time to get her house prepared for the youngster.

She would still go to Pittsburgh on Tuesday and John and Vivian could return to Charlottesville early on Monday. Vivian would only miss one day of each of her classes. Since spring break had started on March 19, she would return in time for her Monday classes. She had set her schedule to have no class earlier than 10am. Originally they had planned to leave on Monday, but decided to leave on Sunday evening instead. Vivian felt it would be nice to get her mind occupied with economics and accounting rather than the last two weeks and the loss of her father and home.

The young couple accompanied their mother to mass and left shortly after lunch on Palm Sunday. They would make the four hour drive and have a good night's sleep before Vivian had to go to her first class at ten. She hated leaving her mother, but knew she would be kept busy. She had heard her mother weeping each night and talking in her sleep calling out "Paul". Although Emily put on a front of excitement during the day, Vivian knew how difficult of a time she was having in dealing with the loss of Paul. It would be worse now that she was going to be alone. Henry and Catherine's rental ended on Sunday and agreed to stay with Emily until she left for Pittsburgh and would then go on with her to New York. Catherine had told Emily where to go in New York to buy the necessary accessories for her new home, but Belle had personally asked Catherine to go with Emily so she wouldn't be alone.

Emily's mind wandered after Vivian and John had left for Charlottesville to the day before when they, along with Belle, Catherine, and Henry had accompanied Emily to select a grave marker for Paul. She decided to get a six foot tall statue of the Blessed Mother with the image of the infant Jesus. A porcelain portrait of Paul would be at the base as well as the inscription, "Paul Black, Beloved husband and father 1901-1945". It would take almost six months to be delivered and after taking care of the marker, Emily asked to go to the cemetery once more. She wanted to place a pot of lilies on his grave and was distraught when she saw only bare ground. All of the flowers that had once been a beautiful carpet were now gone. Emily shook hard and could barely stand as she wept at the sight of the sunken ground above her Paul. She placed the lilies on the site and whispered a promise to Paul that she would return soon. She would have to get a concrete border placed around his grave and have a wild rose bush planted to bloom where the base of the statue would be. She would also have a cast iron fence to enclose the grave as well and have dirt and then gravel placed to be even with the level of the concrete. It was at the gravesite that Emily felt the furthest from Paul. Here she was reminded of how they were separated forever, in fact, they were an eternity apart. The peacefulness of the cemetery did nothing to quiet the pain in both her heart and her soul. Although she was with friends, she had never before felt so utterly alone in the world. She missed the sound of his voice, his joking, and his kissing her forehead each morning. There were so many little things that she missed and it was difficult to list them all.

In church on Palm Sunday, she had listened carefully to the long reading of the Passion of Christ and thought of how humans today were like those of Christ's time to make innocent victims suffer needlessly in Europe due to the horrors of this awful war. What had innocent children like little Paul Miklos witnessed during the war? She had thanked God for giving her beloved a relatively quick death. How many in Europe and Asia had suffered for months or even years at the hands of others before dying? How much had his cousins suffered before they had died? She hadn't shared her thoughts with anyone but knew that she needed little Paul to renew her faith in human nature and in God. How could he have taken the love of her life when she hadn't been ready for him to go? How could he have let it happen at the one place where Paul loved the most, his little farm? It was then that she realized Paul had gotten to die at his favorite place on earth doing what he loved the best! She should be grateful that God had let it happen that way. She had felt torn in two going through the last several weeks with only half a heart. As she left the cemetery, she realized she still had her heart but that the part she had felt was missing wasn't really missing, but only changed. As long as she remembered how much she had loved Paul and his unique qualities, then he would be alive. She would tell Paul Miklos about her Paul and hoped that he would be the man she had always hoped a son of theirs would become. No one could ever take Paul away from her memories.

Vivian and John had arrived safely in Charlottesville and Emily invited John's parents to stay with her. She could not bear to be alone for the first time in more than twenty years. They had been so kind to her, such dear friends they understood she needed them without uttering a word about it. It was an odd feeling sitting at the table with only the three of them, but thank goodness they were comfortable enough together that it wasn't out and out awkward. Emily insisted that they talk about Paul if something reminded them of Paul.

"Many women may choose not to talk about their deceased husbands. Others may talk as if they were merely gone or on a trip, but not me. I understand that our life together on earth is over, but I have faith that we will be together after death," she openly shared with her friends. Her faith would get her through those difficult times when she wished he was still there, but her practical side knew the truth.

Henry brought up the subject of horses and how much Paul loved to ride horses. Emily had to laugh when he mentioned her lack of experience with horses and how they chose the gentlest horse at the club and she had still been so petrified. Emily shared her thoughts openly about how it felt the first time she was in a saddle. "What you didn't know was Paul had introduced me to the horse as if it was a person. I had to talk to it, he said, and get to know it, but most of all trust it. I thought he was out of his mind, but I did it anyway. Paul could talk me into doing those kinds of things with his charm. Paul was a lot of my strength in trying times at the beginning of our marriage, and he let me develop my own strength. If it hadn't, I couldn't have survived these last weeks. Do you remember how he tried to get me to do my first jump with the horse?"

The friends continued with a pleasant dinner and Emily led them to the living room where she had placed the radio and phonograph. She turned on the radio and they listened to the news about the allied troops surrounding Laurenberg. Surely the war would end soon. The Soviet's offensive was on some city on the Danube. They laughed as they listened to The Great Gildersleeve's radio program, "Old Flame Violet" that came on at 6:30pm. Gildersleeve's a character on "Fibber McGee and Molly" had been one of the favorites in the Black household on Tuesday nights. It was a new show and they enjoyed it immensely.

Henry played a few phonographs and when he put on Benny Goodman's "Sing, Sing, Sing" Emily smiled as she remembered how Vivian had his band play at her wedding reception as a surprise for her. She patted her foot to the beat and Henry and Catherine danced. It was so nice to see someone enjoying themselves and especially her friends. They listened until almost ten and went to bed with smiles on their faces.

Monday was a busy day as Emily packed her clothes. Catherine went shopping with her in downtown Welfield to get a variety of underclothes boy size 6 and 7 for little Paul. They knew that little Paul would probably be thin, but didn't how tall he was going to be. They purchased some socks, sweaters, and shirts in the two sizes as well. Any that he couldn't wear would be donated for other refugee children that arrived without many belongings. Emily decided to purchase items for little girls as well. She might as well donate clothing for them as well. Catherine purchased several dresses, slips, underclothes, and socks as well as several smaller sized pairs of shoes.

With the major offensive of the allies building, the war would end soon and so many refugees would be arriving in the United States. The two women had fun buying for children as if they were buying for grandchildren. It was a pleasant distraction for Emily. When she got to New York she would send the clothing to the refugee camp at Oswego, New York. Emily would buy more masculine luggage like the ones from Swaine Adeney Brigg when she arrived in New York. They were the brand that she used for Paul but she only had one piece for him. Little Paul would need several for his new clothes. Belle and Emily needed to go to Pittsburgh and Caroline and Henry needed to go home to check on business issues as well as get some appropriate clothes for New York.

Caroline helped her pack the clothing into Emily's smaller travel trunk and the two women had their own luggage to pack. Caroline would be going to Bluestone to catch a train to Richmond and would be riding with Emily and Belle in the Pierce Arrow together to the train station. Catherine would fly to New York from Richmond in about a week to help Emily select items for her new home. Emily held her tightly and thanked her over and over for being so kind to her and Vivian. They promised to call each other frequently and Catherine invited her to Richmond during the summer so that she could get extra time with both Emily and little Paul.

Belle and Emily traveled in the private rail car while Mr. Blakeman would sleep in the adjoining sleeper car. Belle went over her ideas of her new proposals that would be put in Emily's name from the onset. There were a lot of ideas between Bluestone and Pittsburgh discussed. They agreed to focus on strollers, high chairs, feeding bowls, bottles, bassinets, changing tables, cribs, and quality blankets and changing pads. They would stay away from foods and formulas and would stick with items needed in a nursery.

Perhaps they could get into nursery jars for swabs, lotions, etc. but for now basic quality items would be their choice.

Emily thought that perhaps, if they could find a baby carriage that folded there would be a great market for it. With so many women driving now, they would want a stroller that they could put in the trunk of their car. Perhaps investing in development of better car seats would be wise as well. The ones they had now only kept children in their seat and did little to protect them. That would probably take years to develop but could certainly be a long-range project. Belle had investigated several companies and wasn't satisfied with the quality of many of their products. She had narrowed the list down to only four and they debated each one for particular products in which to invest or purchase. There was a new company that was just starting out that needed capital on the list of prospects. Belle and Emily chose the company that produced most of the items that happened to be on their list. They could purchase more than 51% of that particular company for a relatively small amount. It was decided that they would invest the money and rename the company Baby Belle. It would take time to change the current factory's machinery and of course a logo would have to be designed. Now that they had made their decision, Mr. Blakeman could begin on the paperwork and transfer funds giving Emily control of the company.

They had completed their work shortly after a late lunch and rested for two hours before reaching Pittsburgh around 3pm. They would go directly to the banks and see what was in the safety deposit boxes. Tomorrow, there would be a board meeting for Belle and Mr. Blakeman. Emily wanted to go to some of the antique shops that Belle had mentioned to her before.

The two women went into each bank accompanied by Mr. Blakeman and completed the necessary paperwork to see the contents of the boxes. The first one contained only a stained pillow case and all of them secretly suspected a mystery of sorts. Why on earth would Bertie have rented a safety deposit box just to hold a stained pillowcase? The second bank's box contained two letters one written by Bertie's mother and the other by her mother, Martha Coleman. Neither Emily nor Belle could believe what they had read and replaced the letters into the box. Belle barely made it to the limo before she broke down and cried as did Emily. Poor Bertie, how could she have kept that secret for so long? How could her mother have been so cruel and so greedy after what she had done to her? Although Bertie couldn't be harmed anymore from the contents of those two letters, William and

Louise would be hurt for different reasons if those letters were ever made public. As the two women entered their hotel, a man that looked vaguely familiar approached them and introduced himself as Louis Carpenter. He claimed to be one of Louise's neighbors in Charleston and Belle recognized him at once as a poorly disguised Jake Turner. He offered his services as an escort and Belle politely declined. She told him that she was familiar with the city, had business to attend to, and did not require an escort since she had Mr. Blakeman. She asked that he tell Louise hello and that she looked forward to her next visit.

Jake immediately called Louise and told her, "I think the old woman is onto me. She declined my offer to be an escort and said she had more business to take care of. They went to two banks already and didn't carry anything out with them from either one. She told me to tell you hello. What do you want me to do?"

Louise said, "I'll casually mention that my mother had said something to me about some safety deposit boxes. How would she know that mother didn't tell me? I'll take over from here. What did you find out about Emily? Why did she move so close to my in-laws?"

"I'll see what I can find out from her maid or cook. That will mean I'll have to leave here and go back to Welfield for a few days. Is that what you want me to do?" he asked.

"Yes, I definitely need to know what she is up to. She and Aunt Belle are making big plans, I can just feel it. Call me as soon as you find out anything, anything at all," Louise snapped and then hung up the phone. 'What are they up to?' she asked herself.

The trio had a quiet dinner and said nothing about the contents of the letters. Belle and Emily were still too shocked to even attempt to make a comment. Mr. Blakeman suggested that perhaps Louise should be told the truth. She was older and could perhaps comprehend how much her mother had loved her and the true character of the grandmother she had adored for so long. Emily disagreed since she knew how much pain it would cause Bertie's children. Once Louise knew, she would blurt it out to William. Emily refused to agree to anything that could harm William or the memory of her best friend, Bertie. Bertie had suffered more in life than they had known. There was nothing to be accomplished by telling the truth to anyone at this point.

Emily tossed a lot that night and had several nightmares about Bertie, Louise, William, Paul, and Belle. She awakened and found her pillow case was wet from tears. She sat on the edge of her bed and buried her face into her hands as she mourned her husband and friend. She needed Paul so much right now, if only to have him advise her about the letters. She decided to bathe and dress and Belle found her sitting in the dark peering at the dreary Pittsburgh sky as the sun began to appear just over the horizon. Belle had not slept well either and could only muster a weak, "Good morning," when she came out of her room for breakfast and added, "Red sky in the morning, sailors take warning. I sure hope that's not an omen for the next few days. We certainly don't need any more bad news."

They ordered some coffee and toast for breakfast and spoke only of today's agenda. Belle told Emily where the best shops were and that they all were within a few blocks of their hotel, the William Penn. The board meeting would end around noon and they would meet back in the hotel for lunch. Emily left the hotel when Belle and Mr. Blakeman left for their meeting. Emily went into the first antique shop and immersed herself into finding treasures for her new home. She found several pairs of sconces, candelabra, beveled mirrors, and some beautiful gas lamps with lovely flowers on the base and shade. They would look lovely in the office. She bought some prints for the bedrooms and after paying for all of her purchases, asked that they be shipped to her home in Welfield. It felt strange to give her new address to the clerks after living in the little cabin for so many years without Paul. She had seen an art museum on her way from the train station to the hotel and caught a cab to visit it.

She found some lovely prints of artwork by Andrew Wyeth in an art gallery. She purchased copies of his *Dil Huey Farm* and *Pennsylvania Landscape* both of which reminded her of her farm from an art museum. She would place those in her own bedroom.

The Carnegie Museum of the Arts was hosting an auction on Wednesday night and she caught a cab to see if preview books were available for the auction. Paul would go to auctions for farm equipment and she had never been to one before. Perhaps she and Belle could go there together. She left the museum with the booklet just in time to meet Belle for lunch.

The meeting had gone well and Belle was pleased with the profits for the quarter. Emily shared the auction preview book with Belle and they made plans to attend. The next day, Belle and Emily went to a few shops to look for some smaller pieces of furniture that Emily needed for her home. She wanted a small chest to hold towels, guest hand towels, and wash cloths for each bathroom upstairs as well as some side tables for the wing back chairs. They went to several furniture stores and found some lovely little drum tables for the parlor and some small tables with a drawer and lower shelf. Vases and picture frames were located in a tiny gift shop. They had lunch in their room and were scheduled to have dinner at one of the board member's homes in the Oakland district.

They had a marvelous dinner and Emily got to meet several of the board members who were pleased to meet Vivian's mother and were also kind enough to offer their condolences on her loss of Paul. Emily accepted their condolences with grace but the pain was deeply hidden behind her slight smile. She conversed with them about the auction they would be attending the following evening and several had intended to attend as well. They assured her that she would not be disappointed in either the items or their quality.

Emily and Belle arrived early at the auction preview and placed some offers on several pieces. A beautiful crystal chandelier they found would look lovely in the dining room. The starting bid was $700 and Emily placed a bid of $1200 to the auctioneer who would bid on her behalf. She also found some bronze bookends, candle sticks with marble bases and crystals, lovely porcelain figurines, a mahogany hall tree, huge mirror for a foyer, and several sterling silver pieces on which she placed bids. She had registered and was #102 and Belle was #103. They sat down just as the auction started. Belle nodded to several Marshall Steel board members and the bidding began. Emily enjoyed watching bids escalate on items that she had no interest in and was pleased when her number was called for several items. She won all of the items except for several figurines and the bookends and paid for them as well as the commissions, shipping and handling. The auction clerk told her that all items would arrive within a week. They arrived back to the hotel around 11:15pm and were exhausted. Emily was handed a telegram at the desk from Mrs. Carlson that informed her that Paul Miklos had gotten on a ship after all and would be in New York within five days. They had planned on leaving the next morning for Welfield and would now have to make arrangements to go to New York. Belle called Mr. Blakeman about the change in plans so that he could get the private rail car attached to a train going to New York. The train to New York would be leaving in the afternoon and they would have plenty of time to finish packing. Emily had mixed feelings of the little boy's arrival as she went to bed that night. Mr. Blakeman had arranged for an attorney to take care of the paperwork at the immigration port who would meet them at the Plaza Hotel.

Catherine couldn't come to New York since she had caught a devil of a cold and now had a sinus infection. She needed rest and plenty of liquids and Emily forbade her from leaving the house! Catherine promised that they would come as soon as she got over the cold and asked Emily to let her know what else she could do for the little boy.

Chapter 6

Emily had called Catherine and Vivian just before she left from Pittsburgh for New York and both of them wished her luck. She paced back and forth as she waited for the Red Cross ship to be moored at the New York port. Wounded soldiers were taken off first and then children with large tags pinned on their jackets or shirts were taken next. Emily scanned the crowd and waited for her name to be called. It took almost four hours for them to call her name and she got her chance to finally meet Paul Miklos Blecoe. He was very small for his age with huge blue eyes and sandy colored hair. He had the largest, saddest eyes she had ever seen. His clothes were little more than dirty rags and his mismatched shoes appeared to be several sizes too large. She signed the necessary paperwork and they quickly returned to the Plaza hotel via a limo. She had chosen to stay at the Plaza since it was closer to the shops that she would need to go to for clothing for the boy.

She walked calmly through the lobby with the little boy in tattered clothes. Belle had informed the concierge about the little refugee boy that Emily was adopting and advised them of his possible condition. They made arrangements for a barber and man's servant to be available to help with the lad. They had discreetly sent for shampoo for lice and bath soaks for children. When Emily arrived to the suite she introduced Paul Miklos to Belle. He spoke no English and she had him practice phrases including: Hello, how do you do, thank you, and good bye. He was very intelligent and by the time his bath and shampoo were finished he said, "Thank you." Emily gave the men a large tip and asked that the rags that had been Paul

Miklos's clothing be disposed of quickly. She only kept the tag and planned to put it into her hope chest for safekeeping until Paul Michael was grown. He clung to her and managed a small smile when he came out in a new pair of pants and shirt. The shoes were a child's size 9 that fit loosely on his feet and the size 6 pair of pants was still slightly too large for him. The barber had trimmed his hair nicely and soon, he didn't resemble the ragamuffin that had entered the suite only an hour earlier.

Belle took it upon herself to try to teach the lad some English. She started with using gestures and before too long he could say, "My name is Paul Miklos Blecoe, I am pleased to meet you." Although he quickly learned their names, he still insisted on calling Emily, "Anya". She repeated her name and he smiled sweetly as he said very slowly, "Anya" instead of Emily. Belle and Emily ate a late lunch with him in their room and taught him the names of utensils, plates, cups, foods. They were pleased with his progress and took him shopping. He would not leave Emily's side and so she had to help him get properly fitted herself. He cried so hard if she got out of his sight even for a moment and would tearfully call, "Anya, Anya!" She had his small feet fitted for everyday shoes, boots, galoshes, and dress shoes. He needed pajamas, house slippers, and a robe as well as suits, vests, and sweaters. He could wear most of the size six clothing she had purchased in Welfield and could wear those clothes to school but all the pants had to be altered with being hemmed and taken in at the waist.

He counted for her in Hungarian and she held up her fingers so that he could learn how to count to five in English. He told her he needed one coat as he held up one tiny finger when she asked how many he needed. After taking a bite from a candy bar, when she asked how many candy he wanted, he held up all ten fingers. Everyone laughed but he still selected only two and smiled at the clerk who tousled his hair. His eyes grew a little less sad over the course of the week as did Emily's. On Easter Sunday, they attended mass at St. Patrick's. He had attended mass in secret during the war, in Hungary, and was pleased that this mass was like the ones he had attended but amazingly in such a large place and openly. Emily purchased an English missal for him to help with his learning of English. He could not read Hungarian, but he could speak it well. He recognized the parts of the mass from the picture and could easily recite the Agnus Dei, Sanctus, and Pater Noster prayers. He was pleased that he could say it along with Emily and Belle smiled over at the pair. Paul Michael sat quietly with Aunt Belle when Emily went for communion and knelt reverently until she returned.

This faith was going to be a bond that the two could share and Belle felt a great comfort that Emily was going to have someone else in her life to love. If anyone needed that little boy to save them, it was Emily. She had a framed picture of Paul in her room and told him who Paul was and what had happened to him. Little Paul looked puzzled until Emily said, "Pal van halott" as Mrs. Novak had taught her. It meant, "Paul is dead." The little boy hugged Emily and wept his little heart out. Emily kissed the crown of his little head and wept as well. Paul had been his last relative and both of them clung to each other for comfort.

When it was time to go to bed, he called out to her several times and she finally showed him her bed and convinced him that she would be there when he awakened. He was a little confused by Mr. Blakeman's presence but trusted him because he had seen how Emily was at ease around him. He slept in the small bed in one of the suite's other rooms. She awakened to see his small face looking down at her and he kissed her and said, "Good morning, Anya". Belle and Mr. Blakeman were at breakfast and smiled when he suddenly came running out of the room to join them. Emily came out about ten minutes later fully dressed with her eyes set on little Paul. He jumped out of his seat and ran behind Mr. Blakeman who threw up his hands for surrender. Emily caught Paul Miklos and tickled him. His musical laughter helped to lift her spirits greatly. She had another nightmare about Paul's accident and had thankfully been awakened by little Paul before she once again saw his bloodied body on the plow blade. Before falling asleep the night before, she had decided to call him either Paulie or Paul Michael. She finally asked him which he preferred and when asked he said, "Paul Michael". He liked the sound of it since it sounded like his name but slightly different.

She wanted to take him to a toy store today to select some toys for his room. He immediately went for a telescope and some jigsaw puzzles. He ignored the toy soldiers, tanks, etc. and actually looked at them rather cautiously and moved away from them. He found a teddy bear that he hugged tightly and his eyes lit up when he saw a chess set! His grandfather had taught him how to play chess just before he was imprisoned and the little boy had to leave his set behind. She made her purchases and they went on to a store that sold framed artwork and prints. The pictures he seemed to like the most had either horses in them or fields of grass with few trees. He seemed to be fond of horses and so Emily took him to a carousel where he could ride a fake horse. He went for six consecutive rides and had to be bribed with a candy apple to get him off of it.

They would be leaving on Wednesday and stopping in Charlottesville so Paul Michael could meet Vivian. John hadn't been able to come to New York as planned and told her he was excited to meet his new brother-in-law. Mrs. Novak had taught Emily a few words in Hungarian over the phone and Emily told John that Paul Michael could hardly wait to meet his sister. The word for sister was "nover" and "Ez testveretek, Vivian" meant "This is your sister Vivian." The maids packed his belongings in his new suitcases and Emily pointed to his initials PMB engraved on the locks.

Paul Michael had enjoyed himself greatly but suddenly got very frightened when he first caught sight of the train and realized that they were going on board. He started screaming, frozen in place, shaking until Emily had to carry him into the private rail car. He was still shaking when the train began to move and he didn't leave her lap for several miles. He loosened his grip around her neck and looked around the rail car after they had gone about twenty miles. His natural curiosity got the best of him and he went from side to side checking the sleeping quarters, dining area, and he spotted his chess set on the table with Mr. Blakeman who motioned to the chair across from him and they began a match. "Ellenoriz tars!" Paul Michael called. Mr. Blakeman said, "Why you sneaky little rascal, you have me in check mate in only eight moves!" He began laughing and Paul Michael was busy setting up the board once more. Mr. Blakeman won the next match and the women heard different versions of "check" and they smiled as Emily sat crocheting and Belle read over more contracts and correspondence.

When they arrived in Charlottesville, John and Vivian waved to them and Vivian ran to Emily. Paul Michael stepped behind Emily as if she was his shield when he first saw John. John had his back towards Paul Michael and the back of his greenish gray suit reminded Paul Michael of the Nazi uniform and he was petrified. Emily greeted them and when he saw how John greeted Emily and saw the shirt and tie he eventually came forward to offer him his tiny hand.

When Emily introduced him to Vivian, he smiled and said, "How do you do?" with a very heavy accent. Mr. Blakeman informed John that Paul Michael liked to play chess and was quite the player. When Emily had called Vivian, she had told her how much Paul Michael liked puzzles and she had bought several jigsaw puzzles as well as a few comic books. She chose those that were actually fairy tales so that Paul Michael could practice his English while learning new words.

John and Paul Michael had their heads bent over the jigsaw puzzle of 100 pieces nonstop for about an hour. John let Paul Michael show him where an individual piece belonged and he would have to say, "That piece goes there," before John would put it in the correct spot. The puzzle was of a puppy and Paul Michael got very excited when he saw the finished picture. He spoke a rapid sentence in Hungarian that no one understood. He smiled and then sat down realizing that they could not understand him.

Belle said, "He may have had a puppy like that in Hungary or wants one. What kind of puppy is that?"

John looked at the box and read."It says on the side that it's a Yorkshire terrier! It's adorable isn't it?"

Vivian said, "I always wanted a dog. Mom, why didn't we ever have a dog?"

Emily answered, "Your dad had a fear of a dog turning on us. When he was young one of his parent's dogs went rabid. Later on other dogs chased him and scared him on his way to and from school. He was afraid that they might hurt you and wouldn't even think about letting you have one!"

"We live in the city and they have veterinarians that give regularly scheduled vaccinations. John, let's think about getting a puppy maybe a small one like that," Vivian suggested.

"They are a lot of responsibility. They have to be trained, fed, walked, and not to mention traveling. What do you do when you have to go out of town? Most hotels especially the nice ones won't allow a dog. When would we have time to properly train a puppy? I'm at work and you're going to be in class all day. I just don't think that getting a dog for us is a good idea," John argued.

"Those are all valid points counselor. I'll take it under advisement," Vivian teased. "Well, how about you, mom, why don't you get a puppy?"

"Me, what in the world would I do with a puppy?" Emily asked anxiously.

"Well Paul Michael could use a puppy to adjust to being in the United States and in a new home. It would certainly keep him company if you had to travel or go somewhere without him even for a few hours and he could practice his English. Little boys need a dog don't they, John?" Vivian questioned him with a gleam in her eye.

"Little boys do, but big ones don't" he countered.

"Well, it would keep both of us company and would alert us to any visitors, both welcome and unwelcome. I'll think about it! It would have to be a small breed and one that is known to be intelligent. Do you really think Paul Michael likes dogs? I'll need to get someone who can speak Hungarian to ask them. I couldn't possibly get one if he is afraid of them," Emily said seriously.

Vivian said, "Mom, look at his face, does he look afraid? Now, tell me about my new brother, Paul Michael." Both women spoke at once about his intelligence, quick wit, and hard work to learn English. They told her that he insisted on calling Emily "Anya". They couldn't wait to ask Mrs. Novak what that meant and could perhaps ask about his disposition towards dogs.

Belle, Vivian, and Mr. Blakeman went into Vivian's home office to discuss the recent Marshall Steel board meeting while John kept Paul Michael occupied with some story books. Emily sat in the living room crocheting. They were talking for over an hour when Vivian offered to get some coffee or tea. Both of the others thought it sounded like a good idea and Vivian went into the living room to ask John and Emily if they wanted coffee or tea. Emily said coffee and John said tea and Vivian went to get them ready. The trio was busy for another hour until Vivian suggested that they go to the Charlottesville Country Club for dinner.

Belle spoke up first, "It might be a little too soon for Paul Michael to go out with a larger crowd. He might get upset if anyone spoke to him and he couldn't understand him. It might be a little overwhelming. I know, perhaps going to a small restaurant would be better and a nice compromise."

"The Blue Ridge Tavern has waiters and waitresses in period costumes and serves food from the 18th century. It's different from a regular restaurant and has small private rooms for parties of 6 or more. I can call for a reservation around 7 or so if you would like or we can go to a restaurant that has good steaks." Vivian offered.

"I myself would prefer the Blue Ridge. Why don't you try to get reservations there first and if not, then we can go for the steaks," Belle advised smiling.

"Okay," Vivian said as she asked the operator to connect her to the Blue Ridge Tavern. They had a room available for 7:30 that night and so Vivian made the reservation.

"Well that's taken care of. Where we will be eating, it's as if we were back in the 18th century. John and I went there our first week after our return from our honeymoon. It's going to be a real experience for mom and Paul Michael. Speaking of Paul Michael, I wonder what the two of them are up to now. With John, there's no telling what those two will get into," Vivian suggested to Belle.

When they went into the living room John and Paul Michael were reading a comic book together about Jack and the beanstalk. John was playing the role of the giant and it was hilarious listening to him change his voice and strike a pose pretending to be the giant and then change to a funny voice as the voice of Jack. It was just like watching a performance of a live radio program. Paul Michael wanted him to read it again and turned it back to the beginning. "Do you want me to read it again?" he asked. "Well, Paul Michael has to say, "Please read it again"" and so Paul Michaels did and John started it over. In another five minutes when John was finished Paul Michael said, "Please read it again." Emily chuckled and said, "He will know that one expression by heart pretty soon!" Poor John read it five more times and each time Paul Michael would laugh when John changed his voice. He fell asleep on John's lap at some point during the eighth reading and John carried him to a bed in the guest room. When he rejoined them he said, "He is so adorable and so intelligent. You should have seen him work that puzzle. He's amazing! My little brother-in-law is the smartest kid I've ever known."

"Of course he is. It's in his genes!" Vivian added.

Belle chuckled and said, "Spoken like a proud sister and brother-in-law."

Paul Michael awakened around 6:00 pm to find himself in the strange room and screamed for his "Anya" who ran up to him. "I'm here darling, I'm here. It's okay, shh, shh my dear little boy." He wiped his eyes and hugged her tightly. She pointed around the room and told him that this would be his room for the next few days. "This is Paul Michael's room at Vivian's house.

He took his hand and showed him her room saying, "This is Anya's room and Belle will be in this room. Okay?"

"Okay," Paul smiled.

Emily wasn't sure if he understood or not, but she wanted to get him ready for dinner. She dressed him in a suit and changed into a tweed suit for herself. He smiled and when he pointed to her nodded as if giving her his approval. He spoke quickly and the only word she could make out of the entire sentence was Anya.

Paul Michael enjoyed the fried chicken, corn, macaroni and cheese, and cornbread at the tavern. He didn't seem to like the stewed tomatoes with okra or collard greens but ate them anyway. The waitresses winked at him and he winked back. Everyone enjoyed their meal and had an enjoyable time at the tavern. The next few days went by so quickly and it was finally time to go to Welfield.

On their last full day, Emily asked Belle about the puppy and she told her that she thought it was a great idea.

"You can always call Mrs. Novak and ask her to speak to Paul Michael and ask him. She could tell you what his answer is or you could wait until we got back to Welfield. If she tells you he likes them you would probably have a better chance of getting a decent one here than in Welfield," she advised.

"But how in this world would we get it to Welfield?" Emily asked.

"Well we could put it inside a wooden crate. If it was walked at each stop, it shouldn't have any accidents on the train. Paul Michael won't let it down when the train's moving. Even if the little thing does, it can be cleaned. Let's check with Vivian and see if there are any pet stores nearby," Belle suggested.

Emily made the call home and smiled broadly when Mrs. Novak translated Paul Michael's response. She repeated the answer to the group and they waited for Vivian to share the experience of getting the perfect dog.

Vivian's Friday classes ended at noon and the three women took Paul to several pet stores. He liked several but didn't get very excited about any of them until he saw a dachshund. He laughed at it trying to run to him and its rear legs kept going out from under it. There were three of them and one of the little females kept smelling towards him and tried to lick his face. The clerk said that they were miniature dachshunds and that they were very intelligent dogs and easy to train. The other dogs they had there would grow to be quite large or were meant for large farms. He felt that for a home environment the dachshund would be ideal for the little boy.

Emily decided on the female and Belle decided to surprise William with the other female. They bought collars, leashes, food, vitamins, toys, beds, and food dishes and water bowls. The pet shop owner gave them a wooden box for the dogs to travel in. He had no idea that the dogs would not be closed up in the crates and offered to include the top of the crate and Belle merely said it wouldn't be necessary. The dogs couldn't climb out and that would be fine for the trip home. Returning to Vivian's house, one puppy rode on Paul Michael's lap and the other one was on Belle's. Belle decided to let William name the puppy and asked Paul Michael what he would name his puppy? She pointed to herself and said, "Belle", pointed to Vivian and said, "Vivian", pointed to Emily and said, "Emily", and when she pointed to his puppy he said, "Poppy". They didn't know if he was trying to say puppy or not, but Poppy suited her. She was a red dachshund and poppies were indeed red. Maybe he had been reminded of the poppies in fields in Europe. It didn't matter. The puppy was to be called Poppy.

John was happy that the little boy had a puppy and showed him how to hold the dachshund under its belly; how to connect the leash; how to walk the dog; and how to train the dog using a newspaper in the crate. Paul Michael insisted that the puppy sleep with him in his bed and at first both Emily and Vivian disapproved, but after an hour of listening to the puppies crying and whining, Poppy was placed in bed with Paul Michael and the other one was snuck into Belle's bed sometime during the night. No accidents occurred during the night and everyone slept much better after the puppies became quiet.

Vivian and John told Emily that they would be coming to Welfield towards the end of May. John would be starting his apprenticeship in June and it would be difficult for them to come in after that. Vivian had already enrolled for an economics class and Business Law class for the first summer term and the second term she was taking Psychology and the second part of the economics class. Vivian wanted to check on Emily more often and would have to make the trip all by herself once John started his law clerk job.

The train trip was indeed an experience. Paul Michael walked Poppy at every stop while Mr. Blakeman took the other one out. It was hilarious watching a grown man in his suit and tie trying to get a tiny dachshund to use the bathroom at each stop. The two puppies followed each other and if one squatted the other one did as well. Emily watched from the door of the private car and Belle chuckled when the two leashes inevitably got tangled. The two little dachshunds got very excited with every trip outside and tried to greet each and every passenger. Mr. Blakeman would twirl around trying to untangle the two leashes and he never lost his patience with the puppies. Paul Michael did wander far from Robert Blakeman and Emily noticed Paul Michael imitating Robert's stance or mannerisms. Evidently, by the time they arrived in Welfield, Robert Blakeman had a new friend.

Emily was expecting all of the furniture, auction items, etc. from New York to be at the house when she returned and could hardly wait to see all of it in place. She held Paul Michael's free hand as they entered the front door. He looked around but held Poppy's leash as they went together to check out each room. Emily introduced him to the maid, butler, and cook. Belle had called the Perkins' residence several times during the trip to check on William and she also asked if any deliveries had been made to Emily's house. Belle had left William with Judge Perkins since Louise was coming to their home for Easter. William had been excited about a little boy coming to live with Emily and was anxious to meet him. Louise had promised to be there for several days before and after Easter and was true to her word.

He told Belle that in fact a large truck had delivered some furniture and large boxes earlier that week. He asked if she wanted to speak to Louise. "No dear! I just wanted to let you know that we will be leaving Charlottesville tomorrow and will be home by the time you get home from school. We will be waiting on you! I love you dear," Belle said with a huge smile.

"I love you too," William echoed.

Louise had enjoyed her visit with William and had gotten a lot more information from him. He knew that Emily and Belle were going to go to two banks in Pittsburgh at some point in time working it around Belle's meetings with Marshall Steel Company. Each time Belle called she would hint at the boxes and he would just shrug and say that he had no idea what they found. He claimed that Belle never told him.

William and Belle arrived at Emily's about an hour after Emily had, and the two puppies acted as though they hadn't seen each other for years.

William introduced himself and Paul Michael said, "My name is Paul Michael Blekoe. This is Poppy," as he held his little dog. William had his puppy and said, "Well, I think I'll call this one Gracie." George Burns and Gracie were two of William's favorites on the radio and he was so surprised with the puppy that was the first name that popped into his head. She was as cuckoo as Gracie and was definitely a little clown. William took Paul Michael upstairs and showed him his new room. The furniture and instructions from Emily had arrived and the rooms were all set up with candle sticks, hall tree, and prints as she had directed. Belle and Emily watched as Paul Michael checked out his room. He turned and said, "Anya room" as he pointed towards her room.

She walked his over to her room and said, "This is my room" and pointed to herself. She walked him to Vivian and John's room and said, "Vivian and John's room," and held up a picture of Vivian and John. He nodded his head and repeated what she had said. She took him to the bathroom that would be his and then showed him the one that would serve the maid's quarters and attic bedrooms. She knew that it had to be confusing, but he seemed to have the house all figured out. Paul Michael pointed to his chess set and William said, "Do you play?" and made a motion with the pieces. Paul Michael nodded and both boys sat down each holding their own puppy on their laps. Belle walked downstairs with Emily who went into the office to check through the tall pile of mail. She had checks to sign for the caretaker and crew from the Sportsman's Club and needed to fill out deposit slips for the bank. She saw a large envelope with a courthouse's return address on it with an attached receipt signed by the housekeeper. She opened it and there were blue legal forms inside. Belle didn't seem surprised to see it and knew what the papers were all about. Judge Perkins had filled her in while she had waited for William to come home from school. Emily had expected sympathy cards, deliveries, etc. but what she didn't expect was a summons to appear in court. Louise had filed a disclosure complaint in civil court charging that Bertie had jewelry in safety deposit boxes and it had not been given to her but to Emily instead. She wanted a full disclosure of the contents of the boxes and wanted Emily and Belle to appear in court to testify under oath about the contents of the boxes.

The last thing that either woman wanted to do was to testify as to what had been found in the boxes in court or even in private to Louise and William. They knew it would do irreparable damage to both of Bertie's children. But both of them knew Louise well enough to know that she would not be satisfied until she knew exactly what was in the boxes.

"Perhaps if we told her it was just papers, she will believe us," Belle offered as a solution. "I believe she has talked with William while we were gone and has milked information from him. She knows about the blue diamond, but does not know that it wasn't set when we found it. If a diamond isn't set, it isn't considered jewelry is it? I suppose the real question is what would a court decide? Do you suppose that we should just offer her the pendant?"

"If we do, then she will assume that there was other jewelry in the other boxes and that we are hiding it. Giving her the diamond will only cause her to persist in the disclosure suit. If we don't offer it to her, she will assume that we are hiding it along with other jewelry. No matter what we do, she will assume that there is more when we both know there isn't. Do you think we could meet in Judge Perkins home and tell her in the privacy of his home that the only thing that was worth anything was the blue diamond?" Emily asked.

"We will have to ask Mr. Blakeman what would be the best course of action. I don't know how we can avoid the court room unless we offer to take her to the safety deposit boxes to let her view the contents and sign a statement that with the exception of the diamond that had been unset and the bearer bonds, nothing else was removed from the boxes. Perhaps that is a choice," Belle said.

The sound of puppies yapping and boys laughing got their attention. Emily was upset that Louise had chosen this particular time to bring the suit. Emily had a lot of things to take care of including Paul Michael's enrollment in school. She would have to explain the situation to the Elementary school principal. She knew that there was only a slight chance that some of the children would understood a little of the Hungarian language if they learned it from their grandparents or parents, but certainly none of the teachers would. She assumed that he would have to repeat the first grade, but he needed to make friends and learn more English as soon as possible. He could learn a lot of American customs at school as well.

The boys said that they were taking the puppies out to go to the bathroom and the two women watched as the two boys easily handled the two puppies. Poppy and Gracie quickly went about their business and then turned towards the house wanting to come back in. They were so adorable, both the boys and the puppies. William and Gracie bid Emily a fond farewell and Belle kissed Emily's cheek as she left to return to her home.

Emily, Paul Michael and Poppy had to decide where the best place for Poppy's bed would be. With her short legs, she wouldn't be able to climb up and down the steps. Emily decided to put the bed in Paul Michael's room and go to Murphy's and buy another one for the downstairs and would set it on her office floor. Poppy would stay with Paul Michael at night and stay with her during the day while he was at school. Paul Michael would have to carry Poppy up and down the stairs.

Emily read a story to Paul Michael in the living room as they awaited dinner to be ready. Poppy was fed that morning, and would be fed, while they ate, a small amount of kibbles in the kitchen. She was not to be allowed in the dining room when they were eating. Paul Michael kept looking towards the kitchen and Emily pointed to his plate and said, "Eat Paul Michael." He ate the roast beef and potatoes, beets, rolls, and pickles. He loved the apple pie and rubbed his stomach. Emily laughed and said, "You're full?"

Paul Michael thought for a moment and shook his head and said as he rubbed his stomach again, "Full."

She took him to take a bath and ran the tub with warm water and added some of her bubble bath crystals to the water. His eyes grew big as the bubbles raised up. She allowed him to undress by himself and when she reentered he had bubbles up to his chin. She motioned for him to wash his face using a dry wash cloth on her own. She used it to show him to wash his necks, arms, etc. She allowed him a few minutes to play with the bubbles and then pulled the plug. She held up a huge bath towel and wrapped him up. She used another towel to demonstrate drying and then pointed to his clean underwear and pajamas. She closed the door to give him some privacy and he called to her, "Anya!" She opened the door and saw that he had put both legs into one leg of the pajamas. The poor little thing couldn't get out and so she lifted him and helped him put on his pajama bottoms. He had washed his hair with the bath water and she combed his hair.

She didn't think twice and picked up the towel and wash cloth and hung them on the rack behind the bathroom door. Mrs. Carlson rushed in to rinse the tub and took the dirty clothes, towel, and wash cloth away to be laundered. Emily apologized for disrespecting her and walked into Paul Michael's room. He was playing with Poppy and she pointed to Poppy's bed and said, "Poppy come here. This is your bed." She pointed to it again and said, "Poppy's bed".

She picked the little boy up and sat down with him as she started reading the story of Jack and the Beanstalk. He laughed as she tried to change her voice as John had and he took over. It was amazing how he remembered the story word for word as well as what the giant said. He pointed to pictures in the book and identified Jack, giant, beans, cow, and "Anya". When Emily saw who he was pointing to when he said "Anya" it was Jack's mother. "Anya" must mean mother to Paul Michael. It was probably what he had called his natural mother.

She tucked him into bed and kissed him on the forehead. She covered up Poppy as well using a hand towel and went to get ready for bed herself. When she awakened around two in the morning, she went to check on Paul Michael. He was sound asleep and Poppy was curled up in her bed. Emily couldn't help but smile and returned to her lonely bed. Tomorrow would be an exciting day for Paul Michael as his first day at an American school.

When morning came, she awakened Paul Michael around seven and had his clothes set out for him to put on. He said, "Good morning Anya," and she answered him with "Good morning, Paul Michael." He ate his oatmeal, eggs, and bacon without leaving even the smallest crumb. The butler had taken Poppy out for her morning duty and now she was eating in the kitchen. Cook felt sorry for the tiny fellow Ms. Emily had brought home and was determined to fatten him up. He was the skinniest child she had ever seen in her life. He smiled at her when she had set down the oatmeal and dug into it immediately. He didn't add any sugar, butter, or cream. He ate it plain and it broke her heart watching him. She had cooked for many a rich family and he was the first one to ever eat plain oatmeal with nothing on it. After that he ate bacon and eggs and smiled once again when he was finished. She mentioned to Ms. Emily that maybe he had a tapeworm and she might need to get him checked. Emily told her he would be checked out once more but informed her that he had come from Europe and hadn't eaten very well for months. She assured cook that she would have him checked by a doctor as soon as possible to ease her own mind that he wasn't ill.

Emily knew that the Red Cross had given him a physical on the boat, but wanted him to get any shots he needed to have and perhaps some vitamins. He might need to take extra iron or Vitamin C. She called for the driver to bring the Ford around and told the driver to take them to the elementary school.

When Emily talked with the principal, he assured her that Paul Michael would be fine and led them to three first grade classrooms to choose from. Emily chose the one with the youngest teacher and beautiful smile for Paul Michael's teacher. Emily decided to stay for a while after telling him that the teacher Miss Wilson was, "Your teacher". He pointed to Miss Wilson and said "teacher?" and Emily said, "Yes". Paul smiled and sat with the other children who were currently doing addition drills. Emily was afraid that he might not know what to do but he watched the children, picked up a pencil and wrote the correct sums quickly and finished before the others did. Miss Wilson said, "That's amazing. Does he know his alphabet?" Emily explained that he was a refugee and had perhaps a different alphabet. The teacher returned to the classroom and set down an alphabet with both upper and lower case letters. She had him write one line of upper and lower A's each and said, "A". He printed another line of each and said, "A". Before mid-morning he was printing all the letters and recognized them even if the teacher mixed them up.

Reading, however, was difficult for him. Miss Wilson pointed to words on the board and pronounced each word slowly. All the children said the words with her several times and then they were given a silent reading assignment. She sat with a group at a table and they took turns reading aloud. Paul was in the last group and Emily was afraid he would be completely lost, but when it was his turn, he read very well messing up on only a few words and those had been words that had not been read by the other groups. He looked up and smiled at Miss Wilson and then to Emily. She slipped out the door when it was time for art. She had forgotten to get crayons and Miss Wilson quickly supplied him with a box of used crayons from her desk. Emily would stay by the door just in case he was frightened, but heard nothing and left.

Paul Michael began drawing and Miss Wilson smiled as she saw what looked like a dachshund. She asked if that was his dog and Paul Michael looked confused and said, "Poppy."

"Oh," she said, "it's your puppy. It's very cute. What's your puppy's name?"

He answered, "Poppy."

She smiled and moved on to the next child. Paul Michael ate all of his lunch in his lunch pail and enjoyed recess. A little boy named George Magyar from his class showed Paul Michael how to shoot marbles. He learned quickly and they took turns shooting. They were best friends by the end of recess.

Emily was driven over to Murphy's where she purchased large red pencils, some primer paper, a box of Crayola crayons, scissors, pencil sharpener, and a jar of paste. She bought a book bag and lunch box with a small thermos having a picture of a cowboy on it. She also stopped at a pediatrician's office and made an appointment for him.

She returned to the school about a half an hour before dismissal and was pleased to find him busy working at his desk. She returned to the principal's office to buy a reading workbook and a spelling book. She paid the $1 instructional fee and donated an additional $100 to be used by the teachers for supplies.

When they returned home he told her a little about each paper he had brought home with him. He showed her Poppy's portrait and she smiled as she correctly identified Poppy. He had gotten all of his arithmetic correct and the teacher had written down his reading assignment and wanted him to practice writing words from his reader. He told her, "Homework," as he pointed to the teacher's note.

When they opened the front door Poppy started yapping and had an accident due to her excitement at seeing Paul Michael. She was so happy to see Paul Michael and licked his face as he bent down to pick her up. He went for her leash to take her outside. He stopped by the mess that the maid was cleaning and said sternly, "No, no, no," to Poppy. He walked her around and said, "Good Poppy, good" when she squatted. He was exceptionally bright and was learning English amazingly fast. Although the Red Cross had given the children lessons in Basic English on the trip across the Atlantic, this was better than Emily had ever imagined possible.

The cook had made liver and onions as Mrs. Emily had asked for and she did although she was sure that the little boy would certainly not eat it. But he ate everything on his plate without complaint. He smiled and said, "Good." She wept when Mrs. Carlson repeated what the little boy had said. The poor little thing must have been starved half to death when he had arrived. She thought as she washed up the dishes, there must be millions more like him in Europe. She decided to buy more war bonds if it helped to end the horrible war and save a starving child. The maid had told her that he was the neatest little boy and returned everything back to where it had been when he first arrived. She told how he had scolded the puppy for making a mess and then took the puppy outside. The household staff had grown fond of both Emily and Paul Michael in just a matter of a few hours.

When Ms. Emily and the boy listened to the radio for about a half an hour after dinner, he liked the music and danced holding the little puppy in his arms. Emily listened to the news and told Paul Michael he had to work on his homework. She took him to his desk and got out the book bag and supplies for him to do his homework. She was going to tell him to write his words when he pulled out a paper like the one he had written his ABC's on. The teacher had written the words down for him and he wrote them several times. The teacher had written that each word had to be written five times each and he wrote them eight times each. He was to say each word and he did after Emily said them first. She pointed to each word and he recognized them. She changed the order when she pointed and he got them correct. The next item on the homework was reading. He read very well and had difficulty with the word pony. She repeated the word several times and when he came upon the word again he correctly identified it. She was pleased when he finished the sums his teacher had given with two column addition without carrying and couldn't believe how quickly he did them.

He bathed and asked for bubbles by pointing to the bottle and she gave in. She closed the door as he undressed, bathed, washed his hair, and dried off by himself. He opened the door after knocking and surprised her with his towel and wash cloth in his hand. He had tried to hang it up but couldn't reach the rack. She smiled and told him to go to his room for a story. Mrs. Carlson shook her head as she cleaned up the bathroom that looked as though it hadn't been touched and saw the little boy sitting on Emily's lap.

She was reading him a different story about the Three Little Pigs. She made the sounds of the wolf blowing at the houses and Paul Michael giggled. She told him it was time to go to bed and he jumped in. He pointed to Poppy's bed and said, "Poppy, bed." The little puppy curled up and the two were soon asleep.

Emily left Paul Michael at the school's main entrance and instructed the principal to call if there were any problems. She would take him to the pediatrician for a physical immediately after school and when she returned home she called Belle about Louise's lawsuit. Belle told her that Louise refused to listen to her or to accept any deal Belle offered. Louise had insisted that it to go to court and she wanted to see everything, she had told Belle. Alfred had wanted to try to work it out without going to the court because he had no idea what was in the boxes and didn't want any more surprises thrown at him. When only one party was informed in a lawsuit, he knew that it had the makings of a disaster. Belle had made it clear to him that it was in Louise's best interest not to see the contents.

While speaking with Belle, the announcement had been made on the radio that FDR had died in Warm Springs, Georgia. Harry Truman was sworn in as president and the nation was stunned at the loss of their 4-term president. He had been ill and had gone to recuperate. He had been sitting for an artist and suffered a massive cerebral hemorrhage and died in a matter of a few minutes. The longest serving president had helped the nation out of the Great Depression and the war was being won. The news had spread like wildfire in the small county that traditionally voted Democrat in the elections since FDR helped them get out of difficult times.

The rest of the country was mourning the loss of FDR and to top it off, Alfred had no idea if those boxes would make or break his marriage. If it had been Louise having the boxes, then there was no telling what would be in there, but because they were Bertie's he knew that she would have only put things in a safety deposit box for one reason and one reason alone and that would be to protect her children. He couldn't help protect Louise when she was so bent on destroying herself.

Chapter 7

Emily asked where they had to go to court and Belle told her that Louise's husband had filed the papers in Charleston and the case was scheduled to be heard in June there. Mr. Blakeman offered to have a copy made of the original notes he had made to Emily about the boxes that had been in the hope chest, but Alfred had declined. He would come to Welfield and look at the papers himself in two weeks. Emily had her receipt for the diamond setting from New York available as well. Meanwhile Belle had Emily call the jeweler who had set the stone and asked him to write a letter describing the receipt of the stone as a loose stone. When Alfred saw it, he said another jeweler could have easily unset it before she had taken it to them. Emily telegraphed the manager of the Astoria and asked for a sworn statement that the blue diamond had been stored in the safe immediately upon their return from the bank and another from their limo driver to state that he drove them directly from the bank to the hotel and had not stopped at a jeweler's on the way. Alfred accepted all of the statements without any additional comments. By the expression on his face, he wasn't happy.

Belle advised Mr. Blakeman to interview Jake Turner, a private investigator hired by Louise Perkins about what he had witnessed and heard at the hotel lobby. When Mr. Blakeman got his statement he sent a copy of it to Alfred and again received no comment from Alfred. Alfred hadn't known about Jake and did not like to find out indirectly that Louise had hired a private investigator without consulting him first.

Meanwhile, that afternoon, the doctor told Emily that physically there was nothing wrong with the little boy that a lot of rest and good nutrition wouldn't take care of. The test for worms was negative and when he called to tell her a few days later, he added, "He will slow down eating when he realizes that food is readily available and there's plenty for him to eat. Soon he'll realize that he's safe and no one is going to threaten him or you, for that matter."

Paul Michael made astronomical gains in his acquisition of learning English. He now read with little assistance from Emily and enjoyed reading comic books. After his homework was finished, he would join Emily in the living room to read his primer or comic books while she crocheted. He liked to listen to the radio with her and especially loved music.

Emily yelled out loud and cried out to her staff when the news spread on the radio that the war was finally over in Europe. Germany had surrendered on May 7 and all of Welfield celebrated. Many of the boys would be returning soon and Emily called Belle to share the good news. Belle wanted to proceed with haste now with the new business venture. She had set the deal in motion about two months earlier and everything was ready. Emily would be very busy in the summer traveling to Chicago and New York to check on factories, production, and research all of the chosen baby products. They would have to do as much of the work necessary before the trial in June.

The weeks had gone by and Paul Michael had finished school and had actually been promoted to the second grade. Miss Wilson had been pleased with how quickly he had caught up with the others and had surpassed the rest of his classmates in less than two months. She commented on how well behaved he was as well as how well he followed her directions.

Vivian and John came to visit for the week between UVA's spring semester and the first summer term during the first week of June. Paul Michael not only remembered them, but he immediately ran up the stairs to get his "Jack and the Beanstalk" book. Poppy remembered them as well and covered their faces with doggie kisses. Paul Michael wanted John to see his room and pulled him up the stairs after John had read the story to him. Poppy whined at the foot of the stairs for her young master and sat looking up the huge staircase eventually lying down to wait for their return.

Paul Michael showed him his books from school and John could hardly believe this was the same child he had seen only a few months earlier. The little boy's face was now fuller and his hair shone. His English was nearly perfect and he still referred to Emily as Anya. John was impressed by how neat his room was in appearance. The little teddy bear was propped up on the bed pillows, books held upright on his shelves, toys neatly placed on shelves as well. Clothes were either hung up or in drawers and not a single cookie crumb could be seen anywhere. John picked up a chess piece to look at it and set it back down. Paul Michael moved it to be almost in the center of the square and John shrugged. Regardless of his shortcomings of being overly neat, he loved the little boy and gave him a piggyback ride back down the steps.

John's parents were coming for a visit the following day and would also be staying with Emily. They would be spending their first summer in their completed cabin near a Roanoke lake and so were driving in to Welfield rather than coming by train. Both were anxious to meet the little boy that they had heard so much about. Emily and Vivian were going to take Paul Michael and William to the farm later that day. It would be the first time Emily had returned to the farm since moving. It would also be Paul Michael's first look at it as well. She always went to the cemetery while he had been at school and thought that she could have Mrs. Novak explain to him in Hungarian before they went there with him the first time. Mrs. Novak explained it carefully to the little boy who looked at Emily while Mrs. Novak's voice calmly told him the story about his cousin. Silent tears rolled down his fair-skinned cheeks as he listened to her and he asked her a few questions. He set the phone back in its cradle and hugged Emily tightly around the neck.

They all ate lunch and then got into John's car. Paul Michael asked a lot of questions about where they were going and had set himself in the front seat between Vivian and John. When they stopped at the old cabin, Emily had mixed emotions. She had called to tell Mrs. Novak that they would be coming and Mrs. Novak came out on the front porch to greet them. Paul Michael looked around and called to Emily, "Anya, what is this place?" Mrs. Novak smiled and asked Paul Michael in Hungarian if he liked it in America. He quickly replied that he liked it very much but his favorite thing was having his Anya. Mrs. Novak translated their conversation to them and everyone smiled as she translated.

Vivian was afraid that she would cry when she first returned to the cabin after Emily moved to Welfield, but was too happy to see that the cabin looked almost as it had when John had first visited there. There was none of the fancy china or furniture to be seen like in the new house, but the old couch and painted table sat in the exact place they had been for as long as she could remember. It was one of her favorite times of the year because the strawberries were getting ripe and they would be picking berries later. Each one got a pail and John carried a large bucket. Vivian remarked, "When the bucket is full, we will have enough to make some jam!"

Vivian showed Paul Michael which berries to pick and the little one set out on a mission. John stayed with him to make sure that he didn't stray or get out of sight. Vivian loved picking strawberries on the farm. It brought back so many pleasant memories of growing up in this hollow and her fun times as a child. Paul Michael brought his pail almost full of berries to show Emily who told him to pour the berries into the bucket gently. She demonstrated how to him, and he grinned and called out, "I'm going to get some more!"

They had picked two extra pails full of strawberries and those would be saved to make strawberry shortcake the following day for John's parents. Josef came down from the barn to greet Emily and he met Paul Michael. He asked the boy if he would like to see the barn and John joined them to see the hogs and chickens. The women would be busy making strawberry jam for several hours and knew that both guys would be kept busy for some time. Vivian carefully washed the jars, boiled them as well as the flat parts of the lids, and slowly melted the paraffin wax in another pot. She removed a wrapped bowl of butter from the refrigerator and set it on the counter. Emily and Mrs. Novak carefully capped, washed, and sliced the berries at the table. The old "jam pot" had been carefully washed and set on the table awaiting the berries. Mrs. Novak had the sugar and Certo Fruit Pectin needed for the preserves. The berries were mashed slightly as they cooked. Emily had on one of her old aprons and dresses she had kept at the farm and Vivian smiled as her mother used the long wooden spoon to stir the berries. When Emily was satisfied that all was ready, she skimmed the foam off and put it into a small bowl and ladled the jam into jars, Vivian ladled melted paraffin wax on the top of the jam and then sealed the jar with its cap and screw ring.

Mrs. Novak had churned butter the day before and had made fresh bread that morning. Vivian could hardly wait to cut herself some bread and spread it with some butter and preserves from the foam bowl. She called to John and Paul Michael who were walking down the mountain path from the barn, "Come and join us in eating food that was meant only for the gods of yore!" She told them to come through the back porch and to wash up out back. Mrs. Novak had sliced the fresh bread and the butter had softened enough to be spread. There was just enough of the foam jam for them to each enjoy the mixture of fresh jam, butter, and bread. John said, "Just when I thought I had tasted the best food in America in New York or Parisian restaurants, you women fix this. This is great!" He winked at Paul Michael who had preserves on both cheeks and a huge grin on his face. Paul Michael, "This is great!" and took another big bite.

The women chuckled as Paul Michael described the little piglets he had seen. He briefly mentioned that his grandfather had chickens at one time and some pigs, but the Nazis took all of them away. His grandfather had saved a few eggs that were ready to hatch and had hidden them and kept them warm until they hatched. They had owned a small number of chickens and then the Russians came through and took those. "We didn't have much to eat but they still took them all. They took our chickens and our only cow. My grandfather's friend found some wild onions and old potatoes. We planted a few of the potatoes and ate on them for a while. Mr. Dudas made potato soup and before I left we ate only water soup when the potatoes ran out and I got very hungry. That's all we had left, until the Russians finally left us alone. Mr. Dudas sent me to you and now, I don't get hungry now that I'm with Anya."

Mrs. Novak wiped tears from her eyes using her apron and John shook his head in disbelief. Emily and Vivian said nothing, but Emily wiped his face with a damp cloth and said, "You will never go hungry with me, Paul Michael, never." Mrs. Novak spoke to him about the war in Hungarian and then told him about Paul dying. He nodded when she asked if he understood what she had said. He came up to Emily and hugged her and said, "I'm sorry Anya about Paul."

The small group walked up the mountain to the upper pasture so that Paul Michael could see all of the cows. They continued up the trail and he saw the old Pierce cabin. The little boy, of course, wanted to go in and check out the strange dwelling, but John warned him that snakes might be in there. They looked about and Emily told Paul Michael that William had actually been born in the cabin. She assured him that the cabin had looked much nicer then. She showed him the fruit trees and told him that his cousin, Paul, had planted those very trees more than twenty years ago. The trees were full of fruit just starting to make their appearance. The bee hives were overflowing with honey. Josef was scared of bees and had not robbed the hives for months.

Vivian had helped her father before with the gathering of honey and volunteered to collect some. She donned her father's bee hat with netting, wore a long sleeved shirt and pants with rubber bands on the openings near her ankles and wrists. She took Paul's smoke pot and lit a charcoal on the bottom on fire and closed the lid. She moved slowly through the hives gently passing the smoke around each hive and removed the screen with the honeycomb and scraped it into her dad's honey pot. She moved to each successive hive and repeated the process. It took a lot of patience and slow movement to complete the task without getting the bees upset.

Paul Michael's eyes got big as he watched the bees swarm and then fall lightly to the hive from the smoke. When Vivian moved with the smoke pot, the bees revived and continued with their work. When he saw the honeycomb he just jumped up and down clapping his hands together. He wanted to try some with a piece of bread and butter as soon as they returned to the house.

The rest of the day was spent enjoying the sunshine on the porch after a wonderful lunch and they left in the late afternoon to return home with several cases of jam. Emily had left six jars for Mrs. Novak to enjoy. They had boiled jars as well as the two part lids with rings and flat seals in which to put the honeycomb. They took six jars of honey with them and left four with Mrs. Novak. After watching Vivian, and seeing that she hadn't been stung, Josef knew how to go about collecting the honey. If she could do it, then so could he.

The group returned to Welfield and all of them were tired from all of the walking, picking, etc. and John carried the berries into the kitchen for cook to prepare for strawberry shortcake. She capped, washed, and dried the berries off and put them in a large covered bowl in the refrigerator. Poppy was excited to see all of them and Paul Michael ran straight outside with the puppy on its leash. John ran out to go with him to view the new tree house. It was his fort and Paul Michael was so proud of it.

The cook was pleased with all of the jars of preserves and honey and tubs of butter. With sugar being so hard to get, the honey would sure come in handy to make goodies. She had prepared a nice supper and smiled as she looked out the kitchen window and then laughed as she watched the puppy raise itself on its back legs trying to catch a glimpse of Paul Michael and John in the tree.

When Paul Michael and John returned inside, they went to play a game of chess. Vivian and Emily both sat in the living room crocheting. Emily was making some scarves and Vivian was working on window panels for her dining room windows. She wanted crocheted panels for the summer months to replace the heavy drapery that was currently on the rods in their home.

Paul Michael carried Poppy up the stairs, bathed and went to bed without argument or delay. He wanted John to read to him and chose the story about the Elves and the Shoemaker. He giggled as John changed his voice for the elves' lines and was asleep before the end of the story. John put the book back on the shelf where Paul Michael had removed it. He went down a few steps and looked back towards the little boy's room. He had forgotten to shut the door and smiled as he saw Poppy curled up in her bed. He gently closed the door and continued down the staircase. The two women had their needles going quickly to the beat of a song on the radio. They enjoyed the music and radio shows until almost ten and they all decided it was time to go to bed.

It was around ten the next morning when John's parents arrived. They had spent the night in Bluestone and had driven the rest of the way to Welfield that morning. Henry and Catherine were impressed with Paul Michael who shared the events from the previous day about picking berries and Vivian's miracle with the bees. He introduced himself and Poppy to both of them and shook Henry's hand. He asked, "Anya, may I go outside and play?"

"But of course. Don't get too dirty lunch will be in a couple of hours. Be careful in that tree house," she said.

"I will," he said and turned to go outside.

Catherine was pleased that Emily looked so much better than she had in March. The little boy had performed a miracle with Emily. Catherine said, "Why did he call you Anya and not Emily or mother?"

"Oh," Emily explained, "that's Hungarian for mother."

The women chattered about all sorts of events. It was the 6th of June and after dinner they listened to the news. The allied forces had invaded a year ago in France at Normandy. It had been a huge success and the Germans, although deeply entrenched, had been on the run. They talked about the end of the war in Europe and thought that perhaps the war in the Pacific would end soon as well. The ship building business was thriving and profits for the second quarter were great. Although war was profitable for them, both Catherine and Henry prayed the war would end soon.

Emily had planned a picnic with John and Vivian up on Filbert Mountain. Emily hadn't gone up on the mountain since Paul's death and had chosen to only speak with the caretaker on the phone instead. Paul Michael was so excited that he could hardly wait. John had bought a baseball and a glove for Paul Michael and had brought his old glove with him. They would play catch up on the mountain and John had promised to teach him the game of baseball. Cook prepared a feast for them with fried chicken, potato salad, coleslaw, rolls, and baked beans. She had made cookies using the honey and packed them in the basket as well. Emily walked by herself to the various sites of picnic areas that Paul had worked on. She felt like she had neglected the property and had asked the caretaker to give her a tour around the grounds. The others joined, but at a distance. Paul Michael's curiosity had him asking question after question. He took hold of Henry's hand and walked between Henry and John constantly looking back at the woods as if searching for something. Finally he asked, "Mr. Henry, are there any soldiers in these woods?"

"Why of course there aren't! There are a few bears and deer, but no soldiers. I'm positive that there aren't any," he assured the little boy. The boy must have been remembering his home and the soldiers. "At my grandfather's village the soldiers always hid in the woods. They killed all the deer and took all of our chickens and even our only cow. Sometimes they shot people from our village and the guns were very loud! They had cannons hidden there too."

"Now, don't get yourself all worked up there, Paul Michael. There are neither guns nor soldiers in these woods. Emily owns this property and doesn't allow hunting near the lodge or cabins. Come on, let's go over there and take a look at the gazebo. That's where Vivian and John were married," Henry suggested.

"What's a gazebo?" the lad inquired.

"Come on, we'll show you!" John said.

The little boy checked all around the gazebo and stood on one of the benches to get a better view. He liked the mountains but he loved the quietness. He spotted a lizard and decided to try to catch it. John said, "And just what will you do with it when you catch it?"

"Why I'll let it go I suppose!" Paul Michael giggled. The two men sat down and watched Paul Michael's pursuit of the lizard. The poor little lizard ran in several directions until Paul Michael jumped and caught it. He was going to hold it by its tail to show them when the tail broke and the lizard disappeared into some tall grass over the edge. "Did you see that?" he exclaimed. The men had and were laughing at Paul Michael's expression when the tail broke. "We saw it," Henry cried out slapping his leg with one hand and wiping his eye with the other.

The caretaker had done an excellent job getting the lodge and cabins ready for the summer visitors. He had added an additional dozen picnic areas and had planted several more azaleas around the main grounds. He planted some wild roses around the gazebo. In just a few years, Emily knew that the top of the gazebo would be covered with wild roses. The others rejoined Emily as she gave Paul Michael a tour and introduced him to the staff.

The next few days were very enjoyable as they fit a visit to the company store and Henry's favorite store, G. C. Murphy's. Henry was fascinated each time he went into Welfield by those two stores and wanted to see what treasures awaited his discovery. Henry asked Emily if he could take Paul Michael down to the pet department where they bought a toy for Poppy and several rawhide chews. Henry took him to the candy department where they had some gumballs and jawbreakers. Henry couldn't remember the last time he had a jawbreaker and Paul could barely fit one into his mouth. The two fellows each popped one in their mouths and a half an hour later with blue lips and tongue they laughed and pointed at each other!

Catherine bought some material to have curtains made for their cabin as well as some oilcloth for their outdoor picnic table. She purchased a few kerosene lamps and stoneware dishes and flatware as well. Catherine wanted their new cabin to be just as cozy as she had found Emily's home the year before. China and crystal didn't really belong there and she found much of what she needed in good old G.C. Murphy's. Emily had given her several hand loomed rugs for their floors as well as some table scarves.

John and Henry eventually found their way back to the toy department. They found some model cars and puzzles and bought several of each. John and Henry would work on one of the new puzzles with Paul Michael after lunch. Belle and William surprised Emily with a visit after lunch and so William joined in with the guys to solve the jigsaw puzzle while Gracie and Poppy sat at their feet. Both puppies were now house trained and were devoted to their masters. William was going to be fifteen the following summer and Vivian surprised him with an early birthday present. She had brought him a baseball autographed by Babe Ruth himself. William couldn't believe it and tried to explain baseball to Paul Michael and about Babe Ruth. Ruth had retired in 1936 but he was still William's favorite baseball player. William showed all the others and he thanked Vivian and John many times. He gave the baseball to Belle to put into her purse. He didn't want it to get scuffed or messed up in any way and so she wrapped it up in her handkerchief.

William had brought Gracie over for a visit every few days and she joined Paul Michael and Poppy to play in the back yard. After the tree house was built, Paul Michael's friend, George, came over to play and soon games of cowboy and Indians ensued. It was a pleasant time had by all. William called Louise as soon as he got home and told her all about the baseball and his days he had spent with Paul Michael.

"Who is Paul Michael?" she asked. "Oh, so that's the little boy that Emily is adopting. So, not only is he some relative of Paul's but is also a war refugee."

"How interesting," she mused. It was strange that a little boy would just happen to appear and felt that perhaps there was some sort of secret there. She would have her investigator check out the unbelievable story. Perhaps the little boy was Vivian or Emily's love child. If he was, then it would be the perfect weapon to use against Vivian and Emily. John's parents would never accept a child born out of wedlock. She asked William about the other visitors and when she heard about John's parents being there as well she really got upset but said, "Oh William do tell everyone that I said hello." She wanted to make sure that they thought only the best about her when she became their daughter-in-law. William followed her directions and relayed the message. They had curtly replied with, "Please tell her that we send our regards to her as well."

Vivian and John left with John's parents a day earlier than planned so that they could check out the new lake cabin. In only a few days, Emily had to go to Charleston with Belle, William, and Mr. Blakeman for their court appearance. They chose to stay at the Daniel Boone Hotel and the puppies and Paul Michael stayed in Welfield at Emily's house with Mrs. Novak. Hopefully it wouldn't take very long for the hearing. Judge George Jackson had been assigned the case and Belle saw Judge Marshall sitting in the gallery as the case was presented. Alfred brought forth the copy of the will and Mr. Blakeman countered with statements and testimony under oath by Belle, Emily, Vivian, John, and William.

The judge had listened carefully to both sides and decided that the diamond had indeed been a loose stone and as such could not be described as jewelry as the will had stated, but he ordered that Louise be allowed to view all boxes and until that could occur that all the boxes would be sealed. Until Louise could view the contents of each box, he further ordered that Judge Marshall would witness the opening of the boxes on behalf of the court to determine pertinence and report to the court. It amounted to a mixed verdict. Belle and Emily would have gladly handed over the diamond, but did not want the contents to be revealed to anyone, especially to Alfred and a judge of the WV Supreme Court. The New York box could damage Louise's marriage on its own and that was for certain. If Belle's suspicions about the December miscarriage were correct, Louise's marriage would be doomed to end abruptly.

Louise was so pleased with the result that she loudly announced her pleasure and told Alfred loudly, "I'm pregnant!" for everyone in the courtroom to hear. Belle turned towards Emily and grimaced as she heard the words. Belle said, "Congratulations on your victory and your news, Louise, Alfred," and turned to leave. William was so excited, "I'm going to be an uncle! I'm going to be an uncle!" The two women couldn't bear to tell him that was definitely very unlikely to occur.

Louise said, "Oh Aunt Belle, I think the fifth of July works for me to go to New York to view the boxes does that sound like an open date for you? What about you Emily?" both nodded in agreement that the boxes would be opened in New York on the fifth of July. Louise was excited about spending a holiday in New York. She felt sure that Belle would make the hotel arrangements, but didn't want to risk being stuck with the bill. "Uh, Aunt Belle, will you make the hotel arrangements or shall I?"

Belle said, "We will be staying at the Astoria with my compliments. I will pay for the hotel, but I will pay for no additional charges sent to the hotel for you or while you are staying at the hotel. Your husband can do that. Is that arrangement all right with you, Alfred?"

"Certainly and I thank you for being so gracious," he answered.

Belle asked Alfred if he would come to her hotel room, after the hearing, alone. Louise at first feared what she was going to say to him, but then, he already knew all about Louise's problems in college. There was nothing she could tell him that he didn't already know and what there was left to tell, Belle had no way of knowing. Her secrets had gone to the grave with Bertie.

When Alfred came into her hotel room Belle was on the phone. He heard her say, "Be good Paul Michael." His curiosity got the best of him and he asked Belle about Paul Michael. She said, "He is a refugee from Hungary. He is a cousin to the late Paul Black and is being adopted by Emily Black. He and William, despite their age differences, have become quite good friends. Please sit down."

Belle had asked the maid to order some coffee and finger sandwiches from room service and before Belle proceeded she offered him coffee and a selection of finger sandwiches. After making his choices and Belle had made hers, Belle said, "Louise and I have not always seen eye to eye especially here recently, but I do still care for her. I now make a personal plea to you, on her behalf as well as William's, Alfred do not let her open those boxes. You may open the ones in Pittsburgh but do not let her open the ones in New York! What is found in those boxes will destroy her emotionally and mentally. All of them, including the ones in New York, will hurt William as well. Please consider opening the Pittsburgh boxes without her, and act only as her attorney and not her husband."

"Belle I have the highest regard for you, but the court has ordered the boxes to be opened and the contents revealed to her. I cannot go against a court order, I would be disbarred! What is in them that could possibly hurt Louise?" he asked.

"I will tell you this much. There are certificates, letters, and other items in those boxes but there's absolutely no jewelry and definitely nothing that is of any value. Louise will find nothing but pain if she persists in looking inside them. Bertie hid those items to protect Louise and William and trusted Emily to do so as well. I will not divulge the information freely to you, but I will tell you that this will be the one time when Louise will not be happy with getting her way. With her court victory, she will ultimately be the one to suffer. When Louise gets into those boxes and sees the contents, she will wish that she hadn't! Please, isn't there some way that the seals can be broken without her being there?" Belle pleaded.

"Belle it is my intention to accompany Louise along with Judge Marshall of the WV Supreme Court to go as a witness for the court as ordered. You know Judge Marshall to be a fair and decent man. He will bear witness that no jewelry was found and what was in the boxes in court if he has to. That is my final answer, I'm afraid. We will meet you on the Fifth of July at 9:00 am at the Chase Manhattan Bank and will proceed to the next ones in an orderly manner. If you have nothing else, I must go. Louise is waiting. We are going to my parent's house and I am sure she wants to know what we have discussed. I have no secrets from my wife and, thanks to you; she has none to keep from me."

"One more question, Alfred, if there is no jewelry; do the papers inside the boxes have to be read?" Belle asked with the slightest hint of desperation.

"Those papers could very well be another will or legal document and so each paper will have to be examined. The judge and I will determine any legal issues connected to any papers found. Now I must really go," Alfred pleaded.

Belle managed to say, "Well thank you for at least listening. But my dear, at least warn her that she may not want to see those papers, will you do that at least? I know you love her and do not want her to be hurt, especially now that she is expecting. A sudden shock could hurt both her and the baby. Take care dear."

Belle escorted him to the door and as he was leaving he noticed Emily returning with William. From the bags they were carrying, they had done some shopping. William told him about his autographed baseball and Alfred invited him to his birthday party coming up in late July. "I hope you will try to be there, buddy. I have to go now," Alfred said to his brother-in-law.

As soon as Alfred returned to his house, Louise wanted to know what Belle had to say that couldn't be said in front of her. Alfred recalled the conversation to her and Louise said, "So she thinks that little pieces of paper can hurt me, how absurd. She's not going to stop me, not this time. I have a court order and I will see it through. Now darling let's go celebrate after we call your parents to tell them that they will be grandparents before too long!"

Alfred's parents were ecstatic at the news and asked when she was due. Louise told them that the baby would be coming in late January or early February. She had just had her first bout of morning sickness and figured she was about six weeks along. After talking with Alfred, she figured that if there were papers and letters that were upsetting it would be a perfect cover for what she would have to do while they were in New York. If she timed it just right, then she would get a nice brooch or necklace this time, and that was for sure.

It was near the end of June when Emily got a phone call from Vivian. Her first summer term was almost over and would end after the Fourth of July holiday. She had good news and couldn't wait to share it. She was three months pregnant. She had gone to the doctor to confirm the pregnancy and had known for about three weeks now. She had waited until she could pass through the nausea and vomiting stage before letting Emily know. Vivian didn't want to risk another miscarriage and getting Emily upset. The baby was due around Christmas. "I've had three straight mornings of no sickness and the doctor is going to watching me closely since my last miscarriage. He wants me to come in every two weeks. John is so excited and loves his new job. It keeps him quite busy and he has long hours. He has already learned a lot from all of the partners in the firm. How's Paul Michael?"

Emily told Vivian how quickly he was picking up English and what good friends he had made with William and one of his classmates, George. His birthday was in September and he was already getting anxious for school to start once more. She had taken Paul Michael and George to the county library to check out some books. Paul Michael told her that only a church was more beautiful than the library. Vivian chuckled when she heard his musings about the library. Paul Michael loved going to mass, reading his books, and playing with Poppy and George. He drew a picture of his tree house one rainy day and had mailed it to John. Vivian later told Emily that John had framed it and hung in his office at work. He wanted her to send his thank you vocally via Vivian and had just mailed a thank you note for the beautiful art work. Emily relayed the information about the thank you note but chose not to say anything about the pregnancy. She would wait another month or two before she said anything to the little boy. She didn't want to build up his hopes of being an uncle.

They would be leaving the next morning, July 2, to go to New York. The bags were packed and they would be leaving early the next day by train and Belle, William, and Mr. Blakeman would be accompanying them. Alfred, Louise, and Judge Marshall were flying later that day to New York and would be arriving at about the same time. Paul Michael and Mr. Blakeman played chess and worked puzzles during the entire trip. Emily and Belle spent the whole day pouring over contracts, orders, and spreadsheets for the infant care venture. Belle had purchased the majority of shares of stock giving her controlling interest and a few other companies she had bought outright and signed them over to Emily. Emily would be flying to Chicago from Pittsburgh with Mr. Blakeman to take a firsthand look at all of the facilities. Paul Michael would be staying with Belle, at the hotel, while Emily was gone to the banks with the attorneys and the judge. He had stayed the night several times to prepare him for this separation and Emily promised that she would call him nightly to check on him.

When they arrived at the Astoria, Louise hadn't checked in yet and Belle asked for Louise and Alfred as well as Judge Marshall to be placed in rooms on a separate floor from their suite. Mr. Blakeman would be in a separate room next to their suite. She would be paying for all of the rooms and the suite of course, which was always at her disposal, had fresh flowers and fruit waiting. The hotel was happy to oblige her wishes for the additional rooms. When Louise discovered that she was in a room with only a small adjoining living space she was livid. Why shouldn't she be in a suite as well? The hotel manager repeated Belle's instructions and she called Belle. Belle told Louise, "If the arrangements do not suit you, then by all means feel free to change them and you can pay for it yourself."

Louise changed her attitude slightly and said the room would be satisfactory. She and Alfred were going to go out for dinner and Judge Marshall was going to call on some friends. Belle, William, and Emily would be going to the Rainbow Room for the Fourth of July and decided to go to a French restaurant recommended by the concierge.

They did some shopping and William wanted to look for a special present for Paul Michael. He wanted to find a carved chess set. They searched and he finally found a lovely jade and ivory set from China. Emily found a beautiful leather bound set of children's stories for him and a few infant items as well for Louise. She bought some lovely infant gowns, just in case Louise went through with the pregnancy and gave birth. At Cartier's, Belle found a silver dual dish for Gracie and ordered one for Poppy as well to be engraved with their names. She also purchased a pair of silver frames with tiny bone shapes etched into them. She would have the children's photographs taken with their puppies to keep in their rooms.

William could hardly wait for the fireworks show over the Hudson River and he espied Judge Marshall at the restaurant and motioned to him with a wave of his hand. He asked Aunt Belle, "Oh can't he join us? I do miss him so much."

"Only if he isn't with someone, my dear," she answered.

Judge Marshall greeted Belle and she asked him to join them. He said that his friends had just left and he agreed to stay with them for a while. William told him all about Gracie and Paul Michael and asked about his news. They talked about Louise being pregnant and how anxious he was to be an uncle.

Emily recalled having met the judge at Bertie's funeral. He had loved Bertie and had actually planned on marrying her. He nodded to Belle and asked him if Belle could do him the honor of a waltz. William agreed and Belle and the judge left the table. Belle took the opportunity to speak candidly with Judge Marshall. She told him what they would find in the three boxes in New York. William's war bonds, marriage certificates, birth certificates, and Jack's death certificate and a few receipts. She then told him about the other papers dealing with Louise. By the time William and Emily had returned from the waltz Judge Marshall knew the whole story of what was in each of the New York boxes. Belle asked him to join her in her suite and she would tell him what was in the Pittsburgh boxes. She hadn't had time to do it during that waltz and did not want to risk William overhearing anything about them.

The fireworks display was fantastic and William cheered several times, but the grand finale was his favorite. Judge Marshall assured Belle that he would recommend that they sign for the contents and return them to the hotel room to Louise. He agreed that a scene at the bank would not benefit anyone. As long as he would keep a record of any of the contents that could legally belong to Louise, they would be turned over to her and any that in his judgment that did not, would remain in the boxes. It would be Louise's choice as to whether they should return with the contents related to her or not.

At nine o'clock the following morning, they entered the Chase Manhattan bank and the safety deposit box was unsealed in the Judge's presence. There was nothing in the first one except for war bonds in William's name. There was nothing else just as Belle had claimed. On their way to the second bank, Louise began to get a little anxious about what could be in the boxes, but she refused to become too alarmed. There were copies of her birth certificate, which she was allowed to keep, one of William's birth certificate, her parent's marriage certificate, and Jack Pierce's death certificate. Jack's death certificate upset Louise when she saw the cause of death was Myocardial Infarction due to alcoholism. A stray piece of paper was picked up and Louise recognized it at once. It was a bill for a treatment given by a doctor in the Welfield hospital for an unusual hemorrhage in a then teenaged Louise. She said, "I vaguely remember going to the doctor when I had a very difficult menstrual cycle and had severe cramping. The doctor recommended a D & C; you know Dilation and Curettage and gave me some penicillin."

Louise was worried when she saw the note and now suspected what they would find in the next box. She begged Alfred to return her to the hotel claiming that she wasn't feeling well. She agreed that he and Judge Marshall could return all of the contents while she rested for a while. He had no sooner left than she jumped up to take care of things. She didn't hear him when he had returned to check on her a few minutes later to ask if perhaps she needed a doctor when he saw the bloody sharpened pencil. "What have you done?" he screamed.

The hotel doctor was immediately called in to check on Louise. He advised that she rest and so Alfred, Judge Marshall, Belle and Emily went on to the last bank to open the last box. Alfred closed his eyes and wept as he read a letter. What a fool he had been, a stupid fool! He handed it to Judge Marshall who read Bertie's Letter and then immediately looked at Bertie and Emily.

Dear Emily,

If you are reading this letter then I have died and you have found the safety deposit box receipts in my hope chest. You are probably wandering why I put a receipt for a doctor in a safety deposit box but I did it to protect Louise. Louise attempted to abort a baby using a sharpened pencil and really messed things up back in high school. The doctor told her she would be lucky if she ever got pregnant again. I have also enclosed miscellaneous bills from a detective agency in Bluestone. The detective sent me the attached folder with a report about Louise and her movements when she went to town with her friends while in high school.

The report told me how Louise had met a boy, Richard Collins, on several weekend nights at the back of the house and they had gone to a hotel in Bluestone. The Collins boy was killed in France in July of '43. Apparently Louise had gotten pregnant in the summer before her senior year. Louise fooled all of them: Belle, Alfred, and Judge Perkins into thinking she was a virgin when she got married to Alfred. She must have bribed the doctor or nurse to change the report after her examination before the wedding.

I had to protect her and now I am asking you, Emily to do the same. I know she has done so many wrong things in the last year or so, but I still love her. Please make sure that she never does anything as foolish as this again. I know that you will show this letter to Belle and hopefully it can then be destroyed. Please tell her I am sorry for being such a fool and hiding the truth from her.

I didn't know about the doctor's examination, I swear I didn't. Belle wanted it done before the wedding and I didn't find out until it was too late. I would have told Belle the truth then, but she didn't say anything to me about an examination. I do not know how Louise pulled it off, about not being a virgin, but she needed to be married and quickly. Forgive me and never let Louise know that you know her secrets. Protect her from herself.

Love,

Bertie

Alfred cried without cease for almost ten minutes. He told them about the scene in his room at the hotel and that the hotel physician was with her now. Judge Marshall could offer no words of comfort and looked first at Belle and then at Emily. She had warned him as well as Alfred, but he had no idea that it could possibly be something this terrible. Judge Marshall had loved Bertie and would have married her. He knew that she must have struggled with the truth and hadn't known what to do. Ultimately, she had chosen to protect her daughter.

Belle had told him that the boxes in Pittsburgh were even worse and had more information that could damage both of Bertie's children. Alfred had to ask, "What could possibly be worse than what they had just learned about Louise?"

Judge Marshall waited until Alfred composed himself well enough to leave the bank and maintain some sort of dignity. Emily had asked someone in the bank for a glass of water and offered it to Alfred. She spoke softly and said, "Alfred, I do not know what to say, but do not say words to Louise that you may regret later. I suggest you give her a few days to recover before you address what you have found here. You will need those days to figure out what needs to be done from here. Judge Marshall, what do you suggest?"

"I believe that you are absolutely correct and very wise. Louise has done some very horrible things and right now it would do no good to confront her about her past. Alfred, you will need a little time to heal as well before you confront her. Remember that you are serving as a representative of a court and must maintain your client-lawyer privilege. You may want to excuse yourself as her attorney at this point in time," Judge Marshall suggested.

Unfortunately a reporter had gotten wind of a possible story, via a phone call from Louise, and a photographer took a shocking picture of Alfred entering the hotel carrying a large envelope. The reporter approached Alfred's party and "No comment" was given by all. William and Mr. Blakeman had stayed in the suite and were not told what had happened at the bank. Instead, Emily just told him that Louise had gotten sick and a physician had been sent to take care of her. William insisted on going to see his sister and was frightened by her pale appearance. The physician suggested that she be taken to a hospital. Alfred agreed and within only a few hours, Louise had to have a total hysterectomy to stop a hemorrhage. She was only twenty and since she had punctured her uterus with the pencil, the gynecologist had no choice and had to perform the hysterectomy. Alfred called his parents and told them that Louise had lost the baby and had hemorrhaged. She was in Mount Sinai Hospital where they had to do a total hysterectomy. Alfred had no idea of what he was going to do next. He knew that he could never forgive Louise for what she had done to their baby.

Later when he watched her sleeping in the hospital bed, he realized that she was either a cold, calculating woman who must have had no feelings for him at all or she was emotionally disturbed. If he asked for a divorce, he was convinced that it wouldn't hurt her at all. She would merely be concerned with the loss of money and position. He had to think long and hard about the course of action he would have to take when she had recovered. He would give her the benefit of the doubt for the time being.

Chapter 8

Louise had needed several pints of blood and once everyone in the group was checked, Emily was the only one found with her blood type. William was too young to donate and Belle was too old. Alfred had A negative and Louise had O positive. Ironically, the baby had the Rh negative factor. If it had been carried to term, the baby probably wouldn't have survived because of the differences in the blood types. The fact was that the fetus had had the negative Rh factor as well and Louise would have lost the baby in just a few weeks, naturally. Alfred visited Louise at the hospital every day and reporters were posted outside the hospital waiting for a comment. They smelled a story and wanted all the details. Emily and Belle would merely say, "No comment," and let Alfred do all of the talking.

Alfred made a statement, "My wife miscarried our first child, hemorrhaged, and required surgery. I have no other comments to make and will not be answering questions at this time."

Belle hired a private security firm to prevent any photographs, reporters, or unapproved visitors from entering Louise's private room. This was the worst thing that could have happened at this time but, unfortunately for Louise, the worst was yet to come.

Louise was in the hospital for more than a week. Belle hired a private nurse to take care of Louise for the next month. Alfred and Judge Marshall would go to the other safety deposit boxes with Emily in Pittsburgh. Belle and William decided that it would be best if they accompanied Louise to her Charleston home to look after her. Mrs. Novak agreed to come to New

York to get Paul Michael and the two of them would return to Welfield on the train. She would take care of Paul Michael and suggested that he come to stay at the farm in Jackson until Emily returned to Welfield. Our Lady of the Rosary was having it summer catechism classes lead by the Sisters of Charity and it would occupy the next two weeks. Paul Michael loved the farm and the church and he would miss her less if he was kept busy during the daytime.

Emily asked Mrs. Novak to have a mass said for Louise and Alfred but to have it read, "Intentions of the donor" in the bulletin. The next two weeks would be trying ones for everyone. Louise needed to heal and so did Alfred. Mr. Blakeman would accompany Emily to Pittsburgh as well and then his wife would join them when they got to Chicago. Mrs. Blakeman had family in Chicago and wanted to take advantage of any opportunity to visit with them.

Emily entered the Pittsburgh Bank and kept her eyes lowered as they looked into the first box. They were just as confused as Emily had remembered she and Belle had been, when they had first seen the pillowcase. A very old embroidered pillowcase that was heavily stained was all that was in the first box. Emily quietly told them that she recognized it as one of a pair that she had given to Bertie for her birthday the second year after Jack and Bertie had moved into the hollow.

"Bertie had never been taught how to embroider and had admired some of mine that had been hanging out on the clothesline. I embroidered the pair and crocheted across the bottom. She had been so happy when she had opened them. She told me they were too pretty to sleep on. I told her that's what they were for. She put them up for a few years and didn't use them again until after Louise was born. I went to visit her and saw them out on her clothesline. She told me she had better dreams when they were on the bed." She paused and tears began to appear in her eyes, "Bertie loved the simplest things in life and always seemed to have a struggle of one sort or another. I beg you; do not go to the next box. Please do not go there. I know I know that you must, but do what you must to protect Louise and William. I know that Louise has done some horrible things but think of William. He will be hurt as well. I will tell you this, that neither I nor Belle had any idea what that pillowcase was doing in the box until we went to the second bank."

Judge Marshall suggested that they leave the pillowcase in the box and report that there was an embroidered pillowcase in the box. They went to a nice restaurant that the bank clerks said that the locals visited. It served nice Italian food and Emily needed to recompose herself before the next stop. The judge noticed that Emily was very gentle and motherly towards Alfred. Mr. Blakeman had revealed to the judge, while they had waited during Louise's surgery, what Louise had tried to do to Vivian Black Williams, Emily's daughter at Comfield College. He couldn't understand how anyone could possibly want to protect someone like Louise and yet here she was trying just as hard as she could, to do just that. Emily was certainly a remarkable woman capable of so much compassion for someone that had tried to hurt her daughter.

Perhaps it was out of loyalty to her friend Bertie, but he suspected that it was her nature of just being a good and decent person. He understood the strength of that friendship by the secrets she had been asked to bear. He knew that Emily had taken on the responsibility of Bertie's care before she died and that she had recently lost her husband. Indeed, this woman had been through a lot of pain in the past year. Alfred had mentioned that she had a refugee child living with her and so he asked Emily about him.

"Alfred tells me that you have a Hungarian child refugee that you are in the process of adopting. What is that like?" he cleared his throat as if under stress.

"Paul Michael is the most amazing child I've ever known that's only six years old. When I got him just before Easter, he was severely malnourished and was absolutely filthy. He wore rags and shoes without socks and had the saddest eyes I believe I have ever seen. You've seen him now and he's nothing like he was when I first got him. He has gained weight, is extremely energetic, is a perfectionist when it comes to being neat and clean, and loves to read. He could speak very little English but you wouldn't know it now. I enrolled him in school thinking he would have to repeat the first grade but he met the challenge and was a star pupil of his class. He can print, read, spell, and do two-column addition," she said proudly.

"You sound like any other proud mother," he teased.

Emily blushed and said, "He also happens to be my late husband's cousin. All of Paul's other relatives that were in Hungary were either sent to concentration camps or killed in the war. Paul Michael was hidden by a friend of his grandfather's and he had written to Paul just before Paul was killed. Paul had kept letters that his parents had received from Hungary and some of the letters had been written mentioning the same man that had contacted me. We had other documentation of his identity and he will legally be my son in late September."

"Sounds like you are going to have many happy years together. He is very lucky that you have given him a nice home and a lot of love. I understand from some of the news reports that most of Eastern Europe is a disaster," Alfred interjected.

"Paul Michael told me about how the Germans came into the village and took a lot of their food and then when the Russians arrived, they took what little the villagers had left. Before he left he was eating what he called water soup. He will not play with soldiers, tanks, jeeps or other war toys like the other little boys at home and is still a little skittish around forest areas. He loves my farm where I used to live but does not like to go into the woods. It took some convincing by my son-in-law and his dad that there were no tanks, no cannons and no soldiers with guns in our woods. He loves to go to church and play chess. We are Catholic and since the masses are said in Latin he has gotten a lot of comfort there. He cries out in his sleep for his parents who were killed early in the war. I bought him a puppy to help him sleep," she added and then took a breath.

"Oh what kind did you get him?" Alfred perked up a little. "I had a puppy when I was a kid and loved mine."

"She's a red miniature dachshund that he named Poppy. He loves that little puppy and I can tell you that the feeling is definitely mutual. William has the litter mate and he's called his Gracie. I want you to know that Paul Michael calls me, Anya, which is Hungarian for mother. He called me that when I first laid hands on him and walked with him through the hotel lobby. He's now staying with an older Hungarian woman who is taking him to summer catechism classes while I'm here. Did you know that I now live only a few houses from your parents, Alfred? Perhaps you can come over and visit with us some time. He loves company and it seems that he bonds quickly with older males. Louise's brother is one of his best friends," Emily offered.

"I would love to meet him, but under the current circumstances I may not get a chance for a while. William has mentioned him to Louise and told us that he got a puppy as well," Alfred gave as slight smile.

"Nonsense, this is a court matter and not personal for me. You're both always welcome at my home. Now let me tell you about those puppies. Believe it or not, Belle actually went to Cartier's to buy them both dual dish pet bowls with their names engraved on them. Those little puppies have sure brought a lot of joy to our homes. Paul Michael and William have had several chess matches. By the way, do you happen to play chess Alfred?" Emily asked.

"I used to play all the time, why?" Alfred questioned.

"William and Paul Michael love to play. Paul Michael has beaten Mr. Blakeman, hasn't he?" Emily turned to ask Mr. Blakeman.

"He is a chess genius! I have never seen someone so young grasp the concepts so well. You should watch him work a jigsaw puzzle or do math. He is very gifted in many areas and a bundle of energy let me tell you!" Mr. Blakeman shook his head.

Alfred said, "I am going to have to meet this little fellow and challenge him to a chess match myself."

They enjoyed their meal and Judge Marshall spoke briefly about his late wife who had died several years ago. Emily asked about the Supreme Court work and how interesting it must be. All of them steered the conversation away from what had happened in New York. They had put it off long enough and after paying for the delicious meal, they left for the second bank.

In the second box were only two letters. The first one was in handwriting that neither Alfred nor Judge Marshall recognized. Emily told them that it had been written by Bertie's mother.

Dear Bertie,

I went by your house after you had left to live with Belle and felt that since you had left stuff in your house that you didn't want any of it. That uppity Belle wouldn't want some of those things but I ain't that picky. Anyways, I found me some pillows that I could use as well as some kitchen goods; shame on you for leaving perfectly good stuff at that cabin. I had to go during the night and leave before morning because those nosey Blacks would have told me to take the things back. I didn't feel like arguing with 'em and had to make several trips down to that old truck of your dad's. It 'bout wore me out.

I want you to know that I was going to keep protecting you but after you made me leave Louise's party and all and then told me not to come to her wedding I decided that you owed me and I mean to collect. You been livin' in that fancy house with your fancy clothes and here I am, 'bout desitute. Well I aim to get my share. Belle has ignored me and the others for too long and oughta pay us our due.

Anyways, I found this here pillowcase that you had hidden in the kindlin wood off the back porch. Now I got to thinking, why would you hide a perfectly good pillowcase? And do you know what I think? Jack didn't die from no heart attack. You killed him didn't you, girl? That's vomit and saliva on that pillowcase. You musta smothered him. Now you either pay me oh say $500 a month or I'm gonna tell the police. Think about it. I'll send the pillowcase when you give me the first payment. The other payments will keep me from telling Louise or William what you done!

Your momma

"Louise's grandmother was blackmailing Bertie! You meant to tell me that woman was blackmailing her own daughter?" Alfred was fuming!

"There are a lot of things she did to Bertie. This was the last stroke for Bertie. She made several payments to Martha as you can see by these copies of the bank drafts. That woman didn't have one ounce of decency in her whole miserable body. She backstabbed Bertie any and every chance she could after she had left home. Ask Belle, she will tell you what the real Martha Coleman was like. She had this strange bond with Louise and I'm sorry to say, she was a bigger influence on Louise than Bertie was, unfortunately." Emily conceded.

Alfred looked at the receipts and then began reading Bertie's letter.

Dear Emily,

I have to write this down so that you understand what happened the night Jack died. If you read momma's letter she accused me of killin' Jack. I killed Jack; indeed I smothered him just like my mom suspected. Jack had started putting his arms around little Louise like my daddy used to do to me. He would kiss Louise on the mouth and "beard" her little face until she cried. He started looking at her when she was asleep and commented on what a looker she was going to be when she got older. It was the same thing my father had done and said to me just before he raped me before I was ten.

I refused to allow him to rape Louise and so I killed him to protect her! My own mother allowed, in fact encouraged, my own father to rape me! She would bring him to my room and lock the door so I couldn't get out. It started just before I turned ten. I recognized the same look in Jack's eyes and panicked. Please forgive me Emily but I had to do it! I had to and would do it again to protect Louise.

I acted when he was passed out. I turned him over when he died so that he would be found face down. I hid the pillow and pillow case and came down to your house the next day to tell you I thought he was dead and Paul got the doctor there. The doctor said that Jack must have died of a heart attack which was what was typed on his death certificate. Please don't ever let Louise or William find out what I have done. I have paid for it every day since then. I know that sooner or later I will have to face judgment by the Good Lord for what I did, but I'm not sorry.

Take care of my children. Louise has gotten married and might need you from time to time. She's really not a bad person, just confused by my mother's bad influence. William, he can still be saved. Just don't let either of them know the truth. Swear to God that you will not tell them the truth. If my mother ever comes near or is hanging around William, please, please don't even let her talk to him or leave her alone with him for only a few minutes. She is mean enough to tell him what I done after I'm dead and gone. I love you Emily as though you were my sister. I wish you had of been. Maybe then I wouldn't have gotten myself into the mess I had with Jack.

Love, Bertie

Both men were quiet when they finished reading the letter. Alfred and Judge Marshall didn't quite know what to say. "What kind of woman would send her husband to rape his own daughters?" Alfred asked. "Louise thought that woman walked on water or something. It's no wonder she's so messed up in the head. I don't know what to say. I wish now that I hadn't read it."

Emily looked down and said quietly, "I know that you must report your findings but, can't the actual letters stay here? They wouldn't do anything except hurt Louise and William. I wouldn't hurt Bertie when she was alive and I will fight to keep her memory of being a fine woman and a good mother alive. You can report that there were some personal correspondences or something, just don't tell what's in them."

Judge Marshall shook his head slightly and wiped his brows with his hand and said, "There is nothing in this box that I would judge belongs to either Louise Pierce Perkins or to William Pierce. It would be my ruling in a courtroom that the letters are yours to do with as you wish. I believe that you like any decent human being would rule the same way."

"The problem is what do we say to Louise?" Alfred asked.

"Belle and I warned you that the contents of the boxes would only cause harm. Now, it cannot be undone. You know how Louise has made very bad choices and now perhaps you can understand why she did if she was in counsel with such a woman as her grandmother. I cannot tell you what to do, but I would suggest that you tell her the truth that there were two letters and an embroidered pillowcase. If she asks about the letters you could say they were about leaving the hollow and her engagement party. I wouldn't mention the contents of the one that was from her grandmother. Louise would definitely want to see it," Emily suggested.

Judge Marshall raised his eyebrows and said, "Well, that is the truth, but you are omitting some important details."

"But would those details, that are being left out, do harm or good? Isn't justice about doing what's right? How would this alter the past, present, or future? Judge Anderson said that you were to decide whether or not she should be given the items from the box. Would it benefit anyone to give her those letters? They were written to me. Whatever you decide I will abide by, I may not like it, but I will follow your judgment," Emily stressed.

Judge Marshall said, "The letters stay in the boxes or may be destroyed. They belong to you now Emily. They are addressed to you and therefore are your property. Let's leave it like that. Now let's go home." He said to Alfred.

Mr. Blakeman had deliberately kept quiet at the bank and let Emily, Alfred, and the Judge work things out. If they were satisfied, he was satisfied. They went out together to eat supper. Alfred and Judge Marshall's flight was scheduled to leave at ten the next morning and they would arrive in Charleston around noon. Emily's and Mr. Blakeman's flight was scheduled to leave at ten thirty in the morning and arriving in Chicago around two o'clock central time.

Emily called Belle first to check on Louise and reported that all was well. She then called her old cabin and Mrs. Novak answered. Paul Michael was enjoying the summer catechism and Mrs. Novak had fixed him some cabbage with homemade noodles served with home-made Kielbasa. He helped Josef in the barn to feed the chickens and helped her around the house. They were going to go blackberry picking in the next few days and make some preserves. Paul Michael was doing well but he reported that Poppy was having trouble with the cows. She yapped at them and they ignored her and he declared, "That just made her madder." Paul Michael talked with Emily about catechism, the chickens, and Poppy. Poppy had run across the field between the house and barn chasing a butterfly. She had gotten a tick on her ear and Mrs. Novak took care of it. Emily promised to call the next night and wanted to hear about all those jars of preserves they had made.

Emily, Alfred, Judge Marshall, and Mr. Blakeman had a rather tense dinner until Emily told them about the adventures of Poppy. They chuckled as they imagined watching the little dachshund barking at a cow. Alfred spoke little and after dinner Emily asked him to escort her to her room. As she neared her room she turned to him suddenly and asked, "Do you love her?" When he nodded his head she said, "Then do what you must. Knowing what you do now, she may need to see a psychiatrist to get her mind straight and to do that she will need professional help. Just dealing with the hysterectomy, the hot flashes, and the mood swings is enough, but dealing with the guilt about what she has done to her own body and your child will need to be addressed. Only when she is ready to begin healing her mind and her heart, will she truly start healing and be like the little girl I remember. It will be hard, but you have to forgive her. You may never forget what she has done, but if you love her, then forgive her. After a while, when she gets better, you may decide to adopt. Now that the war is over there will be more refugee children from Europe as well as all the orphans right here in the states. Don't decide now when you are hurting so much, but give yourself time to heal your wounds." She kissed his cheek as she turned to go into her room.

Everyone caught their flights on time and as Emily landed in Chicago, she hadn't realized how tightly she had been gripping the armrests. When they went to pick up their luggage, Mr. Blakeman's wife was there waiting for them with Robert, Jr. Emily liked her a lot and greeted her with a kiss on the cheek and shook little Robert's hand. They drove Emily to the Palmer House hotel where she would be staying in the Penthouse suite. She would be hosting dinners in her suite with her new business associates as well as the Blakeman's. The large living area of the room allowed her to receive guests for cocktails or for them just to visit. The marbled surround tub and luxurious robe made it a comfortable room for the next week. She called Belle for further details and the agenda was set.

The current owners of the companies Belle had purchased set up tours of their facilities over the next few days and she met the employees. She took notes about the facilities and interviewed employees that she chose at random. She wanted to get a good idea about current working conditions and their input. She asked poignant questions and checked for herself on any problem areas. She made various suggestions to the current supervisors and watched their reactions. Some seemed open to the changes while others seemed to ignore her. She fired the latter and promoted the former. Products were only as good as the employees. Happy employees would make better products. She expected all of her employees to listen and support her decisions from the top down.

Mr. Blakeman had each of the corporations' attorneys on hand about the legal issues concerning current conditions. One facility had union workers and Emily wanted to meet with the union representatives in the factory lounge. She ordered a meal to be delivered and listened to their complaints. They had come prepared to ask for a 30 minute lunch and she offered them a 45 minute lunch and a 15 minute break. She offered split shifts for women who had children so they could be available when their children were at home. She wanted better health insurance for the employees and a better lounge area. Overtime would be offered to those employees who had the best ratings by their supervisors and by seniority. Salaried employees were to alternate weekend shifts. She asked for each employee to be committed to making the best product and would be given a discount on any purchases they made. The attorneys were shocked and the union reps weren't sure that she was serious until she told all of the company's attorneys to "Make it happen."

She invited the reps and top executives to dinner and held it in her suite. The dinner was strained at the beginning, but open conversations were being held by the end of the dinner. The end of the war would bring veterans wanting their old jobs back. Emily had no intention of firing anyone and decided to expand the business to accommodate the returning veterans. With split shifts and working weekends, there would be a lot of openings once they expanded.

The second company that made playpens was a nightmare. There was little ventilation and the lighting was extremely poor. She decided to shut the factory down and keep only key personnel around until a lot of improvements could be made. The other 100 employees were given two weeks of paid vacation. The single employee bathroom was disgusting and she insisted that not only was another one needed, but additional stalls in each were to be installed. The machinery was new, but some of the wood stock was old and she initiated a cycling system of inventory so that new would be placed behind the older wood with date received written on the ends of the boards. The lathes were in good shape and so were the sanders.

She hired four full-time custodial staff to keep the factory clean, as well as the break room, the bathrooms, floor, etc. The wood shavings were to be recycled into pressed wood particleboard that could be used for the base of the play pens and cribs. In two weeks time the employees would return to a brighter cleaner work space that would be organized. The news about the additional bathrooms was well received and she asked the employees to elect a spokesman to sit on her board. They weren't union workers because of their size but she wanted a spokesperson that she could speak with about any issues. She was exhausted but pleased with the results of her efforts.

She made frequent calls daily to Belle to tell her about her suggestions for improvements and Belle was well pleased. When Emily told her that she had prototypes made for the new cribs and playpens and she wanted a closer look at the one that could convert from a playpen to a play yard, Belle knew that Emily was going to be a success. Emily had concerns about the rails and so they were moved in closer together to prevent little heads from getting stuck between them. She did not like the ones that converted from a crib to a playpen due to possible flaws in the design. She wouldn't trust it and she didn't think other mothers would either.

She had called Paul Michael each and every day and one day he bragged about Poppy answering commands in Hungarian. Emily had treated each of her companies' employees to a Chicago Cubs ball game. She had purchased Cubs hats for William and Paul Michael as well as pennants. She purchased several board games at FAO Schwartz and bought Paul Michael some clothes for the upcoming school year.

She caught a flight to Charleston and she planned to ride back to Welfield along with Belle and William in her limo. While she had waited at the airport to be picked up by Belle and William, she was surprised when she was paged by Judge Marshall. He drove her straight to Alfred's house and was she was warmly welcomed by Belle and Alfred. Louise was now recuperating in a sanitarium just outside of Charleston. She was currently receiving psychiatric help. Alfred told Emily that he visited Louise on the weekends and the doctor had said she could be there for up to six months. Alfred had purchased a Bishon Frise puppy as a surprise for Louise. William was responsible for the house breaking and so far he had been highly successful. Alfred had named the puppy, Gigi and Emily couldn't help but laugh at the white powder puff running towards her. Alfred and Louise had a beautiful home with gorgeous furniture and Emily commented that obviously Louise had exquisite taste. It was definitely the most sophisticated home that Emily had ever been in and the white fur ball fit in nicely.

William loved his hat and pennant and other gifts that Emily had gotten for him while Belle was very pleased with the contracts and changes she had made at the factories. Emily was a born business woman capable of organizing them as well as she did her own home. Belle had gotten rave reports from all of the attorneys, union reps, employees, and company executives. Production was already up and morale was high in one of the factories. It took more than three hours for them to go over the contracts, stipulations, and plans. Belle decided that Emily was going to need a secretary and when they returned to Welfield she would call Mr. Blakeman to help find her one.

Alfred took everyone to dinner at the Daniel Boone hotel and Emily stayed the night there. She did not want to agitate or cause Louise to have a relapse by finding out that Emily had stayed in her home. Judge Marshall joined them for dinner and reported that Judge Anderson was satisfied that his orders had been followed in regards to the safety deposit boxes. The issue was now considered closed.

Emily felt a bit fatigued the next morning and was ready to get home. Vivian had called her a few times and was excited to have another month, without any problems, completed in her pregnancy. John teased that she was showing a little bit and claimed that she now glowed. She had two more days of the first summer term left and would begin the new one on the following Monday. She was taking Intro to business management and Microeconomics. Emily tried to visualize her baby girl being pregnant and could hardly wait to see her.

It seemed like it took forever for them to get to Welfield and she was exhausted but happy to finally be home. Mrs. Novak called and told Emily that she would have Paul Michael home within the hour. Emily was amazed at how much he and Poppy had both grown. He came running from the car yelling, "Anya, Anya, Anya!" He looked at least an inch taller and was now slightly tanned. He had freckles on his face now and a huge smile. Poppy seemed almost twice as long as she had been and was now a whopping three pounds in weight. Her ears were still longer than her legs and she gave doggie kisses to Emily. Poppy had been given a bath and Emily bragged about her shiny red coat. Paul Michael presented Emily with jars of blackberry, cherry, and raspberry preserves. He told her that he had also been very busy. She gave him his baseball cap and pennant and when she explained how it went on his wall he asked for it to be done immediately so he could see how it looked.

She had him model his new clothes and chuckled when he hammed it up a bit. He posed like he had seen the mannequins in GC Murphy's. Mrs. Novak had taken him to the store on Fridays to buy a comb and some Calamine lotion. She was surprised when they went by the candy counter and he had only asked for one extra large jawbreaker. It set her back a whole 2 cents.

Paul Michael had unfortunately discovered the only patch of poison ivy anywhere around the farm and had gotten it onto his little arms and neck. It was now almost healed after Mrs. Novak had suggested that he use water weed, found along the railroad, on the pustules. It dried them up in only a couple of days. She told Emily that he had been well-behaved and she had enjoyed speaking Hungarian with him. Josef had been glad to have the company in the barn and Paul Michael did a good job feeding the chickens and weeding the garden. They had picked more strawberries and he helped wash up the dishes.

Paul Michael had told her that she cooked like his grandmother and was pleased when she had made jellied pig's feet. That had been one of his favorites and she told Emily that he had eaten until he could hold no more. Emily said, "Paul tried to get me to make it, but I tried several times and gave up. Kocsonya was one of the few Hungarian dishes I couldn't learn how to make. Paul made it for us and I have to admit, I loved it. Thank you again for taking such good care of my boy."

Chapter 9

Emily caught up on her mail when she returned home and was pleased when a secretary finally arrived two days after her return from Chicago. Emily had already purchased an oak file cabinet and boxes of file folders. Within three hours stacks of folders with contracts, spreadsheets, employee rosters, blueprints, etc. had been filed and cross-referenced. Her new secretary was a WWII veteran who had been injured in the Philippines and was missing his left foot. He had a prosthetic foot and could get around as well as anyone. He had once been an aide to General McArthur and had been in a jeep when they were hit by a mortar shell. Mr. Jethro Jenkins was his name and he had asked Emily to just call him JJ.

Emily was pleased that she could once again able to see the top of her desk and since JJ would handle all packages, mail, phone calls and telegrams, she could now focus on local issues. She wanted to go up to Filbert Mountain and asked the driver to get the car ready. She was almost ready to leave when JJ told her that she received a call from an Alfred Perkins. He was visiting his parents and wanted to walk over to meet Paul Michael and Poppy.

Emily called Judge Perkins and asked to speak with Alfred. She told him, "By all means to come down and bring Gigi with you." In a few minutes time, Poppy jumped up and began barking towards the front door. She ran to the front door and sat down with her tail wagging. Emily's butler answered the door and announced that Alfred Perkins and Gigi had arrived. Paul Michael squealed with delight when he saw Gigi. The two puppies started chasing each other so fast that their little legs went out from under them each time they completed a lap through the living room dining room, parlor,

163

office, kitchen, etc. They finally stopped when they got worn out and sat down by their respective masters.

When Emily introduced Paul Michael to Alfred, the little boy shook his hand and said, "I am pleased to meet you." Emily smiled as Alfred returned the greeting. Paul Michael asked him questions about Gigi and sat down timidly beside Alfred on the couch. Since Emily had a cast iron fence with a stone wall on the lower part of the back yard, the two dogs were let out to play. Emily said that she was going up to Filbert Mountain and asked Alfred if he would like to join them. "Sure," he answered. "Why are you going up there?" he asked. "Are you having a party up there?"

"No, I'm just going up to check my property," she offered. "Alfred, I'm the owner of the Sportsman's Club and cabins. I was the one who wrote the contract for your rehearsal dinner you had last year."

"You're kidding me!" he laughed. "I have a friend up there now, Judge Marshall, but you already knew that, right?"

"No, the caretaker has been signing the contracts while I have been out of town and JJ just filed them for me. I'm sorry I didn't introduce him to you sooner. Let's take care of that right now. JJ is my new secretary and Belle found him for me. So do you want to go with us or not?" she asked again as they walked towards her office.

"Sure, I'll drive!" he offered.

Emily called her driver to tell him that she wouldn't need him after all after introducing Alfred to JJ. The driver pulled the 1939 Ford back into the garage. As they walked to the Perkins home, she mentioned that she needed to buy a new car but had no idea of what kind to even look for. Alfred set Gigi into the house and got his car keys. When he opened the car door, Paul Michael parked himself in the front seat between Emily and Alfred and when they went by the underpass in Jackson, Paul Michael said, "Anya has a farm up there."

"She does?" he asked.

"Yes sir and my Anya has chickens, bees, pigs, and cows on her farm. I picked berries up there and I found some poison ivy all by myself. Do you know how to milk a cow Alfred?" Paul Michael asked with a grin.

"No, I don't believe I have. Have you?" he shot back.

"Yes sir, Josef showed me. I helped Mrs. Novak make some jam. It's very good. We will be making apple butter in a few weeks. We will be picking peaches this weekend, maybe you could come and help," he paused and asked, "Anya, can, I mean, may Alfred help pick peaches this weekend?"

"If he wants to help, he may certainly come and help," she answered. They had come to the bottom of the mountain and Paul Michael pointed out some heavily loaded berry vines. "Josef told me to be careful because there are briars on the vines. They'll poke your skin and you have to wear long sleeves. You want to pick some berries?"

"Well if we find something to put them in and the owner doesn't mind, we can come back here some day and pick some while your Anya takes care of business. Ok?" he smiled down at Paul Michael.

"Ok!" Paul Michael said.

"I hope you know that he knows exactly where the cook in the lodge keeps the lard buckets. I'm afraid that you are going to be picking berries today! I'll only need about an hour or so," Emily said seriously.

"There's Judge Marshall," he pointed at cabin #15. He pulled into a parking space and Paul Michael took off in the direction of the lodge. Emily knew he would be a few minutes while he greeted everyone in the lodge. She heard his light knock on the back door of the kitchen and heard a familiar voice call out from the main lodge, "Hello Paul Michael, come on in."

Alfred walked over and called to Judge Marshall just as Emily was going towards the caretaker's cabin. She saw him rounding the back of the lodge and he waved and walked her way. "I knew you were here when the cook recognized Paul Michael as he came into the kitchen. He is in there catching up on the news and is inspecting the kitchen. He found a few pots and pans out of order and is asking for three lard pails." Emily laughed and told him about taking a young friend berry picking. Alfred was walking towards her while the caretaker walked behind Paul Michael who was running towards her from the other side with three lard buckets.

Alfred introduced Judge Marshall to Paul Michael and explained that the judge wanted to help them pick berries. He had mentioned about the berry picking and the judge asked if he could join them.

"Ok! With the three of us picking, we might be able to pick enough to make some preserves. We better go before the sun gets on those vines. Snakes come out when the sun shines on the vines," Paul Michael stated with such authority that the two men grabbed their buckets. Judge Marshall said, "You heard him man, let's get going" and laughed.

Emily toured the lodge and looked over the reservations for the cabins and lodges. She had thought on her way home to have a check out card made which would give guests an opportunity to rate the cabins and/or lodge with categories like cleanliness, comfort, friendliness, accommodations, service, and value. She asked for his input and he thought to perhaps add the option of having food available in case they wanted to eat at the lodge when there wasn't a special event planned on the contract. They could also add a comment or special request section so that they could get ideas of how to make the resort area more pleasing. She didn't want to add too much to the area because it would lose the atmosphere that she wanted so much to create on top of the mountain.

All of the cabins were rented through Thanksgiving now for weekends and the lodge was usually booked solid through Halloween for weddings, family reunions, and celebrations. Winter was the slow season and unless they could provide perhaps a sleigh or wagon for the guests to get up the mountain it was going to be difficult for them to get more guests to stay in the cabins during the winter months. She asked him what he thought about putting a second parking lot at the bottom of the mountain and arranging for a lodge taxi to carry guests to and from the cabins. It could run from 9:00am to 5:00pm on the hour and every half hour in the winter. The resort would need to have at least two cars and the caretaker said his wife could drive one and he could drive the other.

"No, she will have to be available if something comes up. There are some lumber men that don't work in the winter; perhaps we could hire two of them to run the taxis. Let me check with my attorney about liability insurance and other costs. What kind of vehicle could get up this mountain in the winter?" she asked.

"Well a truck could do it, but an army Jeep, like they use over in Europe would be even better. It definitely would be able to make it," he suggested.

"I have no idea how we could get two Jeeps, but I can buy us two trucks. In the spring and summer we can use them to transport equipment, groceries, etc. If we had tarps we could protect the guests' luggage from the weather and any dirt. Let me talk it over and find out the costs versus income to see if it's cost effective. If we could advertise the service, we could perhaps fill about a fourth up to half of the cabins in the winter. Any more than that and we could definitely pay off both of the trucks in a single winter season," she reasoned.

They continued the survey of the property and Emily noticed a few areas in the parking area that had deep dips and could mess up a vehicle. "We will need to get some gravel to fill those holes and smooth it out with rakes," she said as she jotted that down on her notes. They continued around the property and had just finished the lap when Alfred's car appeared and Paul Michael was grinning from ear to ear. "Anya we have more than enough berries to make some pies!"

Judge Marshall indicated that it had been a while since he had berry pie and Paul Michael said his Anya could make him one. The judge told Emily the plan they had cooked up while they were picking the berries. "Paul Michael invited us for dinner and said you could serve us the berry pie." Paul Michael was nodding and she thought, 'He can't be offering dinner invitations without my knowledge beforehand.'

The judge must have read her mind and said, "I informed Paul Michael that only the owner of the house could invite guests to meals and so I invited Paul Michael, Alfred, and you to dine with me and have berry pie."

Emily was about to decline when she saw Paul Michael looking up at the judge biting his lower lip. "Well if I can call cook before she starts supper that will be fine. May I ask who will be making the pie?" Paul Michael piped up, "You, Anya!"

The guys laughed and she shook her head as though defeated and said, "I would be honored to make the pie." Emily went into the lodge and called her cook. The cook was preparing lunch and had not yet started on their supper. Emily gave her the afternoon off and told her that she and Paul Michael had two pies to make this afternoon for his friends and that they had been invited to dine out for supper. When she told the guys the news, they all grinned and the Judge said, "I'll see you around 7pm then."

Emily smiled and waved as they left the parking lot and Paul Michael told her about their berry picking adventure all the way down the mountain.

Emily asked Alfred if he knew anything about the new model cars and he offered to take her the next day to the area dealerships to select a car. She thanked him for an enjoyable morning and for the berries. Alfred offered to drive them once more up the mountain.

Alfred unloaded the three buckets of berries and he carried two of them and Paul Michael carried the third into the kitchen. Cook approved of the plump berries and Paul Michael said, "Anya is making us some pies."

"Oh she is. Did you give her permission to cook in my kitchen?" she asked with a wink.

"Yes ma'am, I did," he nodded.

Cook told him to go wash his face and hands for lunch and the maid set the table. Emily asked Alfred to join them, but he declined. He would be eating lunch with his parents. Paul Michael ate his lunch and then went out to play with Poppy. Emily took her lists of tasks that needed to be completed at the club to JJ. She asked him to create a comment card with the categories she had given him. He would need to order gravel, check on the price of trucks, tarps, and liability for transportation of guests with Mr. Blakeman.

She changed her clothes and donned her apron. As cook cleaned up the lunch dishes, Emily had mixed her lard, flour, salt, and ice cold water to make pie crusts. She rolled out two round of dough and lined two pie pans. She cleaned and dried the berries and poured one-fourth into each pie pan. She sliced some butter into thin slats and placed them on top of the berries about two inches apart. She mixed flour, sugar, and spices and poured one fourth on each pie and then split the remaining berries into the two pie pans and repeated the process with the butter and flour mixture. She rolled out two more rounds and cut slits into each. She gently unfolded the top crust and with her fingers, folded the extra crusts under the top crust and used her thumbs to primp around the edges. She brushed the tops with egg whites and when the pies were cooling about an hour later, cook told Mrs. Carlson that the pies looked like something out of a magazine. Her mistress not only could cook, but she could cook well.

Emily insisted that Paul Michael take a bath before leaving for dinner. He did so and asked if Poppy could have one too. Poppy was bathed by Emily's driver who volunteered for the job. Paul Michael wore a pair of shorts and shirt while Emily had on an afternoon dress. Alfred came at 6:30pm to pick up the rest of the judge's dinner party. Cook had covered the pies with towels and Alfred set them in a box in the back seat. Everyone and the pies arrived to the Judge's cabin a few minutes before seven.

The judge's cook had prepared a lovely dinner with a salad, fresh melon, grilled chicken, creamed cucumbers, and pilaf. The dinner was wonderful and everyone ate their fill of pie. Paul Michael had berries on his cheeks and his chin. The four of them had finished an entire pie when the men had seconds!

They sat out on the porch and Paul Michael asked Alfred to help him catch some lightning bugs to put in a jar. The two had quite a time catching the lightning bugs. Judge Marshall and Emily spoke little as Emily carefully watched Paul Michael. He ran up to show her his jar of bugs and it was like having a lantern when the bugs lit up! She told him that he would have to let them go or they would die. "But I caught them, why do I have to let them go? The Germans didn't!" That innocent comment caught the judge's attention.

"What do you mean Paul Michael?" he asked.

"The Germans never let anyone go. Once they caught someone they didn't let them go," Paul Michael said sadly. "Sometimes they took them to camps far away. That's what happened to my grandfather. They took him away and didn't let him go."

The judge gently suggested, "That's why the Germans surrendered. They were the bad guys and now everyone they took away that didn't die is being released. Do you understand?"

"Yes sir, I do. My grandfather will never come back for me though and that's why I'm here with my Anya," he whispered.

The judge countered, "And wouldn't your grandfather want you to be with Anya and be free?"

"Yes sir," as he unscrewed the lid. Some of the bugs flew out and others stayed inside the jar.

"Look Judge Marshall, some of them don't want to leave! Can I keep those?" Paul Michel asked.

"Just watch," the judge said with a smile.

Slowly the bugs climbed out of the jar until all had flown away. Paul Michael said, "We can catch them another day!" Emily said it was his bed time and to thank the judge for dinner. Paul Michael thanked him for dinner and asked if he could come again. "Anytime, my friend, you may return anytime."

By the time they were at the bottom of the mountain Paul Michael's head was in Emily's lap. Alfred carried the little boy to his bed and thanked Emily for a lovely day. He was glad that he had met Paul Michael. It was the first day in over a month that he hadn't worried himself over Louise's recovery when he wasn't at work. Alfred told Emily he would be by around nine in the morning to take her to the car dealerships.

Paul Michael was ready for a new adventure the next day when Emily told him they were going to go and look for a new car. He almost choked on his breakfast trying to eat too quickly and she told him to slow down. The car dealer wouldn't be open until nine. Emily had asked the driver to follow them to the dealerships to help select a car since he would be the one doing most of the driving.

When Alfred knocked on the door, Poppy was waiting for him. She attacked his shoelaces with vigor until she remembered JJ and returned to the office to go after his. Alfred had done some serious thinking and told her he was thinking about adopting a child. Louise couldn't have his child, but they could always adopt a child. He adored Paul Michael and told her that there had to be thousands just like him in Europe. He would raise the subject with Louise when she was a little stronger. A child might heal some of the deep wounds that had almost killed their marriage.

Alfred took her to a Chevy dealership and she didn't find anything she liked. At the Ford dealership Emily and the driver looked over a '45 Lincoln. It was a beauty and had a wooden dash panel with ivory knobs. The seats were real leather and the dealer offered to take them on a test drive and she agreed. By noon, the driver returned her home in the new Lincoln. Emily gave the driver the '39 to use as if it was his own personal car. Any staff member could borrow it for shopping, holidays, etc. and would make the arrangements to use it through JJ.

Emily decided to purchase two Ford trucks for the club and both had truck beds with raised sides. Two passengers could ride with the driver on each trip. She bought a used truck to carry supplies, etc. and had the new trucks painted with the Sportsman's Club logo on the cab doors. Those would be used for guests' transportation and a custom wood cover was ordered that could be used on one of the trucks.

She had the dealer deliver the trucks to the lodge and asked JJ to type up an ad for the winter months advertising taxi service up and down the mountain. Also, she told him he would need to find someone to level a parking area at the base of the mountain for guests to park their vehicles. A small cabin would be built with heat and a restroom would provide protection for guards to keep 24 hour security for the guests' vehicles. The two trucks together cost $8000 and the used truck was $475. She would get her money back with only 2 months' rental fees.

Paul Michael called to Anya from the living room to ask if they could visit Belle and William. When she had a clear calendar she called Belle and told Belle that apparently it was time for a Paul Michael and Poppy invasion. Belle was delighted and the trio rode in the back of the new Lincoln at once to her house. William was keen over the new car and looked it over with interest. Paul Michael went to look for Gracie and her yap gave away her location. Gracie was in the living room waiting and the two dachshunds greeted each other and began their game of chase. Paul Michael talked to Belle about their dinner with Alfred and Judge Marshall and Belle smiled as he described the lightning bug round up.

Belle thanked Emily for taking such good care of Alfred during his visit. She told her that Louise was going to be discharged in September while Emily told Belle about buying the new trucks for taxiing guests. Guests in the summer could arrive by train and could now be driven up to the mountain instead of trying to hire a car or possibly catching a ride themselves with a local, friend, or relative.

Emily finally told Belle about Vivian's pregnancy and her Christmas due date. Belle was absolutely ecstatic. Belle would now have to complete some of the arrangements for the various business ventures once the baby arrived. She was so happy for Vivian and John who were the kind of people who were born to be parents. They were so good with both William and Paul Michael. As far as Belle was concerned, John and Vivian were two people who needed a whole house full of children. Belle was happy for Emily as well. Paul Michael had given her a reason to get up each day and renewed her zest for life. Paul would have loved being with Paul Michael. It was a shame that Emily couldn't have had more children. But then, God had sent Paul Michael just when she had needed him the most.

Emily invited Belle to go with her to Bluestone to do some back to school shopping. Belle agreed and they decided to go on the upcoming Saturday. In exactly one month, the boys would be returning to school. They made a list of needed items and asked the boys if they had forgotten anything. Paul Michael heard the word school and was eager to go at any time. Emily had to take him to the library to get some new books. He was reading 40 to 50 page books and his vocabulary was growing by leaps and bounds. He would retell Emily the stories and needed help every now and then with longer words. William was spending his summer days with his best friend, Marcella, a girl who had been in all of his classes since the first grade. They were going to be painting Marcella's living room with her mom and he was looking forward to it. Marcella came over to the house to work on school projects during school months and the two worked on a variety of special projects during the summer months.

The women went shopping and Emily was pleased to find that Paul Michael now wore a size 7 and his feet had also grown one full size. There were sweaters, jackets, socks, new underclothes, and pants to buy. Paul Michael needed a new belt and Emily bought one that would fit a size 7/8 waist. Several more weeks passed and Emily received a call from Charleston. Judge Marshall told her he was arriving for an extended visit with Judge Perkins and wanted to invite her as his guest to a special dinner in his honor at the Country Club. Emily declined the offer but told him how honored she was to even be asked. The truth of the matter was that Emily had no intention of ever going out with anyone. Her Paul had been gone less than six months and she still mourned him as if it had only occurred.

Judge Marshall called a week later and asked if he might come over for a brief visit. He came to apologize for the insensitivity he had exhibited with his recent invitation. He assured her that the invitation was merely to be as a dinner companion and not a date, but understood her predicament and apologized. Paul Michael was so excited when he came to the door that Poppy ran to see who it could be that had caused him to jump up and down. She didn't recognize the judge and backed up a little and barked with great ferocity. JJ called to her and she went off to the office in search of his shoe laces. The judge stayed for coffee and returned to the Perkins home a few minutes later.

Cook looked at the maid and winked when the judge had left. Mrs. Emily shouldn't be lonely and he seemed like he was such a nice man. They knew her husband had only died in March, but she was young and so nice. They wanted her to be happy. They would contact the cook and maids at the Perkins home and see what could be done from that end. Emily had thanked him for his kind offer and for his acknowledgement of her mourning. She watched as he walked down the front walkway and returned to her work. 'He's a very nice man but he isn't my Paul,' she thought.

Belle's maid received a call from her sister, Judge Perkins maid, and happened to mention a dinner honoring Judge Marshall was going to be at the Country Club and wondered if Belle was going to attend. She found out that Belle was going and had asked William to be her escort for the evening. When she had lunch with Emily a few days later, she asked if she had been invited to Judge Marshall's dinner. Emily told her she had received a very nice invitation in the mail after Judge Marshall's visit. The dinner was scheduled for Saturday and she had not responded and tomorrow was the cutoff date.

"I received the invitation and haven't sent my regrets. I'll have to get JJ to do it for me," Emily shook her head. "I have been incredibly busy and just didn't get around to it. Are you going?"

"Of course I'm going. He was a dear friend to Bertie and William thinks the world of him. I will never forget how he helped us out with that sticky situation with those boxes. I would never even consider not going to the dinner. I suppose you have your own reasons, but I do think you owe him something for his assistance with Louise. Perhaps you will reconsider," Belle hinted.

The maid removed the soup bowls and spoons from the table and reported to the kitchen that their plan just might work. Mrs. Coleman was talking about the dinner right now. The maid returned with the luncheon plates with chicken salad, sliced tomatoes, and a roll. Belle and Emily were deep in conversation and didn't notice the kitchen door slightly ajar. Emily was speaking, "I know what you are saying, but it's just too soon after Paul's death. I cannot go and be seen with another man so soon, I just can't."

"Well, what if William was your escort? I can go with Judge Marshall. He asked me after I had asked William. It might not be too late," she stressed. "No one could criticize you for going with William, no one."

"I don't know. I just hate leaving Paul Michael on a weekend night. He will be going back to school soon and I don't like leaving him," Emily argued.

"But the dinner isn't until 8:00pm and he will be in bed by 7:30pm. Now why don't you go with us? It would mean so much to me to see you there," Belle said.

"Well I guess I could go if only for a little while. Just long enough to put in an appearance you understand," Emily said as she finally surrendered. "You understand that it would only be for a little while. I'll have my driver take me for only an hour or so and you ride back home with me."

In the kitchen the cook and maid were celebrating. They would take extra care to make sure she looked her best. After about twenty minutes the maid went in to freshen up their tea and removed their plates. When she returned with a mousse dessert, she reported that the two women were talking about their gowns.

"I suppose I could wear my black gown with a high collar," Emily said while Belle thought, 'Oh dear' and said, "I was thinking of that lovely blue gown we bought last year. The one with the matching cape we bought at Clarice's on Madison Avenue. It would be so beautiful with Bertie's blue diamond pendant. After all, I'm sure that he would want to see it after it started all that business with Louise."

"You don't think the gown would look too forward?" Emily asked.

"Of course it wouldn't. This isn't the Victorian age, dearie, where you would have worn black for a year. Now have your maid set it out to loosen some of the wrinkles. She'll know what to do," Belle stated in a matter of fact manner. Belle glanced up and winked to the maid looking out the kitchen door. The maid quickly moved and told the cook about the gown.

Emily enjoyed the rest of lunch and Paul Michael returned from a visit with his friend George. Poppy came running out of the office to greet her young master and Paul Michael picked her up to go outside. He wanted to play fetch with a little ball that George had given to him for just that purpose. Emily had gone to the cemetery every Saturday and sometimes she went with Paul Michael and other times she went without him. Because of the dinner, this would be the first Saturday that she didn't go to the cemetery while being in Welfield. She would have to go there sometime during the week.

The women adjourned to the living room and as Emily passed the office and told JJ to accept the judge's invitation to the dinner. He grinned and said eagerly, "Yes ma'am!"

He rang up the Perkins home and the maid answered. He told her, "Mrs. Emily Black is accepting the invitation to the Marshall banquet," and then whispered, "So far, so good!"

Emily's maid suggested that she have her hair put up into a pompadour. It would look better with the gown. "I could do it for you ma'am. My sister is a hairdresser and showed me how." The maid added a capful of bath scents the bath she drew for Emily. She fixed Emily's hair and added some crystals attached by bobby pins that she just happened to have. She suggested just a little rouge and powder, after all "You don't want folks to think you're sick or something, now do you Ms. Emily?"

The maid looked onto Emily like her pet project and was satisfied with the results. She was naturally a pretty woman but now with a little help, she looked spectacular. The blue diamond pendant sparkled at her throat and she had on blue and white diamond earrings. The diamond bracelet had been last year's birthday gift from Paul and it was the first time she had worn it. He had surprised her with it by placing it on his pillow so that she found it when she awakened. Emily smiled to herself as she remembered he had made her breakfast in bed that morning. He had a lot of chores to do but had gotten up early to make her breakfast. Her eyes became teary when she remembered finding the bracelet. He had simply said, "I dreamed I bought you one of those bracelets. Well, what do you know? Dreams do come true." He had gotten up from the table, kissed her on the forehead, and had told her, "Enjoy your breakfast. I need to go check on things in the barn."

Emily's driver called to tell Emily that he had a terrible bout of nausea and vomiting and couldn't possibly drive her to the country club. He suggested that perhaps Judge Perkins had room for her in his car. Emily told him to rest and quickly rang up Judge Perkins. Judge Perkins and his wife were just leaving when they received her call and assured her that there was plenty of room in their car. She would have to ride in the back seat with Judge Marshall. Emily didn't have a choice since Belle had called her just a few minutes earlier that she was leaving. Emily could either not go and be talked about or go and be talked about. She would go, but only if she could sit with Belle and William.

When the Perkins car arrived at the club, photographers took pictures of Judge Marshall and the lovely Emily Black he helped get out of the car. It was at that moment that Emily realized that it all had been a setup. She smiled and walked into the country club and found Belle and William. She was about to sit down when another lady informed her that was her seat. The table was full and they had all been assigned seats. "I suppose your seat is somewhere else, my dear. You were seated last and that was probably because you waited so long to respond." Emily's face had reddened because of the lady's rude remark and was about to leave when Belle called a waiter over for her. "Please ask Mrs. Perkins where Emily Black is to be seated," Belle spoke softly as the other lady snuggled into her seat. He returned and guided her to the head table. Emily found that she was to be seated right beside the Judge at the head table looking down upon the rude woman sitting several rows towards the back. He stood up as she came near the table and assisted her with her chair. Emily felt her face burn as she felt all eyes of the club were upon her. She just knew they were thinking how terrible she was to be seen so soon after Paul's death with another man.

The speeches given by other justices were entertaining as they told funny anecdotes about the judge. One of his assistants told of his interest in refugee children in the last few months and how he had personally assisted in getting a little boy from Hungary on a Red Cross ship for a friend in Welfield. Emily's mouth opened to say something but she couldn't speak until the assistant was finished. So that was how Paul Michael had gotten to the states so much sooner than planned and the judge had never said a word to her about his intervention.

After the speeches dinner was served and Emily whispered, "I'm grateful you got Paul Michael here sooner, but you should have told me."

Judge Marshall whispered, "You can thank Belle she's the one that got me interested. I placed my 100th orphaned refugee last week. I am stepping down from the Supreme Court after this term and devote more time to the effort." He asked about her children and she told him about Vivian expecting her first grandchild. He smiled and said, "You will make the world's most beautiful grandmother for sure."

Emily blushed and could only manage a, "Thank you." She told him about Vivian's miscarriage a year ago and how long Vivian had waited to tell her about this pregnancy. "She's getting ready to start her sixth month and I'm dying to see her. She can't travel now by doctor's orders until the eighth month or so. The baby can survive after the eighth month and Vivian and John are coming for Thanksgiving. I'll be going at the end of August to Charlottesville before Paul Michael starts school."

The dinner portion was finally over and the band began to play. Emily declined to dance. She would not publicly disgrace Paul by dancing with another man so soon. Judge Marshall danced with Mrs. Perkins and Belle and Alfred came to sit beside Emily. He asked about Paul Michael and told her that Louise would be returning home in a few weeks. She asked him about Gigi and he told her that he had taken her to visit Louise and both seemed happy to see each other. Belle walked over and offered her a ride home around eleven and she took her up on it. She thanked the Perkins for the invitation and assured them and Judge Marshall that she had enjoyed herself. Belle was quiet on the trip home but William told her how pretty she looked and how everybody there had said so too. Emily felt her face flush and she felt a little dizzy. Thank goodness the car was dark inside.

The next morning her picture appeared on the front of the *Welfield Express* newspaper. Emily was so embarrassed when she saw the picture as she prepared for mass. The maid was humming as she hung up the gown and told her,"That sure was a nice picture of you and the judge, ma'am." Emily was putting on her gloves as she checked over Paul Michael's suit for possible dog hairs. Finding none, she called the driver to take her to Sunday mass in Jackson.

Several parishioners nudged each other as Emily and Paul Michael walked down the aisle. Mrs. Novak smiled at her and slid over for them to sit beside her. Paul Michael was so well behaved during mass and shook Father O'Brien's hand at the end of mass. Father O'Brien complemented Paul Michael on his behavior and smiled at Emily. Of course there were a few disparaging remarks overheard by Emily and surprisingly, they were made by two of Marshall Steel Jackson mine foremen's wives. The ladies from the altar society welcomed her and told her that she sure looked nice in the newspaper picture. Mrs. Novak had gone over to say something to the two criticizing women and returned speaking in Hungarian. Paul Michael chuckled and said something to himself in Hungarian. Mrs. Novak heard him and laughed and then Emily and Paul Michael rode up with her to the cabin for lunch. They now went to the cabin each Sunday for lunch after mass. Paul Michael would change clothes and "help" Josef. Emily was sure that he pestered Josef more than helped but had never heard a complaint from Josef.

Emily helped prepare lunch and the women talked about the dinner. Mrs. Novak said, "Emily, don't you pay attention to those old biddies. They're just jealous. Mr. Paul would have been proud of you. He loved you dearly and without a doubt you loved him, but he wouldn't want you to be dying slowly yourself while you're still so much alive. There is no shame in admitting you're alive. Live and live happily. You have a son now who needs a happy mother and not a living corpse. Don't you ever be ashamed for being pretty and enjoying yourself without Mr. Paul! He wouldn't want you to be alone, no ma'am, he wouldn't."

They ate lunch and Paul Michael told her the apples were just about ready to be picked. They would be picking them that week and Mrs. Novak would be making apple butter. Emily was coming to help as well as peel and slice some apples that were bruised to put into the freezer for winter. The other apples would be stacked in barrels in between layers of straw. Emily was going to make some apple cider as well. It was going to be a busy week.

When they returned home, Emily changed into an afternoon dress and Paul Michael went out to play with Poppy. The cook and maid had Emily's picture cut out and had passed it around the staff. Everyone congratulated each other on a mission accomplished. Now if they could just give that one little extra nudge to take it to the next step. Opportunity came when somehow Poppy got out of the backyard and Paul Michael came in crying, "I can't find Poppy!"

Emily ran out to help look for the puppy as did the maid, butler, cook, and driver. All were calling, "Poppy" and walking down the street looking from side to side. When they approached the Perkins house they saw Judge Marshall coming their way. He was holding Poppy in his arms. He explained, "She showed up at their door yapping and I recognized her." He was returning her and Paul Michael ran to meet them. The judge tousled his hair and waved to Emily. "Thank you," she called and he called back, "No problem."

The butler nudged the driver's side who quickly said, "It wasn't me!"

Paul Michael took Poppy into the house and scolded her for running away. He sat down on the floor and played tug of war with the puppy. Vivian called that afternoon to give Emily an update on classes and her pregnancy. Emily told her about the dance and Vivian sounded pleased. She said, "Mom you need to get out more! Dad would want you to! If you're ever asked again, please go. Now when are you guys coming to see us? I can't wait to see you. You have to bring Poppy. John insists on that." The women laughed and chatted for several more minutes as Emily admitted buying things for her expectant grandbaby. Paul Michael wanted to talk with Vivian and told her of Poppy's escape and the judge's rescue. He asked about John and then returned the phone to Emily. The two talked a little while longer and Emily hung up the phone with a smile on her face.

The rest of the Sunday afternoon was spent listening to the radio and phonograph. It had started to rain and Paul Michael was bored. He said, "I sure wish John was here then we could play chess. Anya, Alfred knows how to play chess. May I ask him and Judge Marshall to come and play chess, and then we could take turns?"

"I doubt that Alfred will come here in this rain to play chess, but you can call him," she said with a smile. She asked the maid to call Judge Perkins number for Paul Michael. The lad followed the maid into the office and he spoke with Alfred and the judge. He returned to tell Emily that both of them were coming. Emily quickly asked the maid to put on some tea and coffee and perhaps prepare a few sandwiches and cookies on a tray. The two visitors were due to arrive shortly.

Alfred drove down the street rather than fight the heavy downpour of rain. Their umbrellas were shaken and placed in the hall tree by the butler when they arrived. Paul Michael had brought down his chess set and had already placed it on the gaming table in the parlor. Poppy greeted both men with her tail in full swing and immediately set upon Alfred's shoe strings. He picked her up and carried her into the parlor. Paul Michael wanted to play the judge first and the match was declared a draw by Alfred almost an hour later. Alfred played tug of war with Poppy as he watched the match. Both players had only their king and queen and it was declared a draw. The maid brought in refreshments and Emily poured their request. The judge stood up and turned his seat over to Alfred to get another chance playing the little boy. Poppy was set down and Emily took her to the office where she wouldn't bother anyone's shoes.

Emily and the judge spoke about the dinner and Paul Michael piped in to tell them about the apple harvest later that week. "We could use all the help we could get, couldn't we Anya?" Emily patiently reminded him that Alfred and the judge had to return to Charleston. Alfred spoke up, "Oh I'm leaving this evening but the judge will be here for another week." Paul Michael turned to the judge who said, "Well I can help on Tuesday, but I'm afraid my other days are full of commitments that I made earlier."

"Okay, Tuesday it is then," Alfred said. Paul Michael looked over the board and smiled. He moved his bishop and said, "Check". Alfred looked at the board, captured Paul Michael's bishop with his queen and Paul Michael immediately captured Alfred's queen and said, "Check mate!" Alfred commended him on a well played match and his distracting strategy. Judge Marshall threw up his hands as he laughed and said, "Don't ask me how to beat him. I was happy to get a draw with him! So, what time are we picking apples?"

"We will be leaving to go to the farm around six in the morning. We have to be finished picking before the bees arrive. The honey bees won't bother you but those yellow jackets are nasty little rascals. We will have to get them picked before eight," she explained.

"Well, thank you for the refreshments and entertainment and thank you Paul Michael for having pity on me! See you at six on Tuesday. We better leave now Alfred while the rain has stopped," the judge suggested and Alfred agreed. The two men thanked Emily and her son for an excellent time.

Emily escorted them to the foyer where the butler opened the front door with a slight smile on his face. Emily returned to the parlor to help Paul Michael pack up the chess set. She told him about their visit in two weeks with Vivian and John. They would be celebrating Paul Michael's birthday while there as a family affair and he would have a small party with friends when they returned on his actual birthday. She told Paul Michael that Vivian was expecting a baby and he looked with his mouth open and his eyes wide open. "I'm going to be an uncle, Anya?"

"Yes dear," she answered.

The judge arrived on time Tuesday morning and they picked several bushels of apples. He had driven his car so that her driver wouldn't have to wait for them. Josef drove the old truck down to the cabin with the baskets of apples.

Emily and Mrs. Novak would separate the apples into several categories. They carefully packed the ones to be put into layers separated by straw in barrels, cut and peeled the ones for the freezer, apple butter, or cider. They emptied the baskets and Josef drove back on the mountain to refill the baskets. By the time he returned there were six more bushels of apples and two of peaches. Emily washed and peeled the apples to make the cider and Mrs. Novak took care of keeping a watchful eye on the apple butter she was cooking in a huge kettle over an open fire in the front yard. The kettle held about five gallons and the apple butter would take about seven hours to cook and once Paul Michael and the judge returned with Josef they would each take turns stirring the kettle with the large wooden paddle. The trio picked up the apples on the ground called drops, and those would be given to the hogs. They returned to the cabin around ten thirty and had given the apples to the hogs. Another basket full of the apples would be given to them later.

Emily was busy packing up the barrels. These would be rolled up a ramp and put on the back of the truck and transported to her home's cellar in Welfield. Once the barrels were packed, she began making the cider. It would take her several hours to make the cider. She ground the apples in her grinder and then put them into the apple press. She covered the pot with a piece of cheesecloth and another on the inside of the press. She would be heating the juice and storing it in boiled jars and lids. She would store some of the jars of cider in the freezer to heat up during the winter. It was a lot of work, but worth the effort. Josef helped to pour the cider into the boiled jars and sealed them for her. She had the spices ready for the apple butter and when she was finished with the cider she would help Mrs. Novak season the apple butter. Emily used cinnamon, nutmeg, allspice, and cloves to season her apple butter.

When Emily finished with the cider she made some beef pot pies for lunch. They were made of folded pie crust over tiny diced potatoes, carrots, onion, and peas with thin slices of cooked roast beef. She called to the others to take turns washing and coming in to eat. Mrs. Novak and Paul Michael came in while the judge stirred the apple butter, then Josef, and finally the judge was relieved by Josef. The judge sat down and Emily offered him coffee to eat with his pies and sat down to eat as well. Paul Michael rose from his chair and said he was going to help Mrs. Novak with the dishes. Emily and the judge ate their lunch and he talked about his morning so far.

"I believe that I have used muscles that I had forgotten about having," he smiled slightly.

"Oh it's hard work for sure," Emily added.

They were awkward at first in their conversation, but with Paul Michael's urging and occasional comments they had plenty to talk about and were soon at ease with each other. He thanked her for a fine meal and for sharing the day with him. "I can't remember working so hard and enjoying myself at the same time. I have lived a sheltered life and never knew how much effort went into making the simplest things. I have learned a lot today."

"Paul Michael said that this used to be your home and that your husband actually built it. It is very well-made and very homey. Why did you ever leave here?" he asked. The judge obviously didn't know how Paul had died and as Emily's eyes became teary he knew he had asked the wrong question. "I'm sorry. I didn't mean to upset you," he said seriously.

"Oh it's okay. Paul died in the upper pasture from a plowing accident. I couldn't stay here without him and moved to Welfield. I have kept up the farm and use it to supplement our meals and sell the eggs, milk, bacon, and hams for profit. Paul loved this farm and I just couldn't leave it entirely," she said biting her lower lip. "We both loved it here and had worked so hard to make it a success for so many years."

"I'm sorry for the loss of your husband and your home. You have a lovely home in Welfield and a fine future with Paul Michael. You will soon be a grandmother and have a lot to live for. Your husband was a very lucky man to have found you. I envy him even now," he said with his head hung low.

"What about your wife? How did she die?" Emily asked.

"She died in an automobile crash at the age of thirty eight. She died instantly and I comforted myself with my work. I was a civil court judge for Kanawha County and spent most of my time in my office. I couldn't bear to be home by myself. Judge Perkins and I were friends in college and he talked me into rejoining the human race," he said and then sighed heavily. "I can still see her face and sometimes I even dream about her. Do you ever dream of Paul?"

"No, I have nightmares about the accident, but he hasn't come to me peacefully in my dreams yet. I only dream of finding him on the plow and he's keeps calling my name over and over," she said.

"He will come to you, but it will take time. When your heart has healed enough so that it won't hurt you, he will come peacefully into your dreams. It took me about six months before I had my first dream of her. I got a lot of peace of mind after having just that one, single dream," he remarked.

Emily talked about their early years in the cabin as well as raising Vivian and how Louise used to come to their house and had spent many nights during the winter months. Emily spoke with a kind voice as she reflected on those early days. She paused and said, "You know I believe that every major decision that we ever made was made in this very cabin and usually it was while we were sitting at this very table."

The two had not realized that Paul Michael and Mrs. Novak had snuck out the front door to leave them alone. Emily turned to ask Mrs. Novak a question when she realized that they were alone. She started to rise and the judge gently put his hand on her arm and said, "Thank you for a fabulous day and for trusting me enough to share your past." He rose and kissed her on the forehead and helped move her chair back.

Emily and the judge did not miss the winks given between Josef and his mother. Paul Michael tried to hold in a giggle but failed miserably. The judge spoke with great authority, "Now see here young man, there's nothing to giggle about. Your Anya and I were just having a private talk and that is all."

The apple butter would cook for several more hours and they finally began to put it in the jars around six that night. With all jars and lids washed, boiled and dry it didn't take long for the assembly line to ladle the hot liquid into a jar, put on the lid and ring, tighten the ring, and wipe the jar off with a damp rag. After another hour they had finished with the last jar and had packed them into boxes. Mrs. Novak had her dozen jars, the judge was offered a dozen but took only four, and Emily would take the rest of the jars home with her.

On the drive home Paul Michael fell asleep and the judge carried him to bed. The butler carried in the two cases of apple butter and the quart jars of apple cider. The judge returned from Paul Michael's room as the maid carried Poppy upstairs to join him. The judge bid her good night and drove immediately back to the Perkins' residence. The next morning he asked the cook for toast with apple butter at breakfast. He was definitely pleased with the fruits of his labor after only one bite.

He returned to Charleston while Emily and Paul Michael went to visit with John and Vivian. Paul Michael's first birthday party with his new family was a success. He got so many nice presents but told them that he liked having his family around him the most. His thoughts turned towards the judge as he blew out his birthday candles and made his birthday wish.

Chapter 10

Louise was complacent in the sanitarium and with only two weeks left in her stay, she was given permission to read a newspaper. On the second day, while reading the paper, she had seen the picture of Emily with Judge Marshall and had suffered a relapse. Emily Black was trying to get her hooks into the judge. If she succeeded, then Emily would certainly try to ruin Alfred's career. She broke down into hysterics and had to be heavily sedated. They had called Alfred and told him it would now be around Thanksgiving before she would be released. He was disappointed and called his parents and Belle to give them the news.

August and September had flown by for Alfred. He had immersed himself into his work and had taken on several difficult cases. He had left Charleston only to go to Paul Michael's birthday party. He had given the little boy a pair of binoculars that he could use on the mountain when he visited the lodge. The little boy was more like a younger brother to William and the feelings were mutual. He was very near and dear to his heart and Alfred enjoyed his company. Emily's final adoption of Paul Michael's was completed and his last name was now officially Black. Paul Michael was doing so well in the second grade and was reading fourth grade level books. His teacher recommended that he should be double promoted to the third grade after only the first grading period and the principal agreed. He easily handled multiplication and division in arithmetic as well as multi-column subtraction with and without borrowing. His life was full since he now enjoyed school, church, Anya, chess, and his puppy.

Gigi was a lot of company for Alfred and now she even went to his office with him on the weekends. She was almost full grown weighing two and a half pounds. When he went to visit Louise, Louise seemed to perk up when she saw the little dog. He briefly mentioned William who desperately wanted to see his sister. She agreed around the middle of August and it had been a total disaster. She was mean and cruel to him accusing him of spreading vicious lies to Alfred. William was silent all the way home his heart aching since only the mere mention of Emily had set her off. William vowed that he wouldn't see his sister again until she was released from the sanitarium.

William worked harder than ever in his all of his classes. He wanted to try out for JV football and made the team as a punter. He could really boot the ball and wasn't easily shaken. In the first game he made the winning point after kick. Although younger than the others, he worked harder trying to get stronger and better. Belle bought him a set of weights to increase his strength. He was a lot taller than he had been and began to gain weight. Girls had started to notice him. He was an adorable fourteen year-old to everyone, but to Marcella he was her best friend, her confidante. Alfred invited him to come and stay with him on the weekends when he wasn't working and they would go to football games together in Huntington to watch Marshall University games.

Alfred and William became quite close during Louise's hospitalization, but Louise, on the other hand, decided that the only way she was going to leave the sanitarium was to take serious control of her emotions. Louise had to get out for Thanksgiving and she would begin paying her debts to all she felt owed her. William had neglected her, Alfred had abandoned her, and Emily Black had tried to replace her mother. All of them would pay dearly for putting her in that awful place. Alfred had mentioned adopting a refugee child but Louise, she had another idea. Why not adopt an American child, one whose parents were poor? She would begin volunteering at the hospital in the nursery. She would convince her doctor and Alfred that working in the nursery would help her accept her hysterectomy better. She would wait until there was an unwed mother and talk her into giving up her child. She could never accept any foreign child, never. Her grandmother had told her how they were good for nothing and Louise knew that her grandmother had been right.

Louise convinced herself that she would prefer a little girl, one she could dress up and play with. Why, the baby would be like her very own living doll. She would hire a nanny and wouldn't have to change a diaper and that's for sure. She would adopt a child maybe two, but no more. She would teach her daughter about the real world and the evils that lurked behind innocence like her grandmother had taught her. She would teach her how to catch a husband and of course several other little tricks. Most of all, the baby could be used to help her repay a lot of Louise's debts. Judge Perkins would help them with the adoption, since he wanted Alfred to have a family and would do whatever it took to make it happen. Belle would give the child money, a lot of it. Yes indeed, a baby would do nicely as a means to get what she wanted.

Louise would be the perfect patient from now on and if she was lucky by the New Year she could be a mother. Louise chose to not get very excited by the news of the Japanese surrender and was happy that things would finally get back to normal. Rationing would finally be over thank goodness. Unfortunately shops would be getting more crowded, but there would be a lot of babies being born and her chances for getting just the right one would increase. Some of the troops had arrived in May and perhaps some of them would be overly zealous with their girl friends. There would doubtless be plenty of unwed mothers to choose from and the baby she got would have to be gorgeous. She cooperated with the counselors, took her medication, and argued with no one on staff.

The thought of having a child drove her so she could leave the sanitarium sooner, but it also drove her to have her revenge and right now, she was closer than she had ever been. When William had let it slip that Vivian was pregnant, she had physically attacked him. How could he, her own brother, be happy for her worst enemy? There was nothing she could do now, but she would get Vivian and what joy it would be for her to watch her squirm. That witch had gotten knocked up on purpose and Louise was sure that it probably wasn't even John's. As soon as she could, she'd get the dirt on that farmer's daughter and then look out; John would be seeking her out to be with him. She had made a good impression on his parents. She was as sure of that as she was that he would be with her and Vivian returned to the dirt. One way or the other, Vivian would return to the dirt from whence she came.

Jake Turner had let her down by not finding out anything about that kid, Paul Michael. She had been very specific in her demands to find a connection between the little boy and Vivian. Jake had told her that the boy came from Hungary and was the cousin of Vivian's late father. It had infuriated Louise when he had told her about Paul Michael coming from Hungary, but she just couldn't accept it. There had to be more to it. She was tired of the Blacks being considered living saints. They had secrets, everyone had them.

The doctors were amazed at her sudden progress and released her one week before Thanksgiving. The psychiatrist told Alfred about her desire to work in a hospital and he recommended that she work in a small one and be around her immediate family. Being around her family would give her time to adjust to life outside the sanitarium. Alfred asked his parents if Louise could stay with them and they agreed. He would come to visit her on the weekends as he had done before when she had been at the sanitarium.

Alfred was very tense around Louise and he tried hard getting used to the idea of her being at home and out of the sanitarium. He had planned to have a two week vacation around Christmas but had to cut it back to only one week since she had gotten released so early. Perhaps they could spend it in one of the cabins on Filbert Mountain. Judge and Mrs. Perkins came to the sanitarium to pick up Louise and they had driven her to Welfield. Alfred would be coming home to join them on the Wednesday before Thanksgiving.

Vivian and John were going to spend Thanksgiving in Welfield. She was in her eighth month and the doctor said she could go home as long as she kept off her feet for extended periods. Emily was so happy to see her baby girl and admitted that Vivian looked especially radiant. Judge Marshall took his time in courting Emily and called her once a week. His term would end in January and he would be returning to a regular law practice. He wanted to move to Welfield after New Year's to be closer to Emily and Paul Michael and his friends, the Perkins. Judge Perkins was in civil court and Judge Marshall, that is Andrew, was returning to practicing corporate law. Emily had asked him to be her attorney for several business ventures of hers and he would be busy with just her case load. She had insisted on paying him the same rate that others received. He had found a house to rent on Sumner Street near Belle's house.

The week before Thanksgiving was increasingly becoming more strained at Judge Perkins' house since everyone seemed to be as tense as they worried about doing or saying anything that might upset Louise. She maintained her self-control and Judge Perkins had taken her over to volunteer at the small Welfield hospital. They needed as many volunteers there as possible. At first she worked in the blood bank and actually did a good job. In a week she was taken to the nursery. She would rock the babies and take them to or from their mothers. Again she got along well with everyone. She would check each of the mother's charts for single mothers and had found only one and that was a little colored girl of fifteen. She would be patient and knew that eventually the right one would come along.

At Emily's, Vivian sat with her feet up on pillows reclined on the couch. Poppy tried to jump up on the couch and Vivian would just scoop her up and hold her on her lap. Poppy would go round and round until she found the right spot on Vivian's lap. Poppy would jump when the baby kicked her and start scratching Vivian's dress and try to circle once more in her lap. Paul Michael and John moved the gaming table into the living room so that Vivian could watch them play chess. JJ was pleased to finally meet the pleasant young woman he had spoken with so frequently on the phone. Emily would bring Vivian's tea and a scone on a beautiful lap table she had bought just for Vivian. Vivian told her that she just about had the nursery ready for the baby. She had chosen all white furniture with walls of light green. Emily had shopped and shopped and had stocked the chest of drawers with plenty of one piece sleepers, sleep bags, stomach bands, t-shirts, burp pads, blankets, sheets, and even booties and socks. The changing table was stacked high with diapers, nursery jars filled with cotton balls, swabs, and baby washcloths. Vivian had plenty of diaper pins and rubber pants and was waiting to get outfits once she knew if it was a girl or a boy. Belle had purchased a sterling drinking cup, bowl, and flatware set as well as a sterling rattle. Vivian had chosen Caroline as a girl's name and John Paul for a boy's name.

Emily was a nervous wreck and would ask her if she was all right at least once an hour. John said that she seemed to be more anxious than he was. Paul Michael was fascinated by how a baby could fit in a woman's stomach. He had even asked her why she couldn't show him the baby now and then just put it back into her stomach. He laughed when he saw her blouse tumble from each of the baby's kicks and Poppy looking surprised each time. Vivian had experienced no problems so far in this pregnancy and her doctor felt that she would do fine when it came time for the delivery. The baby's heartbeat was strong and Vivian was taking her vitamins and iron pills daily. Thanksgiving Day Vivian ate quite well and Paul Michael said, "Are you sure that's only a baby in your stomach and not something else? That baby must have two stomachs!" John bragged on the feast and John and Paul Michael did some Christmas shopping on Friday at the company store and downtown Welfield. John set aside some brother time and enjoyed a trip to Murphy's with Paul Michael.

On the Saturday after Thanksgiving, Judge Marshall came for a visit. He was happy to see the young couple again and had even been a little nervous about seeing them again. This little lady was a great part of Emily's life and he hoped to make a good impression. When Poppy heard the judge she whined and cried to get down. John lifted her to the ground and thought she had to go out. He went to get her leash and when he turned around he saw Poppy raised up on her hind legs tapping the judge's leg. The judge reached down and picked her up. She covered his face with her classic doggie kisses and Vivian laughed and said, "He's Poppy approved!" Everyone enjoyed a pleasant evening as a champion chess tournament was held and it was declared a three way draw. They planned to go to mass at Our Lady of the Rosary on Sunday. Andrew, Judge Marshall, asked if he could go with them to mass. Paul Michael offered, "You can sit beside me if you want!"

On Sunday, after mass, Emily whispered to Vivian that she needed to use the bathroom and asked Vivian if she needed to go. They walked into the new hall and Vivian smiled as she saw a table of presents and a beautiful cake complete with baby booties made from icing. Emily looked at her and said, "You know what, I don't have to go anymore." The men felt a little out of place and decided to ride up the hollow and stay at the farm's cabin for an hour or so.

The ladies had all knitted a variety of blankets, caps, sweater sets, and booties. There were bottles, pacifiers, brushes, baby sets, and hot-water dishes. You filled the hollow dish with hot water and sealed it with a plug that turned. The dish kept cereal and other foods warm. Vivian was ready for the baby to arrive and could hardly wait until he or she arrived. She thanked the women for the beautifully crafted items several times and had held each piece up so all could admire them when she had opened the gifts.

The men returned in an hour and were offered a piece of cake and some homemade mints. Paul Michael helped his sister load the car with the gifts and helped her get into the car. He was happy when he saw the gifts and knew that the one he had bought wasn't among them. He had bought a baby book and matching picture frame. He also had his school picture in another frame so that the baby would know what their uncle looked like and he decided to give the items to Vivian when they left for home. Vivian and John left that afternoon and they called Emily when they had arrived in Charlottesville around eight that evening.

The judge stayed for Sunday dinner and played a chess match with Paul Michael. He enjoyed those quiet times the most. Paul Michael would talk about what was going on in school and would often read some of his assigned readings to the judge and work out his math or ask for him to check over the problems. Emily often played records on the phonograph or listen to radio programs on Sunday afternoons. Emily never crocheted on Sundays because her mother had told her many times, "You don't ever sew on Sunday. Every stitch on Sunday will bring a tear on another day."

The following week Vivian had gone to her doctor for a checkup and the doctor said it would be at least another two weeks. The baby hadn't dropped yet. Vivian had another week of classes and then was going to come home for an early Christmas. She and John wanted to be in their own home for Christmas and get ready for her delivery. With the doctor's approval she returned to Welfield to celebrate an early Christmas with her new brother. John walked with Paul Michael up the hollow of the old cabin near Emily's farm and selected a tree. They put it into the tree stand and filled the stand with water. Vivian stood up and told her mother that she didn't know what happened but all of a sudden she could breathe so much easier. The baby had noticeably dropped overnight. John strung up the lights and Paul Michael clapped as each garland was added. When it was time to put on each ornament he had to look over each one before it could be hung. He would step back and point to where it belonged. John proclaimed, "I was hoping to get this tree decorated before Christmas came, but now it looks like it won't be ready for next Christmas." It made no difference to Paul Michael how much John teased him; he wanted it to be perfect. John moaned when it was time for the tinsel because, sure enough, Paul Michael wanted the tinsel placed one strand at a time. John gave up around eight o'clock at night and helped Paul Michael bathe and go to bed.

The next morning Vivian had more energy than she had in past weeks. She ate a hearty breakfast and helped wash the dishes just to have something to do. The maid whispered to the cook, "Uh oh, watch out for her, she's nesting for sure." They enjoyed a lovely lunch and dinner and went to sit in the living room to admire the perfect tree. Emily had asked Vivian to help her look over the reports for the infant care products and showed her how they had increased production to meet the baby boom that Belle had predicted more than a year earlier. John and Vivian would be leaving the next day and wanted to get a good night's sleep.

Vivian had a doctor's appointment on Wednesday and hoped he would give her a better idea of her due date. Vivian kissed her mother and brother good night and went to bed early. It was around three in the morning when Vivian knocked on Emily's door. "Mom," she said quietly and then knocked again, "Mom, can I come in?"

Emily opened her door and said, "What's wrong dear?"

"I think that I might be in labor!" Vivian answered.

Emily yanked open the door and said, "How close are your pains?"

"I don't know about every ten minutes or so," Vivian said.

"Well you are going to have to go to Welfield hospital for sure. You certainly don't want to drive all the way to Charlottesville in labor. It's too dangerous for you and the baby. We'll go get you checked and make sure that it's not just a false alarm." Emily awakened John and the maid and then called the driver to warm up the car.

When they arrived at the hospital Vivian was taken into the emergency room and a nurse came out to tell John and Emily that Vivian was, in fact, in active labor and should be delivering by early evening. Vivian was taken to the OB/GYN floor and John and Emily waited until it was time to wake up Paul Michael to get ready for school. Emily left only long enough to take Paul Michael to school and when she returned to the hospital there was still no news. John had been allowed to go up on the floor and Emily sat with John in that floor's waiting room. It was around two in the afternoon when the nurse came out and told John that he had a little girl. Vivian had done well and would be in her room in about an hour. They would be bringing the baby to the nursery momentarily.

Louise was busy in the nursery and saw a new baby being brought in. It was such a beautiful baby girl. The very sort of baby she was looking for to adopt. There was another baby girl that came in almost at the same time and although Louise had no medical training, she could tell that it was very ill. Louise stepped aside for the nurse, who had to fill out the information on the baby bracelets and that was when Louise saw Vivian's name on the beautiful baby girl's bracelet. Louise couldn't believe her luck. The nurses put the bracelets in the small bassinets holding the babies, next to the newborns. They would put the bracelets on after getting the report from day shift. While the nurses had their backs turned to Louise, busy with the shift change, she offered to put on the bracelets for the two baby girls. The nurses were busy talking about the babies and one of them told her, "Sure." Louise smiled as she heard one of them say, "We have to go and check on Mrs. Miller and tell her about her little girl. I don't think either of them is going to make it by what day shift told us. Let's check on the baby and see how she is doing." The evening shift nurses, who worked the nursery and the mother's ward, turned around and were surprised at how well the little Miller girl was doing now and double checked the bracelet. They looked at the Williams' baby girl and shook their heads. That baby would be lucky to survive the night. Obviously the nurses on the other shift had mixed up the names because the babies were born at about the same time. Mrs. Williams would be informed when she got on the floor in her private room.

One of the evening shift nurses went out to speak with Mr. Williams in the waiting room. John was ecstatic about his new baby girl and the nurse asked him to follow her into a small room. She told him his baby was very ill and she may not make it through the night. He asked to see her and the nurse led him to the nursery window where he saw a little pink blanket inside of an incubator. The nurse asked him if he had anyone in particular that he needed to contact and he told her that he would take care of it. He asked how long his baby girl had to live and she told him that she doubted that the baby would make it to see the sun rise. John immediately called Emily and asked her to come to the nursery. He told her what the nurse had said and she joined him there in what seemed only a few seconds. She had made arrangements with JJ to pick up Paul Michael from school and was at John's side.

Louise left through the back door of the nursery so as not to be seen and went to the employee's lounge to make a phone call. She called Judge Perkins to tell him she wasn't feeling well and needed to come home early. While she waited in the reception area, she couldn't keep from smiling and actually whistled as she got into the Perkins car to go home. The driver opened the door for her and she went up to her room to lie down. She had the best sleep she had in months, and that was obtained without the use of any medication.

John went into Vivian's room to check on her and she told him she was very tired and very weak. He told her that Caroline was very sick and had to be put into an incubator. She wept as he told her that the nurses and doctors didn't think their baby would make it through the night.

"But John, I don't understand. The doctor who delivered her said she was perfectly healthy. I have to see her!" she cried out. John knew that Vivian wanted to be taken out immediately to see her baby and he helped her into a wheelchair and pushed her to the nursery window. She looked at all the babies and the nurse pointed to the incubator. Vivian pecked on the window and the nurse pointed to the jaundiced baby. The tiny baby was definitely having trouble breathing in addition to being jaundiced and they told the new parents that she also had a severe heart murmur. Vivian wept as she felt so helpless to do anything for her little baby. She asked John to call Father O'Brien to baptize little Caroline and insisted that he went home to rest. Around five o'clock in the evening Father O'Brien came into her room and told her that Caroline had just been baptized. John had called his parents from Emily's and told them the grim news. They told him that they were on their way and that Emily had offered them a place to stay after the baby had been born. Emily was going to stay the night with Vivian and went to Emily's to get some rest.

Around 4:30 am, a nurse entered into the room with a doctor that Vivian didn't recognize. He told her that her daughter had been born too soon and that she had a severe heart murmur and undeveloped lungs. "We gave her oxygen and put her in the incubator. She seemed to improve but at four she took a turn for the worse and expired at four fifteen." Emily gasped and looked at Vivian.

Vivian was stunned and said, "What did you say? She wasn't born too early! She was only a few days before my due date."

"I'm very sorry, but your baby is dead," he immediately gave her a sedative injection as she tried to get out of the bed and the nurse held her down. And he heard the most heartbroken wail that actually sent shivers down his spine that he would recall several years later. The young mother had taken the news much worse than he had thought possible. Surely she must have suspected it was in trouble when the baby was born. Anyone who saw the baby would have known that the poor baby girl hadn't a chance of survival. What he didn't know was that at the last few minutes in the delivery room, the doctor had anesthetized Vivian to use make an incision for the delivery since the baby was so large and Vivian was so petite. Vivian's first glance at Caroline had been in the nursery.

"Oh God no, not my baby, my beautiful little baby girl! Why, why did you take my baby away from me after letting me carry her for so long? If you were going to take her, why didn't you take her like you did the other one?" Vivian sobbed, she tried to scream but found that she had no voice. "Where's John? I need John!" Emily went out of the room to call John. She told him that the baby was critical and that he needed to return to the hospital as soon as possible. She didn't want to tell him about Caroline over the telephone. The nurse brought in the pink wrapped blanket around the baby for Vivian to say her goodbyes and Vivian opened the blanket to get a closer look at her baby. She smoothed down the brown hair and made a mental note of the long lashes on such a small face. Vivian kissed the baby gently saying she couldn't believe she was gone. All of her hopes for their future were lost. The sedative began to take affect and Emily took the tiny bundle from Vivian. She kissed the tiny girl as well and handed the baby to the nurse. The nurse removed the baby from the room and waited until John had arrived to send the baby down to the hospital morgue.

John heard Emily crying inside and immediately knew what had happened before he entered the hospital room. The sedative had taken affect somewhat by that time but Vivian was still thrashing on the bed like a zombie with silent tears running down her face. Her eyes were wild as she pleaded for her baby and then she let out mutterings that were incoherent. The doctor had ordered an additional sedative at 5:30am and her body finally relaxed and she went to sleep. Every once in a while she jerked in her sleep as though she was still weeping.

Emily stayed with her and had called home. She awakened Mrs. Carlson and told her what had happened. She asked her to get Paul Michael dressed and ready for school but asked her not to say anything to Paul Michael. John was asked by the doctor if he wanted an autopsy but John said, "No, I don't want my little girl to suffer any more."

He was told that he had to sign for the death certificate and the release of the body to a funeral home. John wept bitterly over the thought of giving his little girl away, not in marriage years from now to her groom, but today, to a morgue. He was allowed to accompany the gurney that was taken to where her little body was lying, still wrapped in a pink blanket and he kissed his little girl on the forehead before they carried her tiny covered body to the hospital morgue. He waited alone outside the hospital morgue for the hearse to arrive from the mortuary. His mind wandered about how he had gone from being totally happy to hitting the lowest point of his life in the matter of only a few hours.

His parents called the hospital from a pay phone around 5:45am and a nurse had found him so that he could be the one to tell them about Caroline's death. Catherine had dropped the phone and Henry told John that they would be in Welfield later that day. Alone again, he once again thought of Vivian. How would she possibly make it through this pain? After losing Paul, Vivian had thrown herself into her school work. Getting pregnant soon after Paul's death had saved her from a deep depression. What would happen to that petite girl that was indeed the love of his life? He didn't have the answers and buried his face in his hands and wept without shame. He had lost his daughter and thought that he may very well have lost his wife as well on the same day. Vivian, his dear Vivian, might lose her mind over the loss of their baby. She had put so much into the pregnancy getting the nursery ready, eating right, getting plenty of rest, and keeping her appointments.

It was a few minutes before 6am, that one of the nurses working the morning shift had worked the day shift the day before. When she came on duty and the nurse asked the late shift nurse how the Miller baby was doing, she was told that she was doing just fine but that the Williams baby had died. The nurse was surprised to hear that since the Williams baby had appeared to be so healthy the evening before. She received the report on each baby and went to check on each of them. When she went to get the Miller baby to weigh her she went to record the weight and immediately noticed a big discrepancy in the weights. She immediately called and asked to speak with the nurse supervisor in person.

"We have a problem, a big problem. Someone has mixed up two babies and one of them died during the night. There were two babies brought into the nursery at about the same time near shift change. One baby weighed 5 pounds and was very sick the other baby weighed 8 pounds 1 ounce. Mrs. Snyder, the larger baby was Mrs. Williams' baby. I know that because I was the one that brought her into the nursery. She was perfect in every way. I was paged to delivery room 2 and Mrs. Miller had just delivered a small baby that needed to immediately go into an incubator. I rushed back to the delivery room with an incubator and when I brought that baby to the nursery a volunteer was nearby with the snap bracelets while I gave my report to the evening shift. The baby that died belonged to Mrs. Miller and not to Mrs. Williams. If you look at the footprints on the birth certificate made in the delivery room you will see the big difference in the footprints. What do we do?"

The nurse supervisor went into the nursery and checked the weights of the baby. She then looked over the delivery room page of each chart. Mrs. Miller's chart said that her baby girl weighed 5 pounds and was 18inches long. Mrs. Williams' chart stated that her baby girl weighed 8 pounds 1 ounce and was 20 inches long. The baby girl in the nursery weighed 8 pounds ½ ounce and the footprints matched. She asked all of the nurses from the evening shift to come into her office. "Why didn't you check these charts before you talked with those mothers? Didn't any of you think to look at the charts? We have to straighten this out and quickly!"

"We were so busy with all those babies and new ones coming in we didn't think there could possibly be a mix-up. Nurse Snyder, there are twenty four babies in our nursery right now. We don't weigh the babies on our shift, only the day shift weighs the babies. We just thought the head nurse must have made a mistake in her report to our shift's head nurse," one of the evening shift nurses confessed.

"How in the world did that volunteer get anywhere near a newborn baby without it having on its bracelet? Who put on the bracelets?" The nurse from the day shift said, "We did. The bracelets were in the infant bassinets and we filled out their bracelets ourselves. We set them in the bassinets and they were in the correct ones, I'm sure of it."

"Well obviously the volunteer switched the bracelets around. This is exactly why I do not like having volunteers in the nursery. I will need to speak with both sets of parents immediately and I'll need to speak to the volunteer coordinator as well," the supervisor said.

John had just watched his daughter's body placed into the hearse when he was asked by the morgue clerk to go to the nurse supervisor's office on the second floor. 'Oh my God, not Vivian too' he thought as he walked into her office. The nurse supervisor spoke first and said, "Mr. Williams I am afraid to tell you that a terrible thing has happened." Before she could begin to tell him what had happened, he broke down and said, "Not my Viv, please don't tell me I've lost Vivian too!"

"Mr. Williams your wife is alive and well and so is your daughter," she stated firmly.

He sat up straight suddenly and asked, "What did you say?" his face swollen and flush wet with new tears as he looked up obviously puzzled.

"I said a terrible mistake was made. Your baby is just fine. In fact she is just perfect. Somehow, the little bands we put on babies got mixed up between your daughter and another little girl. A volunteer accidentally put the snap bracelets into the wrong bassinets!" she stated clearly. "We are terribly sorry for the mix-up and I assure you that this is the first time this has ever happened and we will make sure that it never happens again. Please accept our deepest apology for the terrible pain we have caused you. Would you like to see your little girl?" she asked.

"Certainly," John answered as he swallowed hard. "But whose baby was it that I just signed the death certificate for? Are you sure this is our baby?" he asked.

"Absolutely, the records match perfectly," she answered.

The nurse supervisor personally escorted John from her office to the nursery. The curtain was closed, but she had one of the other nurses to hold his baby up to the window. Instantly his face changed to one of pleasant surprise as he looked into the face of a sleeping angel that resembled his beloved Vivian. The nurse smiled at him and returned Caroline to her bassinet. John turned to go into Vivian's private room to tell Emily who had fallen asleep in a chair. A nurse had just come out of the women's ward and reported to another nurse that she had just told Mrs. Miller that her baby had died during the night and had given her the sedative that the doctor had ordered. John knew instantly when the nurse held up Caroline that she was indeed his daughter. He was smiling to himself as he recalled that tiny head's thick brown hair, Vivian's chin, and his nose. She was going to be a beauty for sure when she got older. The nurse had shown him the bracelet which had been changed and he beamed like the proud father he was.

Meanwhile, Emily was sleeping in the chair beside Vivian's bed. Vivian had been heavily sedated and was tossing in her sleep. The nurses told him that she would sleep for at least two more hours. John gently shook Emily and asked her to come out into the hall. She was exhausted herself but managed a hug for him and cried on his shoulder. "I am so sorry," she said, "I don't know what to do to make this better for either of you."

"Emily, listen to me. There's been a mistake, a terrible mistake. Someone accidentally mixed up two of the baby's bracelets; they mixed up Caroline's and another baby's by the name of Miller. Caroline is alive! She's alive I tell you! Come see for yourself," he said as he squeezed her tightly.

"I don't believe it. I just don't believe it. How on earth did they find out?" she asked as they walked towards the nursery. "I'm not sure how it happened but the nurse supervisor is the one who told me. All she said was that there had been a mix-up. Wait until you see her, she's beautiful!" he asked. The nurse supervisor was just leaving the nursery when she saw John with Emily so she returned to the nursery and once again Caroline was held up through the barely opened curtain.

"Oh my goodness she's a doll, an honest to goodness living doll," she mused. "We have to tell Vivian, she has to know!"

"We can't; she will be asleep for at least two more hours. She mustn't be awakened suddenly so she won't know until the sedative wears off. Look I'm going to stay here in the waiting room so I can tell her as soon as visiting hours start. Can you get me the biggest bunch of flowers you can find for Vivian?" he asked. "I want to be here when she wakes up. It's almost seven o'clock now and the florist won't be open until nine."

"Of course I will darling. Oh my goodness I have to call home. Hopefully the maid hasn't said anything to Paul Michael!" Emily said quickly. John told her to go on home and he would call to tell the maid about Caroline. Emily called the driver from a different phone to come and pick her up and he showed up in just a few minutes. Emily could have walked home but she was exhausted and it was still dark outside. When Emily got home, the maid came out to meet her and hugged her screaming, "It's a miracle, a miracle Mrs. Emily. Dat baby is alive! Mr. John called and said Miss Vivian's baby is alive! Thank the Good Lord I didn't tell Paul Michael."

"There was a mix-up with another baby. I have to call Father O'Brien. He's baptized someone else's baby. Gee I'm exhausted," she admitted.

"What you need Mrs. Emily is a good cup of cook's special coffee and a nap. Come on, cook will fix you right up. I'll take care of Paul Michael. Now come on and get in bed and get out of this cold," the maid smiled up to her.

The cook gave her some coffee with several ounces of Irish whiskey and made her drink it. The maid helped her get ready for bed and once Emily was settled in, she went to get the little boy up for school. Paul Michael was very quiet when the maid told him about her needing to sleep and how beautiful his new niece was. She also told him if he was quiet he could go and see the baby that afternoon.

Emily awakened around nine and was startled at first to find out it was daylight and then remembered all that had happened. She called for JJ to come up and through her closed door she asked him to call Father O'Brien. She needed to speak with him as soon as possible about a mix-up with Vivian's daughter. She also told JJ that she needed him to order two large floral arrangements for Vivian and to call Belle about her new great-granddaughter. By the time she was dressed, JJ had already ordered two large arrangements one with red roses and the other with pink roses. He also had just reached Father O'Brien and Emily told him that the baby was alive.

Father O'Brien said, "Are you sure Emily? She was very ill when I baptized her last night."

"There was a mix-up with the babies. That wasn't Vivian's baby but was one that belonged to a couple by the last name of Miller. The nursing supervisor told John early this morning! Can you possibly come by and see Vivian?" she asked. "I don't know how we are going to convince her about the mix-up. She was so terribly upset and shocked by the news. I'm afraid she is so distraught that she might not be reached. I'm afraid we will need your help to get through to her!"

Father O'Brien told her that he would be at the hospital after the ten o'clock daily mass. Emily thanked him over and over again. She had no information about the other couple, but asked him if he could check and see if the Millers were possibly Catholic. Emily tried to call the Williams' Richmond home and was told that they had left several hours ago and should arrive there shortly. Henry and Catherine wouldn't know until they had gotten to Welfield about Caroline. Meanwhile, Emily needed a cup of coffee and breakfast while JJ got hold of Belle. There were a lot of things that needed to be done, but first and foremost, she would have to go and see Vivian.

Emily quickly ate her breakfast and left word with JJ that if the Williams happened to call to tell them Caroline was alive and that it had all been a horrible mistake. She called the driver to warm up the car, brushed her teeth and walked through the opened car door and sat down with a smile on her face. As she neared the hospital she saw a volunteer's cap and thought that she recognized the woman but had only caught a side glimpse of the woman since she had been looking out over the town of Welfield through the car's window.

John hugged her as soon as she had entered the waiting room. She told him that the flowers were ordered and should arrive later that day. "Father O'Brien will be here after daily mass. I hope that he can help us get through to Vivian. She may not believe us, I'm afraid. I do not know what state her mind will be in when she awakens," Emily said in almost a whisper. "I also have asked him to determine whether the couple of the dead baby he baptized was Catholic or not. This is a mess and I pray that the Millers are Catholic."

Chapter 11

Louise had awakened from her restful sleep early and had gone down for breakfast with a smile on her face around 7am. She wanted to get to the hospital early. She had called at 5:30 and had inquired about the condition of that poor Williams baby. The nurse told her that the baby had died about an hour earlier. Louise spoke the expected words, "I'm so sorry to hear that," and went to bathe. She would have to get dressed and go to the hospital to comfort John and Vivian in their time of need, well, comfort John anyway.

She had gotten out of the car and walked into the hospital with her volunteer smock over a suit. She went first to Vivian's room and was very disappointed that Vivian wasn't sobbing loudly but was sleeping instead. She was livid that her moment had been stolen, but only for a little while. When Vivian would awaken she would make sure that she was there. John would not be allowed into the room until visiting hours at 9:00 am. Hopefully Vivian would awaken before that time. She thought to go by the nursery but decided that perhaps she would go to the ER for about a half an hour or so and return to Vivian's room then.

The ER was crowded with only a few cases of a broken ankle and a miner who had almost cut off his finger. They didn't need her help there and she went to the hospital cafeteria to get a cup of coffee. John had just left and was returning to the waiting room and had chosen to go up the stairs rather than wait for the elevator. Louise caught the shadow of someone going through the staircase door but didn't take the time to look.

She sat at the table with a smug smile on her face and greeted each person that came through the door of the cafeteria. A particularly haggard looking man came into the cafeteria and she got up to help him with his cup of coffee. The saucer in his hand was shaking and she helped him to sit down without spilling the coffee. He thanked her and took a sip of his coffee and then put his head down and silently wept. 'Someone has died and he just found out. Maybe I should say something to him,' she thought.

"I'm sorry sir to bother you, but are you all right?" she asked.

"My baby died and my wife is doing poorly. They don't expect her to make it either ma'am," he managed to say.

"Oh I'm sorry. If you like I can sit with you for a while," she offered. Surprisingly Louise was very compassionate and listened as he told her what had happened. The tiny baby was born too early and had been born with a heart defect. Louise assumed that the baby had been born earlier that morning and comforted him. She excused herself and left him around 8:45am to check on Vivian, who had just awakened.

"Why Vivian Black, if it isn't you! How are you darling?" Louise said in her most gracious voice.

"Louise, what are you doing here? I thought you lived in Charleston. Why are you here?" Vivian said with guarded speech.

"I work here as a volunteer. I was just in the cafeteria and something told me to come up to this floor. It must have been fate drawing me here. Where are John and your mom? Did they leave you all alone?" Louise replied.

"No of them is here, I'm sure of it," she said as her mind was confused by the drugs. She was having difficulty focusing or tried to stay awake. "Well if you say he's here, then he's here. But why are you here? Did you have to have surgery?" she asked as if interested in the answer.

"If you must know, I gave birth to our child yesterday and my precious baby died during the night," Vivian answered.

"Oh I'm so sorry to hear that. Maybe that's why John isn't around. Men have no use for women who can't bear them children. He'll probably stay around for a little while but, believe me; eventually he will find someone that will provide him with a child. Alfred loves me although I had two miscarriages myself you know. I know how hard it is to lose a baby. Mine never made it past a few months of pregnancy and I can only imagine how hard it must be after all those months of waiting. It's a shame that you won't get to see your baby grow up. Was it a girl or boy?" she asked.

"It was a little girl, Caroline. I caught only a glance of her in the nursery and never even got to hold her while she was alive. She was perfect, absolutely perfect," Vivian wept once more and her body shook with pain.

"Oh my dear, if she had been perfect, then she wouldn't have died. And Vivian, don't worry about John, I'll see to it that he is taken care of, well taken care of," Louise said cruelly and watched as Vivian's body stiffen before breaking into loud sobs. Louise left to see if the nurse could sedate Mrs. Williams who was obviously in need of additional medication. As she approached the nurses' station she overheard two of them talking about the mix-up of the babies and she turned to walk away. Hopefully they wouldn't remember her as being the volunteer in the nursery. She would leave the hospital and not return for several days. After all, with their smocks and caps on, all of the volunteers looked the same.

She was about to leave and recalled the utter destruction of Vivian's countenance and realized that Vivian didn't know that her daughter was alive. Obviously, the nurses thought that she was still sedated. Perhaps she had a few more moments and she could do more damage before Vivian could learn the truth. She saw the nurses were still at the station and returned to Vivian's room. She left with a smile on her face a few minutes later. Vivian was teetering on totally losing control over that fine mind that everyone had bragged about so much during Louise's brief stay at Comfield College. Well that fine mind was all but lost now and Louise whistled a tune as she decided to walk to the Perkins home rather than call for the driver. She wanted to savor her victory for just a little while longer.

She would go home, change clothes, and return to help John who would no doubt be worried about his mad wife who would need to be taken to a sanitarium. Vivian in a sanitarium left to rot in her own wastes, there was an image that inspired Louise. John would appreciate her concern and would not refuse her comfort and later he wouldn't refuse her kisses as he had once before. She would speak kindly to him and tell him how sorry she was that she couldn't apologize to Vivian for that trouble at Comfield and perhaps never would be able to ease her conscience. Louise quickly changed clothes and asked for a cup of coffee to warm up her inside. She dabbed perfume on her neck and put on a beautifully fitting suit. She had removed her cap and restyled her hair. She put on her earrings and put on the suit's matching hat. She checked her teeth and lipstick after sipping the warm coffee. She called for the driver to warm up the car. She would go directly to John and hopefully his parents would find them together with her leather covered hands holding his. He would hear the sweetest voice she could muster as she comforted him.

She would let him tell her about the baby and his distraught wife. Perhaps she should wait until after his parents had arrived. It would give her another chance to make a good impression on them as well. She would walk slowly into the waiting room and would just happen to notice him there. She would claim to be coming there to visit a friend. John in a vulnerable state would accept her hugs and soft words. Louise knew how to manipulate a situation and this one was perfectly suited for her needs.

She entered the hospital about fifteen minutes later to seek John and didn't see him in the waiting room. It was now visiting hours and she figured that she had just missed him. She had taken too long to look her best. She started to go down the private room wing and saw Emily come out of Vivian's room in tears. Louise stepped back and turned so as not to be seen. She listened as she heard John say, "I hope Father O'Brien can reach her. She absolutely refuses to see our baby! I can't understand why she won't accept Caroline as ours. She is convinced that all is lost!"

Emily whispered something and Louise couldn't make out but decided that she would have to leave, hopefully unnoticed by either John or Emily. Louise was ecstatic at the prospect of Vivian being committed and was disappointed that she hadn't got her chance with John. At least she had succeeded in breaking Vivian and walked to the judge's home happy with the knowledge that she had finally gotten her revenge. She entered through the back door and went up the rear set of stairs. She called the hospital from her room and asked about Mrs. John Williams. "Are you family?" the nurse asked. "Yes," she lied. "Mrs. Williams is doing well considering the night she had. She and the baby are doing fine."

Louise knew that was a cautious reply that she had been told to say when you weren't sure to whom you were speaking. She smiled to herself knowing what the truth must be. She decided to do a bit of shopping and went down to ask Mrs. Perkins to join her. Alfred was coming later that evening and she wanted to buy a new negligee for him to admire that evening.

John sat on the edge of the bed and held onto Vivian as Father O'Brien calmly explained to Vivian about the mistake. He told her repeatedly that her beautiful baby was alive. He admitted that he had indeed baptized a baby but now knew it hadn't been hers. He explained that he had found out that the baby's mother was Catholic and he had visited Mrs. Miller in the ward who belonged to the Coalston parish. He told her that the mother wasn't expected to live and that he had performed the last rites before coming to see her. Vivian looked up at him with a look of sudden recognition and simply said, "Father O'Brien." He smiled at her and reminded her that he had taken a solemn vow not to lie to one of God's creatures. She looked at John puzzled at first and remembered what Louise had told her. Louise had claimed that she had seen John making out with a curvaceous nurse in a stair well and was on the prowl for a new mate. Louise also told Vivian that John had left town when he had gotten the news. That had caused Vivian to become despondent.

John held her hand as he again told her about Caroline and asked if she would like to see her. Vivian sat up in her bed and asked Emily to help her get ready. Emily brushed her hair and washed her face. Nurse Snyder had told them it was against regulations for a baby to come to a patient's room during visiting hours but an exception would be made due to the circumstances. But she insisted however, that Emily would have to leave the room and that John wouldn't be permitted to be in the room either. The nurse had asked Father O'Brien to step outside as well. From the happy sounds coming from the room, Emily and John began to cry together. Vivian was crying and soothing her baby. "Oh she's so beautiful, isn't she?" The nurse said, "Yes she certainly is. Would you like to feed her?"

"Oh yes!" Vivian said with excitement. Sounds of her kissing the baby was heard from the room out into the hall. Father O'Brien nodded to them and said, "She will be just fine now. That wee lass has performed a miracle. The baby has saved the life of her lovely mother. Call me if you need me."

The nurse entered with a small bottle of formula. Vivian was quite small and feared that she would not have enough milk in her breasts. She had decided to use formula instead. When the nurse opened the door to leave, Emily caught sight of her darling baby girl feeding her angelic granddaughter.

When the nurse returned for the baby about fifteen minutes later, she left with the pink bundle and went immediately to the nursery. The tiny pink bundle was put into her bassinet sound asleep. The nurse told John that the two of them would be in the hospital for three more days and John told Emily that he had to go and buy some cigars. He would need at least a dozen! Emily promised to stay with Vivian and when she entered the room she was amazed by the incredible transformation in her daughter. She was positively glowing!

Around noon, both of the rose arrangements were delivered. Catherine Williams called the hospital exchange and the call was forwarded to Vivian's private room. Emily answered the phone for Vivian. She told Catherine about everything that had happened and Catherine began to cry out of relief. She turned and called to Henry and repeated the good news. She had only enough change for another minute and said, "We should arrive there around one or so. We are in Bluestone." Emily gave her the directions to the hospital and waited for their arrival.

Emily hung up the phone and suggested that Vivian rest for a while. Catherine and Henry would be arriving in another hour. The nurse brought in a lunch of chicken broth, gelatin, coffee and juice. She told Vivian that she would have a regular meal for supper. Vivian drank all of her broth, juice, and coffee. She ate her gelatin and in just a few minutes was sound asleep. Emily sat and waited for the elder Williams to arrive but smiled at her daughter's sweet face enjoying a much needed rest.

Emily had dozed off for what seemed like only a few minutes when she heard the door ease open. Catherine came over and whispered to Emily, "We just saw her and she's the most beautiful baby I have ever seen in my life." Emily rose to speak with Catherine in the hall. "Vivian fell asleep after eating lunch. She was in bad shape earlier, refused to believe Caroline was alive. Father O'Brien finally got through to her and she got to feed Caroline. Oh Catherine, I thought I had lost her; she teetered awfully close to going mad. I am so glad you made it here safely. Would you like to go and look at our granddaughter again?"

"But of course, Henry wouldn't leave the nursery window and was pointing her out to everyone. I don't believe that there is a prouder grandfather anywhere else in the world! Ah, look at her. Oh she's awake!" Catherine cooed as she peered through the window. All of the grandparents stood watching Caroline as she looked around. She must have had a bit of gas and smiled. Henry said,"Oh look. She smiled at me!" Neither woman had the heart to tell him about the gas and instead said, "She sure did!" Henry was smitten by another female; the tiny, adorable granddaughter had captured her heart.

John arrived with the cigars and presented the first one to his father. Henry slapped him on the back and congratulated him. John walked down the hallway and sat in the room as he watched his beautiful wife sleep peacefully. He dozed off himself until he heard his name being called softly. Vivian was awake and he rose to kiss her gently. He told her that his parents had arrived and asked her if she liked the flowers. "Oh yes they are lovely dear! What do you think of Caroline?"

"She is precious. Mother and father are with your mother at the nursery. I'm sorry to say that they won't want to leave, but I'll go and see if I can get mother to come here to visit," he whispered. He walked down to the nursery and told Catherine that Vivian was awake. Catherine was excited and told Henry, "Henry, order the biggest bunch of flowers for the girls!" Henry nodded and asked Emily to take him to the nearest pay phone.

Catherine gently hugged Vivian and admired her two vases of flowers. They talked about the beautiful baby and the welcome home they were planning. Catherine wanted to go shopping for infant girl's outfits that afternoon. Emily entered the room a few minutes later and John left the women together to savor their women's talk. Catherine asked Emily to go shopping with her and just as they were leaving another vase of flowers was delivered. Vivian asked Emily to open the card. Catherine of course thought they were her arrangement. Emily opened the card and said, "I don't believe it! How on earth did she know Viv was here?"

"Who is it from mom?" Vivian asked.

"It's from Louise Perkins," Emily said.

"Well that's nice so nice of her. May I see the card?" Vivian asked. Her mind tried to recall seeing Louise and thought it must have been some sort of a dream or nightmare.

"No, I think its better that you rest now. Catherine and I have some serious shopping to do!" The women kissed her forehead and Emily put the card into her purse. John and Henry would stay with Vivian. She waited until they had entered the Williams car before she exploded. "That witch! That horrible wicked little witch! Read this Catherine," she said as she held out the card. It read,"So sorry to hear of your loss. I hope you feel better soon. I'll see you again, later. Louise Pierce Perkins"

"What does she mean 'see you again, later'?" Catherine posed the question with a look of confusion.

"Louise must have visited earlier this morning before we heard the news about Caroline. I called Belle after William had already left for school so he didn't tell her. Oh Catherine, I wonder if she might have had a hand in the mix-up. If I find out that she did, then look out! I won't hold anything back. I will tell her everything and I do mean everything!" Emily vented.

"Surely you must be mistaken. No one would intentionally do anything as cruel as that, no one," Catherine protested.

"You don't know Louise; it's in her genes to be cruel. I'm so mad I could chew nails! I can't believe that girl! I need to get out of here before I really lose my temper. Let's go shopping and I'll check this out when we return to the hospital. Do you mind if I purchase the christening gown?" she asked with a cross expression on her face. The two women went into every shop buying one of every infant girl's outfit, pink blanket, pink dresser set, and more. Emily went to the Welfield Bank and opened a savings account for Caroline Williams with $1000. Catherine added another $1000. They were both as giddy as schoolgirls when they carried their purchases into Vivian's room and presented her with the savings account book.

Vivian just nodded her head and smiled as she held up each outfit for John and Henry's approval. It was time for another feeding and they would have to leave the room. They all kissed Vivian and as they left to go into the waiting room Emily took John aside and told him of her suspicions. Emily was acquainted with the volunteer coordinator and would ask her if Louise ever volunteered at the hospital. John was beside himself at the implication and found it hard to believe. "Find out for me, but do not say anything to Vivian just yet. She had shown me the flowers that Louise sent and thinks they were to congratulate us. I will confront Louise with you," he said, "If she had anything to do with this horrendous affair I will make sure that she regrets it."

Emily walked down to the volunteer coordinator's desk and was told that indeed Louise was a volunteer. She had worked in the blood bank, nursery, and ER and was well liked by all of the staff. Emily asked if she was there today and the coordinator looked at the schedule and said, "Well she wasn't scheduled but she signed in to work the ER early this morning and signed out after only about an hour or two later."

Emily pursued it a little further, "Do you happen to know where she worked yesterday?"

"Oh yes, she was assigned to the nursery, the day shift. That is when they are the busiest up there. Would you like to leave her a message?" the coordinator asked.

"No, that's all right. I wanted to thank her for some flowers she sent. My daughter gave birth yesterday and Louise sent the loveliest bunch of flowers. I'll call her at the Perkins' residence," Emily said with conviction.

Emily asked John to go with her to Belle's. Belle didn't know about the unfortunate affair and needed to be told everything in person. Emily told John about her conversation with the coordinator. She was sure that Louise was responsible for the switch and that it hadn't been accidental. When she thought of the state Vivian had been in this morning she was sure that had been Louise's handiwork as well.

When Emily and John told Belle about how beautiful Caroline was, Belle was ecstatic but when they revealed the horrible events that had passed in the last few hours Belle's mouth opened in horror. She had been extremely busy and was planning on going to the hospital with William later that afternoon when he arrived home from school. Belle had known that it was a special day for the grandparents and wanted to give Vivian time to rest. Emily showed Belle the card that Louise had sent and relayed the information gathered from the coordinator. Belle was shocked and horrified by what she had heard. She had never believed, at any time, that Louise's mind was that twisted. At one time she had even suspected that Louise had faked the breakdown, but now she was sure that Louise was beyond help. Who else but a mad woman would devise such a cruel plot?

Emily disagreed and said a mad woman wouldn't, but a detestable, jealous woman would. She intended to ask the day shift nurses about Louise and asked Belle if she could borrow Louise's wedding photograph that was in a frame in Belle's office. She would have to work quickly since Paul Michael would be returning from school in another hour. Emily felt a little faint and realized that she hadn't eaten anything that day. Belle called for the maid to bring Emily and John a sandwich and something to drink. Emily could only swallow a few bites of sandwich. She had a mission and could only think about that and the strength she was going to need to finish it.

Emily returned to the hospital and showed each of the day nurses Louise's picture. One of them distinctly remembered her receiving both babies and had volunteered to put on the bracelets since it was the shift change. Emily looked at John and told him that she would take care of it herself later and left to get Paul Michael.

Paul Michael was so excited about Caroline and saw Louise's photograph. Naturally he wanted to know who the pretty lady was. Emily said she was a lady who had known Vivian for a long time and was married to Alfred Perkins. "Oh, she is very pretty. She must be something special if Alfred married her!" he mused.

"Oh she's something all right!" Emily said sarcastically. "Would you like to go and see your new niece?"

"Will they let me?" he asked.

"For a few minutes I'm sure they will, but you won't be able to go into Vivian's room. Do you understand?" she asked.

"Yes ma'am I do. I'm too little, right?" he reasoned.

"That's right Uncle Paul Michael!" Emily smiled. "You are the handsomest uncle of the most beautiful niece in the whole world."

The nurses agreed to let Paul Michael look at Caroline but only for a few minutes. She whispered to Catherine what she had found out about Louise and Catherine's face turned red with anger. Emily assured her that she would be taken care of once and for all. Paul Michael was amazed by Caroline and pointed out her tiny fingers and nose. He had never been into a hospital before and informed them that he liked the smell. He was one of the few that any of them knew that actually liked the smell of antiseptic, wax, and cleaners.

He couldn't wait to tell Poppy about the baby when he and Emily returned home. John carried the baby girl items in and went to lie down for a few hours. Belle had gone by the hospital with William and had arrived about an hour later at Emily's house. Emily had called Judge Marshall to tell him about Caroline and about Louise's ploy. From the sound of his voice she could tell that he was extremely upset and disappointed. "What are you going to do?" he asked.

"Belle and I will confront her. She knew what she was doing Andrew, and deliberately set out to try to drive my poor Vivian insane," she answered.

"Alfred is coming down later today. Let me cancel my schedule for the next few days and I'll come down with him and go with you to confront her. You will need someone there that will have a level head and can serve as a witness as well. I won't mention any of this to Alfred. I want him to arrive there in one piece. I can't wait to see you, Emily, and can hardly wait to see that grandbaby of yours. Meanwhile, try to calm down and I'll see you later," Andrew counseled. "Settle down and enjoy your new granddaughter, grandma!"

She laughed and told him that she would definitely enjoy her grandbaby and admitted that she looked forward to seeing him. The judge called a florist and ordered two bunches of flowers, one for Vivian and the other for Emily. They should arrive, the florist told him within two hours. They asked if he had a preference and he answered, "A potted chrysanthemum for Vivian that she could plant in her garden and a mixed arrangement for Emily." He gave Emily's address and asked that the potted plant be delivered to Vivian at the Welfield hospital.

As he hung up the phone he thought of the other calls that would have to be made and asked his secretary to cancel all of his appointments for the rest of the week but to call Alfred Perkins first.

When Alfred was reached, Andrew asked if could ride with him to Welfield. He told him about Vivian's new baby and Alfred told him that of course he could get a ride with him. It would be nice to have company on the three hour ride to Welfield. Alfred called his parent's home and was told that his mother and wife had gone shopping and should be returning soon. He advised the maid that he would be arriving around 8:30 that night and that Judge Marshall would be with him.

Alfred and Andrew left at 5:30 and arrived promptly at 8:30. The cook had warmed them some supper and both men were tired after a long week plus the drive. Judge Marshall went to bed after a light supper after talking briefly with Emily. Louise waited for Alfred to show him her new negligee holding it in front of herself and welcomed him with open arms. It was around nine o'clock on Friday morning that Emily and Belle both arrived at the Perkins' residence. They asked to meet with Alfred and Louise and invited Judge Marshall, Judge Perkins and his wife as well to join them. Mrs. Perkins asked them into the library and sent for Louise, Alfred and the two judges. Louise was in a good mood and had just agreed to adopt a child with Alfred. She was happy until she saw Emily and Belle sitting on the leather couch. She turned to leave but Judge Marshall spoke up and said, "I strongly suggest that you stay."

Emily told the events as she understood them up to Louise's morning visit with Vivian and Louise stood up and said, "I don't have to listen to this dribble. She's just upset that her precious daughter couldn't deliver a healthy baby and is trying to somehow blame me because her daughter is unfit to have a healthy baby."

"Sit down Louise, we are not finished," Emily said in a stern voice. She continued with the day shift nurse's findings and Louise's expression changed from one of triumph to an ashen color. When Emily revealed that Caroline was alive and her subsequent investigation into Louise's participation in the mix-up, Alfred looked at Louise and said, "Louise, darling tell me you didn't do that! Louise!"

"I didn't know it was Vivian's baby. It was an honest mistake dear! How would I know she was in Welfield? I thought Vivian was in Virginia. I didn't even know she was pregnant," Louise said through her crocodile tears.

"Louise, you made such a scene with William when he told you about Vivian being pregnant, don't you remember?" Alfred asked.

"Well, I had miscarried and it had upset me to find out she was pregnant. I forgot about that until you just mentioned it. I swear," Louise started wringing her hands and reached for Alfred's arm to steady her.

"Well if that's true, then how did you know that her baby had been pronounced dead? Louise, why did you visit her and say such mean and vicious lies? Why in this world did you tell her 'If she hadn't been perfect she wouldn't have died?' Why did the day nurse identify you as the one who volunteered to put the bracelets into the bassinets? You had never asked to do that before. Why would you do such a cruel thing to Vivian?" Emily asked.

Belle joined in, "What did Vivian ever do to you for you to treat her so abominably?"

Louise looked trapped and said, "I don't feel so well Alfred. I need to rest."

Alfred looked at her and said, "Louise, did you or did you not cause the mix-up?"

"Yes I guess I did but it was so hectic in the nursery with all those babies. I was too busy to look at the bracelets," she insisted.

"I'm sorry; I can't believe it was an accident. The mother's name was on the bracelet and you knew it was Vivian. You even went by her room when she thought her baby had died and made some very hurtful comments and accusations against John," Emily prodded.

Alfred asked once more, "Louise, did you do these things?"

"All right I did it and I would do it all over again! She has everything and has ruined my entire life. She stole my future with John. That should have been my baby, mine, do you hear me? I hate her for stealing everything from me. She's the reason I had to leave college, she's the reason for me having to be married to you, and she's the reason I can't have any children. She drove me to act the way I did! I have to scrape for every penny to spend and should have had a life of ease by now," she was breathing heavy now and looked first at her in-laws and then at Judge Marshall.

"No Louise, you brought everything on yourself. Your dishonesty and laziness made you leave college and you know the real reason why you can't have children. Or would you like for me to enlighten everyone here!" Belle warned her.

Alfred looked shocked and once more said, "Louise, darling, tell me you married me because you loved me. Why are you so upset over the man who married Vivian Black? We have a beautiful home and are going to adopt a child so why do you say those things? We have a future together one full of promise with an adopted child. Louise, what are you saying?"

"Wake up Alfred; we don't have a future together. Have you met John? He is perfect and I mean perfect. He's rich, good-looking, and has some personality. He's nothing at all like you. Trust me, if you knew him then you would know why I am so upset for having to settle for you. Did you honestly think I could love you with your nasal-toned voice and thick glasses? No dear, I shivered every time you touched me and wished every time that it had been John Williams. Why do you think I destroyed your babies? I couldn't bear the idea of them growing inside me! Now you know the truth. You're nothing but a pitiful sham of a man, a weakling," she spat her words at him. "You're worse than those two put together. I wouldn't be surprised if I found out you were in on that fiasco with the boxes!"

Belle shouted, "Louise that is enough!" In a calmer voice she said, "You insist on the truth well get ready sweetheart because here it comes. Do you want to know what was in those safety deposit boxes the ones your greed drove you to find out what was in them? Well, I'll tell you! They contained papers including a doctor's bill for your supposed hemorrhage when you were in high school. What you don't know is that another box contained a detective's report of your escapades in high school with that Collins boy! Bertie hired a detective and he followed you to Bluestone. Judge Perkins, Louise wasn't a virgin when she married Alfred. She had aborted her own baby in her junior year of high school and had made a mess of things back then and needed a D and C."

Judge Perkins and his wife both looked at Louise and he asked, "Is this true Louise? How on earth did you get the report that said you were a virgin?"

Louise looked at him and with pure venom in her voice said, "Money talks, Judge and Aunt Belle forced me to marry him. She was going to cut me off without a cent if I didn't marry him."

Belle continued, "I never paid any doctor money to be quiet. I would have sent you packing to that grandmother of yours. Do you remember at your engagement party how Bertie had asked Martha not to come to your wedding and had a confrontation at your engagement party about her dancing with Andrew? What you don't know is that right after that party Martha wrote a blackmail letter to Bertie. She had figured out something about your mother and had blackmailed her. Your wonderful grandmother, the very one who had been your lifelong coach, blackmailed your mother. In one of the other boxes were copies of the payments Bertie made of $500 a month to keep your grandmother quiet. Didn't you ever wonder why your mother wanted nothing to do with her own mother?"

Louise screamed, "Lies, nothing but lies. Grandmother told me all about how my own mother deserted her when she was only fifteen and how stupid and lazy she had been her whole life! Anyone just had to look at our cabin to know how lazy and stupid she was. She drove my father to drink and you," she pointed to Emily, "did nothing to help us. You made fun of her, you along with that stupid foreign husband of yours."

Emily couldn't help it as she jumped up and suddenly slapped Louise hard. "Don't you ever, ever, talk about me or my late husband in that tone you despicable little witch! Paul and I tried to help Bertie and her children. Her good for nothing mother never taught her how to do anything. Bertie couldn't read or write because her dear mother was too sorry to send her to school. That's the kind of mother she was! She was the lazy one and a poor excuse of a mother! What's more, she made things worse for your mother. Bertie didn't desert your grandmother; she left her family to escape your grandfather!"

"What do you mean escape? Grandmother told me how much she had loved him and what a fine man he was! Mother wanted to marry my father only so she wouldn't have to work at home and nothing you can say will ever change my mind," she said with an evil smile.

"Well Louise you are mistaken, ask Alfred or Judge Marshall. There is a lot you don't know about your grandmother and your grandfather. I was widowed at a young age and your dear grandmother, the wonderful mother, sent her own husband over to my house to rape me! He beat me up, broke my arm and raped me, his own late brother's widow!"

"No, he wouldn't have, she wouldn't. You were jealous of her and her daughters! I know, she told me so!" Louise yelled.

"Did she tell you everything? When Martha wanted custody of William I had my detective's investigate her. Here are the affidavits I received from Bertie's sisters telling about how all of them had been raped by their own father. She forced them to let their father rape them repeatedly just as she sent him over to rape me!" Belle said with conviction.

"No, no, mother would have told me. She would have said something. You're the one responsible; you, you must have seduced him!" she countered.

"Oh and I suppose that I broke my own arm? He came back to rape me again and I shot at him. Here read Dr. Sherman's statement for yourself He's the one who treated me. Your dear grandfather messed me up so badly that I almost died. It was weeks later that I found out I was pregnant and had to hide out in my house for months!" Belle confessed.

"Pregnant? You didn't have any children everyone knows that! You will try anything, won't you, to cover your lies! Where is this mystery child that no one ever saw?" Louise asked with her eyes glaring.

"She is right here," Emily spoke up. "I am Belle's daughter. I didn't know until last year after Bertie died when you sued Belle for custody of William and you wanted Belle's endowments to me and Vivian overturned. It wasn't until she had investigated Vivian, as you had requested before that fiasco at Comfield, that she found out who my parents were and put the pieces together. I never knew I had been adopted until she told me."

"You are Belle's bastard? Well, what do you know? A whore and a bastard preaching to me like they are so much better than me when it's evident to everyone here that you knew all along. And you, Aunt Belle, crying over the brat of a bastard. You are worse than my mother who was such a weakling. She couldn't keep house by herself and you had to take us in. If my father or grandmother hadn't died I wouldn't have had to deal with all of this," she leered at Belle. Turning to Emily she said, "You could have at least tried to help, but instead you let us almost starve to death. I remember everything," she spat out at her.

"Your mother never knew that I had a child and as for Emily and Paul, they rescued you many times. Have you forgotten all those nights you spent in their home? Who do you think brought you to my house? Paul planted us a garden and worked on the barn and garden for several days. He gave your mother food and offered to help her run your farm, but she had refused. She had to leave the hollow; she had to get away from that house. Do you really want to know why she left? Your father used to beard your face didn't he?"

Louise looked as if she had just awakened from a dream as Belle continued. "He used to kiss on you when you were only seven remember? Your mother had given birth to William and your father wanted to have sex with her.

She couldn't since she had a difficult delivery with William. He told your mother how pretty you were and started watching you sleep."

"My father loved me. He worked real hard to make us a good home and I remember how mother couldn't keep our house clean and used to lie in the bed until after noon," Louise said sternly. "You're the one who doesn't know everything that my father had to put up with her."

"Bertie couldn't get out of bed on most days, because your father had almost beaten her to death so many times. Ask anyone in Jackson about your father and they will tell you he was a mean drunk and he beat her senselessly. She was petrified to tell him she was pregnant with William and hid it from him. He always beat her savagely, brutally when she was pregnant, and caused her to have numerous miscarriages. She hid both of her pregnancies so that she could have children. Bertie loved being a mother more than anything. Paul had to fetch the doctor many times to tend to her broken jaw, broken ribs, broken bones of every sort. One time she had so many broken ribs that she could barely breathe. Paul wanted to have him arrested and Bertie asked him not to," Emily explained. "Your mother was one of the strongest women I have ever known to put up with that man, and her family, all of them, just stood by and let it happen."

"You only say that because you are so much worse of a mother than she was. You married that foreigner who thought he was better than everyone and look at that mousy daughter of yours who had to trick John into marrying her. Did he know about you? Huh? Did he know that you were from the wrong side of the blanket?" Louise gave a wicked smile.

"He did and because he loved me, he personally thanked Belle for giving me to my parents," Emily said proudly.

"Just as I thought, he was dumber than I remember. What did he do, buy you some flowers?" she asked, "Did he tell you about our little secret? He used to tell me how pretty I was! He used to have me sit on his lap and rub me all over with his hands! Didn't know that, did you? Your precious Paul was a child molester. He's the one that kissed on me and bearded me, not my own father!"

"No Louise, that was your father and you know it. Your mother knew what your father planned to do and in fact during one of his drunks he admitted what he was going to do since your mother had tricked him and had hidden

219

her pregnancy with William. He was going to rape you! Your mother saw that he looked at you just like her father had looked at her before she had been raped and so your so-called weak mother did what she had to do. She suffocated your father with a pillow," Belle continued.

"You have transferred all the things that your father did to you, to Paul! You always took your grandmother's view of things over your own mother's. That precious grandmother of yours had blackmailed your mother. She had found the pillow and pillowcase that your mother had hidden. Bertie had to get away from that cabin to escape from the horrible memories of what she had done. Neither Emily nor Paul caused your father to drink. It was your grandfather that had introduced him to moonshine when he was just a boy!" Belle finally sighed with shame and disgust. "Your father was an alcoholic."

"You don't expect me to believe any of this, do you? Where is all of this so called proof and letters? Mother couldn't have killed my own father. The doctor said it was a heart attack!" she screamed and was shaking violently now.

"The proof is in the safety deposit boxes. Judge Marshall and Alfred have viewed all of the evidence in those boxes you were so bent on looking at. Go ahead ask them," Belle declared. "Your grandmother was confronted with the evidence of the rapes and did not want to face you or the truth in court. She couldn't bear to lose custody of William because of what she had done. That's why she committed suicide. You wanted the truth, well there it is. Did you know that your mother wrote letters to Emily about what had happened to her? She hid them in the safety deposit boxes so you wouldn't find out. She wrote about how her father had raped her when she wasn't even ten years old. Your grandmother locked Bertie's bedroom from the outside so she couldn't escape! That's the kind of woman Martha Coleman was my dear, and you are just like her." Belle sat down exhausted from her exchange with Louise.

Louise's eyes darted to Alfred and then to Judge Marshall and both of them nodded sadly in agreement and Emily continued. "We left the letters and pillowcase in the safety deposit boxes," Emily sighed. "There is nothing to gain from showing them to you now. I never would have hurt you Louise, but you gave me no choice. I would have kept it from you and would have protected you from the truth. I would have, but no, you just had to try to ruin my Vivian by driving her insane and that my dear I will not let go unpunished."

Belle interjected, "I will have to tell poor William everything as well."

Alfred was shocked by all that he had heard about Vivian while Andrew hugged Emily tightly and Belle finally broke down for the first time since Bertie's death and openly wept. Louise looked around and said, "So, you want to tell William the truth by all means do so. Make sure Aunt Belle that he knows about that whore of a daughter of yours that couldn't wait to jump into Judge Marshall's bed when her husband wasn't even cold in the ground! Tell him she's a chip off the old Coleman block."

"That my dear is a lie! I haven't even kissed Emily. You are a sick woman to even think of such things. You need help! Alfred, she needs to go back to the sanitarium," Judge Marshall observed.

Alfred finally spoke up, "She's not sick judge, she's just evil. Mom, dad, she deliberately caused those miscarriages using a pencil and perforated her uterus. Yes mother, she performed a self-abortion! That's why she had to have the hysterectomy. I had believed everything she had told me, but after reading what was in those boxes and getting to know Emily, what Louise has told me was nothing but one lie after another."

"Oh Alfred grow up! Women do that sort of thing all the time. Do you think all of us want to have your brats and ruin our figures? What's the big deal then? Huh? We want to lead our own lives and have fun! You are such a loser!" Louise looked around, "Your parents look shocked! Well let me tell you something about your precious Alfred. He works all the time and has a crush on Emily Black! Oh Judge Marshall I wish you could see your face!" she laughed.

"That will do Louise. Emily told me to forgive you. This time you've gone too far. I forgave you when I learned about what you had done at Comfield and had gone prowling to bars. I forgave you for aborting our child, but to deliberately try to steal a woman's child and try to drive her insane thinking her beautiful child had died. That is unforgivable and now, you disgust me!" Alfred stood up and yelled at her.

"You think everything is about you and everyone else in the world is like you. I was the one that encouraged Judge Marshall to meet Emily. I admired her and how she had adopted a refugee child. You are not worthy to even stand in her shadow. I admit it, I love her! I love her like another mother and nothing more. We're through Louise! I want a divorce!"

"You can't divorce me! Divorces aren't allowed when one is mentally ill. I've been in a sanitarium my dear. Tell him judges!" Louise smiled.

"You're right Louise he cannot divorce you, but he can get an annulment!" Judge Marshall said.

"I recommend that you begin the process immediately," Judge Perkins said.

"And now dear, if you would be so kind as to pack your bags and leave our home," Mrs. Perkins said

Belle said, "I would recommend that you return to Charleston as soon as possible. I will send my car for you in an hour. William, will you come in here please?"

William Pierce looked at his sister, aunt, and the others. He could not believe what he had just heard. "Louise, did you really do all those horrible things?"Louise ignored him as he asked, "Why? Why did you do it? You have a beautiful house and a man who loved you, don't you? How can you forget all of us that have loved you and do those terrible things to people I love? I have read many books and stories but not even the great writers could have conceived someone like you that could be so cruel, so driven to destroy the innocent! Many wicked men have lived throughout history but none were of the likes, such as you. Right now I find it difficult to love you myself."

"I never asked you to love me, brother! I don't need any of you! Do you hear me? And you least of all," as she spat into William's face and ran out of the room.

William hung his head and Emily walked over and wiped his face with her handkerchief. He stood still and then looked up. "Only God can help her now," he said. He turned to Emily and said in disbelief, "Your Belle's daughter? That means you really are my real aunt, my mother's half-sister! Oh I will call you Aunt Emily if that's all right and I am so sorry for what she did to Vivian, so very sorry! I might slip every once in a while and call you Emily but I can't believe she did that to poor Vivian. Is Vivian all right now?"

Emily nodded and said, "They are both fine. You'll have to come over to see your new cousin. Vivian is your cousin, William. You have relatives that love you and will never hurt you. Perhaps with distance and time, Louise will come to her senses." William nodded and although he had tried to be strong, wept as others had done earlier in the day. Others in the room had teary eyes watching Emily hug him as a mother would tend to any child needing care. In William's heart, Emily became his surrogate mother that evening. She was so much like his mother.

Belle spoke quietly to the Judge and his wife, "I am sorry for intruding on you and washing our family's dirty laundry in your home, but it all had to come out. I will try to get Louise to return for psychiatric help, but knowing her, she will refuse. I will give her an allowance to live on Alfred. My dear boy, I am so sorry for ever having involved you in this mess." She hugged him and he put his chin on the top of her head.

"It's all right, Belle. I will file for an annulment after I return to Charleston. I will have to get my things out. Mother, may I use the phone to call our maid to pack up my clothes, shoes, and things? I will move into the Daniel Boone until I can find another place," Alfred said with resignation.

"Of course you can dear," his mother answered.

Judge Marshall stepped forward and said, "You can live in my house, my dear fellow. I was going to sell it and move here. You can just stay there. That way, if I have to come to Charleston, I'll have some place to stay. Would that be satisfactory?"

"Thank you judge you are indeed a good friend," Alfred said looking down.

"Thank you my young friend. You have grown up a lot in the last year and have really proven your worth with everything you have gone through with Louise. You have given me someone that I cherish as the dearest of friends if she will have me as hers. Emily, I speak from my heart in front of these witnesses that I will forever be in Alfred's debt for leading me to you, one of the dearest persons that I have come to know. I want you to know that

I hold you in the highest regard. Alfred, I will help you write your petition for an annulment," Judge Marshall stated emphatically.

Belle excused herself from the group and went to call her driver to come by and pick up Louise. She picked up the phone to dial and heard Louise's voice on the extension, "Hello, is this New York Times?"

Chapter 12

Belle listened as she heard Louise trying to speak to a reporter. When the reporter answered, she told him that she had a story that anyone else would kill for about the richest woman in eastern United States, Belle Coleman. She offered the story but insisted on meeting face to face with the reporter. "I can be in New York by tomorrow afternoon," she said. The reporter was cautious and said, "Does this have anything to do with her ward, William Pierce?"

"Oh no, it's about her own dirty little secrets!" Louise replied.

"Ma'am we aren't interested in smearing people, but you might want to try *The Inquisitor* I can give you their number if you would like," he offered.

"No thank you I will call them myself," Louise said as she slammed down the phone. 'I will have to get what really happened out before Aunt Belle can ruin my chances at reconciliation with Alfred. I better wait until I get to Charleston. There is no way that Grandmother Coleman did those horrible things that they said she did. There's just no way. Aunt Belle is just trying to cover up for her own loose living. She sits in judgment of me when she did the same thing. Well, like mother, like daughter' as she thought of Emily and Judge Marshall. 'By the time I'm through with them, they will rue the day they messed with Louise Pierce,' she thought to herself.

Belle's driver arrived an hour later and Louise left with bags hurriedly packed for Charleston. She made a mental list of what she wanted to be in the newspaper and made a list on the notepad that Belle always left in the back seat to write down concerns, ideas, etc. Louise wrote down the list for story ideas. She had heard that *The Inquisitor* paid good money for stories and boy did she have them. She would get her revenge on all of them by revealing all of their dirty little secrets in nationwide newspapers.

She had no more walked through her front door than she screamed at the maid, "Get my bags unpacked and throw Alfred's things out! Did you hear me? Get them out of here this minute!" The maid nodded and began to unpack her bags. Mr. Perkins had already called to his belongings packed and had given the address where they were to be delivered. It had been taken care of promptly and Judge Marshall's butler had come for them about an hour before her arrival and Alfred's belongings were now at Judge Marshall's house.

Louise called *The Inquisitor* and told them about how Belle Coleman had an illegitimate daughter and if they wanted the details she would need $500 cash. She smiled as she thought of all the other stories she could tell, the ones that had been revealed to her earlier that day. She knew that Belle would pay and so would Emily not to have the story printed, but at this point in time she didn't care about blackmail. Oh no, they would pay for treating her the way they had. *The Inquisitor's* reporter was very interested, but said he would need confirmation from a second source! She then identified herself as Belle Coleman's niece. That got the reporter's attention and he told her he would meet her the following morning.

She bargained with the reporter the next morning for each story he got printed and he told her that she would get $500. He counted out $500 and she began her story. "Belle Coleman has an illegitimate daughter all right. Do you remember when she gave all that money to Vivian Black a little more than a year ago?"

"Ma'am there is no way Vivian Black is her illegitimate daughter. She's way too young," the reporter stated.

"Do you want the story or not? Everyone wondered why she gave her so much money and I'll tell you why, Vivian Black's mother is the illegitimate daughter of Belle Coleman. You want confirmation call Welfield 5692 and ask that question. Go ahead you can use my phone," she smiled as she handed him the phone.

He dialed the number and waited for an answer. "Good morning, Belle Coleman's residence may I help you?" was spoken on the other end.

"Yes ma'am, this is Clark Johnson of *The Inquisitor* and I need to speak with Mrs. Coleman please," he asked politely.

"Sir, I will see if she will take your call." Clark Johnson waited a few minutes and then heard, "This is Belle Coleman, how may I help you Mr. Johnson."

"Mrs. Coleman it has been brought to my attention that Emily Black is your illegitimate daughter, would you care to confirm?" he asked.

"Mr. Johnson, Emily Black is my daughter as a result of a rape. If you want the details I will be happy to tell you. I am sure that you will get a much different version from Louise Pierce but I will tell you that her grandfather, Luther Coleman, beat me and then raped me and as a result, I got pregnant. Luther was my late husband Carl's brother. Now if you think your readers want to know more about something that happened more than forty years ago, and then by all means print it. But ask yourself this question, why would my niece want this story printed now? What has she done to risk being left completely out of my will? I would be curious to hear her response. If you have further questions please feel free to call me at a later time. I have a lot of business to tend to. My granddaughter just had a baby and both of them will be coming home in a few days," Belle said and then hung up the phone.

The reporter told Louise what Belle had said and that infuriated Louise. She threw the money at the reporter and screamed at him to get out. He told her, "Thanks for the tip," and left without the money. He would write the story as being confirmed by Belle Coleman herself, but first he would call Emily Black. Why had Vivian Black been given so much by Belle and Emily so little? There was a story in here somewhere; he could smell it.

Belle called Emily to tell her about the reporter and told her to prepare for the release of the story. Within an hour Clark Johnson had called Emily. She was very open and told him about the endowment Belle had given to her and the new business ventures that Belle had started for her in the baby business as well as the Sportsman's Club with cabins on a mountain. He asked her about Louise Perkins and she immediately said, "No comment."

The reporter knew then that the story, the real story, was going to be one about Louise Perkins. Who was she? Why wasn't she given an endowment of her own? What had she done that Belle Coleman had hinted at disowning her? He was staying at the Daniel Boone and decided to start his investigation in Charleston. He asked around and was told that Louise Perkins was married to an attorney, a well respected attorney, who had only been open for only about a year but had made quite a name for himself in the local courts. He was married to Belle Coleman's great niece and his father was good friends with Judge Marshall of the WV Supreme Court and was known to be a fair man. People who were best acquainted with Louise could be found at the country club where she went almost daily. When the reporter went to the Kanawha Country Club, he had found out not only was the young couple was a member there, he also heard a lot of gossip about Louise.

He introduced himself as a guest of Alfred and Louise Perkins and explained that he was just visiting the area. The club called Louise and she confirmed it and gave them her member number to pay for his lunch. He was doing a story that would ruin Belle, Emily, and Vivian. The least she could do was feed him and the club had some of the best food in the area. He ate lunch as he listened carefully to other guests speak candidly with each other without lowering their voices, "She came back yesterday. Her maid supposedly packed up all of Alfred's things and moved them to Judge Marshall's. They're going to get a divorce I'm told, ask Marcy," one lady said. Another conversation he overheard coming from another table was about Louise's parties. "You know I think he must have spent a small fortune on last year's Christmas party. She spends money like she was still living with her aunt. Perhaps her mother left her a lot of money, because her husband sure can't be making that much money. I hear that her mother was the nicest lady and nothing like Louise. It was sad the way she suffered with that cancer and all."

After eating his lunch he asked for the dessert menu. While waiting he heard, "That Perkins girl must have been found out. You know, she had a miscarriage last year. My husband was her doctor. He was disturbed by something then but never said anything to me. Perhaps she tried to take things into her own hands again." The other woman said, "They say that she was sent to that sanitarium for her nerves but I heard she had to recuperate from surgery. They say that she was going to be released early, when something came out in the paper. I don't remember what it was all about dear, but it was sometime this fall. Whatever it was she had a relapse or something around the first week of September and was released just before Thanksgiving."

A new pair of women appeared at the club as Clark's dessert came. "Did you know that Louise Perkins has a charge due of more than $1000 at the dress shop on Kanawha Boulevard? And I heard she was brought home in Belle Coleman's Pierce –Arrow, a Pierce-Arrow! The driver told my driver that Mrs. Coleman had asked to be driven to her the parents of Alfred Pierce's house and then came out a short while later and told him that he was to leave in exactly one hour with Louise Perkins whether she was packed or not! I dare say Louise has been worse than a little naughty for her aunt to treat her like that."

Clark had finished with the dessert and was waiting for his bill when he happened to hear a passing couple say, "Alfred Perkins must have found out about all of her other hobbies, shall we call them, and you know what I mean."

"Indeed he must have. I don't know how a nice young man like him got mixed up with such a manipulating little liar. Did you know she told my husband that I was the one who was asked to leave the Woolworth's store? She called him before I could tell him about what really happened. I was the one who saw her; I'm telling you it wasn't me, but she was the one that was caught shoplifting. The store detective caught her and she saw me witnessing the whole incident. She twists everything around and wouldn't know the truth if it came up and bit her! I had to get the detective tell my husband the truth," the other woman spoke as they sat down close enough for Clark to hear the rest.

Clark had heard enough and now had a better picture of Louise Perkins. He would go to the public library and look at their old papers for articles about Alfred and Louise Perkins. Hopefully they had all the major newspapers and had a good vertical file on the society scene. If so, perhaps he would find out what had set her back in the fall.

He caught a cab to the library and found a very organized vertical file and found several articles about Louise Perkins. There was a story about a trip to New York with a variety of pictures with different escorts as well as one taken in California just after her wedding. There was even an article claiming she had a secret romance with Stuart Plexur, star of screen and stage taken for *The Inquisitor* in the file. Her picture was taken with him wearing a revealing swimsuit on his yacht. There were pictures and a long story about her wedding to Alfred Perkins. From the article, he could tell that no expense had been spared for the nuptials. Her great aunt must have paid a lot of money for everything. It said in the article that they moved into a newly built house that had been furnished and built by her aunt. He tried to recall the inside furnishings and remembered how elegant they were. There were articles about a suit for custody of her younger brother but from other articles, it seemed it was suddenly dropped. She had later filed a lawsuit for the contents of some safety deposit boxes and won a mixed verdict. She had wanted some blue diamond that had belonged to her mother and the court ruled in favor of Emily Black. There were only a few articles about her hospitalization and release but nothing more about the safety deposit boxes.

He asked the librarian to see if there was a vertical file on Belle Coleman. He traced her story back to the initial contract with Marshall Steel Company and followed article after article of her acquisitions and wealth. She had made unorthodox donations to a hospital for miners and steel workers. Some articles were duplicates of the ones he had read in Louise's file. The stories of Vivian Black's endowment had been the big news and there were several articles about it, but none about Emily Black's. He would have to try to learn more about that and exactly what it had included.

Emily had told him something about a lodge, yes a Sportsman's Lodge. He looked over his notes and found it also mentioned in Louise Perkins wedding article. She had rented all the cabins for her guests and the lodge as well. If she didn't like Emily Black, then why on earth would she have given Emily so much money to for her guests and rehearsal dinner? He would have to check on the date of the transfer of deed on that property.

He asked for the file on Vivian Black and was impressed by the young girl's academic accomplishments. She had attended Comfield College. 'What a minute, didn't Louise Perkins attend Comfield? Maybe something happened there to cause problems between Louise and Vivian. One of Vivian's bridesmaids lived right there in Charleston, Amelia Jones and another one lived in Huntington, Peggy Clarkson. Vivian must have met them at Comfield College and perhaps they could shed some light on the situation. He was going to pay for lunch and the waiter told him that it was all taken care of by Mrs. Pierce.

Clark got directions to the address given in the article and Amelia Jones was more than interested in talking about Vivian Black. She told him that Vivian had to be the smartest and nicest girl she had ever known. Amelia was currently on winter break in her junior year at Comfield College and had a lot of interesting information about Louise Pierce Perkins. She related the facts of a scandal involving Louise, Vivian and John Williams. Louise had tried to get Vivian thrown out of Comfield in disgrace and had even tried to steal Vivian's boyfriend, now her husband, John Williams. Amelia told him how to get to Peggy's house before he left.

When the reporter arrived in Huntington he found Peggy Clarkson who confirmed Amelia Jones story and added even more details. Apparently Louise was quite the popular girl with the fellows. Clark had asked Amelia not to mention anything to Peggy and he could tell from Peggy's body language that she hadn't. She elaborated on Louise's plot and also about Louise having a maid to clean her dorm room. She told him about Louise forging notes from her mother giving permission to go into Bluestone. All the girls knew she had been frequenting bars and cut classes due to hangovers.

Peggy told him about Vivian's forgiving nature of the other girl involved and how well suited Vivian and John Williams were for each other. She described John as being from a very wealthy Virginia family and told Clark that Louise had set her cap for him, but he only had eyes for Vivian. Peggy told him about Vivian's endowment and how it didn't change her from the girl next door type. She also told him about Vivian's recent delivery of a beautiful baby girl. Emily had called her the day after the birth as a favor to Vivian. Peggy and Amelia still kept in touch with Vivian, albeit usually through letters, cards, etc.

Clark had a better picture of the characters involved in his story, but he had a long list of information to gather. He wanted to know about those boxes, Vivian's child, deed transfer, court records, etc. Louise must have been a difficult teenager. Perhaps some of her high school friends could enlighten him about her teen years. He caught a taxi back to his hotel and rented a car to drive to Welfield. There was a story, he had told his editor, one that would make him famous across the US.

He rented a cabin on the mountain of the Sportsman's lodge and had left his rental car at the foot of the mountain. The lodge not only provided a truck to go up the mountain but had also provided a security guard for the cars. He would unpack and then speak with the caretaker about the owner and his opinion of Louise Perkins. The caretaker remembered Louise as a very difficult person to work with while she was planning her rehearsal dinner. He told Clark how he had to hire people to hand-pick leaves smaller that a pea from the front porch and had to rake over the grounds numerous times. He told the reporter that he really liked Mrs. Black who was so nice to him and his missus. Her husband, God rests his soul, had been a hard-working man who would work side by side him to make improvements. Mrs. Black had taken his death particularly hard, since it had been due to an accident with a plow. He told about Mr. Blakeman coming in the spring of '44 with the Blacks to look over the property and said that there were no finer people than the Blacks in his book. He told him that Vivian and John Williams were one of the nicest couples he had ever met. Real down to earth people as well as his parents are is what the caretaker had said. Clark had taken many notes and would have to find out about Mr. Blakeman, the attorney of Belle Coleman. The caretaker mentioned the little boy, a war refugee that Mrs. Black had recently adopted from Hungary. He told Clark that the boy was some distant relative of Paul Black, Emily's deceased husband.

Tomorrow, Clark decided, he would go to Welfield and check on the transfer of deeds for the resort property. Perhaps he could also find out more from some Louise Perkins' high school friends. He would check over the city and see where the popular hangouts were for teenagers. Those particular proprietors would know exactly who the friends were of the richest girl that had lived in Welfield. He had a lot of questions for those friends of hers. What kind of a person was the real Louise Pierce Perkins? He was getting enough, not for just a story, but a book! He settled into the extremely comfortable bed of his cabin and slept like a baby.

Clark was in the drug store when a handsome young man that looked familiar walked in. "I have a prescription for Vivian Williams. When will it be ready?"

"In about 15 minutes, would you like to wait, Mr. Williams?" the pharmacist asked.

"I'll wait," he answered and sat down.

'So that is Vivian Black's husband. Yeah, I recognize him now. I wonder if he would speak to me about Louise Perkins. Probably not, but I will mention Amelia and Peggy.' "Ah, Mr. Williams, I am Clark Johnson with *The Inquisitor*. I'm writing a story about life in southern WV and the millionaires among the poor. I spoke with your mother-in-law Mrs. Black, a charming woman, and Belle Coleman. I was doing a follow up on some information given to me by Amelia Jones and Peggy Clarkson. Do you know them sir?" Clark asked.

"Yes I do. They were both in our wedding, but you already know that don't you? What do you really want Mr. Johnson?" John asked poignantly.

"To be honest with you I am doing a story on Louise Perkins. She wanted to sell me a story about Belle Coleman, but I believe that the better story would be one about her. So do you know anything about Ms. Perkins, Mr. Williams?" Clark looked hopeful.

"No comment," John said. He got up and walked to the counter and said, "I'll send someone for that prescription."

"Good day Mr. Jackson," John said as he left.

The pharmacist looked at Clark with a puzzled expression on his face. Clark read it and went over to the counter. "Do you know Louise Pierce, I mean, Louise Perkins?"

"Yes, as a matter of fact I do. Her great aunt owns this pharmacy," the pharmacist said.

"Oh, I see. Do you know any of her friends from high school that still live here?" Clark asked.

"Well there's Lydia Stone, Sadie Livingston, and Luanne Montgomery. They still live here. In fact all of them were in Louise's wedding to that Perkins' boy. They will be coming in here before too long if you don't care to wait. They usually come in for a fountain drink about this time of the day. Did you need anything else?" the pharmacist said hurriedly.

"I'll have a Coca-cola please," Clark answered.

Within a few minutes, three giggling girls walked in and Clark heard the names Lydia and Luanne. These girls had to be Louise's friends. Clark rose and offered to buy each of them a fountain drink. He introduced himself as a writer for *The Inquisitor* and told them he was writing a story about Louise Pierce Perkins and if they said anything he could use, their name would appear in his newspaper. The girls gave him their names and after they had gotten their fountain drinks, they sat down with Clark.

"Well, we have known Louise for some time now," Lydia started. "We were her best friends in high school."

"Oh really, then perhaps you know what happened at Comfield when she was sent home?" he asked as he watched each of their expressions and reactions. He noticed that the one named Luanne was literally squirming in her seat and he decided to let the others talk first. "Oh yes, she got sick or something and had to come home. She was in her house for two weeks without coming out with us a single time. Later she told us that some people had gossiped about her being loose and her aunt had yanked her home from college. Louise told us that gossip had been spread by people that were just jealous of her. She always liked having a good time and somehow her aunt must have found out," Lydia answered.

Sadie added, "Louise wasn't the best student and was having trouble in math. She got a tutor and was suddenly doing a lot better. She loves to go shopping and I have to admit that she has exquisite tastes. She can always spot quality and could tell you the cost of any dress, coat, shoe, bag, or jewelry. She loves jewelry. Her mother left her all of her jewelry, but that Emily Black, she cheated her out of a blue diamond."

"How did that happen?" Clark asked.

"Louise's mother had left in her will that Louise to receive all of her jewelry. Well there was a large blue diamond, unset mind you, in a safety deposit box that Emily Black said was left to her. Some judge in Charleston ruled that the diamond was merely a stone and because it wasn't set, it wasn't jewelry. That was wrong, Louise deserved that diamond that belonged to her mother, besides she told me doesn't have a blue diamond," the girl continued. Clark thought, 'This girl is almost as shallow as Louise Perkins.' But rather than stop the pursuit he asked, "Did they find any jewelry in the any of the boxes?"

"No only some papers, I think. Louise called me of course and said that there were other boxes and she had every intention of looking into the boxes herself. Poor thing got sick in New York and then had to be taken to a hospital. She miscarried you see." Clark noticed Luanne squirm again and asked the girls if they would like some ice cream. They all answered yes and

234

he asked Lydia and Sadie to go and get them each a cone. He gave them $5 and said to go next door to buy some gum as well. He turned to Luanne and said, "Now what do you know, Luanne, that the others don't know?"

"I don't know what you are talking about, Mr. Jackson," Luanne said averting Clark's eyes.

"Oh you know what I'm talking. What do you know about the boys, the drinking, and the sneaking out? You might as well tell me everything," he led.

"Well when we were in high school, Louise used to sneak out with different boys. She left town several times with one of the Collins' boys when she was supposed to be out with us at a movie. One day she asked us if we knew how to take care of an accident," Luanne leaned over and whispered, "You know what I mean, a pregnancy. Lydia told her that she could run real hard around a house. She asked us if we had ever heard about using a sharpened pencil and we told her we didn't and besides, who would do such a dreadful thing to themselves? She never told us she was actually knocked up, you understand, but I believe she was. She missed over a week of school a few days later."

"Is there anything else?" he pursued her because she still looked like she was holding something back.

"Well, Louise used to shoplift and drink. She didn't think I saw her steal things, but I did. The store detective at different stores saw her as well. He must have told Mrs. Coleman and she paid for the things. Louise always had plenty of cash with her but liked the excitement of stealing. Mr. Jackson, I'd be careful if I were you. Louise can be very dangerous when she wants to be. She will pretend to be your friend and then steal you blind. I know from personal experience. You see, she knew I liked the Collins' boy and we were on the verge of going steady and she took him from me. I loved him but she set her eyes on him. He got killed in the war shortly after it broke out. They only dated a few times but she didn't shed a tear when he died. She didn't care that she had hurt me dating him and all; she just wanted the thrill of seeing if she could take him from me and she did. She never loved him; she had only used him like a toy and didn't even go to his funeral." Luanne said sadly.

The girls returned with their purchases of gum and ice cream and gave Clark his change. 'So Louise had gotten rid of a baby. Did she do that anymore? What was it that woman at the country club had said in Charleston? He looked over his notes. Ah, here it is, did she take things into her own hands again? And didn't another lady mention an incident in Woolworth's? Louise Pierce Perkins was getting more and more interesting,' Clark thought. "Well ladies, I thank you for a delightful time, but I have to be going. Thank you again," he said as he left to go to the Courthouse.

He went directly there and found the dates of the transfer of property just as Emily Black and Belle had said he would. Both of them appeared to be above board so far and he then searched probated wills. He read over Bertha Pierce's will several times and it clearly stated that anything connected to a hope chest belonged to Emily Black. 'How was the blue diamond connected to the hope chest? It had to be or she wouldn't have been granted possession of it in court. Was there any evidence of what was in those mystery boxes? There had to be, but how could he find out? Only the attorney and parties involved would know and they weren't going to talk, but who else knew, who else would talk with him? The attorneys weren't going to talk since they would claim client-attorney privilege. Who else could know and would perhaps tell him? Ah, yes the younger brother he was only fourteen or so. What is his name?' Clark looked through his notes. William Pierce had given away his sister at her wedding. Perhaps he would tell me what had been in the boxes?

Clark drove his car by the Coleman residence on Sumner Street and noticed that no car was in the driveway. He parked the car further down the street and waited. The school bus should be arriving before too long. He checked to make sure that he had his business cards and watched. The bus stopped and William was the only one getting off the bus. Clark walked up to the young man and handed him a business card. "I was wondering if I could talk to you about what was in those mystery safety deposit boxes. Do you know what was in the boxes?"

"Sir, I have no comment," William stated clearly.

Clark walked with him and said, "Could you just give me a hint?"

William answered, "There were bonds, letters, and a blue diamond. Now if you will excuse me I have nothing more to say." The young man walked quickly down his driveway and Clark watched him. 'So there were letters.

That poor kid certainly looked horribly sad. Something must have happened between William and Louise. Did it have to do with those letters? What had Vivian Black's friend said about her having a baby? Could it be that she had the baby while visiting here? He would check at the Welfield hospital. If he hurried, he could be there before the business office closed.

He asked a mailman on his route how to get to the hospital and drove directly there. He asked at the visitor's desk if Vivian Williams was a patient there. The receptionist said that she was due to be discharged at any time. He asked what room and she told him. She also reminded him that visiting hours would be over at 6 pm.

He rode the elevator up to the given floor and saw John Williams walk out of the room. He softly walked down the hall and stood outside of Vivian's door listening. He heard a lot more details about Louise in only five minutes time standing in that hallway. Somehow, she had tried to convince Vivian Black that her daughter had died by switching bracelets. What a woman! What a story! There had been a show down of sorts with Belle and Emily and that was why Louise had been alone in Charleston.

Clark drove back to the foot of the mountain and waited on the truck to take him to his cabin. He would write everything down before he forgot it. His story would be front page news! Clark stayed up late and wrote his story complete with the recent plan that almost ruined a good and decent family's life. He wrote until almost three o'clock in the morning. It was December 17 and with driving, editing, and rewrites his story would definitely be in the papers before Christmas. If it was as big of a story as he thought it was going to be, he was going to be famous and would be getting lots of job offers from other newspapers.

He slept in the next day and checked out early telling the caretaker that something had come up and he wouldn't need the cabin for the rest of the week. He had paid for the full week and it just gave the caretaker and the maids extra days to get the cabin ready for the Christmas full house that had booked in early November.

Clark returned the rental car to Charleston and then flew to New York. He went home for a good night's sleep and decided that he wouldn't go into the office until the 18th. He had a feeling that he was going to be up late the next day. He took his story to the editor's secretary and she took it into the editor and closed the door behind her. In about thirty minutes the editor called him into his office. "Did you confirm this about the baby?"

"I heard it from a conversation between Vivian Williams, her husband, and her mother, Emily Black. The other sources that I have named gave me permission to use their names. So what do you think?" Clark asked.

"We need some file photographs of Louise Perkins and Vivian Williams. We also need to get a picture of that baby! Why didn't you take one of her in the nursery? She's definitely home by now and we will never get one now. I tell you what; take a picture of some other newborn baby. Pay some woman for a picture of her baby in a nursery of a hospital. Only a few people will know that it isn't the real baby! We gotta move on this! I want it in the Saturday, let's see, Dec. 22nd, edition. Let's roll with this one!" the editor shouted. He called the research department for pictures of Louise and Vivian. He asked for any pictures of Louise Pierce Perkins that made her look a little frazzled and told them to get any of Vivian Black's wedding pictures. He screamed at them over the phone and told them that he needed the pictures yesterday!

The research department sent up all the pictures they had and the editor made his final choices. He called Emily Black's home as a courtesy and asked her to comment on the recent mix-up involving her granddaughter. She was very polite and thanked him for the warning of the article before it was actually released. She explained that it had been a very difficult time for the family and would appreciate if the newsmen would respect the family's wishes to be able to relax and enjoy their newest family addition. The editor could not speak for the other papers, but promised that he wouldn't send anyone from his newspaper.

The story not only made the front page of *The Inquisitor*, but was discussed on every radio news program across America. Feedback was positive and *The Inquisitor* had to do a second printing because it had sold out in only a few hours. It was the first time in the history of the paper that they had to do a reprint of a story. Around eleven o'clock Clark Johnson received a call from Louise threatening to sue him and the newspaper. He asked if he could quote her on that and she had slammed the phone down.

Louise was still fuming when she called a friend of hers, Daniel Furgon, from the Comfield College days in Bluestone. He was known for having friends that had hot tempers and big fists. She asked him to do her a favor for which he would be well compensated. She gave him the name and location of the newspaper and wired money for a plane ticket for three people to fly out of Bluestone to New York on the 23rd. Clark Johnson was found on Christmas Eve almost beaten to death found by a paperboy on his morning rounds with his wallet and watch stolen. He was taken to the hospital and had no recollection of that day or of the attack. Louise smiled to herself as she read the article about the mugging of Clark Johnson. She called Daniel once more, but this time he was in one of the reserved rooms for himself and his friends at the Waldorf. She told him that she had another job, but that it had to be done on Christmas Day. The man that answered the phone in the other room told her that they would be flying back to Bluestone late on Christmas Eve. She stressed that the job absolutely had to be done without any of them being seen or leaving any witnesses. The man hung up the phone and couldn't remember the last time that he had so much fun as he had these past few days.

Chapter 13

Vivian and Caroline came home to Emily's house amid a forest of flowers. Every member of the board for Marshall Steel had sent arrangements as did her friends from UVA. All of her professors had agreed that they would give her an incomplete and had agreed to give her their final exam when she returned to campus. Her doctor in Charlottesville wasn't surprised that she had gone into labor so soon after his examination the previous week, but was pleased to hear that everything had gone smoothly.

"Smoothly," she chuckled, "if you only knew what I have been through?" Vivian was glad to be out of the hospital. John had paid all of the expenses at the hospital and Emily driver had driven very slowly from the hospital. Vivian was pleased to find that Emily had purchased a cradle for Caroline and watched as Poppy found a spot to lie beneath the cradle. Poppy stayed there until Caroline cried, and if either Vivian or John wasn't in the room, Poppy would go to where they were and whined until they followed her. She acted as though Caroline was her baby! She would lift her nose to look at Vivian as if she was making sure Vivian was holding Caroline correctly.

Paul Michael had held Caroline for only a few minutes and went through the house strutting with an unlit cigar he had gotten from John. John and Vivian were going to return to Charlottesville in another week or so after Christmas. Emily had gone out the day before Vivian was released and had quickly turned one of the guest rooms into a nursery. She had purchased a duplicate cradle for Vivian and John to take home with them. She had placed a changing table, chest of drawers, as well as a portable baby bath tub in the nursery. Belle had insisted on stocking the nursery with diapers, powder, oils, and lotion. Emily had extra blankets, sheets, and pads in there as well. When John and Vivian visited, they would only have to bring Caroline with them. Everything she could need for the first year could be found in the nursery at Emily's house.

Vivian followed the pediatrician's release orders on how to take care of Caroline's belly button and wiped her thoroughly with each diaper change. John became somewhat adept at changing diapers, but Emily, she was the expert. They took turns feeding Caroline so that Vivian could rest. Paul Michael was all smiles when he had gotten a chance to feed her as well. He put her across his lap to burp her with some assistance from John. William was thrilled holding Caroline who looked like she was smiling at him. Catherine and Henry were pleased to do their part as well helping Vivian take care of their newest grandchild. Vivian took naps only after Caroline had been fed, changed, and fell asleep. Vivian loved feeding and changing her baby girl. While she was changing Caroline, she spoke in low tones but with her regular voice and not using baby talk. She was going to be an excellent mother, Emily noted with pride. Vivian would stay upstairs for a week at Emily's and John carried her down the stairs to eat dinner with the others.

Paul Michael had volunteered at first to assist with the diaper changes and did so without complaint until Caroline had her first bowel movement and he was on "diaper duty". He ran to the diaper pail with his nose pinched. He used a pair of tongs to dunk the diapers in the commode before putting them into the pail. He actually got pretty good at it within a few days. He would not step down from his responsibility as he so eloquently put it. He had asked Henry to take him to GC Murphy's to buy the tongs and they had both returned with blue lips, no doubt to the jawbreakers that they had purchased. Anytime someone needed something from Murphy's the two of them always volunteered to go and get it. Whether it was baby powder or shampoo, they would go and return with blue, green, or red lips from their jawbreaker treats.

Emily told everyone about the article in *The Inquisitor* that was coming out on the 22nd and to expect fallout from it on the 22nd and the 23rd. She told them that she did not know how the reporter had found out but she wanted to warn them ahead of time. They had gone to mass on Sunday and everyone was sympathetic to the entire family but they were all curious about the details of the article. Belle and William attempted to go to church at eleven and could not get out of their driveway from reporters. It was even more horrible for Emily's group at her house. They had to creep through the driveway and newsmen were beating on the windows of the cars asking for pictures or comments. Henry wanted to talk to the reporters for the family. They had written a statement the night before and he read it out loud to them.

The newsmen were disappointed that no questions were answered by the family but were especially upset since they all wanted to take pictures of Vivian, John, and the baby. They were given a resounding "No!" by Henry who waved as he turned and walked back into the house when asked about a picture of the young heiress.

Christmas was now only a few days away and Paul Michael was so excited. He insisted on saying prayers before lighting the advent wreath at supper. He let Henry light the candles because he was the oldest male. Another day he would tell Emily to light the candles because she was the Anya and he would light them for Catherine, the youngest of the household. He was keen on keeping track as to whose turn it was each evening.

Emily turned on the radio for Christmas songs and Paul Michael's favorite was without a doubt Bing Crosby's "White Christmas". He liked the melody and would hum it to little Caroline. He also read to her while she was sleeping. William was fascinated by the baby and he liked it when she tried to turn her head to look around. Her head would bobble at first and Emily told him that within two weeks she would be able to follow movement. He had found a bright faced rag doll and he made it dance on the edge of the cradle. William would have been an excellent uncle if he had only been given the chance by Louise.

Emily had purchased a rocking chair for Vivian's bedroom and another one for the living room. Emily and Catherine took turns rocking Caroline if she had a stomachache or was a little fussy. John would also sit in the rocker and set the baby in the crook of his arm and she would be asleep in less than five minutes. The women teased him saying, "Why did you let us wear ourselves out? You use your long arms to get her to sleep so fast and didn't say a word."

"Mother, you should know that you didn't raise a fool!" he returned the tease.

Emily had knitted Paul Michael a hat, scarf, and mittens. She had also bought several classic novels, drawing pad, Crayola crayons, and clothes for him. She wanted to give him a big surprise for his first Christmas with her and had also purchased a piano for Christmas. Paul Michael had wanted one and she asked him in November what he would want to ask Santa Claus to bring to him.

He had said, "Anya, Santa Claus can bring me whatever he wants, but if Santa could find me a piano that would be fine. I just don't see how he will put it in his bag! Perhaps he can get someone to help, hmmm?"

She paid men $50 to load the piano onto a truck and to bring it into the house sometime after Christmas mass which would be at 10:00am. They would get another $100 if they brought it inside before noon. Vivian and John had bought Paul Michael some easy sheets of music to learn. They found sheet music for "White Christmas" and felt sure that it would be his favorite. John would slip it into the piano bench along with a learning to play piano book.

Vivian had bought him a UVA sweater and some baseball cards with gum. Henry and Catherine bought him a box filled with 250 of the extra large jawbreakers. John bought him a phonograph and some records for his room. Emily would be given a mink coat and hat from Vivian and Paul Michael; a tiffany lamp from Catherine and Henry, and a drawing of Poppy from Paul Michael. Henry would receive a new ink pen from Emily and a small bag of jawbreakers from Paul Michael. Vivian and John had purchased him a new cashmere coat and hat. Catherine would be given a watercolor by Andrew Wyeth of a cabin from Emily, a sable stole from Vivian and John, and Paul Michael had made her a candle from beeswax and melted crayons.

On Christmas Eve, Emily had invited Josef and Mrs. Novak for dinner and did all of the cooking herself. There was a ham, turkey, stuffing, mashed potatoes, yams, rib roast, canned green beans, potato rolls, cabbage and homemade noodles, potato rolls, Kolache, and fresh apple cake. Vivian was so happy to have a meal like they had always had on the farm when she was growing up. Emily had bought a new dress and coat for Mrs. Novak, and coat and tie for Josef. Vivian and John had decided to buy Josef a small farm in Virginia. It was only 100 acres but would be able to support a family, if he ever had one, one day. It would be waiting for him when he was ready to start his own family. Henry bought him a new hat and pair of gloves for church.

Vivian and John bought Mrs. Novak 100 shares of stock each in Ford Motor Company and TWA. The dividend checks would supplement her income for years to come. They were grateful for the couple's assistance taking care of Paul Michael and the farm. Mrs. Novak had been indispensable when it came to helping Paul Michael adjust to life in Welfield.

The dinner was fantastic and Paul Michael wanted to go to bed early but insisted on reading "'Twas the Night before Christmas" to Caroline. Henry promised to tuck him into bed and John read him the story of the first Christmas from the Bible. They would be going to mass the next morning at ten and would have to leave no later than 9:30am. Everyone would be going and Vivian decided that she and Caroline would be going as well. Paul Michael was so excited that Caroline would be going to her very first mass. He had bought a Hungarian missal with coins he had been saving in a bank when he first found out that he was going to be an uncle. He would show her the pictures so that she could follow along. When Christmas morning dawned the ground was covered with about 3" of snow. Paul Michael was whistling or humming his favorite Christmas song several times that morning. Cook would have a big lunch waiting when they returned from mass. Emily had given each of her servants $100. Cook cried as did the maid. The butler thanked her and then quickly returned to his post. JJ was totally speechless. For all of the staff, the money was almost two month's worth of their salary. Paul Michael drew the cook a picture of an apple tree for the cook. She cried more when she saw his colored drawing than from the $100. He bought the butler and JJ a new pair of shoestrings to replace the ones Poppy had chewed. Paul Michael had chosen a small bottle of lotion for the maid and a pair of socks for the driver. He had picked out the presents himself and felt very proud when each shook his hand or gave him a hug after receiving their gift from the little boy.

Caroline was snug in her little pink dress, sweater set with booties and matching cap and then wrapped in several thin blankets and a handcrafted a that Emily had made for her using a print with kittens playing with strings of yarn. Paul Michael introduced his niece to all members of the congregation at Our Lady of the Rosary. He stood the entire time except during the consecration. He turned the pages in the missal he had given as a gift to Caroline as the mass progressed. At the end of mass he handed the missal to Vivian. She had smiled and gave him a kiss on the top of his head. John had decided to convert to Catholicism and would be receiving his first communion on Easter. Vivian asked Father O'Brien if he would baptize Caroline before they returned to Charlottesville and he agreed. Paul Michael asked, "Anya, am I baptized?"

"I don't know Paul Michael Mr. Dudas didn't tell me. Hm, I'll have to ask Father O'Brien what to do and make sure that you are baptized," she promised. She asked him right after mass and Father O'Brien told her that he could indeed baptize him on the same day he baptized Caroline. The Russians had burned all the records at Catholic churches that the Nazis had missed and told her he would need the date of his baptism when he received other sacraments.

When they returned home it had started to snow again. Poppy had her new toy and was thoroughly enjoying it when the men had brought in the piano around 10:30 or so. She didn't like to be disturbed and took her toy into the office and curled up on her bed. The maid had directed the men to where the piano was to be placed. She asked one of them to make deep boot tracks in the snow as she handed him the envelope containing their bonus pay. They had left with more than ten minutes to spare. Poppy jumped up when she heard the cars and immediately started yapping. She noticed the piano and started barking at it as well. It hadn't been there before and she didn't like things to change.

Emily led Vivian holding baby Caroline through the door the butler held open and Catherine and Paul Michael followed. Paul Michael ran into the dining room directly from the front door and hadn't noticed the piano. He had insisted on fasting the way Emily and Vivian did although he was much too young to receive communion anyway. John and Henry came in last and pointed to the piano. Emily had invited Belle and William to brunch after mass and they arrived about five minutes after the others. Emily was directing people where to sit when Belle came in with a stack of packages. Emily told the butler to set the packages under the tree. Cook had outdone herself for brunch. She had waffles, pancakes, ham, bacon, eggs, biscuits, and grits. Everyone was hungry and dug into the buffet she had set up on the sideboard in chafing dishes. The dining room grew quiet as they began to eat.

Vivian was about to take a bite when Caroline started crying. She must be wet and Vivian quickly took a bite and went to check. Caroline was changed and Vivian brought her to the table and she finished eating. John put a drop of honey on her tongue for a Christmas treat. Caroline's eyes grew large as she tasted the honey. Paul Michael giggled and said, "Anya, she likes our honey."

Vivian said, "John, now you know she's too young for honey. What if she's allergic to it or something?"

Emily said, "Now Vivian, she will be just fine. You were only two days old when your father did the exact same thing to you!"

Catherine and Henry had eaten their fill and pronounced it to be the finest brunch in America. Henry called for a toast to the cook. She came out of the kitchen when the maid told her she was asked to come to the dining room. Henry and the others drank a toast to her and she wiped her eyes with her apron. She was working on a huge roast, stuffed goose, and roast duckling for Christmas dinner. She had made vegetable soup and would serve it with liver dumplings for the dinner's first course. A salad of mixed greens and tomato slices would be their second. The entrée would follow with winter vegetables, garlic potatoes, and hot rolls. Cook made a red velvet cake with cream cheese frosting and black walnut apple cake for dessert.

After brunch, Emily invited everyone into the living room to open presents. Paul Michael's jaw dropped when he saw the piano. "Anya, how can this be? It wasn't here when we went to church." He went to ask the maid who shook her head saying that she didn't know anything about it. Cook shushed him out of her kitchen for talking nonsense and the butler assured him that he was aware of no visitors or they surely would have left a card. He returned and said, "Anya, Santa Claus must have brought it!" He looked out the window and saw the boot tracks! "He did bring it! Look there's his tracks, do you see them?"

Poppy had received another new chewy and attacked the wrapper as she waited patiently for Paul Michael to open it. Everyone opened their gifts and an ooh or ah was heard at various times that afternoon. When Paul Michael opened the knitted scarf, hat, and mittens he began to cry. Emily asked what was the matter and he replied, "Anya these are the nicest mittens I've ever had for sure, but my grandmother made me a hat just like this when I was little. I lost it when the soldiers came and thought I would never have another one like it, oh thank you!"

"Well now, you are very welcome," she smiled and kissed his little cheek.

Everyone was pleased with their gifts and when Paul Michael received his sheet music all eyes were on the youngster. He seemed confused by the lines and notes and so John sat down at the piano and played the tune for him and explained the keys and notes. Paul Michael watched him and repeated the movements. His legs were too short to reach the pedals like John could, but he played the first line without a single mistake. John would play the next measure and Paul Michael repeated it. After several renditions of the song, John played several Christmas carols on the piano and the family group sang along.

Judge Marshall called around five in the evening and extended his holiday best wishes. He had stayed in Charleston to finish up some court decisions that were due before his term expired. He would be moving in mid-January to Welfield. He and his wife had never had children and his closest friends were in Welfield. The judge had asked to speak with Paul Michael and was given the list of what he had received. He went on and on about his hat, mittens, and scarf that Anya had made. The judge asked if that was all he had received and the little boy mentioned all the gifts. "I got too much judge, just too much. My friend George said Santa never brings him anything for Christmas. He is very good. I should know, so why doesn't he get anything?"

The judge said, "Perhaps he didn't get his letter written in time."

"Oh my goodness, I bet that's what it is. I'll have to get him to write his letter earlier next year. Thanks Judge Marshall!" he answered with great jubilation.

Emily asked what that was all about and the judge told her about Paul Michael's friend. They spoke for a few more minutes before Emily rejoined her guests. Emily told the judge that she had given George's mother money to buy Christmas gifts and she had personally wrapped George a drawing pad, crayons, and train set. George's father had gotten hurt in the mines and they only received $75 a month to live on. George's oldest sister worked as a clerk at JC Penney to help out her parents. She was such a nice girl who always helped Emily and others with a beautiful smile at Penney's.

Belle had brought jewelry for Emily and Vivian, a sled for Paul Michael, a set of Virginia code of law books for John, and for Henry and Catherine she had purchased a Waterford crystal carafe and matching glasses. Belle received a copy of a photograph taken of Paul, Emily, and Vivian at Vivian's wedding reception. It was in an ornate frame. On the back of the picture it was signed, *"We love you grandma, Vivian and John."* She cried when she read the message and told them she would treasure it forever. Emily had bought her a chair that reclined and it had been delivered on Christmas Eve. William received a pair of ear muffs and matching scarf and gloves. Emily had also had made him a crocheted scarf for his dresser in a square block pattern with his initials in the middle.

Everyone ate their fill at the Christmas dinner and listened to the radio into the evening hours. Other phone calls were received from some of Emily's friends that lived in Jackson as well as some of her new friends she had made in Chicago. Chess matches, jigsaw puzzles, and crossword puzzles were attended to by several. Emily, Belle, William, and John played a game of Rummy until it got dark. Paul Michael was exhausted but tried to stay awake.

Paul Michael was too excited to sleep that night, but once John got him settled into bed and read him a story, he was sound asleep. John closed his door after Henry carried up Poppy and placed her in her bed beside Paul Michael. If it snowed during the night, they had promised to take him for a ride on the new sled down the hill above his house.

Caroline was asleep in her cradle after eating and being changed. It was a tranquil evening and the group reflected on their many blessings and went to bed. Around midnight, Henry and John snuck into the kitchen for another slice of the delicious red velvet cake and John looked out the window towards the garage to see if it was still snowing. The back porch light had been turned on when cook had left to spend Christmas evening with her family. John thought he had seen a shadow running behind a tree, put on his coat and went outside to investigate and said, "Dad, dad there's somebody out there by the garage!" Henry grabbed a coat and went out to join him. As Henry left the rear door, he heard a crash and saw flames coming from behind him and then felt a sudden pain and he fell. John ran to his father's side that was coming to when John looked to see the back porch roof on fire. He rolled out the garden hose and screamed "Fire, Fire!" as he hosed down the flames. He had put out the fire and hosed it extra in case there was any chance of it starting again. Thank goodness the temperatures had warmed up in the early evening and the hose wasn't frozen. Emily and Catherine had run out while Vivian was calling the fire department from upstairs ready to get Paul Michael and Caroline awake.

The fire department came and told them that they were lucky to have gotten the fire out so quickly. By what they saw and found, someone had soaked a rag with kerosene and stuck it inside a single kerosene filled quart-sized canning jar and had set it on fire. After tossing the torch onto the porch roof, they must have run around the house after hitting Henry in the back of the head and gotten into a car. He needed stitches and John drove him to the hospital along with his mother. When the fireman asked if they had any enemies, everyone had only one single thought of who it could be, Louise!

It had to have been a man though that had hit Henry with such force. The footprints in the snow and mud were large prints of men's boots. John described the person that he had seen out the window was about six feet tall and stocky in build. He didn't see any features only his back as he turned the corner of the house. He had been busy with his dad and flames and didn't pursue the arsonist.

The children were left to sleep and the Emily and Vivian went into the living room to discuss the fire. "Thank goodness the men just happened to be in the kitchen for their snack. All of us could have been killed if we had been in bed."

Emily observed, "Whoever it was, had waited until they thought we were all asleep. I agree with you, they didn't just want to burn the house down; they wanted all of us to be killed as well. I pray to the Lord to keep watch over us until John and his parents return from the hospital. I'll go make some coffee."

Vivian went into the kitchen with her mother and looked out the window as John had done. "The man must have been startled when John turned on the kitchen light. I think there might have been two of them mother and not just one. What are you going to do?" she asked.

"I will hire an armed security guard. I can't feel safe now knowing that someone is out there trying to burn us out of my home. I will have to get some large dogs as well. Poppy will have to be taken out the back yard before it turns dark. The large dogs will be kept outside Paul Michael's play area. I will see if I can purchase or at lease the property to the top of the mountain and have the security guard a small house and dog quarters as well," Emily sighed.

"I just hope no one has tried to hurt Belle and William. I asked the fireman to get a police car to check on them and I suppose no news is good news. I cannot go through life waiting on Louise to make another move mom. She is insane and her schemes are getting more and more dangerous! I'm sure she was behind this attack, but how can I prove it when we don't even know for sure what either of them looked like?" she asked.

"Mom, perhaps you and Paul Michael should stay somewhere else. I mean until school starts back up and the guards are hired." Vivian was very worried about her mom and little brother. Paul Michael would have been terrified to awaken to flames in what he had considered a safe place. He had seen too many fires and explosions during the war and sudden noises still made him jump. There was no telling how much damage had been done to the back porch roof, but perhaps it could be repaired before he knew anything about it.

"Coffee is just about ready dear. Vivian, I made you some tea. They will be returning before too long and I'm sure they won't be able to go to sleep either. Do you want a cookie or some cake with your tea?" Emily said with a smile.

"No just tea will be fine. Mom, why does Louise hate us so much?" Vivian asked.

"I don't know, I just don't know," Emily answered.

"I believe she has built some sort of wall around the truth and her perception of how it should have been has overcome her sense of what is truth to block out the past and that unpleasantness with Jack. She truly believes her warped and twisted version of her past happened. She has cast all the blame for her actions on others, mainly you and me. I believe it's called transference or something like that. We talked about it in my psychology class. She is consumed with what she perceives as justice for what she believes we have done to her," Vivian shook her head and sat down dejected. "Mom, she may be sick, but deep down, I think she is just an evil woman with the devil in her heart. Her grandmother must have twisted the truth to cover everything up for herself and Louise is doing the same thing."

Emily patted her only daughter's shoulder and added, "Unfortunately, Louise has chosen the darker path of life and didn't take after her dear mother. Thank goodness Bertie is not alive to see just how evil Louise has become."

"In my psychology class we studied about psychopaths who lack empathy. They use violence, charm, or sex, whatever it takes, to manipulate people. They have no guilt or shame and they will often act impulsively without thought of the consequences. We studied, "The Mask of Sanity" by a Dr. Cleckley and I have to say that I truly believe that Louise is a classic psychopath. There is no cure mom and no treatment for a psychopath. She will only get more manipulative with each counseling session she has and will only get worse. Mom, psychopaths are said to be born and not created," Vivian said with finality. "I don't know if there's anyone who will be able to prevent her from actually killing someone."

"So what can be done?" Emily asked.

"She will eventually be caught and possibly imprisoned for one of her schemes. She's not going to improve and will of course blame others when she's caught. At this point, she is still manipulating others to do her dirty work. Her schemes are getting more complicated and at the same time escalating in severity. She lied to Bertie who made excuses for her over the years. Bertie must have realized Louise had a problem when she hired the detective and I think that Bertie also realized there was nothing she could do to save her. It would take a miracle, but I wouldn't expect one to occur with someone so full of hatred. I only hope she does not seriously hurt or kill someone in the process, before she is caught," Vivian conceded.

John and his parents returned after about two hours and Henry told the women that he had required 5 stitches. He was advised to be kept awake for at least the next twelve hours since he may have a mild concussion. He relived the flame and crash over and over in his head and couldn't remember anything when suddenly he thought of a smell. The man smelled like old pipe tobacco. "Say John, I just remembered something. That man smelled like old tobacco, you know, like when it's been in a pipe for too long. Our attacker smokes a pipe! We will have to report that to the police in the morning."

Catherine told him not to get excited and to drink his coffee. She cut each of them a slice of cake and set it in front of the guys. John was still visibly shaken about his father being assaulted. The police had followed Henry to the Emergency Room and had taken his statement there. He was to write down anything else he remembered. Henry had taken a piece of paper out of his pocket and wrote down about the pipe tobacco.

The next morning the cook came in and found the outside light had been turned off. She was muttering to herself when she entered into the kitchen and found Emily, Henry, John, and Catherine sitting around her kitchen table. "What's going on in my kitchen?" she asked.

"We had an intruder last night on the property that tried to burn the house down!" Emily stated calmly.

"What?" the cook asked. "Who would want to hurt this nice family?"

"We don't know for sure but the police are checking into it. Henry and John went outside and someone hit Henry and cut his head and needed stitches. It's a miracle that John put out the fire in time. Thank goodness there was snow and ice on that shady part of the house. We are going to go out when it gets lighter outside and see if we can find any more evidence." Catherine said.

"If we hadn't come back down for some of your cake, we could have all been killed," John said.

Emily smiled at the cook and said, "I guess we need to get out of your way now. We will all be in the living room."

Vivian walked down the steps with Caroline and everyone seemed to suddenly get wide awake to greet their precious living baby doll. Vivian had gone to bed around three in the morning and still looked tired. Emily suggested that she go back to bed and Vivian said that she would once she had fed Caroline. Emily volunteered to make up the bottle and Caroline said that she would feed the baby. Vivian was ordered to go back up the stairs to get some sleep by her two "mothers", Emily and Catherine.

At first light, John and Henry went out to check the back yard. Paul Michael wanted help and said, "My footprints are small and I am closer to the ground. I will look hard to help you!"

They went back and forth over the area where John had seen the shadow and where Henry had been hit. They were about to give up when Paul Michael found a green piece of paper with a number on it. Henry recognized it as a dry cleaning ticket. John went around the corner where the man had thrown the jar and found a book of matches from a Bluestone nightclub. They didn't find any other clues. Henry told him that there were two different sets of prints, one slightly smaller than the other, but both had been made by men. They went inside and called the Welfield police. They turned over the two pieces of evidence, as well as the fact that Henry remembered the scent of an old pipe or old pipe tobacco, and showed them the two sets of prints before they melted in the snow.

Belle and William were called around eight o'clock in the morning to give them the information about the attempted murder. Emily told her that there wasn't much damage and the plans she had made for her home and suggested that Belle consider the same. Belle called Marshall Steel and had two company guards immediately posted at each house until arrests were made or full time guards could be hired. She came over to Emily's house to look over the damage, but while looking over the damage the carpenters and roofers, promised a bonus showed up within an hour. The roof was almost completely repaired by noon. Emily had asked Belle over and had also invited Alfred, Judge and Mrs. Perkins to come for a breakfast. They discussed the fire and evidence when Alfred mentioned that he had heard about a story on the CBS news radio program about the news reporter that had one the story about Louise being mugged and almost beaten to death on the 23rd and found early on Christmas Eve. The guy had survived but had no recall of the beating. It was reported that a witness had seen the mugging and reported seeing three men together just before the beating someone at that location. One was about six feet tall and heavy set and the other attacker appeared to be thinner and shorter. The third one she had heard, but didn't get a good look though because he was in the shadows more. The tall one was looking to his right when the third voice spoke and he must be about the same height. The two she could make out were both described as white and one of them wore a fancy overcoat. The thinner, shorter one was heard to say, "Let's go Dan," or something like that. NYPD is looking for them in New York.

Emily calmly told everyone what had happened and Alfred grew pale. He said, "I believe it must have been the same two men who almost beat that man to death. What color did you say the ticket was from the drycleaners?"

"It was green," Henry offered.

"Thousands of drycleaners are in the country, but some use green, pink, blue, or yellow tags," Alfred said. "If they check in that bar from the matchbook, they might just locate the two men. I suggest that you let the police do their job and be on guard. Mother and father, I suggest that you go on an unannounced holiday. They came to destroy and not to rob. I suspect that the robbery in New York was staged. Someone is going through a lot of trouble to cause the greatest amount of harm and destruction. I know what you are thinking and unfortunately, I cannot disagree with you."

Judge Perkins spoke up, "Perhaps we should tell our suspicions to the police. Phone calls can be checked and there couldn't have been that many passengers with tickets from New York to Welfield or even to Bluestone. They would have to come by train, bus, or car into Welfield or Bluestone. Since no car was found out of place near your house, I believe that a third person was waiting in a getaway car. Belle did you happen to hear from Louise on Christmas Day?"

Belle said, "No, she didn't call William or me on either Christmas or Christmas Eve."

John said, "Alfred, call your house and ask the maid if Louise was home yesterday."

Alfred called his residence to speak with Louise and was told that she was not at home but had left for New York on the 22nd and would not be home until after New Year's Day. He asked where she was staying and the maid told him she was at the Astoria of course.

Alfred called the Astoria and asked to speak with his wife, Louise Perkins. He hotel clerk informed him, "Mrs. Perkins left strict instructions that she would not accept any calls from anyone except Daniel Furgon. Perhaps if you would call him and give your message sir they would be passed along to her. Otherwise I am afraid I cannot possibly intrude upon our guests. You understand my position sir don't you?"

Alfred wrote down the name and returned to the group. "Does Louise know a Daniel Furgon?" Alfred asked.

Belle answered, "Not that I know of, why?"

Alfred said, "Well, he's the only one she is receiving calls from."

"How odd, even for Louise," Belle mused aloud.

John and Henry looked at each other and John immediately went over to phone the police about a possible suspect by the name of Daniel Furgon. The police told him that they would question him if they caught up with him.

Around three that afternoon, the police located Daniel Furgon in Bluestone and he confessed to driving the getaway car. He told them that two brothers had left for New York that morning and would be arriving around 9pm at Grand Central Station. He didn't know where they were going, but Alfred informed the police, saying he felt they would be going to be paid for their work at the Waldorf Astoria. Daniel had claimed, at first, that he didn't know who had hired him.

Louise had been disappointed when she received word that the fire had been put out so quickly, but she was pleased that at least no one could possibly have seen the fools. She was expecting Daniel Furgon and his hired thugs to return to New York for payment at any time and told the maid to let her know when her guests arrived. She had sold some of her jewelry, a diamond bracelet, brooch, and her engagement ring to pay them for their silence. When Daniel arrived she would pay all of them for services rendered even though they had failed, this time.

Louise was dressed and ready when the maid opened her door and told her that someone had come to see her about a payment. Louise asked her to have them shown in and she was shocked when she saw only two men and no sign of Daniel. She had no idea how well he was acquainted with these two characters but they, however, recognized her immediately and called out, "Well what do you know if it isn't our Cousin Louise!"